Finola Moorhead is a novelist whose work continues to break new ground. She has written for theatre and directed several plays. Her novel, *Still Murder* won the Victorian Premier's Literary Award. Her other books include a manifesto, *A Handwritten Modern Classic*, a collection of prose, *Quilt* and her extraordinary literary epic, *Darkness More Visible*.

Other books by Finola Moorhead:

A Handwritten Modern Classic

Quilt

Still Murder

Darkness More Visible

REMEMBER THE TARANTELLA

Finola Moorhead

SPINIFEX PRESS

First published by Primavera Press 1987
This edition published by Spinifex Press 2011

Spinifex Press Pty Ltd
504 Queensberry St
North Melbourne, Victoria 3051
Australia
women@spinifexpress.com.au
http://www.spinifexpress.com.au/

The National Library of Australia Cataloguing-in-Publication data:
Moorhead, Finola.
Remember the Tarantella.

ISBN: 9781876756932 (pbk)
ISBN: 9781742193809 (ebook: pdf)
ISBN: 9781742194585 (ebook: ePub)
ISBN: 9781742193816 (ebook: Kindle)

I. Title.
A823.3

MIX
Paper from responsible sources
FSC® C001695
www.fsc.org

CONTENTS

Australia Council for the Arts

Publication assisted by the Literature Board of the Australia Council, the Federal Government's arts funding and advisory body.

AUTHOR'S NOTE

Perhaps *Remember The Tarantella* started with Christina Stead's challenge to me: it's very difficult to make an interesting novel with no men in it at all. But she took me to lunch at Monash University, where she was writer-in-residence, and discussed the mathematical aspects of my first chaotic attempt at long fiction, *Lots Of Potential.*

Two or three years later, I was writer-in-residence at Monash University, wondering what and how to write, suffering the culture shock and absurdity of changing from 'taxi-driver' to 'writer'.

Since 1974 I have been developing theories of the feminine aesthetic in literature. I had been hunting for an 'everywoman', the free archetypal female, to underlie a possible Hamlet, Peer Gynt, Candid of my gender. I was sick of sorry women, in my own and others' stories, who were not in control of their own downfall. Fiction is a literary composition wherein the writer creates above, below and around the real world. Simply screening an accurate description of one's life with a facade of false names and places was not satisfying to me either as a writer or a reader. I could not squeeze this 'everywoman' out of my mind. It was necessary to get to know a mob of women, all searching for their own freedom. I mean freedom of the soul. 'Everywoman' was women; the singular does not compute when one investigates the nature of the feminine.

A worker, no longer a taxi-driver, now a writer with an office and a title, albeit for ten weeks, my job, then, was to put my theories into practice: a daunting project when it became clear to me what I had to do. Christina Stead had given me two clues with her mention of maths and 'no men in it at all'. The daring to make a novel from geometry was possible in the rarified air of a 'sinecure'. Thanks to Monash University.

The first draft was a series of diagrams, and nouns. No sentences. That was to ensure a symphonic and historic depth. The first level of attack was structure.

The second draft was *flow-prose*. It is dependent on inspiration, excitement, the tides of language and having the time. The merging of the diagrammatic and chaotic was a poem.

Throughout the many drafts, I had readers, arguers, encouragers, critics and researchers who worked for the book, the idea, their own reasons, with implicit faith in my purpose to uncover a truth; to tell the truth and not resort to a gossipy theft of their ideas and their lives. I absorbed it all with gratitude and worked with a discipline and strength I felt I owed them. Thus my ideas weigh with those of others. The *I* becomes an *alphabet,* the *my* becomes *ours*. The first person singular is plural.

This book is dedicated to those who helped me write it.

F.M.

If, going astray,
a reader can enter the mosaic
of chipped experiences, employing
the wings of dream,
then come…

Alphabet of Characters

ARACHNE. Alice Audrey Farr, born Mosman, Sydney, New South Wales, on August 1, 1956.

BEATRIX. Beatrix Unsdatter, born in Denmark under the sign of Libra, parents migrated to Australia in the middle fifties.

CERRIDWEN. Cerridwen Colleen Flynn, born Rio de Janiero, Brazil, January 25, 1960.

DAWN. Dawn Nerida Clancy, born Phillip Island, Victoria, under the sign of Aquarius.

ETAMA. Elsa Hannah Gluck, born April 26, 1952, Springvale Victoria.

FRANCES. Frances Veronica Furriskey, born November 9, 1947, Mildura, Victoria.

GRUNDHILDE. Grundhilde Schmidt, born September 15, 1955, Zurich, Switzerland.

HELEN. Helen Hoffman, born January 7, 1945, Union City, New Jersey, U.S.A.

IONA. Iona Josephine Flynn, born March 16, 1947, Healesville, Victoria.

JAY JAY. Janice Judith Jansen, born August 5, 1940, Christchurch, New Zealand.

KATE. Katharine Tasma McMillan, born June 29, 1922, Hobart, Tasmania.

LESLEY. Monica Lesley Nicholson, born September 25, 1951, Alice Springs, Northern Territory.

MARY. Mary Joanne Monday, born June 5, 1941, Melbourne Victoria.

NISABA. Nisaba Diana Kirby, born April 10, 1921, Manchester, England.

OONA. Oona Strider, born Febuary 21, 1938, Perth, Western Australia.

PAMELA. Pamela Ruth Scarf, born in Caulfield, Victoria, under the sign of Scorpio.

QUEENIE. Terese-Avila Quenelle, born July 20, 1955, Quebec, Canada.

ROSE. Ellen Rose Croft, born in Ipswich, Queensland, under the sign of Pisces.

SOPHIE. Sophia Maria McKennan, born May 10, 1947, Wangaratta, Victoria.

TREES. Therese Dimnsey-Green, born in India, under the sign of Gemini.

URSULA. Ursula Miriam Trap, born March 23, 1930, Traralgon, Victoria.

VANESSA. Vanessa Dorothy Sheppard, born November 28, 1944, Penrith, New South Wales.

WINIFRED. Winifred Jane Stevens, born in Traralgon, Victoria, under the sign of Sagittarius.

XAVIERA. Francesca Xaviera Marquez, born Cuernevaca, Mexico, under the sign of Leo.

YVONNE. Yvonne Margaret Smythe, born London, England, under the sign of Virgo.

ZORRO. Laura Quezeda, born December 23, 1955, Barcelona Spain.

1

NAKED AS the queen of heaven, Iona is born, covered in blood.

She has this pleasure in a pristine Catholic hospital with walls of pale blue and grey, white sheets and chrome instruments. Deep red gladioli stand in a glass jug beside a pile of detective novels on the cupboard next to her mother's bed.

It is the Autumn of 1947 in Melbourne.

Several concurrent events exist in the moment she first observes her mother's curious, distant gaze.

Her father cannot be found. He is in Margaretta Webber's bookshop anticipating the day his own titles will be displayed near those of Joyce and James. His ever-distracted eyes wander to the destination of a ginger-haired student, a young bluestocking. She smiles a great big country girl's grin. Then they are chatting in a coffee shop.

Mrs Flynn, her mind full of murders and mystery, therefore quite far away from her personal experience, tries to hug the baby with unabashed maternalism. Fails. They stare at each other across a question mark neither can dissolve.

The soul inside the chubby cheeks, jelly bones and jutting limbs is reeling from the spin of karma landing her suddenly back on earth, registering some confusion. It is all too intriguing to cry.

The regal features of her mother's face relax a little and she smiles at her fifth. The fourth, Nola, had been born defective, and the third, Veronica, was a screaming handful. Even at rest a sad countenance on her little fine face foreshadowed her tragic destiny. The fifth, Iona, grimaces, gurgles and goes about the business of living with the curiosity of a kitten.

The other insignificant occurrence of this day in 1947 happens up the 'Paris end' of Collins Street in the same city. A girl of about seventeen with a ghastly puce stain on her facial skin is sniffing the odontal odour of panic, waiting to have a rotten molar removed, with an old copy of *The Ladies Home Journal* on her lap. She flicks through the pages until a couple of coloured rectangles glow with meaning. As she reads the article about the artist, Nisaba Diana Kirby, she forgets the smell, the impending dentistry and her fear, just loving this woman and her art. In a shy agony, she rips the page out and sneaks it into her handbag. When in the chair, prone to the smooth shaved chin and probing fingers of the all-powerful professional, she faces the pain with courage.

Himself, the Irish impregnator, the ne'er-do-well, would come and go in more ways than one, always apologetic in the tongue of a poet without poems. Accommodated on his person when visiting the hospital would be whisky flask and violets in a posy. Fancying the easier life, nevertheless he is charmed by this chubby cherub into staying around the family home for another three years. But the lugubrious presence of the older girls, one in her idiocy and the other in her precocity, the forebearance of the sons and the reprimands of his wife send him into the arms of the redhead, for seven years.

For Iona, the youngest, a veil falls across the knowledge of her first three years. Fatherless, she experiences a mortal ignorance and consequent melancholy. Wanderlust chained at its ankles in her being, it is she who sustains the guilt of his leaving.

She sets out on the track to the great abstract diagram of it all, the co-ordinate geometry of the One, seeking the sense of belonging. An emotional task. She, the companion of her mother's lonely mind, goes about it intellectually. Thus, she considers herself a writer, a fictioneer, a worker in the literary craft. But for all the intents and purposes of this world, she drives a taxi, a yellow Falcon, G17, radio code, 'Gay-one-seven'.

Alone in the cab, early 1980, she thinks of Kierkegaard. Doubt and illusion. Delighting in the clip-clop chess game pace of her thought, she considers the historical logic of Existentialism. Christianity supports a speculative philosophy that distorts the reality of man's existence in, with, illusion, becoming the residue of pure thought, an abstraction of existence, not existence itself. The only object of thought is one's personal being, within which lies the potential of a supreme ethical choice.

A supreme ethical choice, which can only be determined by thought. Teenagers in a deserted Altona street all wave frantically. A fare.

The moon is a pale reflection of fire in the military blue of the sky. 'And', 'yet', but', conjunctions, tick-tock like clocks. Therefore, they can—no, should—be used frequently in a piece, in English anyway. She reaches the very hump of the Westgate Bridge. A late-rising Luna hangs like pregnancy over the eastern suburbs.

There is a tiny tape-recorder on the front seat of the Falcon, underneath the Melways Street Directory beside the change dispenser. She has driven a cab long enough to know that a lot of the time the top light will gleam 'vacant'. Her tapes are not for the grubby journalism of eavesdropping, she wants to record her own thoughts. There are a few books beneath the dash. If you read a novel on this job, especially an exciting one, you get no passengers. The books are for dipping into, for booting along her thoughts if they run down, a poem, a paragraph, a phrase. The secret is to stay awake and aware, one eye on pedestrians, one hand on the radio mike. Attend!

Who owns thoughts? Who knows? Her rule is to spend no more than twenty minutes on one rank.

Outside a night club in King Street, she reads George Meredith's sentence: "Masculine ideas are one thing; but let feminine ever be feminine, or our civilisation perishes."

—Now, there's a nice verb I never use. 'Perishes'.

Along her next journey, she amuses herself with sentences joining 'perishes' with the new world, a task she believes worthwhile: her generation of women must attempt to change civilisation, or, as some of her friends maintain, the world will end. Will we, the women, rot the regime like bacteria in old socks?

Caught in a chip
of the hologramic plate,

time,
which is also a wave,
a relentless undulation bringing thirteen moons
to the zenith in four seasons,
is everything:
the dance,
though the dusts of centuries have blown
over the place, brought bones to the surface
and dug them deeper beneath the paving stones
of buried civilisations;
carnal life and blood—primal clay.
All caught in the beam, changing.
All time is.

Oona Strider was born in the middle of February in 1938 somewhere in Perth. Her first years were spent in an orphanage, a musty, underprivileged place. Then it was foster home followed by foster home. Why such unsuitable people wanted others' children bemused her. Her first job was as a nursing assistant at the age of fifteen. Several years later, when a student psychiatric nurse, she discovered drugs. Before completing her training, she vanished into the nether reaches of heroin addiction. In the early sixties, she served a jail sentence in the West. Later in the sixties, she escaped from Fairlie Women's Prison in Melbourne, and thenceforth has been an outlaw.

Now wandering through the dry lands, the bulldust puffing up between toes like powder between fingers, she decides only a few can survive the outback without losing some sanity, the endless copper horizon, the sudden winds giving voice to the sheoak strings, the harps of harpies. None walks here untouched, as it were, by the Never-never. Heat shimmers ahead taunting. The vast dome of the sky as solid as porcelain weighing, the perspective of distance is awry. Solid things like the pathetically thin rotors of a windmill near a bore appear like fantasies, a detail which is an omen, a cause. Few hold their own in such a sandscape.

It is the audacity of the planet that such emptiness should exist composed of rock and minerals, vegetation and insect life, wild flower, emu and lizard. The emptiness is the lie, but it is what the heart must love, comprehend, to pierce. The mind grips the body to continue blinking, beating, anchoring the soul in the rhythmic depths of staying alive.

The tan figure of Oona is the largest moving object in the scene. Her toes make four little red clouds as each bare foot pads the ground. Her legs are beyond complaining. Her body in surrendering has reached a state of exhilaration which is in tune with the trembling of her emotions. Earth, flesh and soul seem to vibrate on a single chord, the healing, tough note that Oona needs to hear.

She comes to a halt. Her hips are humming. The glassy screen of sameness lifts. Her long sight scans the landscape for a stand of trees, any herbage, a gathering of birds. There's a clump of mulga to the north.

I am echo. I am emptiness. I observe. I am in the lovely howl of the desert, and eight feet from me is a bright Sturt desert-pea. Here I can see to the end of the earth, for the big world is a huge penny. The horizon a circle, not a curve.

She freezes. Her body assumes a hard tranquility. It is the shush of a snake. Nothing is so alive as a dead calm that ensures continued existence. One move and it's curtains, kid. The olive brown serpent executes a lightning figure of eight and disappears. She pulls out her dogeared book of facts: death adder; tiger snake; brown snake; black snake; copperhead; taipan. Oona loves the shape of eight. The symbol of infinity she saw in a diagram in a book somewhere she adopted as an okay. Thumbs up. The octonary action of the poisonous brown snake is good.

The sunset is rich and ferocious, indigo to the east with a slither of moon high in the true blue. A chip of bone. Where, when there is nothing left to search for in this hard land, are the bones? The blood-defying desert is neither my retreat nor my challenge, it's my weapon. Being capable of being here is my knowledge. My inner stasis, my freedom. She makes a tiny cooking fire with twigs and pebbles. As she kneads the flour and water and raisin mixture, she grumbles to herself. She has been ousted, she feels, from her home in the highlands.

Way into the Blue Mountains she had found a loggers' hut made of stone. There she squatted, until they came. The white dykes. Then they accused her of theft. I only ever take what I need, I never take from greed, everything belongs to everybody. They get so disturbed when their purses go, it's worth the laugh. The litany is a preamble to her task. She must distinguish right from wrong, friends from shits, pearls from onions.

Some people are onions. They're not really empty. They are simply composed of layers, all exactly the same in texture and strength. Once you've worked out the surface, you can be pretty sure there's more of the same underneath. If it's hypocrisy, jealousy, meanness, it's all still there, layer after layer, level after level, right into the belly of it. But other people are round and solid, with all the colours of a rainbow. Like pearls. I just have to figure out who is which. Yeah, who is which.

The damper slowly cooking on the hot coals, Oona worries. The note of her serenity has been knocked out of earshot by her considering the poor forked animals. Being outcast is not having the one you want, while rejecting those I don't is a piece of cake. It always happens, in all my forty-two years, those I love don't love me. The fancy emotions of love and care are shit kept in some people's mouths and never allowed any lower.

She is at a moment in her life wherein she must resort intently to the mirror of self-reflection. No matter how long it takes, out here in the simplicity of survival.

She read once, 'democracy does violence to our archaic instincts' and she keeps the phrase with others she has collected like butterflies on pins in her head. 'Archaic', the word, sings, for in her blood there is something truly ancient. Even though she didn't know her mother or her father, she knows that one of them was black. Real black and the other was really fair, blond. Her own colouring tells that story, Aboriginal features with light brown hair and tawny skin. And 'democracy', well that's sharing, right? Everyone equal. Okay, what's this 'violence'?

There's a bloody mob of 'em.

A mob of bloody women. They had five million words to say and every conceivable way of saying them, from haranguing to soft social work shit, from promises to threats. Their world is an aura of words and ideals, of daydreams and dramas. I tried milking those words for something real, something you could use, but uh uh. Ratbags and rebels. Or, as Amos reckons, 'university sheilas with knives slung to their waists'.

As a martial artist has no visible weapon but his skill, I have the desert. I can have their company if I want it. Who needs to rake through all the crap to get it?

That thought doesn't make Oona feel any better. She needs to know who her real friends are, or else the future may undo all those years enticing the addiction out of her brain. Descending into it, ripping it out again. Alone in the bush, struggling with her own inner serpent, she learnt from snakes. Fear of their slithering beauty and power turned to respect and from respect to a kind of understanding. She owes to the snake her attention to the wild, her ease with nature. The fatal bite, she fantasised, would be like the hypodermic needle she squeezed up her veins. Either way, she would be a victim and she did not want that, finally.

Dying and no one caring, just being dry bones in the desert or lying blue in some city gutter was not walking over the edge to the Dreamtime proudly, having lived.

Her boots under a thin little pillow filled with scented herbs for her head, the bed-roll half-inch foam-rubber and grey blanket, she looks at the sky. The few pearls in her pocket include one on a string, as she has a self-taught way of divining with a pendulum. Her tiny antique scales are wrapped in an Indian silk scarf—she trades in dope when she has to. She has flour, a few potatoes, big bag of raisins and an army water bottle. For fresh water she rigged up her enamel billy underneath a piece of plastic weighed down by three stones around a hole. The first thing she will taste in the morning will be dew. Then tea …

Which reminds me, that windmill, I wonder if the bore works. Brackish water's okay if the tea is very strong.

Her hands behind her head staring up at the stars, she thinks of the windmill. What does it, being an omen, a cause, mean? Where did those words jump from into my head?

2

FOR ETAMA the sky is as blue as the exquisite eyes of the fickle Beatrix, blue as the flowers and monkey in the fresco at Knossos.

Etama's own eyes are brown, her eyebrows dark and her skin is an even tan on which the vibrant colour of lime green looks great, regardless of cut or fabric. Blues, except for aqua or turquoise, look rather dull on her. The weather at Zakros on Crete is equable, There is an insect hum in the grasses.

She is sitting on the stone steps of a recent excavation, with tourist brochures and an airmail writing-pad on her knee. Beatrix is as wicked as a huge pretty child, with china blue eyes magnified by glasses, as tall as the Minoan women in their full tiered skirts, elaborate jewellery and exposed breasts. She told Etama she didn't want to sleep with her anymore, ever. Rejection, Here on the isle of the labrys, the powerful double-axe, a tiny golden replica of which she wears around her neck, her spiritual home, her sign being Taurus, her heart being feminist, she is given the boot. It is intolerable. The sky is smug.

She is a potter, a craftswoman in clay. She has studied the neolithic, the magdalenians, the megalithic, the periods of the white goddess, collected pictures of pots and sculptures, to come as a kind of homecoming eventually. She looked forward to Kamilari, the place of the dancing dead in the womb of the large tomb, expecting to feel uplifted.

She feels dreadful.

All the way on the bus from Ayios Nikolaos she is preoccupied by her own loss. Beatrix delivered the wound, and, in hectic compensation, Etama wants one of the most exciting archeological finds in recent years, these undisturbed ruins, to distract her. In terms of time her obsession with Beatrix may be as small as the ant speedily making its way across the stone in the sunshine, a black skerrick of life on immortal white, but she is in the heart of it and it is everything.

"ZAKROS" she writes.

"Dear Frances," Etama loves to write letters; on paper, she can scream at the world. Considerations of form are dashed like vodka glasses into the fireplace. Her mind focussed by solitude throws words, opinions, metaphors by the dozens along the broad path of her thought. Her handwriting is that of an artist, fine flourishing capitals and clear words evenly cover the page.

"You said my brown eyes under their long lashes were like gem stones with lights of the yellow sun, that they had a sensual balance between light and dark, that my intense gaze arouses trust in a lover. But that was years ago. Lovers ago. Later you changed that, saying it was because my appetite shows. That eighteen months we were together were the most passionate in my whole life. You and I were capable of total immersion beyond the realms of pleasure into freedom. The moon is exalted in Taurus. And your moon is in Taurus and my sun, but that alone doesn't explain it. Every time I am rejected it is a resurrection of your rejection. You said I was flattering, so jealous and possessive. I was secure with you on those lazy, rainy Sundays we'd spend in bed when nothing else was required but love-making and kisses and reading the paper and drinking camomile tea. Your moral confidence made me feel so stable. When I got into clay—excuse the expression but that is literally how it was—and my first pot whizzed around in my fingers, I felt it again. Drinking at the breast........... As if all my sensuality, all my sexuality could be at my fingertips with the proper concentration.

Feminism came for me like a Revivalist faith, tailored to my cut. I could be as idealistic and angry as I chose, well, as I am! Oh the crowds in '74, '75, '76 at conferences, gatherings, dances. It was the right time for our love, the whole environment was with us, was as we were. Crazy. Remember me claiming madness at the Woman and Madness Conference, let's embrace it, let's be it. Why not?

I believed in the Movement, I believed it was as great as the one started by Christ at the beginning of the Age of Pisces, that we were the baptism of the Age of Aquarius, we women with Pluto in Leo.

Why am I writing in the past tense, I still believe it, but I suppose you don't. I wanted women who could fight, who could argue without holding back.

My faith has got deeper. I think. But so has my suspicion of other women. They disappoint me, especially heterosexuals.

I haven't written to you for ages and I don't know if I'll send this. It's just that I'm alone and you and I journeyed deep into each other so therefore we must mean something to each other always. Oh the nostalgia for five years ago, or is it only four? Anyway there was a cornucopia of handsome women around. You came out of Gay Liberation so I guess Women's liberation for you was Lesbian liberation. That's okay for me, I was born lesbian, but it's not great, not universal as I imagine the great changes associated with the beginning of the Age of Aquarius must be. Must have religious dimensions. I know you hate this kind of talk.

Why am I here, in Zakros, Crete? I needed wider horizons, to find my spiritual roots. And why am I sitting on 4,000-year-old steps writing to you? Because I was sleeping with somebody, in fact we started travelling together, and now she doesn't want to any more. It's not another woman either, it is the place. She is seduced by a sense of beauty, she says. I am snubbed by her, and by Crete. It gives me the shits. I need contact. It's a torture for me to sleep alone. Just to stay close. Especially here.

Oh bugger it, I'm going to Brussels. I'll come back to Greece when I'm in a better space.

I was thinking of her, consumed by a desire to deliver heartache and revenge, and I ended up writing to you, forgetting the oceans of tears I shed over you and I don't know if it adds up to forgiveness. I know you're not interested in that. The best sex ever was with you, Frances. Beyond all our disagreements, there is trust. I trust your soul.

I think, in fact, you might have given me strength to crack hardy and continue by myself, without Beatrix and her easy commitment to women, her Libran grace and taste, always surrounded by friends.

Remember our love, your lonely,
Et."

—Arachne has disappeared.

—You mean Alice, Alice Farr?

—Yes. Arachne. She felt a lot better after she changed her name to Arachne. She's gone.

—No one's seen her? Heard from her?

—Not for two months! No one. She's disappeared. Iona lies back on her mattress in the shed, while outside Rose and Dawn talk of the absence of Arachne. Their voices are airbrush rhythms in her chimerical thinking. She is in the hypnogogia of half sleep. Her mind is turning a mandala of right angles. Memories shimmering in the pool of the present, never cameos frozen on a date, are always changing, reinterpreting themselves and commenting. Shifting illusions. Her vision to the future intrudes as a refraction of light in the water. Her thoughts map themselves on the pattern of streets. She opens her eyes. The blowflies seem to circle but turn angles. She drifts. Rose's voice is indolent, with an sardonic edge. Humour suppressed into a whine. Dawn's is a voice that could say everything if there were time, measured and punctuated with consideration of the next sentence. The best thing about working nights is sleeping days, hugged by the sounds of life and living.

—Perhaps she's finally gone overseas. Become a sufi.

—Well, Etama and a bunch of women are in Crete. I know she knows that. I hope she's all right. I mean she's not robust, is she?

—Whatever she does she'll get away with it. Wherever she is.

—Anyway, I'm worried.

—You like worrying, Rose.

Iona has dozed. Many dark Indians of the south in flagrant shining clothes are at a small store buying and selling jewellery. A wide sweep of garish countryside is in the background. Everyone is black. It is familiar. Iona has never been there. A figure in a rich yellow sari turns. The face is white. An electric shock of closeness, the dreamer and the dreamed in full recognition. The dreamer attempts to follow the dreamed crying, 'What?' The roads she is on have high walls in the architecture of Asia Minor.

The egg-yolk sari with golden threads is all she sees of the figure which is moving too fast, too perilously close to sheer drops. Her own feet feel cemented down. The dreamer, Iona, sees her own body, in a narrow street walled by teeming houses and into her disembodied ears comes the answer to her call, 'Journey'. Again the fair figure is in front of her, this time not catching her eyes but having the customary vague look of Arachne. A suffusion of warmth enters the dream, something Iona never felt for Arachne in consciousness.

The dream of Arachne etches itself into her catalogue of memories, as if the feeling in her dream were as real as any emotion she had had, and she returns back through the groggy pool of waking, which synthesises all in the present, to the talking of Dawn and Rose.

Rose lives in the house proper, pays more of the rent and reluctantly let Iona transform the old wood/tool shed into a bedroom as long as she does not disrupt her independence. Rose is not a house-mate you would yell at to bring a cup of coffee. Iona emerges into the sunlight.

—Arachne, I think, is in India. Is that tea warm?

—So we can expect an illegible postcard from Poona?

—Didn't she say she was going to hitch across West Pakistan and Afghanistan?

—That was ages ago. No one took her seriously, she can't even look after herself in Melbourne.

—Anyone want a bet? Fifty bucks says she's in India.

—Iona, you'd take a punt on anything, but with fifty on it you've got inside information.

—No she hasn't, Dawn, I told you no one knows where Arachne is. She's disappeared. I'd know.

"On days like these, we are inside the lung of a huge breathing machine. A panting, excited lung."

Ursula would seem to be a conventional old maid, nurse to her invalid mother, a spinster more unfortunate than most because of the right side of her face. The skin of her eyelid is pinched in and stretched through her eyebrow. The cheek is bulbous and pulls down the corner of her mouth. A slight dribble of saliva is always visible. The colour is maroon-purple, permanently spotted with whiteheads. It has closed her off from the world as effectively as a Carmelite's grille. The left side, which could have relieved the unsightliness by pure force of character, habitually wears an ungracious expression.

After forty years, self-sorrow can descend intensely but is not indulged. Defences against one's own vulnerabilities are stuck, as it were, on automatic.

She puts her diary back in her coat pocket and continues along the "plasmic" sand. Her dog, Flush, scampers ahead on the scalloped tideline, where caught in the black tangles of seaweed are treasures: the half-dome of a tennis ball, plastics of toys and soft drink containers, an abandoned set of dentures, waterlogged citrus fruits, white polystyrene, fish bones, shells and encrustations, green sea-frosted glass, smooth driftwood of natural shapes and hairy wood of the milled variety. It is the lace on the hemwork of Port Phillip Bay.

The wind blows out in short fierce gusts, licking up the sea into spitting waves. These equinoctial days suit Ursula's type of angry energy. That mark of Cain, the scar that forces her to be a saint, frustrates her. Growth has been stunted. Activity must always be nipped in the bud, the instinct to be gregarious ruled off with a frown, her desire to gasbag on about the meaning of life stifled. It has twisted in her, bent her character savagely into antagonism, loneliness. She pursues her rapid constitutional every morning at ten, covers miles of the foreshore in a couple of hours, with her diary in her pocket. The scavenging of her irrepressible terrier is a canine projection of her own searching.

"The wind cry, the wave cry, the vast waters of the petrel and porpoise" give Ursula her best communion. T.S.Eliot's words are Ursula's knowledge, for the sea is her great mirror. The sea is as she is inside, behind the shell of appearance, beyond the unopened door of her hymen. Virginity does not describe her state of mind. She dreams all.

For Ursula, waking from sleep is the running aground of a small yacht from a turbulent sea. She is all a-shudder, having to take her bearings while being dumped by breakers.

In a bit of a pickle, panicked and brittle. She is racked with feelings, wave-motions, dismayed and bored by the heavinesss of the body. Every night is the same. She's off adventuring on the high seas. Her dreams are crowded with personalities. Flying about the night sky with the fittest of astral bodies, she drops in wherever she is called, whatever the age, place, society, materialising and dematerialising. She is free in her dreams, but on waking, she is as helpless as a beached whale. Consciousness is an arrest of a velocity as could only be described algebraically. It is a slow clearing of smoke, a desolate landscape. Concussion.

During the day, what does Ursula have? She has her walks along the foreshore. And she reads.

With her cups of tea, she reads. When she has a moment, she reads. Apart from her mother, her sister and her sister's sons, Ursula has one friend in the world, Jocelyn, a demented dog-show lady with kennels. None of these give her the intimacy she gets from reading. Fine literature over the centuries has provided some great associates for the price of a book, a stop at the Regional Library. She keeps diaries, dozens of exercise books, each with a colour print stuck on the cover, a habit which started thirty-three years before with a couple of reproductions from *The Ladies Home Journal* of the artwork of Nisaba Diana Kirby. The picture, often cut out of a magazine, names the diary for Ursula, it recalls her mood, the date and the matters inside.

When Ursula goes to her church, to whom does she pray? Jane Austen, Joan of Arc, Cleopatra, Mary Shelley, Leibnitz. In her time, Ursula has talked to all the dead creators she has met. Ursula does not waste her time beating her breast. 'Mea culpa' would be a lie, her conscious life is a purgatory. She has nothing to say 'my fault' about. Neither Lucifer nor God would be interested in her petty sins, nor, if the truth be known, is Ursula. She has not conjured up heavens of purity and bright light and is scared of no hell she can imagine. Somehow salvation must be lived in the life she's got.

"Mimbo settled with tea and crumpet.

The other evening she said my diaries look like a collection of Dickens, an entire shelf of uniform height and spines of dark green canvas. I wonder if all mothers have such cunning ways with small flatteries.

On such a day as this I saw the wave-dancing girl.

Ocsar Wilde: 'Art is out of the reach of morals, for her eyes are fixed upon things beautiful and immortal and ever-changing.'

My facade puts me out of the reach of immorality. Another one, Oscar: 'A little sincerity is a dangerous thing. And a great deal is absolutely fatal.'

We were inside a Turner seascape on that day. In the winter of 1970, the wind was howling and the waves were cracking down on the shallow beach. I was wearing my gent's gaberdine overcoat, with the huge pockets, and my hat was pulled down at the ears. I was the watcher and she the watched. We were both in a moment of art, immortal and ever-changing. Clad in black rubber, she was such a slight thing battling the surf. Her knees wide apart, her arms weighing this way and that, it was a performance just for me. To show me it could be done, ballet on the sea.

'My dear, aren't you cold?' I said. Her feet and hands were purple but she assured me that the wet suit worked. She was training for some surfing competition. She came from Bells Beach. 'It is not a girls' sport,' I said. But not for this androgynous creature, my shy Valkyrie, she could be better than the boys. 'Indeed, how old are you?' I said. Thirteen, neither man nor woman, boy nor girl, but an embodiment of all human potential, a spirit, a myth. How I managed to talk to her I don't know. The unique. She would not be taken aback by my looks. Or rather, that didn't matter a fig.

'80−'70=10. 10+13=23.

Now she must be twenty-three.

She instigated a faith I find returns every time the wind blows from the south-west. She brought to me a belief that my wishing life could be the one I live some day. I often trouble myself over how this can happen. Now instead of praying to dead writers, from which communication nothing can come, I have taken up hunting for a live one, listening to the radio and reading the newspapers, looking for the hole through which I might slip to meet the real…she must be great…no, I check myself, it is through her work I will know her. Her characters must be able to give me the intimacy that I know from so much reading. I have my rules and they are by no means easy.

The local library sadly lacks Australian work, except that of the most popular and vulgar kind.

Time laps in me like the seasons. My constant round, to the beach, to the shops, attending to Mimbo's every need is monotonous, except for Flush. Every minute is new to him, that way he loves routine. Except for my secret expedition. Will it be an Elizabeth Barrett Browning? An Emily Bronte? I hardly think we'd hit it off. With one of her sisters perhaps. I fancy I'd get along with a George Eliot, actually."

3

IN AFGHANISTAN, Arachne, traveller, came on sudden green and fertile valleys and confetti-covering of purple flowers scattered on the seemingly arid soil. She went along the Hindu Kush where empty desert sands border with Iran. Alongside Islam, the Persian influence was also grand. Alexander the Great, here for only four years, left huge garrisons behind. And war still raged. In the mountains of Ghor, the World Burner, Alaudin Jahansoz, butchered his captives, mixed their blood with the soil of their native town and built victory towers thereof. And Tamerlane of Samarkand embellished buildings so richly and commissioned works of art so beautiful in the wild *avagana* where his troops tobogganed on their shields to invade. Though Tamerlane was lame, it triumphed his Ghengis blood.

In December the invasions began again, this time the USSR. But the Afghan is the same and will not be tame. Barbur who named Kabul after Cain wrote of the place: you can go in a single day from where the snow never falls to where the snow never melts. Nadir Shah erected towers of the heads of those he tortured.

In the high country where the women hide in purdah and chadhuri ritual and privacy, and sweat in the embroidered burqa, and men hold one another's hands in romance seeing in each beloved the Warrior Poet, *Pushtanwali* protected Arachne. Pathans with fierce black eyebrows and carriage as high and proud as the mountains themselves gave her hospitality as a matter of honour. Mercy towards someone so weak and odd was a spiritual obligation. No Pathan is such a coward as to shed the blood of a god-given fool.

Arachne's nostrils were assailed by the odour of the earth on fire as pungent as flesh scorching. Eve's beauty plucked from the tail of a deadly serpent is perfume and the hot black hills surrender marble as if from the mouth of hell.

She pursued her shining path with trust, never carrying food upon her back. An eager expectant spirit shone in the body of a wandering beggar. Asexual and too intelligent to be cunning, Arachne crossed Afghanistan.

In Saudi Arabia, she was arrested.

BRUSSELS

Dear Jay-Jay,

You wouldn't believe this, but I'm sitting in a cemetery. In Belgium it drizzles. The trees are as green as huge silver beets and every gravestone is grey. I've been on trains looking out windows at moving countryside.

Beatrix disappointed me in terms of loyalty, and I decided to go on alone for a while. Visiting cemeteries has become a habit. I don't feel hassled by anyone here. Southern European men just don't get it that you're a lesbian. A woman is a woman to them and that's all they care about. They just want to grab you. But I discovered they respect their dead. The women in black have a kind of confidence, more than the men here in, as Oona would say, the dead heart of the city.

I've been staying in this feminist household. It's kind of wet and sad, and everybody only speaks English if they have to, so I've been reading. I was reading on the trains and I've continued. I had a dream in which gods and goddesses were making children under five cry…

Have you heard of St Unburdyne? She is a descendant of Aphrodite, but hermaphrodite and bearded. She is a saint, or demigoddess, who has nothing to do with fertility. Women pray to her to be relieved of the burden of their husbands. I've adopted her. And wonder which of these self-important widows under their bat-like umbrellas have in fact reached their new status through the intercession of St Unburdyne…

Anyway, how are things on the land? Much mud? Many leeches? And the mares? I heard on the grapevine that Vanessa, or someone, had a big argument with Oona over some of my things. Did Oona take them? What? Was it the pot pourri dream pillow that Lesley made for me? My I Ching? There was a gold coin I had taped in the back with the Chinese tossing pennies. Jay Jay, could you check on that? It's very important to me to have a piece of gold and a piece of silver protecting my things, my spirit. Is it true the argument was so bad Oona took off threatening to never come back again?

I wrote a poem called *Fear Of Dying Plants* in the cemetery yesterday. And Grundhilde, a Swiss-German woman who had arrived while I was away, read it. She says I have captivated her through my poetry. She read it over and over again, saying, things like "there is no self in this poem, no sense of individual destiny. A force is taken out of the deserts of Australia. The writer is rock and sand." My work has never been criticised so thoroughly before. I didn't even know I was a poet, but I suppose every woman is, if she just sits down and writes.

I've got to go now, it's getting cold. I'll enclose the London address. Love to everybody,

Et

4

PAPER LITTER dances down the track from the station at the whim of the wind. Before midnight on the Moorabbin rank, waiting for the Philip Morris call, ten cars, twelve cars? Iona is about the eighth. She is breaking her own rule, been here over half an hour already, and never liked this part of suburbia.

Today's newspaper says voters in Catalonia elect the first regional parliament since 1932. Under the dash is a Black Sparrow book of an Australian poet, Mary Low, who was there with her lover to fight in the International Brigade against the fascists... "gun barrels gleamed in the dark and a kitten played in and out between the rows of canvas shoes."

Iona looks down at her own sockless feet in Dunlop Volleys. The radio is dead. The cabbies ahead lounge in each other's cars.

"The night we arrived a well-known French poet was standing guard, among others. We saluted with a clenched fist as readily as shaking hands, drank wine from long-necked bottles. Wearing canvas shoes with rope soles and blue jeans, we rolled cigarettes fondly and dextrously and seemed not tired at all, but restless and excited. There was no sense of discipline but great friendliness and a desire to collaborate. I was amazed at first at the lack of personal criticism...the women who lined the way thrust flowers into the barrels of our rifles.... I wondered why they were going down and joined the line, forgetting the strange indifference of Spanish peoples to their own death and the powerful attraction that death itself exercises over them."

Sure enough a good book proves disastrous. From being eighth on the rank, she is now thirteenth at the factory gates, and is not likely to get a long fare. If any. Fatalism takes over. She reads, she dreams.

Who sits in the Automatic Cafe now, under the brims of low-slung lamps, while up and down the aisle people with secrets whisper together?

She remembers jogging towards it, keeping up with Zorro's long strides, across the Plaza de Catalunya.

Zorro is taller than most Spanish men. Her sombrero is deep green, almost black. Her woolly zamarra is worn with flair, falling from her shoulders fully, going no further than her waist. A few dark hairs grow on her upper lip and her eyebrows meet in the centre. She looks dangerous. Those of the underground are dangerous because their passionate belief is the stuff of martyrs and revolutionaries. The authorities, however, are more dangerous as their functionaries are cowardly, so robbed of free will they know no truth. Rumours of anarchism on the European continent set their guns a-blazing at movements in the grass, rabbits, terrorists escaping from impossible holes.

Zorro's war is a holy war against individual selfishness. Her politics are a religion to her. *La gente* verses *numero uno*.

Her mind is cool and razor-sharp from constant rubbing on the whetstone of idealism. And yet she is histrionic. She removes her Hasidic hat and slaps her forehead with wide arm movements and exclaims, *Mi madre, mi madre,* when troubled or annoyed.

Zorro's mother is a dumpy Spanish-Jewish woman who punctuates her long silences with rapid bursts of Catalan. This is done with the same busy determination housewives in tenements all over Barcelona thrust their washing out their windows to flutter and dry in the wind or sun. Zorro's mother has another daughter, Isabel, who is a Communist, doing socially and financially very well as a teacher. The truth is that she has, in fact, got Zorro out of scrapes all over Europe, so the curious mystery is that the exclamation, *mi madre, mi madre* or the slap of palm on forehead is communication. It must be telepathic as Zorro rarely returns to Barcelona for long, and her mother never leaves.

Zorro is perpetually busy on some errand. She has roamed from Israel to Northern Ireland, has associates in all the cities of Europe and an everyday facility in German, English, French as well as fluency in Castillian, Catalan and Hebrew. If she is not understood in words she speaks in gestures, definitive actions, her eyes. She has slept in jails, in factories, on the docks, under the trees, in brothels with saunas, been at home in the dwellings of the famous and the poor. Seldom does she pay for her bed, often does she provide the whole household with breakfast. She is in love with underprivileged peoples. It is her mission to right wrongs. There is a room for her everywhere.

Except England.

Iona lets out of her cab three migrant workers who have neither grace nor gratitude for her but, she suspects, healthy totals in their Building Society accounts.

The romanticism of politics is always brought down by something, at least for me. Something lived. These Southern suburbs look like the 'void', abyssmal. Is there an essence beyond the duality of either/or, neither conscious nor subconscious, but simply unknowable? Is there a void? There is a sense of one—a kind of vast sea upon which both our known and semi-known bits are tossed about—a terror past positive and negative—you know its edge. And fear to tread…

—Birmingham, that wet and miserable night. Zorro and I hitching across the horrid foreignness of England. The coldness in the people that night exascerbating the harshness of the climate. My bourgeois charm cracked and shattered and I bellowed at her. My benefactor. Me, passive little Australian in search of experience, to have on the face of it more experience than Frances, who was shivering away in a London dump, shooting up. Something I considered, consider, disgusting. Yet I reckon I paid for a hit. Hindsight. Frances had been so righteous back here, when we were lovers, finding fault with all my assumptions, being holy in the words and thoughts of Simone Weil. Well I'd found the real thing, Zorro. I got as naked as King Lear in that Birmingham storm. Sleet, rain and wind howling round the tangle of motorways, spaghetti junction, I was panicked for a little comfort, screaming through the cacophony of lorries at Zorro. She, too, was cold, but on some frightening business to do with political prisoners in Belfast. I was seeking the land of my father. I wanted to escape the mean shame of hitchhiking and moneylessness. All Zorro's contacts turned us out. Her caring so well for me filled me with anger. The sound of her tin whistle I hated. I felt guilty.

Now Helen has written, True freedom demands a commitment to social actions which terrifies you…for you are really shackled with recurring bouts of melancholy'.

Iona, getting back onto the Nepean Highway, regains her peace of mind by thinking of Zorro who is now so far away from her, and, unlike Helen, not threatening to come to Australia.

Zorro travels best by night. She knows the Moon intimately, grows mystical in its light. She plays her shepherd's whistle without musicality, without ear, yet with a haunting quality reminiscent of a secret language devised by the Resistance to resemble creatures of the night to confound the Nazis. She hears, when she arrives, the politics of resentment and the theories of hope murmured in doorways and cafes. She can lurk in the shadows like a street urchin, almost invisible.

'If' is the love story of fiction. 'If' is the mental escape from guilt, from melancholia. The nebulas of the Milky Way move in spirals. Beginnings are beginnings again, each a little further on the way?

'If' alone can be a reason to be a writer.

—No-one, Iona says to her tape-recorder, holds a spiral in a box without running the risk of being punched on the chin by a boxing glove on a spring.

Oona picked up a copy of *Gray's Anatomy* in Victor Harbour at a St Vincent de Paul op shop where she had intended to buy a shirt. A few weeks camping on The Coorong, perhaps at Policemans Point or Salt Creek, and I could be a genius. Knowing all about the insides of myself. The spinal cord and its membranes. The Osseous Labyrinth of the inner ear. The relations of the large intestine with the kidney. Yeah.

Like self-educated people everywhere, Oona has a fascination with books containing information, especially diagrams. Except for its weight, *Gray's Anatomy* is perfect. Published 1901. Age in books impresses her as well. The physical item standing the test of time has somehow proved its classical worth. A hardback that has been around for eighty or a hundred years is like a tree or a rock in human knowledge terms.

Having the book is enough for Oona most of the time, she can always look into it. Her memory, an untrained and almost loose mental faculty, tends to scramble rather than retain facts. It is a free bird, relentlessly collecting and flying on. Migrating from one field of knowledge to another as if the *Encyclopedia Britanica* were Asia and Ramon Mascord's *Australian Spiders* an island in Bass Strait. Short on the saving side, her mind is tireless in curiosity. Phrases such as 'Genito-crural Nerve' are as intriguing as the hundreds of beetles she has observed. Knowing the little thing has a birth, a life, a place to live, work to do and a death is okay, but you never know what, where, when, how. The anatomical phrase is also descriptive of a truth she believes rather than knows. She can read that 'the genito-crural nerve passes obliquely through the substance of the Psoas' as easily as she can watch the coloured drop of the ladybird sprout wings and fly.

Indulgence in fascination and curiosity has her in two minds whether to visit her friends outside Mount Compass or to hitch around Lake Alexandrina to the Princes Highway. Her friends will have a crop at this time of year and maybe there would be some money in it if she took a couple of pounds to Melbourne. A girl's got to stay alive and I don't want my scales getting rusty. Trouble is if I go there before I go down The Coorong I'll smoke it all myself.

The Coorong, with its sweeping coastal grasses and calm enclosed water sustaining such a magnificent variety of sea and land birds including pelicans, seems sweet as she imagines it. Lake Alexandrina is pink with lime. It looks like a chemical waste dump but it is natural. The pale rock bordered by browner stone is great in the houses, built last century on acres of land which look like they carry nothing. No stock, no raggedy horses, nothing. Looks like some part of France where they have those wild white horses with long manes and tails. I could squat that place over there, but it looks so bloody lonely and exposed. And even though the land shouldn't be worth a deal of dope, I reckon some regular bastard owns it. Probably hunt me off with a shotgun.

Policemans Point, okay.

As she walks she has forgotten the myriad curiosities of anatomy and she is used to the new weight of her gear. Walking is a rhythm she loves. It's in my blood. She doesn't have to concentrate, thoughts float through her attention like wracks of mist in the mountains. Or they are eagles. Some inform her. Some attack with sudden substance. Some exist outside her immediacy, like scenery.

Onions, Oona muses, either boast about how cheap something was or about how expensive it was. Pearls know real worth or everything is valueless and so, valuable. But if I'm going to trade I can't just lump all onions together. There are all sorts of onions, there's spring onions and onion weed, garlic, white ones and brown. Is garlic an onion? Anyway, if I'm dealing I figure is this one going to appreciate expensive grass or cheap. There's those who'll pay more if you give them some free for a start…

The driest state in the bloody Southern Hemisphere and it begins to rain. The Coorong is a beautiful place but no shelter. Oona crosses the road. Faces west.

Standing under a gum with a mighty trunk shedding long sheets of bark, Oona's mood changes. She resents her homelessness.

A year or so ago, she was secure in her mountain hut. The bushmen's cabin made of stones rudely piled on each other and stuck together with the clay from around, which you slip on in the wet, with a rusty corrugated iron roof and chimney, was her home from the moment she found it. And no one bothered her. Amos flexed his muscles a couple of times at the Warribuck Hills Family pub, saying it was rightly his because it was his mother's. Oona gave him the odd twenty dollars. Or argued with him. Peace and quiet. She grew her own crop then, and all that was left of smack was dreamy half sleep. Survival, the bare essence of life reasserting itself over the downward suction that had been the life of addiction, was turning her into a strong woman.

They found her in the middle of the day sleeping on her ticking mattress. She heard them but snakes and various other creatures of the bush had taught her to stay put without a glimmer of a movement until the situation was assessed. They left the hut in shocked hurry. Humans, they didn't go off into the scrub but talked right there on her doorstep.

Their car was parked at the end of the track and streaked with red dust. They were travelling from Lithgow to Richmond doing the penultimate leg of a Melbourne to Sydney journey. No Hume Highway trip this. The five women in the old grey Holden had a dream of land. They dreamed of a place where men would never come, a kind of refuge for women in the womb of nature.

—Some women are frightened, for nature is cruel as she heals.

—The women who know that the inexpressible excitement beyond the inner end of their vaginas is like the face of god on Judgment Day—it can't be looked upon unless it has been approached with love—will know this is right.

—For the women afraid of the dark and the suggestions of the nocturnal gods, the mountain, this mountain, is not the place for comfort.

—The interconnected points of the triangle are spirit, sex, and money. It is the tripod of our politics. We've got to get the money together to buy this place.

—What about…?

—Obviously, she is one of us. Whatever is wrong with her we can heal her.

—We've decided, without deciding.

—As soon as we saw the FOR SALE sign nailed to that tree.

—And as we passed the orchards and grazing paddocks, and as it got steeper, we were more and more certain.

—Coming to the gate, through that avenue of pines, the trees were singing, sighing, humming, keening, calling …

—The pines were chanting, like us, introduced onto this continent, yet yearning somehow.

—The tunnel of pines was muscular, drawing us in. Moving, pulling, massaging.

—And then there was the gate, with the rickety old sign saying BRIGADOON, which name we will change …to what?

—I want horses, mares. I've always wanted horses, to run together as brumbies.

—I want dreams, nightdreams as, if we get this place, my daydreams are settled.

—Isn't 'nightmares' sexist?

—Sure is. No-one would come to Nightmare Mountain.

—Not even women. We must get other women involved or otherwise we won't be able to get enough money together.

—Instead of relating to each other with reference to our sun signs, here let's treat each other as if our sign were the moon. For instance, instead of you thinking of me as a Taurus you think of me as a Pisces which is my moon. And so on. It'd make life different.

—Let's have no boy horses, no boy dogs and no boy children, because even though they're not men, they will bring male energy to the place. And we want to live in a totally female environment. The earth is already feminine.

—What about boy dingos and boy kangaroos?

—What about Moonmare Mountain?

—That has a hum to it, I like it.

—Mountain of the Moonmares. It's a bit romantic but joins the equine and the feminine while subverting the sexist 'nightmare'.

—Fancy naming a place before we even own it. Fancy agreeing on a name so soon. Collective decisions usually take months.

—Must be a sign that it'll be ours.

—It will be ours.

—I feel sure, too.

—And we had just about got to Sydney without luck.

—I knew we'd find it. We've found it.

—I reckon we have.

—Now we just have to organise a fund-raising campaign, after we check with the agent.

—It's for sale, it's cool. I know it. I know things like this.

Oona on her bed had her eyes wide open straining to hear every verse of this Utopian chorus. Instinctively she knew that Amos would not like these girls. And yet their certainty was unanswerable. She got up. Opened the door and looked at them.

—Suppose you could go a cup of tea. Got three mugs.

So I met Beatrix, Etama, Vanessa, Jay Jay and Lesley. Within months they had the money and were paying off the loan. And they moved up with tents, tarpaulins, caravans and began building the house. My hut became the kitchen-meeting house. I was never one of them though, no matter what their idyllic politics say. Anyway the food was good and in a way they did heal me, but they had no right to assume I was one of them. I am an outlaw. Everything belongs to everybody. They smoked my grass. Sure they planted more. But they took what I had, all I had. Every bloody dyke that hears about the place, Moonmare Mountain, thinks it's hers. The first five, well I have to say I've got a soft spot for them. But Beatrix and Etama are gone, overseas. And these young ones, I don't know.

An old Bedford truck pulls up.

—You look wet, the farmer yells, get in.

On the speedometer, the geriatric hand shudders at no more than thirty miles an hour all the way to Strathalbyn, while Oona and the old fella discuss the state of affairs in the district. He arranges a ride for her with a young buck which gets her to her friends' property in time for tea.

The roof of their house is like a slouch hat being doffed on the left. A brim sagging under the weight of rain, the uneven verandah runs around three sides. On the fourth side a group of very high peppercorn trees grows dangerously close to the wall.

—What do you want? The young man on the other side of the screen door does not know her.

—Is Roge around?

—Roge? You a friend of his?

—You could say so.

—You might as well come in.

Oona feels the slight tremor which moves through the group, two men and three women, as she enters—the fear she sets up in people. They never know with her whether they've brought a viper or a christ disguised as a beggar into their home. Oona herself chooses which to be.

—It's wet.

—That it is. It's great, just what we need.

—How are you Roge? Cec?

—Okay. This is Simon. He's a jesus freak.

—Ah, to see again the visions of Ezekiel, I was the lamb.

—Will you be okay on the verandah? All the beds inside are taken.

—Are there enough vegies, Sal, for another?

—I reckon.

The sky clears completely about ten o'clock and there is the wide expanse of stars, no moon. Simon, the jesus freak, is young and skinny, vibrating with constant praise and gratitude to the Lord. In Oona he has found a listening ear. He stands with his back to her and she lounges on the couch-bed.

—I cannot think of it as night, he says enthusiastically to himself or to Oona or the Lord, there being no night there. Instead I try to remember this black surround with lights streaking across it as part of my native orbit, part of my world. And I reflect that these electron missiles are probably everywhere, moving even through the darkness of my own body.

—I like the Bible. I have a leather-bound King James version that's about a hundred years old at home. But now for spiritual reading I've got the I Ching.

—The world has changed since the parting of the Red Sea. Now the Lord works in different ways, through our minds. If we could even partly conceive of how big and how little the things that he controls are, we must sink to our knees in amazement. He knows about nuclear physics. He also inspired the Chinese mystics. Even women's liberation is a part of his plan. It's his way of saving the earth from destruction. He knows about drugs and the peace movement. He sees all. He knows all. He forgives all.

Reminded that she has Etama's paperback of the I Ching, Oona rummages through her pack to find it. The bare globe screwed to the rafters of the verandah and shaded by a tangle of cobwebs throws barely enough light to read by. She feels the cover and carefully taped on the inside of the back is a small packet of coins. There are four not three. Odd.

His talk of god brought Janice to mind, and when he has gone, Oona thinks of her. Hers is a zealous faith. She is like Sir Galahad seeking some holy grail. They call me a thief, but with Jay Jay 'thou shalt not steal' does not apply. With her shiny black hair, she is like a black cat, a cat burglar out on the tiles. With her, and it's just the energy of her faith, the diamond is turned into the chalice. They are the same for her. How she got the money for the thousand acres of mountain country is constantly intriguing for Oona. Vanessa, I know, organised dances, wrote letters, instituted a Moonmare Mountain Collective and newsletter and offered city women shares to have a kind of retreat in the bush, away from the city and their jobs. But from some of the arguments those two have had, I know Janice provided most of the deposit. How? My theory is that with Beatrix's help she did a few credit card jobs, she's good at disguises and accents. The thing is she could, and she remains guiltless, because then it's all given away. She wants to create a society. She has vision. And she is a leader. But Jay Jay eats her own tail. She's monstrously monogamous and murderously jealous while demanding devoted loyalty from all. Jay Jay, the magnet, I love her. Black pearl, she is.

Oona's knuckles whiten over the packet of coins. She is still sore about the disagreement that obliged her to leave. More women had come to live on the Moonmare acres and Vanessa, having her name on the deeds, was worried about money, and the formalising of collective. She argued that everybody who lived there should buy shares. At least, one, at 500 dollars each. Janice fought back, saying it was open women's land. Oona refused to pay, she argued that she lived there first, that it was hers and they were her guests. Trees said she did not have the money, but would put in as much work as she was capable of. The night wore on and the meeting became more fractious and everybody except Oona believed that the responsibility to pay was everybody's. Janice had turned. Lesley and the others, including the mothers and their children, all accepted the duty of payment. Oona said no. No. It was not the first uncomfortable meeting on that subject. They all found Oona intransigent and stubborn and bloody arrogant. Then Quince, holding her little girl on her lap, had suggested that Oona had stolen Etama's things from the tea chest in the house. The smugness of the allegation's delivery took away all Oona's rationality. No-one asked how Quince would know. She smashed a log of wood onto the mugs and tea cups and went out into the night and walked down the mountain.

At Bilpin in the wet mist of dawn, Oona decided not to go to Sydney, but outback.

5

————————here is how it is when the lion thrashes the serpent for the fight is terrible and the darkness is a boa constrictor strangling the world almost to death before the lion comes with a mane of rainbow sunbeams so golden and triumphant in this i believe and i am a loyal leo here it is how with my right finger i write on the floor of my cell in the sand in the night i have no light i have one window facing east too high up to see out only the sky my bed is a pallet on the dirt covered by a carpet the walls are very very old————————————————

EACH EXERCISE book of my journal requires a new picture and a formal address.

Dear diary, do you like your cover?

I chose it specially for my years and your charm. A sunset scene across the sea. Waves of liquid amber finishing at burnished rocks in foamy locks of gold. Artistically quite dead. Remember the Vermeer? The pregnant lady reading in that beam of light, oh dear, it was so difficult to write in you then. And the Bruegel? It quite defeated my intention to be truthful, for I was forever imagining myself among crowds of hungry peasants enjoying the Wedding Feast, and trying to wipe the pig-grease off my chin.

Truth, up there, firmamentally so to speak, something to reach for…

Oh remember the cows my daddy called Heat, Light and Sound? My past, my childhood, on the dairy farm in the Strzelecki Ranges, is painted by Hans Heysen now—the mud and the gumboots—as if I never lived it at all. It is crisply framed and consigned to the gallery.

Dear diary, I chose this most carefully. Each morning I walk along the shell-line of the beach and how green grows my envy of the graphic artist. I fancy the driven souls of the great painters, but this, this sunset even I could paint, given a couple of classes.

Lately I've had one of *those* books from the library. Tears crept out.

I am not like Eve. I am not like Abel. I am like Cain bearing the mark on my head. The mark of god's disapproval of me. But Cain is a murderer and a man, bearer of the weapon and the scar, but not the weeping wound. *The Bell Jar* by Sylvia Plath. She talks of Mrs Willard 'braiding a rug out of strips of wool from Mr Willard's old suits. She had spent a week on that rug… instead of hanging the rug on the wall the way I would have done, she put it down in place of her kitchen mat…'

I am not like Cain. I am like Mrs Willard's mat, and unfortunately it is not possible to meet Miss Plath as she did away with herself.

This awful sunset allows me self pity, that is what it is.

If one could freeze a brazen second that is how it would be—a platitude, a dead truism. There is no still point in the sea. Such death Van Gogh could never paint.

Jocelyn! My dear. What a horror she is!

Any rate, I've been striding on old shank's pony out past the factories to do a bit of work for her in the kennels. Her laugh, diary dear, is like a wall of mirthless sound.

My shell of lies upsets her you know, quite upsets her. I should have charity but I don't need to have it. My face brings out vices in others. They look at me and they're faced with their own lower sides. She tries not to look at me, pretends she is, but it's my left shoulder she talks to, like someone on TV reading the idiot board. Disconcerting. She welcomes me because of her boneheaded stupidity. I couldn't understand why the dogs could love her so. Now I see it is her selfishness they love. They are her kingdom.

You see, a thoroughly selfish individual cannot see beyond power over others.

She is their white goddess, their jealous Io, dispensing food, affection, punishment quite arbitrarily.

Troubling happenings in the garden! I think the big gum tree is being taken over. The crows seem more in residence than the magpies lately. Does this mean a death in the household?

Flush found me an abalone shell this morning. A gift with meaning, don't you think, diary dear? The mother-of-pearl on the inner side of the tough and ugly outer shell so that the fish itself has a very pretty home.

————————in this part of the world civilisation is very old the ceiling is low on the west side where my pallet is and high on the east side where the window is and it is the same clay as the walls i don't know how it stays up it has a crack in it from north to south and that is my boa constrictor because most of the time it is a dark snake before dawn everything is dark so it has eaten everything when i write in the fine sand i put my back to it————————

One relapse into guilt drops her into all her depressions, all her guilts. Iona emerges from a TAB on Whitehorse Road trying to toss off cloying melancholia with betting tickets on trotters chosen for their names. Too lazy to study the form. Frances introduced her to the delicious fatalism of gambling, the mug's game. The cab is unlocked, engine running, 'VACANT' glowing on the roof.

The wide road is shiny with rain and reflecting amber, white and red lights. She hates driving in this weather. It is a fallacy about getting more customers, fewer people are out. Yet another thing annoys her: it is the road itself. Melbourne is a radial city, major arterial routes come to the centre like spokes of a wheel. This is the vein to her mother's house in Healesville. Its familiarity caused by so many faint-hearted trips of duty gives it a dull patina.

Mary would say her mother was spiritually dark, full of emotional blackmail, a lowering cloud. Iona cannot judge so harshly.

She fought that 'blackmail' once. She sold everything she had to go overseas. Her mother's face among the lesbians' at the airport was tragic. Its age, its cragginess, its sadness haunted her most of the time she was away with its stubborn refusal to forgive. She had a right to her independence, she argued, you want me to be strong, well I must be free to be fully responsible. You're too impressionable, her mother said, it is because of one of 'those women' you spend your time with.

In fact it was. It was Frances. And the argument was just ideals verbalised preceding their own realisation. Frances had left her without farewell. Frances had judged her complacent and insular. In the months between the two departures, she could see no beauty but Frances', no wisdom but her words. The struggle between black cloud and thunder raged in her psychic sky. Her sun hardly shone in those months. She probably seemed mad.

Do we never grow up, never ever? Her mood is that of the burdened teenager she was, bussing back along this road from university or from school sporting events; somehow, not only responsible for her own fatherlessness, but also for the death of her sister, Veronica. For her mother's sadness. For Nola's infantilism.

Bad tempered taxi-drivers get no fares, not out on the Maroondah Highway in the rain.

Frances had gone without her. If she could not have Frances, she could be Frances. She copied her, first in travelling like that, the moss gatherer becoming the rolling stone and secondly, in her clothes sense, she aped her taste. The way she had of walking. The thoughts in her head were Frances-quotes. 'Love is a myth if it pretends people are not alone.' 'Families are economic units, cells in a structure designed to exploit the powerless.' As most people met are passing strangers, Frances' style ironically became Iona's natural asset. On Frances it was won and worn, wrought, sincere and tarty, aggressive, sulky. In contrast it gave Iona an artless air, a cool aristocracy, as if she had pulled on the rags nearest to hand and forgotten them. Where Frances goes there go I, what Frances does do I. That was my rule of travel.

Frances had taught Iona one crucial thing. To trust her sexuality, to trust sex itself, divorced from the claims it made on partners. All the romantic myths were illusions which, if you looked through them, had sinister chains beneath the cigarette-ad surfaces of conformist happiness.

An arm waves under a street lamp. To Healesville. To Healesville? He is drunk. He sleeps alongside her in the front seat in which all men sit except some poofters and those necking with girlfriends.

Mrs Flynn's anger with Iona for leaving her alone those twelve months was inextricably linked with her anger at her husband. They both dared to steal their own independence when it was actually her personality which would use independence best. Nola thumped in her wheelchair. Nothing would grow on Veronica's grave. After fifteen years of trying she had finally given up. She had sea pebbles thrown over it and once a month she raked them. Veronica with her fragile femininity and her sharp precocious tongue was the one who understood her. She had threatened her father with genius: how dare a girl so young beat a dashing man consistently at chess? Watching Veronica slice him up in so subtle a way had been a revenge.

Privately she was furious with the girls. Nola's blessed innocence was pointless idiocy. She thought of euthanasia almost as much as she remained determined to keep her out of an institution. The older ones, the boys, Frank and Terry, were dutiful, normal. Good Catholics, Terry, a Christian Brother, and Frank with his family. The other Mrs Flynn, her daughter-in-law, was beyond the pale, a woman who buried her small miseries under a mountain of food. Yet when Michael left for good, it was Veronica, then aged nine, and Iona, aged three, who gave her strength. Again and again the blows seemed to fall on her. The harder they fell the more proud she became. 'Atheism indicates strength of mind, but only up to a certain point', Iona had written, quoting Pascal's *Pensées.* It seemed everyone had a deeper religious streak than herself, and Iona, she suspected, was more truly spiritual than Terry. Even Michael in his perfidy was the sentimental Irish Catholic to the end. She had his papers: drunken ramblings. There was no mistaking the hand. Half crabbed, half generous, the Greek e's, the flying d's, the t's like lonely crosses planted on the hillside of the upward slant of the lines. Guilt and religiosity, morbid rubbish. There was nothing in the world Mrs Flynn hated more than depravity.

Now, as her body was getting too weak to carry on, the vulnerability of the flesh seeping into that strength of conviction, she found love returning to main place in her thoughts. She loved Iona. With a passion. It was the one thing that kept her from despair.

If Iona had chosen to reflect Oona and not Frances in the big cities of the Western world, she would not have been so successful. Somewhere behind the style and sophistication was the dream of riding camels across the Nullarbor Plain, the grubby fingernails, loose-fitting overalls. The future, a dream, put a dimension into her need. The melancholy sense of duty brought a quality of care into her already quite beautiful eyes. She made love on the Island of Hydra, in Spain, Italy, Paris, Amsterdam, had lovers in London, New York, and she spent a great deal of time questioning her motives. Running herself through the wringer of self-examination, on the run. Away from the quagmire of home, it was impossible to wallow.

She wakes her passenger. He is aggressive, inarticulate.

—Listen mate, I only want to know your address, and take the money you owe me.

It is a credit card. The address is down the road from where her mother will be probably watching the *Don Lane* Show.

In the middle fifties certain outdoor angles of the house were photographed for *Home Beautiful.* Now this archway path of wisteria and jasmine vines is dripping and overgrown. The scent of the shrubs and phlox near the verandah dismisses the swampy feelings Iona had of home. There's the warmth of being loved, a womb-cosiness in the comfortable rambling walls.

—You're so like your father, her mother says, just coming in through the night like that. Any night, unannounced, always knowing I'd be here.

—Guess I am like him, unsuccessful writer and all. She kisses her mother's soft, sagging cheek.

—You are a better writer than he was. And more successful.

—Mm, I recorded something for the ABC the other day.

They talk, make a cup of tea, have a brandy, converse easily about the state of the world and Mrs Flynn's interests. The native shrubs outside the windows move with water. Nola grunts in her sleep. The house is smaller than it looks from the outside.

—Do you think I am a wastrel?

—That's for you to prove one way or the other. I've been thinking, Iona, I'd really like a holiday from Nola. To go away by myself. Perhaps on a houseboat down the Murray or the Hawkesbury, the Myall Lakes. Maybe I'm dreaming, but I really am exhausted. She's getting heavier, and I'm getting weaker.

Panic about the old familial duress sets into Iona's nervous system. The desperate pull of her need to say no automatically wars with sympathy for her mother.

—Yes, you do need a holiday…

—I think about euthanasia, I think about suicide. I'm crying more than I ever have. I wish it was Nola who died, not Veronica, and I know I am committing a sin in doing so. You could write here. It is lovely in the Dandenongs, especially in Spring. Time and comfort, only Nola. Better than a shed in miserable Fitzroy.

—Listen, Mum, I'm losing money by being here, an empty cab out the front. I don't know. I just don't know.

Her mother looks so old as she gets up to say goodbye, standing on the verandah hugging her cardigan around her breasts. Iona feels drained.

—'Night.

She turns on the two way radio as soon as she is in the cab. She is hungry for work.

—Where are you, Gay One Seven?

—Healesville, Base.

—There's a bloke wants to go to Tullamarine at Lilydale, can you make it?

—Ten minutes. Is it mine?

—Roger.

—Roger, beauty.

————————they picked me up at the airport i dont know why because i could not understand the language at all not even the gestures it was late at night there was a SAS jet stopping at 3 am and i was going to get on that and off it at athens but i was sitting down and there was one airport attendant in long white robes and a uniform blazer and there was one man behind the food counter getting dips and unleavened bread ready for a flight that was coming but going in the opposite direction to mine then suddenly six policemen were jabbering excitedly and the attendant pointed to me and they raced over and disturbed me and pulled everything out of my pack and wanted to undress me but they didn't touch me i was talking in english but that made no impression________________

ANDORRA

Dear Trees,

These incredible mountains, the Pyrenees, are magical—it wouldn't be hard to believe in appearances of the Blessed Virgin Mary arriving through the sky in a rainbow bubble out of this landscape. Each village is dominated by a church.

I'm not in love, neither with this environment, nor with my present sleeping partner, but I have a kind of urgent contentment, if that makes sense. I am talking all the time. Grundhilde is so interested in Australia, which she constantly refers to as Terra Incognita, the feminine land of the unknown. Is it unknowable? She has a trained mind. She is good for me. Her questions and my answers—I don't know—are like solids and the spaces around them. Sculptural, does that make sense? Australia, I say, allows no death, no quittance, only mystery, disappearance and magnetism. We did have sex a couple of times but it's important to neither of us. At least, not to me. I've been giving history lessons, geography, geology …and I told her that John Macarthur found the sheep which started the economy of the jail colony in Spain. She says, Let's go there. So here we are, on our way, an expedition of exploration.

You know I was homesick until I found Grundhilde; there's always light if there's shadow. From being in the shadow of Beatrix's defection I've come into a light of Grundhilde's interest in me, in us, Australian women (lesbians). There's something more than passing interest, politeness, in her greed for knowledge. She's searching. I agree with that. Nothing's wasted, not time, not movement, it's reinterpreted to make it worthwhile. She read Patrick White's *Voss* in French which I found in Paris.

Is it because Europe has become so small, always been so small, that they're hungry for frontiers? Well, Switzerland's very small, of course, and narrow if Grundhilde's right. As masculine as I say Australia is feminine.

In talking of our wide-open spaces, the explicitly female shapes of our rocks and hills and trees, I can't help mentioning, well I'm always infusing my descriptions with our womenpower, our land, Moonmare Mountain. I think I've challenged her, deeply, her own sense of superior destiny is rivalled by my talk of eccentric Amazons, living in the wild like pygmies, like the Bushmen of Africa. In the tribe situation. A lot of what I'm saying is bullshit and I know it, but I love to say it. It's like I'm blowing mirages out of my mouth and she sees them as real places to discover, to arrive at.

Incidentally the power is not all mine. She knows so much, about reincarnation and mysticism. She knows Jung better than Jung himself. (Being a woman.) And she can make music with anything! A plastic band pulled from her teeth she can get more out of than a dill like me can get from a guitar.

She is fascinating. Travelling is fascinating, and annoying. Men in uniforms everywhere. I'm on a voyage of discovery, Trees, an apt and appropriate venture for my Saturn return, don't you think?

I sent my London address with Jay Jay's letter, but I'll include it here too. So please write,

Your good friend, love,

Et.

P.S. Is it true Arachne is hitchhiking through Afghanistan? What a moron! E.

——————you probably want that shifty crowd i was travelling with for the past two weeks well they just deserted the combi van leaving the keys in the ignition and me in the back they took a couple of canvas bags and ran away and while i was sorting out my thoughts i heard a light aircraft take off that was about fifteen miles away i drove myself to the airport very slowly because i did not know i could drive the combi van is in the carpark but i suppose you know that i talked all this in english very quickly it was keeping me on the track and everybody was talking so i was too______________________________

6

UPDIKE: "OUR actions, our decisions, our vows matter: what can fiction tell us more than that?"

A very sick old chap sits in the back of the cab, next to a nursing Sister.

—I feel I'm followed through crowds by an invisible person with Parkinson's disease. The ghost of St Vitus himself.

Nurse and patient pay and get out in Phoenix Street, Braybrook. They had depressed her. The night is full of weirdos. Iona is vulnerable to it.

—To indicate a fundamentally illogical sameness is the stuff and use of poetry.

The moon is a fat yellow deity, eventually setting about three a.m. When it has gone she is lonely. She is abused by a wharfie in the pre-dawn for running over his foot. He is going to sue her and the Cab Company, and, if she were a man she'd be waking up in hospital. Yes sir.

Dicky, sticky. She accelerates right out of Port Melbourne pretending she is in a car chase, living a fantasy of TV crime and innocence to get her to the north side of the city in record time.

She cruises up Nicholson Street, a certain swagger in her fingers on the wheel, a whistle from her lips, ignoring the radio calls which are coming thick and fast. Outside the Exhibition Buildings she is hailed by a woman with a suitcase. Bird families in the oaks are deafening and there is a sort of charcoal light in the east.

An odour of familiarity. She looks for the first time at her passenger in the rear-view mirror, frowns.

—Iona!

—Pamela? I can hardly recognise you.

—It's me. I've hennaed my hair.

—Your nose is different.

—Nose job.

—Why? And you've lost weight.

—Anorexic, darling.

—You're completely different each time I see you. Remember when you had such a hold over me? You with your prediction of white witches gathering in Melbourne. I always imagine you with that huge garbage bag of grass hanging over your shoulder, like Father Christmas, standing in the middle of the road. Your hair was yellow and curly. You had nice big thighs and you wore floppy Indian things.

—Let's have a coffee.

—L'Alba?

—Haven't been in Melbourne for ages.

Over long glasses of milk coffee between ribbons of cigarette smoke rising from a square dance round the ashtray, they talk. Light takes over outside.

—My nerve broke. Suddenly snap, thwack, gone, I was a shivering jellyfish.

—You?

—Spent some time in the bin, came out making decisions to change. Everything.

—How's your asthma?

—Nearly died last summer. Janice and her mates tried to cure me with potions and hexes. Had no ventolin. Couldn't breathe. Miles into the inaccessible craggy mountains. You're lucky to see me.

—You went up to the Mountain of the Moonmares? You?

—Why not? It's for women isn't it?

—You're not what I imagine the type, that's all.

—Apart from nearly dying, it was stunning. Between earth and sky, city and country, birth and death, basic you know.

—Mary was talking about asthma the other day. She says it's unshed tears.

—That's me. How is the old witch?

—She's good, reading a lot of spiritual stuff. The phlegm in your lungs are tears which won't come out your eyes.

Iona laughs.

—I cry all the time.

—I don't and I don't have asthma but it's typical of Mary's thinking these days, if you see what I mean.

—Who's she on with?

—She also said, on the matter of love and sexual relations, that she thinks one has strong connections with certain people forged over lifetimes, and reforged, so one cannot have endless sexual relationships. Feminists, she now says, have a death wish that is downright dangerous. The desire to use magic exclusively for women is to practise black magic.

—She ought to know.

—So, what are you up to? Another cafe latte?

—I've been living in Sydney. Been fucking with this young physicist, learning about vectors, quasars, and so on with a view to two things, to understand the Apocalypse and to get pregnant.

—But you don't look happy, and you're here in the dawn with a suitcase.

—I got a lift with a truckie.

—Why?

—Well I left him. Arrogant little shit started to use the arts I taught him to seduce fresher girls.

—Why do you want to get pregnant?

—Narcissism, I suppose. Anyway I don't think I was successful.

—Suddenly I'm really tired, Pamela, I've had a hard night.

—What's Mary's address?

Iona writes it down on a paper napkin, picks up her change machine and rises to look down on the now pathetic figure of Pamela.

—Will you be all right?

Pamela's presence is surprisingly debilitating for one so amusing.

Why do these odd-bods drain Iona's energy? It's like a self-sorrow overtakes Pamela and she'll use her to the limit, drag her to a psychic edge she doesn't want to know about. Iona has to escape.

—My partner will be waiting for the cab.

—Iona, can you pay for the coffees?

—Do you want a loan?

—No way, you'd never get it back.

The tragic tears integral to some nights transmogrify into the obscene laughter of hopeless dissipation of night people at daybreak. We can't be earnest.

—See you.

—'Bye.

There is a quote on her scribble pad, from Helen's most recent letter, 'you are a traveller and among your personal things is the self-required baggage of sanity, so rigidly defined that you have virtually no room left for passionate emotion'.

—————————i am not being strangled by the overhanging snake because the sun beats it everyday i am being stifled by a stuffiness my little window has three bars and no glass it is not air i crave by the sound it makes my door is locked by a steel shaft in a bracket i am stifled by a stuffiness inside myself i am annoyed i cannot believe a strong man out there is going to risk his neck to save me_________________

Dear Diary., a computer error in the States nearly gave us nuclear war. Second time in a week. I should be scared, but I'm not.

What on earth possessed Marion to give me Dorothy Richardson for my birthday?

Her reading group must have a new member, perhaps an energetic young wife with feminist leanings. Marion lives always one step from primary sources. She is adept at vicarious living. Except child-bearing, but that's well over; any rate, she lives vicariously through her sons.

She said she sent to England for them, poor Marion.

More important than anything is to give me a significant present for my birthday or Christmas. I'm not to be a maiden aunt with drawers full of boxed handkerchiefs and talcum powder.

Four thick volumes: *Pilgrimage*. I loved the title. She saw my face and she was satisfied. So much so that I haven't opened them in weeks.

Now I have and she has given me a friend. Dorothy and I will go on for some time.

When will I meet my own living scribe? Can Dorothy Richardson turn up alive?

How exciting it must have been for Virginia Woolf when she first read this lady!

Oona is driving. Simon holds a Bible on his lap in the passenger seat.

—The trees went forth on a time to anoint a king over them.

—Read on.

She had stayed a couple of weeks under the hat-brim verandah at Mount Compass until Simon's friends turned up in a van to take him for a jesus weekend in the Flinders Ranges. She decided to go to Broken Hill.

—And they said unto the olive tree, Reign thou over us. But the olive tree said unto them, Should I leave my fatness, wherewith by me they honour God and man, and go to be promoted over the trees?

The two other young men, children of the lord, are in a pleasant state of euphoria in the back seat owing both to their enchantment with the divine and several puffs of Roge's marihuana. They utter encouraging hallelujahs as Simon reads. Oona listens. The neat vineyards either side of the road suit the reading from the Old Testament. She likes to drive.

—And the trees said to the fig tree, Come thou and reign over us. But the fig tree said unto them, Should I foresake my sweetness and my good fruit, and go and be promoted over the trees? Then the trees said unto the vine,…

One of the boys in the back rolls down the window and shouts along with Simon,

—Come thou and reign over us.

—And the vine said unto them, Should I leave my wine, which cheereth God and man, and go to be promoted over the trees? Then all said to the bramble,

—Come thou and reign over us, the boys shout.

—And the bramble said unto the trees, If in truth ye anoint me king over you then come put your trust in my shadow; and if not, let fire come out of the bramble, and devour the cedars of Lebanon.

Oona frowns, grins, thinks.

—Well, that's the word of the lord, Book of Judges.

—It's great. It is a prophecy which I reckon has happened.

The Jesus lads do not wish to discuss it and soon Oona's own mind wanders. The riddle of the rows of trellised vines.

Before Janice came with her friends and took Brigadoon and made it Moonmare Mountain, Oona had a way with nature. Each tree could talk. Each tree could stand alone. So it seemed, although lantana and blackberries were a problem in some places. Staghorns seemed like little kids getting a piggyback. There was a sense, an evenness which was like the bible said, before The Book of Kings. But something had happened, and did happen, and was happening. She was trying to figure what grapevines were like in their natural state. What did they hang on to, or did they run along the ground and climb over dead stumps?

The way the Bible has it, the trees don't have a choice once they've asked for a king. The bramble has to be boss or burn the cedars of Lebanon. No going back, it seems.

Well there's no going back for me either. I found myself fighting flood and storm and fallen trees and fires. Janice was fighting the women. Each of us kind of protecting the other. My aloneness was shattered. I am by myself, now, and it is still shattered. Crowds followed Jay Jay up there, most didn't stay for long, but they were allowed to come and go with their rolls of toilet paper, be selfish and destructive. Every time I found a new and remote part for my camp, Janice would follow. And behind her, the others. I threatened her once. And she did try with tricks and fisticuffs, escapes and tantrums, to keep it for me and her. For a short while.

But they just couldn't seem to find their own places. They wanted a village, well now I reckon they've just about got it. Vanessa would come crashing through the undergrowth, snapping saplings with a flick of the wrist, measuring the width, the possibility of a track for motorbike or four-wheel drive. And along that track, which you couldn't see when it was mine, the others would walk and stop and there are little circles of stones filled with blackened earth and charcoal where they've made a fire or had a camp. It is walked on. There might as well be neat and tidy rows of grape vines or apple trees. Practically everybody who walks there walks along a track, like cattle or sheep. Except me, but trackless places are getting more and more inaccessible or uncomfortable.

Peterborough is a fairly big place. A Commonwealth Bank.

Although she has discovered that the fourth of Etama's coins is gold with St George on a horse slaying a dragon and 1914 on one side and George V of the British Empire on the other, she has no idea of its financial worth and suspects its sentimental value is something. It is a talisman, she keeps it with her pearls. Her invalid pension, kept up from the detoxification days, is paid into the Commonwealth.

She parts ways with the stoned Christians and goes out onto the Barrier Highway. It's a hundred miles to Broken Hill.

Moonmare Mountain is her home. I feel that it is a place I can always go back to, where, whether or not I get on with the women who might be there, I can always find a place to be.

In fact, Oona is feeling what she never felt in childhood, homesickness. As she sits in the high cabin of the big bulldog Mack speeding towards 'the silver city' she daydreams about that bush surrounded by the rugged escarpments of the Blue Mountains.

Her favourite place was not exactly on the women's land. It was on the top of the next ridge. The bones of an impossible shack, with the remains of a chimney and one wooden wall, fortunately on the windy side. The rest, just hairy grey three-be-twos, simply framed the majestic views to the south, east and north. How that went! She smiles now, to herself, but at the time it was not funny.

Lesley appeared between the planks of the eastern side, gorgeous and statuesque like a eucalypt in the foreground. Beautiful, as an empress or a model, she thought she could have anything she asked for. She asked for sex. She stripped off her clothes and demanded. Oona responded with scorn. But Lesley had whipped herself up into a state of desire and was as shrill as the ringing cicadas. She wanted the rock, the loner, the ruddy passion of the outsider. She had assumed, as most did, that Oona's lonesome vulnerability was what it seemed, loneliness, an absence which could be corrected by a presence, a caring, love-making, love. The proposition was grotesque. The circumstances something Oona was suspicious of, the motive was to do with them, not her. Even though I know Lesley better now, I still think of them and me, but then it was definitely them against me. I was paranoid, and that was a couple of days after a huge ruckus. There was no way I could answer Vanessa or Janice with all their words and logic, and it seemed to me Lesley was a kind of emissary coming to attack me from a different side. I was angry because Jay Jay had taken their side. She was, I thought, my defender. She was the one who should have appeared making apologies and wanting to sleep with me. But Lesley just couldn't take a rejection. First she cried real tears. Fancy me, plain old Oona, pissing off the lovely Lesley. Then she screamed. She really did want me. She had got herself all wound up for sex. And I laughed at her. Then she was really mad. Out of control, I suppose. She wrecked the joint. Total destruction.

The truck-driver and Oona go into the Working Mans Club as soon as they arrive in Broken Hill. He buys her a schooner. The poker machines flashing coloured lights and names and promises of hundreds of silver coins attract her like an adult penny arcade. She plays. Wins a bit, loses, drinks.

Outside, it is late-night shopping in Broken Hill and there are well-dressed family folk crossing the street, walking along, meeting each other. In this melée, Oona is sure she sees Lesley walking beside a very beautiful older woman. Her mother? She waits.

——————i am aghast at myself i am liking my four walls

i am becoming fond of them not that i prefer them to being taken outside and whipped i am innocent and i am interested to see what can be achieved by keeping me but if they whip me i will find out what extreme pain feels like and maybe the difference between being punished justly or unjustly or for masochistic pleasure am i required to be heroic in my own eyes to be heroic i am in another world within these walls that have many stains and shapes and subtle changes of colour______________________

7

A SICKISH BABY tries to sleep in a manger of books. During a meeting. In a cramped apartment. In a narrow street. In the old city. Of Barcelona. Attached to the ancient walls are neon signs. Cigarette smoke hovers thickly in the room patiently waiting to escape through the narrow slit of window. Meanwhile the pall of it changes from reddish to bilious green at clicking intervals. The many passionate faces of the exiles, home for a gathering, are lit by this surrealistic miasma.

Zorro's dark eyes flash beneath the rim of her hat like radar as she stands in the doorway. One long leg is high as the boot rests on a spare square inch of sideboard. As a dog identifies one in a swirling mass of scents, she detects a distinctly Mexican accent in the overlapping Spanish voices. It insinuates its softer sibilance through the aggressive Catalan and gutteral Castillian.

Los Indios is one of Zorro's romantic passions. But does this woman speak like a conquistadora or does she talk of conditions?

Xaviera is telling anecdotes about the gringas and gringos lining up their cars at Tijuana and El Paso, using as much gas getting there to fill up on cheap Mexican juice. Ah our oil, our boom, it never came because all of the time it has been spilling into the Gulf. They cannot plug the leak. They never plug the leak. *Stupido, no? Eh.* Coca Cola country presses down on us like a great big tin can full of who knows… Here members of the company contribute names of all things they find despicable amid bursts of laughter. No-one in the room likes the United States of America.

When Zorro smiles her face changes from the severe and handsome to the vulnerable and feminine. Her teeth are white. She is noticed.

Ah Zorro. *Estas aqui.* The room falls quiet. Zorro tells of her travels, of situations, of rumours, of arguments, of theories put forward here and there, of activities planned and those botched, of the long-running struggles of falsely imprisoned anarchists in the United Kingdom and elsewhere. The comrades become impassioned and articulate. Interruptions. Interjections. Worries about the ETA. Basque nationalism is not the only Separatist Movement in Spain. Since Ferdinand and Isabel we've all been colonised. The wine is passed around and gulped from the bottle by individuals in the middle of their sentences. Matches flare up savagely, and go out. Franco is dead, but what exactly has changed for us? You are comfortable in your exile. We live here. I love Catalonia. What do you know, you have your little business in Notting Hill! You can't forget the thirties. Old memories die with old men. The room is heated by argument and human bodies and everybody is having a good time. The reality of their politics is as speedy and exhilarated as bolero music.

Laughter and shouting and scorn and whispers.

Amid the fine fracas, even though both say as much as anyone, Xaviera and Zorro catch each other's glance. When Xaviera goes to the kitchen sink for a cup of water, Zorro sees how small she is, how dignified her movement, her wide hip bones, her big breasts which stand high on her squat body and the graceful surefootedness.

—That is an aristocratic head. A head which has carried baskets without the assistance of hands.

—Bravo.

—Olé.

—*Ayi, si.* When I was seven and my sister was ten, we did carry flat straw plates of bread loafs on our heads, even in the buses on the way to the market, where we sold it in the hot sun. Everybody in Mexico sells something if they can make something. Sensible, no?

Later the two had thick black coffee together in a dingy cafe in a front room of a house only open throughout the night. Drugs changed hands. Prostitutes had a rest. Anarchists continued their conversations. Xaviera and Zorro sought to know as much about each other in as short a time possible. Yet they spoke of Jesuits and pyramids, of gold and glory, the draining of lakes, of how revolutions fail, of mountains and oceans.

Zorro takes it upon herself to show Xaviera Spain. She changes her plans.

In the Prado, in Madrid, Xaviera stands in front of Bosch's *Garden of Earthly Delights* with tears in her eyes. Zorro places her feet squarely as she does when travelling on the seatless subway to counter a rocking, for even Zorro's zeal can hardly withstand the intensity of extreme courage which blazes in the young Mexicana's coal-black eyes. She looks at the painting busy with naked bodies, shells, eggs, membranes, beasts, birds, fish, flowers and fruit all serpentining up and around the canvas. It confuses Zorro at this moment. But for Xaviera it seems to be some kind of revelation. Truth. Comprehension.

Zorro is reminded of the concept of the transfiguration. She frowns.

She has been walking around Madrid, telephoning, discussing, arranging and hurrying for three hours. She has organised a lift, in an army vehicle driven by a conscriptee friend of a friend, to Toledo. Then another, in the Mercedes Benz of a Communist through La Mancha to Granada. Then, maybe, maybe not, the old bomb of some anarchists to Valencia. To be there in less than three days. She is excited to go to Valencia for in the country are olive groves on the rocky hills which is her Commune. Her romantic heart pounds with impatience. *Mi campo.*

But Xaviera has grasped her wrist and is pointing to things in the painting, laughing with glee at the humorous vulgar bits and seeming to cry at the same time. Zorro looks down at the hand, the tendons and blood veins stand out like an old crone's.

The first lift leaves within the hour. Come, *mujere,* come.

MADRID

Dear Trees,

Hell, damn, have you heard?

I've been talking to Beatrix on the telephone—incredible coincidence—(to be expected among us-mob)—someone she was with was ringing someone in the house we are staying, and I got to talk to Beatrix who happened to have something important to convey. I never have doubted our telepathy, anyway, and you certainly haven't, so why am I wasting space?

It goes like this. Beatrix and her friends leap off the ferry at Piraeus, fresh with excitement to get the mail at American Express or Poste Restante, Athens. Catch the underground to Omonia Square and queue downstairs at A.E. among hundreds of American students with backpacks who hug each other when they get a letter. You can imagine tall Beatrix standing in a crowd like that, her specs like a beacon, her height like a lighthouse, bending to advise or ask advice. Anyway, the only letter there is one for me, in a cheap paper envelope postmarked Saudi Arabia!

Written on buff paper, Beatrix said, she read, 'Jeddah, May, Et and 'Trix, have been detained by authorities. Do something. Arachne. P.S. This is sole communication allowed.'

We couldn't talk for long.

What can I do?

I told you about Grundhilde, the mystic. She was a tower of strength on this occasion. I just fell into her arms and cried. She, on the other hand, was smiling. I couldn't wipe the smile off her face, and she wouldn't tell me what it was for.

Anyway we'll meet up with Beatrix and co in London. Meanwhile I'm in the hands of Grundhilde who still seems to think our expedition to the land of the merino is important. It's all part of some pattern, she says. She calls it the spider's web. Arachne, the thirteenth house of the zodiac, the month stolen from the Moon societies by the Sun religions for easier calculation. Etc etc. It was to Grundhilde as if Alice's chosen name, Arachne, was something mystical, something terribly important in her vision of her destiny. Yet how she responded was to be almost lethargically patient. She spoke of some story by Borges in which the trapper is the trapped in the centre of a maze.

We're going across Castille to Valencia, tomorrow. This is written in haste, to tell you, but maybe you've heard already?

Please write. I'll be in London in a couple of weeks

Your faithful, sincere, loving,

Et.

8

GENTLE DAWNS greet her like spinster after spinster in pastel mohair cardigans. Thick denier stockings and silent soled shoes? Sad? Not because of the absence of bickering family breakfasts, the further you get away from them the less you need them. The sea of darkness laps on the beaches of day, as blue as cold feet. The sea is aluminium grey along the Esplanade between Elwood and St. Kilda. Sad? Because of a secret memory, these spinsters in their gardens hang out on the fence bunches of geraniums for the glass jar on her desk. 'They're really cuttings, dear, meant to strike root.' In the mass of humanity, individual loneliness wilts like tired flowers and burnt leaves hanging on the fences, overlooked, or feared, free of dirt and water. The sand is a Georgia O'Keefe colour, grey-yellow. Iona fancies she sees the skull of a longhorn, half-buried at the high tide line. The rest is smooth, glassy across to the petrol silos at Williamstown, the jetty and marina in the foreground. From some well in fate's village, Iona draws encouragement.

—I speak with unnatural huskiness and shadowbox spectres from my conscience and imagination. Something anonymous and deeply personal, being in the nights has skinned me once more, I should sit on the shore with an embroidery frame and play a make-work game, juggle fiction and reality, dream and work. To juggle is made tense by the verb to drop. And what about make-work quilts? Their colours and patterns seem all over the place, yet they're humble and functional and warm as toast.

She cannot get the idea of spinsters out of her head, even though the sun has risen and joggers in designer track suits grimace and pant along the path. As more nuclear bombs are tested, as more mangrove swamps are laid waste to heavy industry, as the murky pink pall of pollution hangs in the air, the idiots get into the health of their own bodies. Narcissus drowned, didn't he, because of his obsession with his own image? As the fabric of civilisation perishes, each puny fibre competes with its neighbour for survival.

—Spinsters, as opposed to lesbians and women, are waking up. No, this is true, little tape-recorder, even though the language makes nonsense of it. Let's try experience. There was Frances, right, in the rigour of her sexuality and honesty. That honesty concerned memory. I would say I don't remember saying that, and she would say I do remember and you are dishonourable, forgetting, and it would mean, eventually, that my supposed lack of memory was manipulation. I could say what I liked if I wasn't going to remember it, therefore I could not be believed. It was a tangle because language was for me expedient, appropriate, contextual, but I spoke in the spirit of truth. To be taken to task on detail was an unfair way of dealing with me, like knowing I was a dancing boxer yet using Eastern martial arts to crush my stance with kicks at the legs. The next person who grabbed my heart to some extent was Yvonne, in London, England. For the English language itself is a pugilistic sport. Freshly sore from Frances I was so careful to remember exactly what I said so as not to contradict myself and recommit former errors; to discover that she not only forgot, or probably didn't forget, but used the word forgot in an elaborate puzzle of lies and language. A game, the objective of which was probably power, but with a style and pattern as elegant as moves in a game of chess, bridge or mah jong—no, the Japanese game of go, where the ritual of lunge and retreat, the way you play is as important as the outcome. Lust, perhaps, is sacred, but emotions are fair prey for the damage the artifice of language can wring.

What one does and what one says are angling ploys. Well, I fell hook, line and sinker. I was such a good mark, being so conscientiously vulnerable, they loved to play me in London. Nowhere else was I ever in such demand, to be finally beaten, a fool. At the end she looked at me as if I wasn't there. Squirming like a fish on the jetty…

Fortunately, there was Zorro.

Yvonne is a spinster. The eccentric British librarian with quaint idiosyncratic ways, fallen arches, a cultivated dullness, horn-rimmed spectacles magnifying her aluminous eyes, a relentless, savage humour and a shamelessness which I suspect is part of her romantic games equipment. Loves to dress up and be queer.

Even though she suffered from Yvonne's method of drawing her in and dismissing her, Iona smiles in memory of her; her shower of crazy gifts, her pleasure at winning the Australian Pisces over old rivals.

A 6 a.m. drunk hails her at the beach end of Fitzroy Street. It is not compulsory to pick up an inebriate. You take responsibility, but hell, there but for the grace of the goddess go I.

——————i am inhabiting an oil painting i am inside the mind of the artist and the mind i am looking at is my own before these walls there were walls i did not see in my freedom i was always getting confused and vague and now that does not matter i have been released from a terrible tangle like i went over the edge when i was not looking and all about me is to be or not to be in a moment or so and aware of right now for it is all to do with falling these walls have caught me in a frame falling and frozen so that i might consider it all______________________

VALENCIA

Dear Lesley,

I'm sitting at an outdoor table in a plaza opposite a church, and I must write to someone and I remember our love as my most poetic relationship. You draw it out of me, how are you?

Incipient nausea of excitement in Spain, drinking strong coffee in cafes where mostly men entertain themselves with backgammon or cards or chess—they use Tarot decks in some yukko symbol of how low the male of the species has sunk. They use the sacred for the profane pleasure of gambling. Laughter like argument, argument like war, police with machine-guns slung at their hips, I distrust Southern Europe. Passions are volatile.

Here in this square the dead El Cid rode victorious.

Out of the crowd comes this tall Spanish woman wearing R.M.Williams cuban heel boots. She must speak to us. She does. With her is a beautiful Mexican, grinning with teeth so white, and hair so black, about half the size of the other. Those boots with the tight ankle elastic brought to me a breath of Australia, of the horses, and a sense of irony, for doesn't Jay Jay sing that Dylan song of boots of Spanish leather? But my feeling of the bush doesn't seem right, for I'm in foreign company here, a Swiss, a Spanish, a Mexican. Beatrix's phone call worrying my mind, I'm confused. We speak about it, Arachne jailed. The beloved Fool as fey as flame captured. Incredible. Everything is too complex. From Arachne the conversation went to witches and witchcraft. I'm only half with it for there's only a little German, only a little English used, mainly French and Spanish. Grundhilde speaks everything and uses language switches to her own advantage, I suspect. It's weird, languages merging like glazes. The main communication is with the eyes, but I don't gather it very well. Too much staring, especially between—her name is Zorro—the Spanish woman, and Grundhilde.

Where did she get those shoes? I ask, abruptly. A fish, she answers, not liking to be interrupted. I run through fishy Australians for something to do. I can only partly understand what's going on and, in defiance and rudeness, I am writing to you at the same time. Grundhilde has said something about how in Berlin in the twenties there was a lesbian bank and twenty-eight clubs exclusively for women. What are they talking about, the universal connection of women? Part German, part French, part Spanish, little words in each I get, the rest is a mess, but I trust them. Diaspora, exodus. Grundhilde saying she has died a thousand deaths and left a thousand bodies rotting in the ground. They don't agree with one another. There is a duel going on. I catch the eye of the Mexican and smile. She smiles and her smile is like sunshine. I am brought into the conversation, it's all English and about astrology. There is a trine of earth at this table, Grundhilde's a Virgo and Zorro a Capricorn and if you have a fairly generous orb, it is a trine: 5 degrees, 1 and 12. And warming us, like flame beneath a three-legged pre-Columbian cooking vessel, is the little Leo, Xaviera.

What am I writing? I am asked. A letter, I answer. You are still at the end of my pen, Lesley, am I being rude? I don't care.

Better stop, Lesley. Love you,

Et.

P.S. The boots were Iona's. Either she has big feet or Zorro small. Or maybe I imagine Iona shorter than she is. Write to me in London, even though you never write letters. I'll hope. E.

9

IONA PERCEIVES herself at the nexus of cowardice and poetry. The matrix of invention and escape? While loving the abstract she is no mathematician. She reads snippets of anthing to plug leaks in her awareness. She has friends like Mary to lend her some certainty. Even though she changes her mind seasonally, Mary is absolutely sure of everything she says. Her breezy confidence is an antidote to Helen's weightier meditations.

To Mary, Iona brings the quotes from Helen's letters which devastate her.

—I might as well pray to my dog, anagram of god, as call the moon more divine than the earth, Mary says enigmatically as she ties her labrador-cross to a tree outside the gates of the Zoological Gardens. Pats her, explains how long they will be, suggests things the bitch might like to look at while she waits, and finally says goodbye. Iona smiles.

—But that's all right, everything is sacred.

Mary, working-class girl from Port Melbourne, had grown up in dire straits during the war years, in a family which bore the cross of poverty with pride, being privileged members of a tiny Christian sect. She knew she was chosen. From the age of ten when the Lord revealed to her the true interpretation of the scriptures, she has known the Second Coming would be in her lifetime. She would bear witness. In front of the tiny congregation she recited three chapters of Revelations in the manner of St John himself; that is, as if she herself saw the Apocalypse. They were amazed as they murmured and nibbled their white bread tomato sandwiches and sponge cakes. A sacred being was in their midst. In the literalness with which such religious folk interpret their path and take lessons from the Bible, Mary's mother treated her daughter as Mary and Joseph treated their son. Miracles were the ways of God. It would be a surprising statistic to discover just how many of those miracles occurred in their own tiny community, whereas the rest of the world seemed seriously short of them. These questions the adolescent Mary answered with a reasonableness that struck her mother and father as inspired.

But when seventeen, at a party, among the skinny waists and rope petticoats, purple socks and stove-pipe jeans, Mary lifted up her skirts, leant back against the wall and let the boys enter her one after another. It was but a small step from the sin of putting on the bright orange lipstick. The parents, in the relative prosperity of the fifties, had a prodigal daughter to pray about.

In the last twenty-four years, Mary has lived in forty-two rented houses, and changed her beliefs almost as often. Still chosen.

—What am I on about? Iona speaks passionately as they pass the parrots. If I don't know love, and only feel a multicoloured maypole of attachments? Chemistry! If we're just amazingly complex designs for the survival of the DNA what use is literature? Music? Sex is a bore. Why do I care? That's a joke, it's my indifference which is considered cowardice.

—You should do yoga or Tai Chi.

Mary has lived all her life in Victoria, yet she has passed through every change the march of time presented, seeking and seeking, reinterpreting the 'elect'. Mary must chatter about matters of spiritual enlightenment. Spread light about the banal.

—Maybe. I'm spending too much time under the moon, in the maze, on the grid of the city...

—The moon is an enormous sponge. Look at that gorilla.

A mother gorilla with the kindest eyes is staring at Iona. Iona stares back. The gorilla blinks.

—It's horrible, I can't bear to see them sitting on that cold concrete. She's lovely.

—The moon is a side of your personality that attracts and magnetises and moulds to suit the situation, in contrast to the ego of the sun. It's instinctive, hereditary.

—My father...

—On a symbolic level, what changes is the manner of solar energy being translated to the earth and its life forms. Although the moon seems the same size as the sun, of course it's not. But it's that degree closer to us, so the illusion is corrected mathematically, four hundred times smaller, four hundred times closer. But I'm not interested in solid mass any more. If anything's important in astrology it's the moon's nodes.

Information splashing into the empty vessel, the stiff breeze picking up papers, fences keeping people on the paths and caging animals, birds, reptiles, platypus, otter …Iona's legs are tired from too much driving. Or sedentary nights. She sits down on a bench and lights a cigarette to handle a sense of urgency, a sense of love, that she is feeling. The rhinoceros is beautiful. The hippopotamus. The giraffe. The confinement is an imprisonment they don't deserve. She would cry if she could, but she smokes. She has her baggage of sanity, a knowledge of the realities. The poachers hunting out there in the savannahs of Africa may have no other livelihood but the greed of some white man offering prices they can't refuse, for instance.

—When god created these creatures he was having fun.

—Iona. You believe god is a he?

—Just a way of saying something. Actually, Jove was probably jovial. The god with a capital G who is a he seems humourless. His devotees far too earnest.

Mary has wandered further down the path, gracefully, her heavy skirt lifting slightly in rhythm with the wind.

The giraffe, the hippo and the rhino were indifferent to Iona in her soggy sympathy for them, but the camels, a particular camel makes an effort to be near her. Iona knows she is communicating. There is too much crushing around them for her to actually understand anything except possible friendship with such a beast. Mary watches.

—I love tameable animals, Iona pulls herself away and talks because she is embarrassed. If you can listen to your cat, imagine how handy a pet camel would be. In Australia, the outback.

—This is a desert continent, there are thousands of wild camels out there. The early explorers brought Afghans and their camels here from another part of the Empire upon which the sun never set to help them ship their pointless junk into the interior. The explorers died and the camels thrived.

Iona laughs.

Mary is a dog maiden, like Artemis, and has an oracular streak in her conversation.

—Something tells me, Iona, that you are spiritually talented but caged.

They go out of the zoo, release the ecstatic dog from her taut and twisted lead and walk back to Mary's car in a different mood from that at the beginning of their excursion.

Mary has a mission in regard to Iona for the next few weeks. She studies her, and studies things to help her. Finally, she persuades Iona to go to yoga as well as dance classes at Mangala Studios. Dance is just exercise for her, she has to find more in it. It is not there just to loosen up the cricks and stiffness from taxi-driving.

—The dance is central, Iona. There has been such a history, such a fight, and still we return over the ashes of our mothers, through the dark. We have to rise above the square houses and the square streets, the square cities, the parallelograms of ignorance they have overlaid our reality with. We will rise, join hands, linking arms and dancing, for the dance is consciousness and the spiral is our dreaming.

Iona is sceptical, yet she likes to humour Mary, while suspending both belief and disbelief in a vague state of relentless inquiry.

—I'm not cut out for meditation and clean living, Mary, the sinister vices of this apathetic materialism are mine. I can't imagine myself giving up…

Mary is impatient.

—Your moon is in Capricorn, isn't it? Well I think you can, looking at your personal chart. In Capricorn the moon stabilises and becomes sensual, craving excitement and entertainment. See? Dance! But to understand that dance you have to do yoga, otherwise dancing for you is some sort of sport.

—Sometimes you talk like Helen. She is coming to Australia, and that scares me.

—Why?

—The very thought of having to be some kind of light, of leader, lover, I don't know…mysticism gives me a headache. I just want to be rich. Said laughingly.

Mary looks so hurt Iona gives in.

—Yoga, okay. But I won't be able to stop smoking.

————————the sharp sun has made a rhombus on my grainy floor and divided the curious shadows and finger mounds into exactly four oblongs it is a square within a square within a cube fingerprinting in the sand in this way part of the painting paints and becomes conscious of itself i feel like el greco and the crucified christ what kind of a high is the son of man getting anyway that makes him look so ecstatically up to the roof was it el greco that understood pain as a masochist would and christ unjust punishment pain or the other way round?————————

10

TORPID SPEEDS along the Silver City Highway to Mildura. Torpid is the name of Lesley's Ford station wagon, for its number plates start with TOR and its colour is the steel grey of a torpedo. It is one of those reliable six cylinder bombs that just keep going and any mechanic anywhere can fix.

—I see where you get your temper from, Oona is struck by the coincidence of having been thinking of Lesley, and then, in Broken Hill, running into her. She has had several days out on the Nicholson station.

—My mother and I always get like that.

—A pair of vixens.

—I don't know why I go home, it's always like that. We fight, fight, fight. We've done it all my life.

—Well, why did you?

—It's a long story, part of a longer story.

—We've got time.

The land is dry and flat and featureless and the strip of bitumen straight.

—You see I'm not frightened of anything. Nothing conscious. So I fight with her. She's frightened of everything, but not me. We disagree on any issue you could name. But there's a connection, you know. She is my mother.

—Well, what's the longer story?

—She says I'm selfish.

—Forget your mother. I don't even have one.

—And my brothers!

—Did I hear right? Did that big bastard call me a boong?

—Selfish could describe me but it doesn't. Yes, he's a racist pig, and look at all the land he's set to inherit. Plus he's stupid. I nearly shot him once.

—Thought he did.

—I'm sorry, Oona, they're just like that.

Back among the grapes and irrigation, Sunraysia. Orange groves. Great river gums.

—'Once upon a summer in the hills by the river

Was a deep green forest where the wild things grew,

There were caves as dark as midnight—there were tangled trees and thickets

And a thousand little places where the sky looked through.

Now way inside the forest where the path was lost in nothing,

And the moss was soft as velvet—dusky, rusky as could be,

Where the day was full of shadows, and the night was full of darkness,

And nobody ever found it—was a big old hollow tree!'

As they drive along the Murray, Lesley teaches Oona a kiddies' story Lesley's mother used to sing her to sleep with. In Mildura, they eat.

The acres of leaning wheat shimmer in the stiff west wind. The whole is a sea of subtle ochres interrupted by broad-trunked gums.

—Next stop Wycheproof.

Lesley, mesmerized by staring at the restless uniform crop, relaxing in the passenger's seat with her bare feet flat to the windscreen, explains to Oona why she is on her way to Melbourne.

—I had a dream. This dream was not usual, not chaotic and disjointed, but perfectly naturalistic. In it I met the most ugly, physically ugly, person. It was like a wet clay head the sculptor has punched and scratched and twisted to one side. The flesh of one cheek seemed carved away and left in a bunch at her jaw. And it was the most lurid colour. All the hair on the front of the skull had been burnt off leaving half her head bald and shiny white. Her ugliness I observed in detail but in the dream I didn't care. I said to her, how can I love anyone as ugly as you? I was genuinely disturbed by it, you know. As if it were a big moral problem. You can, she answered. Your face? No, she said, you can't go away from me if you come to me. And Oona, going to her seemed the most important thing. Like a mission given a knight in a vision, to slay the dragon, find the grail, seek in a rock Excalibur, you know. But I was shaking my head. Then one huge tear like in an animated cartoon came out of her good eye. Drink it, she said. The tear had transformed into a cup. It kept changing until it looked like a mixture of blood and water in a champagne glass. She offered it to me again and this time I saw her beauty, I mean the one beautiful thing about her face, her nose. The nose was perfect. And then I loved her. When I woke I had this feeling of peace and pity. It wasn't a dream you could forget…

—But you always remember your dreams don't you? You always talk about them.

—Do I? Yes, well, some dreams are hard to remember or at least to work out. This one stayed with me during the day. Vanessa, when I told her about it, gave me some serve. You did not drink her cup, she said, you didn't take on her suffering because you wouldn't, not because you couldn't.

—How are you two getting on?

—Well half and half, she's still into me, but I think it's finished. I admire her, and it was fine up until I had this dream, I mean it brought things up you know.

—What things?

—I think she's jealous of me. She said, I would not drink the cup, the champagne glass of blood and water, because I wouldn't know what it was to be ugly or to suffer. She said I think things happen for me, not to me. We had a screaming match. She accused me of being a wealthy grazier's daughter, probably as bitchy as my mother underneath, that I had beauty, brains and fortune. And that my beliefs in reincarnation etc all just supported my privileged lot in life, and that I had no real politics. She took the wind out of my sails that night.

—Anyone can see that.

—What?

—Well you're five foot ten and healthy and I dunno…

—The funny thing was the night I went to sleep after this horrendous argument, I dreamed of the ugly woman again. She was on a beach gliding away from me. I was running after her. A classic. Well, I gave up and wrote in the sand 'i luv u'. When Vanessa was apologising and everything, I told her of the new dream. That was pretty insensitive. She was really upset, but she's strong you know. She cleared her throat, and tried, tried to help me understand it. The cup is an archetype of search and suffering, she said, of nobility and quest. She thought I was frightened of it because it might be poisoned. The day in the dream was sunny, primary colours, like a postcard, blue sea, yellow sand. Or Vanessa said, perhaps I was fixated on her awful scar and that there is probably some disfigurement deep inside me that I have to learn to love or something. She maintained that everything in every dream is yourself.

—Could be.

—The next day, Oona, Vanessa said she thought she was ugly and that I was dreaming of her. Some trip. First one thing and then the opposite, I really had to go away for a while. She said physical love had a lot to do with looks and that I was never really into her. After a while I didn't know any more. Not up there. There's a big barney going on about an electric fence and the goats.

—Has she got one yet?

—Yeah, she did. It's not a bad idea really. It was agreed to put it around the vegetable garden, but I think they'll pressure her to put it around the goats soon. Wilhelmina had twins just before I left. Two little billies.

—What do you know.

—Anyway, after thinking a great deal, I decided that Mary was the best person to talk to. Dreams and visions, you know, have changed lives a lot. In mythology and history. I'm convinced this woman exists. What about you? Where have you been, and where are you going?

—I've been thinking and hitching. Trying to sort out who are my friends and who aren't.

—Who you'd want to be cast off on a raft with?

—No, I'd be alone then.

—Come on.

—In my head it's onions and pearls. Funny, I was thinking of you on the ride just before I met you with your mum.

—Had you come to a decision?

—Nope. You owe me for wrecking my home though.

—I've been thinking about you, too, because if this woman does exist and I meet her, I've got to remember the lesson you taught me.

—Yeah, what's that?

—I dunno. I just might want to sleep with her, that's all.

—Well don't ask.

Lesley laughs. Wycheproof. Change of drivers.

As they come into Melbourne late at night, along the Tullamarine Freeway, as Oona has confessed to Lesley that she wants to write an opera, they improvise a moon chant. The moon has been dominating the sky since Bendigo.

—Limitations of the psychic.

—Amoral moon. Appears to condone rape and murder.

—Shines equally on debutantes and heroin addicts.

—Lends an ominous feel to certain things. Footsteps. Movements in the leaves.

—Storm-blowy cracking the windows.

—The clear eye of Cyclops. Bright white pupil and the ring of the iris.

—Has been offered the blood sacrifices of black magic.

—Endorsing all things shady. Leading adulterers down the path.

—Hanging over drive-in cinemas which show senseless violence and gratuitous sex.

—Seeing vampires stalking the innocent white necks of virgins.

—Bringing out of the woods werewolves.

—And marauding packs of hungry dogs.

—Exciting the mentally unstable to self-destruction.

—Unholy pumpkin of hallowe'en.

—Medieval mummies tormenting the villagers, dancing with terror. Flirting with the unnameable. Copulating with darkness.

—Assisting smugglers.

—Sinister cats scream like newborn babes being slaughtered under the light of the moon.

—A bottle smashes against the wall, and poor people are bashed and robbed.

—Moon's snake eye is icy and indifferent.

—Lover of ghosts and poltergeists.

—Laughs at innocence and fears. Rippers and strippers roam in the moonlight.

—Prisoners escape, a Mordred to Camelot, thief, dissembler, fallen Lucifer.

—When men walked on it, they found nothing but their own achievement and worshipped their technology which videoed the earth, jewel of the solar-sphere.

—Went mad. Anarchy!

11

——————they found someone who speaks english he is an impatient man which makes me think you need more than words to understand someone the english words he does use make no sense to me i am afraid he thinks i am clever he gets angry he says golden crescent and rubs his fingers together and i look confused until i light up with an idea so is it a piece of jewellery i ask because if it is i have not got it i speak slowly because english is certainly his second language if not his fifth or sixth to be helpful i detail every piece of jewellery i have ever had starting backwards from india compiling this list is diverting and i carry on in an animated fashion——————

THE NIGHT she is on radio, Iona is working and does not hear herself. She has been out to Doncaster and back three times.

Her mother hears it.

Ursula Trap on her antique Radiola hears it.

And Kate Tasma McMillan.

Kate, queen of the theatre, with a name known from Darwin to Wellington, was in a bar owned by her friend, Jack Kerr, some thirteen years ago. She was drunk, with a trinity of spirits beneath her belt, and was ignorant of the subtle mottling of malice and sensitivity in the place, which, in the idiom of the time, was as camp as a row of tents.

Jack had been generous with gin-slings, whisky sours and brandy crustas, trying to impress the forty-five-year-old elegant actress, before he opened the bar to his regular customers. Kate, in her pink mood, was ready for pathos. She saw the shy girl student come in with her lecture notes and her novel, set herself on a stool near the corner, croakily order a house white and pay for it with a pile of coins.

Kate's sympathetic nature was touched as she saw Iona try to prop the crisp-bound paperback open with a pepper pot and her folder. She could see she was caught in the deep blush and terror of her immaturity, her grubby hands trying to conceal her pitiful cash. Kate's voice, trained to carry itself through the doorpost of the worst auditorium in Australia, asked her what she was reading.

—Is it a love story?

The few people there looked around. Iona had to take her fate into her own hands. Some style was compulsory in this place. Wit city.

—I don't believe in love, she said, nonchalantly.

—How often have you been in love? Kate was ironic, still with Kerr in her conversation.

—Incessantly, since I was thirteen. Iona looked back down to the clever words of Gertrude Stein, understanding nil.

For Kate was it love to be loved? She had been in love with man after man, traversed the parabola of courtship, intimacy and estrangement, neither mountain nor molehill a dozen times. She tended to believe the girl believed herself and felt encumbered to make her experience love. She was in the prime of her womanhood. Her face, always interesting, her body tall, slim, flexible from ten years of regular warm-ups. She glided over to flick a strand of hair from Iona's forehead. Iona looked right into her, past the veils of art, through to her fervent fairness. Kate wanted to devour her, to suck and suck at the juices of her youth, to have her. The electric magnetism of the virgin female ripe for the plucking was a fruit she had never taken. A sex in which she could be master and masterful was exciting. Somehow it didn't matter if the worst was the worst and the whole trip became an indulgence of self-love.

She played upon Iona's body as if it were her own, she fed the places which had hungered for touch. The pork sausage of a virgin boy she had once had in this same anticipation turned out to be just that, quite a common meal when it was done. But not Iona, the unbroken hymen flooding open was a doorway into an underground labyrinth, an uppermost point giving entrance to the mysterious depths in her own being. She was Iona's first sexual lover, the incessant love was a crush on her sports teacher.

"In search of the intrinsic value, after the moral of endless interest, in love with the hallucinatory depths of improbability, driven, as a writer, upwards and outwards, flinging pale rays on insights, in short, in the general imbroglio…contemplations on I, but yes, we play so gently on the delicate rein between us, i plead my case with some shyness for i too am more excited than i seem."

Kate remembers taking her in the toilets at Kerr's grimy bistro, and hearing, as she did, through the thin wall, poofters making it in the Mens. And what is this writing, experimental, avant-garde?

Coming back along the Eastern Freeway with a middle-aged couple in the back seat, Iona thinks vaguely of Kate McMillan, as she often does, hearing a certain cadence, seeing a certain gesture. She recalls the pain of being dispatched, of being cast out of her life, not with a clean swipe, but her hope being continually cut to shreds with sarcasm.

Kate is a spider, a manipulator.

Yet when Helen meditated with her eyes open, staring at the candle flame, looking crazed, Iona sat in the lounge of the New Jersey apartment watching an Australian mini-series on American Public television just to see Kate McMillan, being, in that case, a prize bitch. Every now and then a slight expression would bring it all back. The whirlwind of her first grand affair, a learning that almost made her fail her subjects that year.

Kate is decadent. I don't want to see her again. I want to hold her in a rosy sunset glow in the slidebox of memory. The night she forced Quentin and me to sleep together, she betrayed herself then. We slept like brother and sister, at home with each other. He was such a queen, even at sixteen. Perhaps that's why she wanted it to happen; she wanted me to initiate him into hetero-normality. What a joke, a bitter joke.

She receives a tip from the woman whose personality must have resembled one of Kate's, outside, of all places, St Martin's Theatre in South Yarra.

————————i giggle when i think of what it must look like from the outside from australia for instance my friends would not think that i am happy because they know i am not a martyr they think i am irresponsible and none of them would be so foolish as to get themselves arrested in the middle east but all this does not matter now that i am in here and outside are a whole lot of arabs they give me a very strong very sweet egg cup of coffee and a tumbler of water in the mornings_______________

Yippee, whoop whoop, diary dear, gallop here gallop there. By jove I think I've got it.

The radio. Now I will go slowly. It was as if we were sitting together holding hands in front of the fire. Sharing thoughts and staring into the flames. We were linked! I know it. She, in the studio with her voice nervous and unformed, with a very obvious Australian accent, and myself eagerly straining over the one-bar radiator heat-mottling my shins, with my elbows on my knees and bumping about inside and sighing. The intensity of her prose and the way she entered it and yet it was me. ME. A woman risen from the sea embracing a seal, whispering with all nature and no human being. A refiguring of the poor mermaid dancing on dry land as if on sharp knives. Heavens, I'm not finishing my sentences.

She is alive, youngish and living in Melbourne.

Her work has not been handled by compositors, editors, book sellers, librarians and so forth. She is undiscovered. But she is uncovered. Come, surely.

Do I really think that my George Eliot, my Jane Austen, my Dorothy Richardson are going to be reborn? Diary dear, Ursula is a cynic. Or is old Ursey mad? …but I have lived half a century and in my adult life only known people through books. Are these emotions, which in me are real as trees, to be ringbarked? Is it the cynic in me who is afraid? But I am different. Ursula de la Trap. von Trap. van Trap. Trapsdatter. I am special. Someone somewhere writes for me.

Don't mock me, sea, with your spitting angry sighs.

You spit and I'll cackle. I'll laugh at you with your restless graveyards of unburied dead.

I imagine her walking under the clocks at Flinders Street station and I am there, too. But she cannot see me, who I am, she is struck by the ghastliness of my face. A perceptive, sensitive lass, she would try to look into my eyes with pity and there she would see the defiance of my soul brutalised into distrust and suspicion.

It's cold and I should be knitting jumpers.

I have listened even more eagerly to local writers on the radio and in what magazines I can find, and none, in my opinion, have it. They're too concerned with surfaces and manners. How can old Ursula care for surfaces?

Before and before and before, the dawn mists of Hans Heysen torment me with my own memories as I lie awake. Before the war, before my father disappeared, before my best friend moved to Deniliquin, and before…

——————he gets so angry with me poor fellow but today his attitude suddenly changed he got someone else in and this one takes notes he goes into what i imagine is a textbook interrogation you are australian yes born where sydney i begin to describe sydney with the words of a copy-writer working for the tourist bureau he interrupts exact address he demands i am not at all sure my crazy mother grandmother and simple brother would appreciate it but i give their address the old family home must be falling down by now his scribe has trouble getting it down so he takes the pad himself and writes it in english he asks me to check it and i am fascinated by the neat little pool of english amidst the arabic————————————

GRANADA

Dear Trees,

What a delight just going into any old Poste Restante and picking up a letter for me from you! You are smart, you Geminis. The answer is yes, yes, yes, of course I'll keep writing, and thanks for the compliment.

What about you and the burnt fruit cake! A thick cinder in the camp oven. I can imagine the eyes of hungry women staring at it. And you thinking of salt. Jay Jay picking at it with chisel and hammer, and Vanessa wanting to kick it. As you said, the Aborigines did clean their teeth with charcoal and they had good teeth before the white bastards came.

Yes, I'm still travelling with Grundhilde, but I'm sad because I'm falling for Xaviera. She is stunning. She and Zorro, a world-wise Spanish Anarchist with one long eyebrow, are meeting us in Lisbon in a couple of days.

Meanwhile in Andalusia, Grundhilde is captivated by gryphons made of stone. There are wild vultures here that swarm, and squabble and gorge themselves to clumsiness. But gryphons are creatures of fable, art and craft.

You know what I've been thinking lately, that Western civilisation has achieved the sublime state of ennui. They're bored. Men are boring. That's what's wrong with them. Even in their violence is the stench of boredom. Greed for power is such a huge yawn it's a black hole. It'll suck everything in, they're terrified of anti-matter. Themselves. Explosions, gelignite, nitroglycerine, gun powder, dynamite and every elegant make of firearm is for the attack on silence, on emptiness, out of fear of nothingness. Fear of exploration beyond existence. So they try to exterminate existence itself, any life. Foliage, animals for experiments, food, glut, rivers, the forests, precious bird and reptile be damned, let's slash the veins and arteries of Mother Earth and exploit every mineral we can find. Mental, physical and emotional destruction is the only power they know they have. That's got to be powerless. I hope the universe is just taking it all in its stride.

Rocks do sing, I've heard the rock-song. Its electricity makes a racket. The rippling of a mountain stream is coarse beside the singing of rock. Yet I've only heard it there where you are, Trees, where men and males are not allowed, and we women live in the virgin scrub, all water for tea boiled over the open fire, carrying everything we need on our backs—by the way, Vanessa hasn't introduced an electric fence for her goats, has she? I'll kill her if she has.

To get out of the grin of the gryphons, at last. Grundhilde's ready. Write to you soon, you're a real good friend, finding me in the Granada G.P.O. when I'm only here a couple of days. Love to Jay Jay. Heard anything about Arachne yet?

Your loyal and devoted correspondent,

love,

Et.

——————toddy mr kangaroo and al i say for the fiftieth time he just does not believe me but they are the names they called each other but there is no way i can convince him have i heard of the golden triangle he asks and i said i had i say i have seen one being played by a brazilian hippie in india he grimaces thailand burma laos he screams i say i have not been there i had a stopover in singapore but by this time i know he is talking about drugs and i do not know anything about that so i stay silent and worry because i know my grandmother is wealthy and i have given her address________________________

12

IT SEEMED to Frances that she had given and given and got nothing, from women. From lovers. Her memory, her mind's great asset, never lost a single detail. Nor did it choose to forget. She would suffer rather than forget, and certainly never forgive. Ha, forgive! Forgiveness is an almighty pain in the arse.

For each arrow fate tossed at her heart, she would score a greater, direct hit, one day.

Revenge might take a lifetime, but waiting to exact it, forever planning it, kept her going with determination when she was at her nadir. Malice made her laugh, she had the right. It was amusing because she had been hurt. Life being what it is, mild sadism has its place.

To love, for Frances, was eventually to hate. Before she left for overseas, her love of Iona had turned inside out, but Iona had no idea. That was planned. Iona chose one Sunday to go to her mother's and look after the simpleton sister, leaving Frances suffering excruciating menstrual cramp in Ackland Street, St Kilda. That day had been horrible for Frances. In the midst of pain and fighting off a rape attempt and struggling home on foot, she started to hate. She had paid for the breakfast and had no money left for a cab or train. They had had a fight about Iona's loyalties, in the street, after the coffee and bagels, and Iona had stormed off. Hardly the moment to ask for money. The climate between them changed from a post love-making sunshower to storm and tempest when Iona said, Well I've got to go.

The hours she had to think about it in agony meant there was no way ever that Iona could make it up to her. The damage had been done. After all she had given her, her complete self, her brilliant sexual gifts, her analysis of the decayed system, Iona chose the family over the lesbian, the conventional over the radical. She was treacherous. A collaborator. Deep down she was a god-fearing wimp. Her mother was a witch. Frances had seen that straight away. How dare a mother impeach the powers of a lover? Frances found it disgusting. Perverted. Below the belt. Mothers have the entire corrupt system behind them, and they use it.

At first sight there was a tangible antagonism between Frances and Mrs Flynn. On Mrs Flynn's side, it was compounded by the likeness in appearance Frances had of Veronica. It is the devil who dresses in the visage of the most loved, the dead daughter. Plus, she displayed her vile depravity, made no pretense to hide the nature of her relationship with Iona. She was destroying her darling, her last-born.

The fight for the soul was on, and Iona, in the middle, looked pinched, worried, sucked dry. In danger of losing her identity.

After the morning and afternoon in St Kilda and walking back to Fitzroy, the future had changed for Frances. Instead of trying to wreak a little happiness with a lover in this pathetic world, she now had the aim of revenge. First she would get the mother, make Iona go away from her, and at the same time she would get the erstwhile lover. She would possess her and then deliver back the arrows of heartache and the slings of emotional pain, confident of success.

So it was she left without any sort of goodbye, having fooled Iona into believing her deeper love and the plans to go to Ireland together. Knowing that Iona would be a fish out of water, alone in the big world, she had a few private laughs at imagined mishaps that would surely happen to the little sensitive thing with her eyes like begging forget-me-nots.

But now she is back. Driving a cab.

Frances had returned to Melbourne six months before Iona. They had had two encounters overseas. Frances relished telling mutual friends how demanding Iona had been. She lied that Iona had taken money from her. She knew that eventually Iona with her easy sociability would have a chance to tell her story, but she, Frances, would have had the jump on her. A certain amount of bad news would have had some effect. First step.

Step two, now. Iona is sitting in a cafe on Lygon Street. Frances sees her. She had waited for this moment. With her are Pamela, with whom Frances had a brief affair in '72, Mary, with whom she spent one night in '75, Lesley, to whom Etama had turned after Frances had gone off with Iona, and Dawn. Doubt is enough; her strategy is, she thinks, cunning. She wanders in, sits at a table close enough to elicit from Iona an 'Hello, how are you?', which she is sure will come, and pretends to ignore them all.

—Hello, Frances.

Mary, Lesley and Pamela wait for Frances to speak before they join in greetings.

Frances does not look up. Iona blushes.

—How are you?

Iona looks foolish. The chemical excitement in her veins energized by the mere proximity of Frances makes her shake. Frances drinks her coffee, reads her book and the others are careful in their conversation. Frances overhears Mary saying,—Well I think Oona is a reincarnation of Ned Kelly. She cannot stop a grunt of scorn escaping. Iona blushes again. Her vast tolerance is finding it hard to agree with all points of view at one moment. Pamela responds to Mary.

—That rip-off merchant, dope peddler? No way. You can believe in reincarnation if you like, but you can't dare to interpret it.

As Pamela continues, Frances slams down her cup, collects her gear and stands a moment by their table, staring straight at Iona.

—Pay me the hundred pounds you owe me when you're ready.

—What? I gave that much to you in London when you looked like you needed it.

—Two hundred dollars will do, whenever…

Frances, her face so like Veronica's with the full lips, high cheek bones and long nose, raises one of the arched eyebrows, turns away, swinging her hips with such insolence that Iona is totally taken aback.

No woman leaves Frances penniless and in pain without paying for it.

Iona is paying for it. She is not guilty but she feels guilty, that is why she gave Frances one of her traveller's cheques, signed, in London, after having a rotten time. Veronica, her sister, who was drowned one summer vacation, had never liked Iona. From what her mother had been saying lately, Iona has deduced that apparently Veronica was jealous of her monopolising her father's affection as a baby. She feels hard done by on every score. Having nothing, but others jealous of what she has.

But Frances' ruse fails to bother her so far as the belief of her friends goes. Whatever they think, who owes whom the hundred pounds, it is none of their business and if they choose not to believe me and believe Frances, well, they're not my friends and time will tell. I know I gave her that money. The facts and the gossip of a situation don't tell the real story. On that level I'm incorruptible.

—Oho, someone's got it in for you, Iona.

Dawn laughs. There is no question what Lesley thinks. She, having had to cope with Etama's misery of rejection, therefore knows Frances better than she could guess. Mary is staring into the air where she was, deciding on the colour of the aura.

—Her aura is too dark. It's very dark. A kind of school uniform blue.

HACKNEY

Dear Rose,

I feel like endlessly flattering you for accepting the call reverse charges. Cash is tight here. I've been worried about her and I thought someone should contact her parents. You're the most respectable. Plus you've met them. Official channels from Australia are as good as any. I was surprised by your reluctance though. It's up to you of course.

England is so green and patchwork. We came across country from Dover after being in a Portuguese trawler for eight hours.

That's the way Zorro travels, somehow, as long as it's free and it's with the workers. I felt I was in some old war movie. Anyway we made it. All four of us.

Now Zorro has settled us into her squat, which is actually three houses with irregular archways smashed into the walls between them. Her room is painted all blue and white. She slaps her head and talks of the frustration of not being able to get back to her art, and here she is, and well… I don't like her work very much. It's sort of heavy, yet untidy, as if she's got loads to say and no talent to say it with. Sad really, perhaps art is occupational therapy for everyone and it's only accidental who becomes famous. Who wants that shit anyway?

My lover here is a traveller, too, from Central America. We have a ball doing all the corny tourist things. Going to the British Museum, art galleries, Hyde Park and Buckingham Palace. Finding out where the dances are, dancing.

Do what you want to about Arachne, okay? She's as much your responsibility as mine.

Yours in sisterhood,

Etama.

Mr Eddie Poe, Dawn's tabby cat, hurls himself at the tin fence time and again. Eventually he pulls himself up by the very end of his claws to teeter on the razor edge with nowhere to go. Except onto a roof, a standing jump of about three by four feet.

—Not possible, Eddie… It is not…don't do it.

But reckless Eddie is a climbing, leaping cat.

The Yellow Cab is parked in a narrow laneway off Rathdowne Street. Not two metres from Iona's elbow, which rests on the open window, is the side door to the factory. The factory is Mary's forty-third place of abode, and the nineteenth she has redecorated and painted.

Lesley and Dawn eat toast and vegemite by hurricane lamplight. Oona sits out in the cab with Iona.

—They don't want me in there.

Iona is always uneasy with Oona and yet she can never oust her. It is as if Oona knows more about her inner self than I myself do—a sort of darker me. My knight of mirrors. Night of my day.

—Give it a break.

—My gear is in there, though. Lesley is on some fanciful dream mission. Looking for the ugliest woman she can find. Dawn reckons she's seen her. Can I stay at your place?

—No. The answer knee-jerks out of Iona before she can hunt around for excuses or think of a soft way of saying it.

She found Oona on the grassy median strip reading the Yellow Pages, looking like a hobo.

—But I've got a present for you.

—What is it?

—A pearl.

—I can't let you stay as I haven't room. I live in a toolshed and Rose is jealously protective of her area which is the rest of the house.

—Don't worry. I've got other places.

Oona is suggesting junkie-pads, disreputable rented houses in the terraces around Richmond and Collingwood which as yet haven't fallen to the developer or the renovating young professional.

—You're not getting back into it, are you?

The addiction to the white *dame sans merci* of heroin fills Iona with repugnance. Not only is it the filthy sinks and fridges in the untidy kitchens of those places, it is the extreme selfishness. Self-gratification. The desperate end of a civilisation of exploitation now feeding off the soul. The thin dripping end of the needle is the final point of power of the corrupt phallus. She has seen so many free women choose it, giving away their power to explore the bowels of their victim-sides. Frances plays with it, enjoying times of squalor.

Whatever the experience is, Oona holds it over her, a darkened theatre of knowledge she has never paid the price to enter. Yet, as both Frances and Oona would have it, she is as ready a candidate as anyone.

—What? Smack? I wouldn't tell you even if I were. But I'm not. I want your help. I'm going to write an opera.

—Opera?

—Uh-huh. Show it round prisons. At demonstrations. Up the bush. You know.

—You do that, Oona. Why not?

Oona, like some others who have thrown off the control of the hard drug, is now a strong woman at the peak of physical condition. Having survived the theatre of horrors they seem to be able to do anything they want.

—Still worried about money? You're jumpy.

—Not that you're interested in anybody else, but I owe some to my brother for my return journey to Australia. I borrowed a thousand. Besides, you always make me jumpy.

Iona is embarrassed. She is guilty. She knows she cannot throw off her own legal moderate addictions without becoming fragile, nervous.

—I reckon you might be a pearl. I loved you.

—I think you attempted to rape me…

—Not true. You came round.

—You can't take no for an answer to anything.

Eddie, the cat, makes a leap and, instead of falling, swings from the guttering. With supreme effort he pulls his rotund tummy over the edge, and disappears.

—Not an opera, a processional sort of chorus.

—Well done, Mr Poe.

A sense of demoralisation assails Iona. The cat is more than a distraction. He genuinely amuses her while Oona—Pamela, Helen—all want something she cannot give. Something she does not even know she has.

—Great cat.

—Mary will let you stay, she's got loads of room in there.

—It'll only be for a day or two. I'm going to Cape Barren Island.

—Cape Barren? In Bass Strait? Where the Tasmanian Aborigines are?

—That's right.

—At least you have a blood connection with this land.

Iona does not have the words to describe exactly what it is about Oona which excites her envy.

—You're full of shit.

—No, I mean it. If I had that I'd be out there, in the centre somewhere, learning the tribal ways.

—You really have no idea. Do you know what black fellas do to dykes? They hate you. They hate it. Even among their own. It's hard. They don't let up. You don't know what it is to be an outcast.

—No, I don't. I'm too fucking popular.

—Yeah, maybe.

—Why Oona? Iona tries to squeeze out of Oona an inkling of that sleazy peace, the lessons of the limits. Why do you want to write an opera?

—I thought I could. There's lots up the bush who could write the music, sing it, you know.

—And I can help you write the words?

—Yep, I knew if I needed anything, you'd give it to me.

—Where did you get that idea?

—You always have.

—What do you need? Money?

—A place to stay.

—I told you. There's no way Rose'd…

—I heard you.

—I'll talk to Mary. It'll be okay with her.

—You know these holy feminists would let you starve in the gutter if you don't smell right.

—Mary wouldn't.

There is a sudden crash on the top of the taxi. A miaow.

—Oh Eddie, Iona opens her door to check, are you all right? You're a silly cat.

He is not a sook and does not admit to any injury.

—You ought to come up the bush with me sometime. Then you'd see me clean and capable of anything. But you never have. You've always seen me bludging around the city, and you can't wait to see me go. I can tell. But up there, shit, I could look after you. And you could help me there, not here. I'm mindless here. And Janice too. With her music…

—Horses.

—Sure there's horses. There's scenery. But anyway, I'm not going back for a while. They kicked me off. Had a disagreement with Vanessa.

—What was it about?

—Just owning shit.

The tabby cat is aiming himself at the side fence now.

—I can't believe that puss. What made you want to go to Cape Barren? I've been there. There are these beautiful geese. They fly low and sound like a short-winded bugle.

—Okay, geese, boongs, anything. I saw a thing on television about mutton birds. Just to visit.

Iona looks at her watch. She has worked out that Oona must have already stayed one night at Mary's. She always does it to me. Wheedles.

—I'm going back to work, Oona. Sorry about accommodation. But I just don't want you to stay there. I'm hassled and I'm busy.

—It's all right. Don't get your knickers in a knot. Here's your pearl.

The tiny pale round thing falls into her palm. She stares down at, holds it up to the interior light. It's a cultured pearl with a minute hole in it. She has a whole necklace of similar ones at home, given her by Frank's wife, which she never wears.

—Thanks.

—I'm searching for a black pearl to give Jay Jay, someday.

—Do they exist?

—Why not?

—I hope you find it. I've really got to go now, Oona. Have a good time on the island. And I'm sorry.

—For what? Letting me starve in the gutter?

—You won't starve. I'm more likely to starve than you are.

—That's bulldust and you know it.

—Cut it out, Oona. Maybe, when we're in the bush together. I've got to drive all night. And I'm tired enough.

—See you.

—By the way, I've got a present for you too. A Mexican poncho. I'll drop it by, later tonight.

—You're all right, Flynn.

Backing out and nearly running over the courageous Eddie, Iona feels that she has done something worthwhile, in talking with Oona.

Mary nods from the footpath, in her arms a box of fresh produce.

A night to hang around the inner suburbs, do small trips.

Hysterical. Hilarious. I never laugh in public. But I must admit to widdling myself here by myself, diary dear. You know Mimbo so well I don't need to explain her personality. She would insist on cooking for Marion, the boys and Allan, well not everything. The scones. I don't know about senility, maybe the taste buds go, anyway she put far too much salt in. She was so proud of herself. Saying things like, 'I don't let Ursula do everything. I cooked the scones.' I'm afraid it was pathetic. No doubt she was an excellent scone chef in her day. But truly it tickled me seeing Allan and Marion consume them with grimaced faces.

I am a naughty old maid.

Mimbo is unrecognisable from Gippsland before I was nine. Winnie and I were outrageous rascals. The twins terrible. My father forever forgiving. La twinnies terreeble, he would say. And Mimbo then, well she was stern and busy, complaining and screeching. Probably pressured—rural poverty in the thirties. But my memories have coloured those days beautiful. Then Winnie went to Deniliquin. We were too young to be letter-writers. Mimbo's cakes and scones were wonderful.

I thought her name was Fiona. I am angry with the ABC man who mispronounced it—Eeona. I find now her name is Iona. Eye-ona I would have thought. I have found a little piece in *Southerly* magazine. It's about a schoolteacher loathed by her students who is seen by one of them as a bag-lady rummaging through a litter bin. There is no judgment in it, you don't know who the author feels sorry for. Probably everyone. It is like a photograph.

Mimbo claiming not to have slept a wink. Many visits to the bathroom, half-washed smalls in the sink. Really this house is falling down. Mimbo can't open the cutlery drawer, and I fight with it. The bathroom's walls are shedding paint, and I have no enthusiasm about getting up there with brush and pail again. The smalls in the basin and she points to the ceiling saying imperiously, Ursula can't you do something about that. So I wash her gussies. Hope she forgets.

More battles in South Africa. Goodness, it must be the seven circles of hell.

I think I have been there through my dreams, I seem to know the place—the anxieties of the middle-class white women slowly going off their rockers.

I lay in my bed thinking of Marion.

Miss Trap is not a Trappist, I was saying to her. My maidenhead is not my choice.

Sometimes the longing to touch has so churned up my insides as to give me ulcers. No one understands that I have pains in my uterus and stomach. As if I were atoning, as if my masquerade creates its own dangers. To she who has much shall be given.

I didn't think it mattered about the truth—by accident or by birth. Well it does. I always compounded it with the loss of my father and Winnie. The great changes which happened. The loss of the animals, the land, the freedom, and our move here, to this Peninsula town, this bungalow…

Old Ursula is not the type to bring up rude truths amid social chit-chat. Forty years. Marion, always so lovely, so cheery, so generous, so maternal, retains that vicious streak. A niggardly spitefulness.

I think I.F. has upset my applecart. I'm scrambling around on all fours picking up pieces of my load. You see, if she should see me and happen to see my sister and my mother, she would see through me, like that schoolteacher. It wouldn't matter about the truth, she'd make it up. But my fair guess is she'd make it up close enough, close enough…

Hence I am seeing myself in pieces.

Oh God I resent it. Marion, do remember what really happened? Are you such a liar?

——————for days i have been doodling with my curved spine arching up at the snake i have been making crescents of all shapes and sizes i have called them moons and wings i have had the whole floor covered in seagulls i have had a street called waratah crescent from the end of the pallet to the door and crescents have led me to rings and circles and i am sure i am entangled in some drug ring some really big racket____________________________

13

THE NIGHT is clear.

I don't know why I take criticism of lady writers personally.

It's four a.m. Iona is the only one alive in this part of the world. The amber vacant light the only light apart from the stars and sterile street lamps which a passenger once told her used but a bit of the spectrum. That's why you can't read very well under them.

—And criticisms of lady drivers. Men don't do that. A man considers himself an individual and every man considers another an individual. His ideas of masculinity, for instance, are his own alone. A level of me is a collective. That's not a matter of faith, it is experienced, inside. And from the outside women are spoken of in the general.

Iona is stiff and tired, but determined to finish her work by the usual time. Determined to stay at it. Determined to keep awake, thinking. Moving. The garbage truck and another truck, cleaning the grooves of the tram lines, are creeping noisily along the road. This is the darkest hour, the coldest.

—Writing is like wringing your daydreams dry, driving at night like robbing yourself of astral travel, or something. I'm living and thinking at the edge of my nervous energy. It's a moral thing, as if ethics were situated somewhere between the nerves and the glands. Is the moon maiden mad with her taste for creamy yoghurt and bathing in dreamy illusions? I am attracted by some wordless concept, a lack in the secular life…

Australian life. Not so in Mexico. But I, as an Australian, couldn't have it. Or didn't think I could.

The art of her aunt, Nisaba Diana Kirby, resembles some Heironymous Bosch. In fact she has painted *a Ship of Fools,* a *Garden of Earthly Delights,* but it was the circus motif of a picture in Ireland that affected Iona. There was a girl as light as a feather balancing on tiptoe on the back of a warm-blooded cart horse dressed up in merry regalia, in the background stripes of the tent and portraits of animals. The faces of these creatures you could stare at for hours. They were human in their expressions but perfect depictions of the species.

Mrs Flynn had referred briefly to her husband's sister who was some famous artist or other. Brought disgrace on the family in the thirties, disappeared to Mexico, has Indians living on the roof, her mother believed. It was not until she was in Ireland, in the house of her uncle, Cerridwen Flynn's father, the diplomat, the white sheep in a family so predominantly full of black ones, that Iona really hungered to meet her. And it was this youthful painting. If she could paint so well when she was fifteen, why wasn't she famous throughout the world? In Feminist and Surrealist circles she is. She is known by the avant-garde. Iona had to research to find out much about her at all, and then it was mainly in Paris, not London or Dublin, New York, certainly, but otherwise it was esoteric to know of Nisaba Diana Kirby. With a determination similar to the one she feels now, driving in the pre-dawn, thinking, she went to Mexico with a couple of hundred dollars lent her by Helen.

Nisaba was no stranger to the peyote hunt, the magic carpet rides of drug-taking adventures, mule-riding into the rugged Mexican mountains, no stranger to mental hospitals and hermetic journeys into her inner self. Although her body was old, arthritic, when Iona met her, her spirit, her eyes were young. The trapped energy came at Iona in riddles, though in English. I had to ask Armand to explain and he would only speak Spanish.

Translated from riddles into Spanish and that partly understood by Iona, Nisaba conveyed: All followers of ancient religions, and many people now living close to nature, bear witness to the existence of normally unperceived classes of beings, entities co-existing in the biosphere of the earth, angels, devas, nature-spirits. But she had said, Ayia the nagual, the nagual. Armand explained that a particular nagual, a great dog, had been chasing Nisaba for years. He appears and disappears through the walls, and he is not all she sees.

Armand would explain, open his long scribe's palms to the sky, raise his shoulders, and drop a book in her lap, as outside the thin air of Mexico City would try unsuccessfully to carry the weight of smog. Iona would sit on the roof on which the Indians were rumoured to have lived and read of hermetics and alchemy, the gospel according to Mary Magdalene and Thomas, the Gnostics, a Western Esoteric tradition among the vibrant, garish spirituality of the Incas' descendants.

—Didn't you know the essence of change was from knowing 'I' to knowing 'we'? Nisaba attacked her one time over lunch prepared by Juanita. Avocado with lavish lashings of coriander, grated cheese and black pepper.

With the grey light of dawn a chill seeps into the Falcon; Iona shivers, and she shivered that day, also. If she answered yes, meaning what she understood by it, she would be wrong. This 'we', she therefore assumed, included the naguals, devas, imps, elves, leprechauns and so on, and she wasn't so sure about that.

Space is not an empty container into which material substances are poured; it is the interrelatedness of everything. Agh, Armand… then she continued in rapid, impatient French. And Armand went to the telephone.

A passenger. The traffic is increasing on Sydney Road, Faulkner. Iona will be busy for the next three hours. Remembering Mexico has caught on a groove in her mind, and she goes about her job mechanically.

Armand rang Juanita's daughter, Xaviera, whom Iona had heard about but not met. Nisaba had said in French, this girl needs to experience peyote. I'll take her down to Oaxaca. You ring Xaviera, make her come. Tomorrow.

Travelling south on a bus, alive with chickens and goats, produce of some kind with every other group, Nisaba became moody, and Xaviera teased Iona with tales of voodoo. Beside Xaviera, she felt tall, clumsy and dense.

They came to the dusty market of Oaxaca City quite early in the morning. Xaviera and Nisaba sat down to a chilli-hot breakfast that Iona couldn't eat. The only alternative was *las comidas de Norte America,* coke and hamburger. She had a coffee and wandered. She came to a woman sitting near three fat geese, glorious creatures. The woman was not unlike her geese, arrogant, smooth and beautiful.

The woman spoke to Iona and Xaviera and Nisaba watched.

Iona stuttered in her abominable Spanish, incredulous that such birds were for sale.

—Squint, and we will see, Xaviera whispered.

As Nisaba told Armand and Iona later,—I tried the art of gazing that Maria had taught me. I saw a fourth goose hovering over the woman. It was an amorphous shape with wings outspread and an extremely long neck. This neck made serpentine movements shooing Iona away. Iona, you, seemed unaware. You continued to smile at the solid geese. They were being affectionate to their owner. Iona took a few steps back. You were pushed back. Then you lit a cigarette and stared at the sand on the ground. Xaviera saw all. It is digging a hole in her head, the crown, with its beak, and then it is swimming inside her, she said. When you looked up she was gone, no? The beautiful witch. You see a lot of them in Oaxaca. But you were not surprised. Iona said, those geese were each worth the equivalent of thirty five American dollars. You had been staring at the ground doing arithmetic? I give up. We were not taking you into the hills. Then Xaviera was nowhere. Nowhere. Nowhere like the witch. You, Armand, and you, Iona, are alike. You carry around a kind of terrible innocence, a brick wall, a blandness. You don't need to climb mountains. I've been climbing mountains all my life, and my lesson, my lesson is you reach the top of a mountain only to see a whole range composed of evermore inaccessible peaks.

Iona drives through the crisp and clear morning, is pleasant and distant to her passengers who mostly seem to be in the process of waking up and are, mercifully, silent. It wasn't an insult to be told she was like Armand. I sure knew what she meant by karmic innocence, it glows out of him.

She speaks aloud to her customer, who is Indian, in a nylon shirt.

—Aren't you cold?

—Where I come from you can make your body skin as resilient as that on your face.

—I once knew a man, she said, needing to talk of Armand, who was a Jew, an orphan. Some time before the war, Nazis blew up the Jewish orphanage. And the little Jewish boys who survived were homeless, scattered. I imagine it was somewhere on the Danube. My friend was twelve and do you know he walked for fifteen years, all over Europe, while Jews were dying in their millions and bombs were dropping and casual violence was happening anyway. He walked to Casablanca. I asked him how he lived, he said he stole, and that always there was someone who protected him when he needed it. He refuses to speak English, but he reads English. He said most of the best books are in English. Funny. I wouldn't have thought so.

—Everybody must know English in today's world.

—How many languages do you know?

—Three, no four. I can read Sanskrit.

She drops the hardy Indian outside the university and goes into Carlton for breakfast.

————looking at me you could say i fit the role of a courier stooge i am just the sort of idiot they would use but they did not use me they gave me a lift they found me suffering with dysentery on the side of the road picked me up did not explain anything and gave me medicine that worked they laughed at my jokes and listened to my music and disappeared in a small aeroplane and that is that and it does not alter the fact that i am here and they are not————————

14

MARION INSISTED on 'helping' while I was washing up. She kept apologising for not knowing where the glasses went. I let myself, diary dear, become irritated. How many years have we gone through this charade? Does she still think she is a princess?

(She is certainly a handsome woman.)

Any rate, I turned on her and said, 'Marion you are wrong'.

I felt like a poet, inspired. A religious teacher whose message is encapsulated in a phrase. I was releasing her from the infuriating obligation to apologise.

Her reaction was frightening. I must have scared her. She started crashing plates and spoons and forks. She was shaken.

Perhaps she wants forgiveness from me. But I, a mere mortal, can't forgive. That is God's job.

The washing-up done, dear diary, I dropped a bombshell.

I said, 'When Mimbo dies you can have everything. The house, her few measly shares, the heirlooms which are jewels would look grotesque on me.' Et cetera.

Mimbo was horrified, more, I suspect, at hearing herself spoken of in the third person. But Marion was annoyed. I had pricked the balloon of her generosity. I had called her a fake in one of the longest speeches I have ever made. Allan and the boys were plainly embarrassed.

Marion's guilt is on my face. I wonder how much Allan knows.

Unsightly. No one says 'unsoundly' or 'untastely'

Unsightly; if Winnie saw me today she would call me unsightly.

Winnie has no reason to suspect that I'm an ugly old crone now. None. She probably believes I'm doing very well. I did beat her regularly at catch the ball and hopscotch.

She was jealous of my skin. Poor Winnie getting so burnt in the summer. Me going golden under my mousy hair. Her hair so red it was like a flame on her head. But Winnie was going to be a success in the world. She had ambitions. I inclined more to the sports. What stories she could tell! Alone in the dark, she'd whisper ghost tales with delightful invention. I haven't seen her name though, in all the years I have had to look.

HACKNEY

Dear Jay Jay,

Got your note, what's it about? I didn't know she had a Supporting Mother's Benefit. They're looking for her kid? Sure I'll tell her, when I see her. I'll tell her it's hassling you too. I was wondering why she didn't want to go to the Australian Consulate in Athens, or anywhere. Anyway she's gone to Denmark where everybody is tall and fair and she'll get lost in the crowd for a change.

How are the mares of the mountain? The horses? You've got pigeons, wow, winged messengers!

There are games of lesbian 'endogamy' going on in London like you can't believe. The promiscuity and freedom of it, the hassles and ecstasy. I don't care, it's sexual, rivers of electricity flowing through a crowd of strangers. I went to a dance first night here. I danced with Xaviera all night. XXX, yum. Xylaphone music, the band had a weird selection of instruments, like C—in the seventies. I'm in love again. Yours, and my Beatrix can do what she likes.

No more room on this card, write again,

love, Et.

————the last time i saw my nutty old grandmother was six years ago i hope they don't blackmail her she would believe anything she thinks i am a naughty flower child she would have no difficulty imagining all this the sort of novels she reads the crescent is a question mark also i am discovering something about love i love my grandmother therefore i worry i worry about my gran therefore i love her————————————————

Iona is in High Street, Preston, surrounded by howling, wailing, yelping sirens of police cars, fire engines, ambulances, throwing her top light into the rugby scrum of vehicles', enmeshed in an emergency of which she is no part, slowing to the side to let excited towtrucks pass. Her heart is far from the sport of urgency.

"I, I, I" whine the alarms.

Tears cannot be shed any easier for the vast number that are shed in the world today. Iona, one huge teardrop herself, can never cry. She, rather, prides herself on her crisp dealings with the world from a vantage of inner amazement. Cynically, she fears another individual tear might be as pointless as another published novel upon the bookshop shelves. By driving through the mouse scuttle of the nocturnal hours, she had upturned the rhythm of normal life, the rise and fall of light and dark. On the linoleum pattern of sprawling suburbia. Trapped by her own inability to take her life into her own hands and live it, live in the consequence of self-determination. Like her cousin, the hermit.

Gay One Seven pulls out from the kerb, and, in front of a cop, executes a U-turn across the tram lines.

Cerridwen Flynn, Iona's first cousin, has a white Celtic face under glittering auburn hair with copper lights. Her small mouth has fleshy lips. Her teeth are pearls, her smile ironic. Her voice is rich, and accent-perfect in Irish brogue, Gaelic, BBC English and South American Spanish. She lives by herself in County Wicklow near a pebbly beach of the Irish Sea and practises privacy. Her maternal great-grandmother was of the Old Faith and lived near New Forest, where Cerridwen spent a summer in her childhood. When Iona visited for a few days, she gave the impression of time-worn wisdom…soft-flowing, as if someone exactly like her had lived in the same cottage for a thousand years. She has a wicker basket on the front handlebars of her pushbike. On a pleasant day she would be out on the Wicklow Hills gathering magic mushrooms, covering them in the basket with a gingham tea-towel, bringing them home, drying them to sell or give away.

She's as pure as driven snow, yet, in her tiny hothouse, marijuana grows among the tomatoes.

Everything in the cottage was natural, and beautiful. She took from a camphor wood box a string of fifty shells and gave them to Iona.

—I keep them as something magical, as if I could wish on them if I dared. But then meeting Frances by accident in Dublin, while I was with Cerridwen on one of her cocaine expeditions, I introduced them. And I heard my precious cousin invite her down. She changed sides in what must have been an obvious ex-lovers' feud. It soured me. Love-hate Ireland, don't trust her, all the cliches are right, the informer, the person who makes the sign of the cross with one arm stabs his brother with the other, all thrive there.

Oh Ireland, my mother's mother's mother had a portrait of Parnell on the wall and when he went off with Kitty O'Shea outside the sanctity of wedlock, she left it there but turned it round. So my mother only ever saw the back of the frame. My father's uncle, a doctor, helped a young black-and-tan soldier who was dying in the gutter outside his surgery. For saving his life, the Irish did not speak to him for the next fifty years, even though he was the only doctor in the village. Love-hate the Irish. It was the only place in all my travels that I was nearly raped, would have been certainly if I hadn't jumped out of a moving caravan with my pack, landing on my clothes only slightly bruised. But…

At the Westgarth end of High Street she picks up a man who is so clean he crackles.

—Do you iron you own shirts?

—Nope, the wife does.

—She does a good job.

—Collect the rubbish from around here I do. You know everything about a house and its people from their garbage bins.

All the way to Glen Waverly, Iona has a fascinating conversation about individuals she doesn't know, who either jump on their garbage to fit more in and therefore have no consideration for the working man or who don't wrap up their smelly prawn shells, those who don't leave out a beer at Christmas and those who sneak their overflow refuse in front of the neighbour's fence. The garbo knows all.

—It's the smart houses that're the worst. They're disgusting.

—I'll remember.

—And they're the ones who are mean in their business dealings. You can tell they're not honest. Not honest workers.

15

—————i must think up a way of getting out of here oona is a mistress of escape make me oona they know i am australian they know whatever they know about toddy mr kangaroo and al from the combi van i am the fish they have in their net i am implicated i listed all my trinkets and i guess they thought i was talking code language and spilling the beans of course they think that i am sca red_______________________________

16

QUEENIE, of the freckled glowing white skin, was born as her mother died on the shores of Lake St John in the midst of the great spruce forests, the single offspring of a friendless man who spoke rarely. He fished and hunted deep in the woods.

Queenie, though destined for a queer career, spent the first twenty-four years of her life as a poor Quebecker peasant. The only two years of her senior schooling were taken by a rabid secessionist who politically refused to teach his charges English. Queenie took a job in the general store. After that it was cleaning in the motel.

Meanwhile, in running the house of her father, she learnt to use as few words as possible in daily intercourse. And, as it happens, an equivalent economy in money matters. There was a savage streak in the taciturn trapper, and Queenie was forced to endure severe beatings in those last years of school. The repressive silence of her father squashed any budding curiosity the girl might have expressed. Her flesh, so vulnerable in colour, had been toughened by rude living and ice-bound winters and withstood the bruising as if it were packed rubber. Her shrewd heart neither forgave nor shed its rage in pointless tears. His beatings ceased when she effectively fought back.

All her life she had accompanied him on a percentage of his wilderness excursions. She could handle guns and traps and skinning knives with ease. Although blessed with a lemon-scented aura, she had as healthy a temper as her father. When trapping and killing are a way of life, blood oozing out of a body gives not queasiness in the stomach, rather a sense of wonder.

Her father had reached his sixties and the cold had entered his joints. His rigidity calcified in his bones. Frustration and pain made him more sarcastic in his sparse use of words. The winter of her twenty-fourth year was almost more than Queenie could bear. She found herself dreaming of absolute change. A life with a little joy, a little love. The insufferable Frenchified bore, her teacher, who arrogantly spoke fluent English and gave none of it away, entered her life again. A bachelor of forty, he began to press a smothering sexual suit. She, whose face under the luxuriant Titian hair had taken on a velvety bloom, was as sensuous as a flower from Zola's *Earth,* he cooed.

The two men in her life were emotional cripples, and instinctively Queenie knew they were also morally impaired. The great Arctic glaciers shift their inch. The old man was more keen than ever to be the first out on the loose water in Spring. His ambition was to bring in the earliest catch, in spite of, or perhaps because of, the despair of aging.

Queenie just wanted to see them sweat with fear, to even the score through action. She flattered the teacher that her father was so old he needed help. She also implied the cabin to be shared was secluded and wild. She told her father that three would be better than two as the ice would not be properly melted. The old backwoodsman knew very well the state of the snows, but he liked the idea of showing a book-learning man the real meaning of masculinity.

They manoeuvred the boat well enough upstream, with vigour and excitement, and settled into the cabin before sundown.

In the middle of the night there was a deafening roar. Both father and daughter recognised it—an avalanche. They set grim frowns as they sounded the direction and proximity of the movement. Neither said a word.

The teacher panicked. For reasons only understood by the panicking brain, he ran outside to meet the disaster. They heard him scream before he was buried and frozen.

Part of the cabin wall caved in, catching the old man's leg under a tonne weight of timber and snow. During the night, Queenie gave him coffee and quinine and boundless attention. By midday he realised his position was hopeless. The pain was addling his senses. He begged Queenie to take his shotgun, which was well oiled from his repeated winter cleanings, and shoot him, just how he had taught her to take a bear, straight through the heart.

She did so.

All her unleashed rage exploded and dissipated with the shot. She executed a sharp, sudden destruction of the old order.

After about an hour of quiet keening, genuine mourning, she had a flash of illumination. She was completely free. She could destroy, therefore she could create. Herself. Her life. She felt no bitterness, no resentment and no guilt. She was a clean slate.

The small community lamented the double catastrophe with due decorum, and felt collectively relieved when the mercy-killer made it known she intended to leave. With her gone, all memory of Old Jacques, the living reminder of a more heroic past, could fade. Become legend. They were eager for a new teacher with more tolerant ideas. The prosperity of the new era, they suspected, would be in the growing industry of tourism. For the moment, however, the Realty Agent, her old boss at the motel, was prepared to handle the sale of her cottage on the lakefront profitably to some hobby fishermen to make into a lodge. There was fine wood in those beams.

She transformed both her father's and her own bank accounts into travellers' cheques in American dollars, and hitchhiked to Montreal.

Shrewd, silent and competent, Queenie hung around on the St Lawrence Seaway, waiting for a galley job on a freighter working the trans-Atlantic route.

______________they are following up leads my passport is not in my new name they will discover that the sydney address is my mother's address they definitely will discover that gran is rich i will say my father who lives with his secretary in coolangatta is a big fella in the middle east meat trade i have not seen my father since i was twelve daddy i need you now i am getting hot and i am getting the shivers i want to shit and i cannot do it there is pain in my muscles fever__________________________

Marion is really the jolliest of people. She did cheer me up on the telephone today.

Virginia Woolf.: "Women are coming to be more independent of opinion."

Strange that something can be written so long ago and accurately apply to one's present state of mind. I am becoming more independent of opinion.

Strolling along with Dorothy Richardson on her pilgrimage.

A certain rigour in my mind. I want to complain she is raving on. Then I realise there's a level of feminine candour that I am simply not used to in books.

"Intellectual achievements among women seem so embarrassing." Where did I get that quote?

But that embarrassment and the candour…

No time to complete that thought. A rumpus at the front door. Mimbo abusing a Seventh Day Adventist: 'Get along with you young man. Get a decent job. Sell something useful.'

Personally, these days, I'd listen to the Adventists, just to see how they think.

No matter. Candour.

Truth is so hard to say.

I've been walking along the foreshore gathering the strength.

Dear diary, I have never told you before—amber sunset, yellow sky—because of a type of cowardice. Even old Ursula, special among old maids, braids her truth with stardust, though not with heavens sweetening the future and rewarding a life of self-sacrifice. Old Ursula blinded herself…

You see we can quite effectively deal with violence done out there…

Well the truth is Marion threw boiling oil at me.

We must remember that I was a cheeky child and no doubt I provoked her. But it couldn't be my fault. Entirely.

She was fourteen and I remember on her face the expression of deliberation. Marion has an uncontrollable temper when she sees red. I can tell the boys have seen it too. Kelvin has a certain look that is fear…especially when he was younger.

I was irritating. You see I loved the place. I was irrepressible. Like my dad.

She hated it. She hated having no pretty clothes. She hated the chores. She hated the old wood stove. And she didn't take Mimbo's orders very well. Daddy and I were always in their bad books.

He was a gambler and a drinker. Probably not very efficient as a farmer. Who could be efficient in those times, when all the dairies in Gippsland were pouring their milk onto the ground?

Soon after my disfigurement, we had to walk off that land, leaving it to creditors.

I remember she was cooking hot potato chips. The smell of them is pungent to this day. I remember anticipating the taste and never eating them.

I came into the kitchen in gumboots all caked in wet mud and my arms loaded up with chocks of wood for the stove. First she yelled at me for the dirt on the floor, but I answered back… I threw the wood down on the tiles. With righteous logic I cried, I couldn't get my boots off without my arms, could I? Bang! A corner of one of the chocks got her toe. She saw red. She had her hand on the handle of the pan of boiling oil. I poked my tongue out at her. She lifted the pan and slammed it upside down on my head.

The pain blotted. It wouldn't. I felt with my hand and burnt my hand. I was screaming. Marion was crying softly.

Mimbo came in, grabbed a tea-towel and went to the tap. She was a zombie. Half paralysed in horror.

My father was suddenly panting at the door, yelling abuse at them. He came over to me and lifted his fist and said gently, 'Keep calm, skipper, there's a girl.' And knocked me out.

I remember those words so clearly. The last words I ever heard my father say.

Now, Mimbo is calling Ursula. Ursula!

Oh dear, it's quarter past eleven and I have forgotten her tea.

'What's wrong with you?' she said.

I put down the pot and cup and saucer and little milk jug and the pill and the spoon and the sugar, quite ungraciously I suppose, as they rattled on the tray.

'Your dog is moulting. There are ginger hairs everywhere.'

Well, I am not going to hoover yet, nor am I taking you for a walk, Flush.

For this moment I am Mary not Martha. I'm talking with Christ.

Next I knew I was in hospital. I was there for months. When I was twelve, we heard my dad died in New Guinea, in the war. A hero, I know it. Though they sent no medals to prove it.

In hospital, I started to read after they took the bandages off. There was no money for expensive operations.

The pain of the oil was bad. Physical pain is like a performance. You remember it, but not the living of it. I mean the actual experience you don't have to have again.

Diary dear, it was the suffering of adolescence that really scarred me. I resented not playing games. Especially netball, as they call it now. I would not talk to anybody. I refused to go to Secretarial School.

Mimbo had such a prejudice against psychiatrists. But…

She worked and I did her housework, and Marion walked out with and finally married Allan.

Mimbo became very busy. She got herself on all the charity committees and had her little bridge circle. For years she was out day and night.

Now I've written it down, diary dear, I fear the grostesque thing is the knowledge of unfairness, not the look of my face.

Well, no more of this. The vacuuming, the shopping and our constitutional, Flush.

——————————hallucinating tossing febrile vile i am so hot i heard the sound of the lash on her back i heard a woman screaming what has she done so many things are not allowed in the lands of allah did she serve alcohol did she go around with face uncovered even though i am sick i dragged my pallet over to the window wall she called out to me in english alice alice i tried to save her i climbed up my pallet and leapt towards the window for a while i hung onto the bars and the pallet fell and i slid down the wall grazing my knees crawling around now on bloodied knees i am so cold_____

17

A GREAT SEA great sea vessel enters the harbour at Southhampton bearing, among its vast cargo, that of lightning wrapped up in the body of a girl who is sick of the sexual harassment and heavy work in its stinky steamy galley.

Queenie jumps ship.

Having tea, three women. Plate glass flush to the pavement of the narrow, historical street. Yvonne enjoying herself, for holidays are few, carefully planned and saved for. Poised like a puss, Yvonne. Sophie, all bubbles and bulges, blonde hair waterfalling down her back and over her emerald green-patterned kaftan. The third, a white African by accent, making ironic glances in Yvonne's direction, saying clever things.

—Revelation can be more perilous than revolution. Says she.

Yvonne's pale skin is stretched over angular facial bones. Heavy rimmed spectacles make her eyes seem fragile until you see they are as sharp as a stainless steel blade. Her little finger makes a question mark over the handle of her cup. Sophie is bored, but too lazy to worry about it. She has never sussed the English pursuit of a conversation wherein anything you mean must be implicated in a filigree of detail and suggested rather than said. Never actually said. Hints. Clues. Anecdotes. Depending on what you already know, or are prepared to reveal that you know. Sophie gives it a miss. She needs the explicit in all things except jazz.

Yvonne's hawk-eyes are captivated by the sudden sight of the diminutive Queenie toting her ragged bags by the window. Quaint prey.

—Go and get her, she directs Sophie.

Sophie calls out laconically and gestures with her plump arm. Queenie responds. Enters. Nervous, tumbles out a lot of rapid French which embarrasses Sophie into good-humoured laughter.

Yvonne, taking her time, goes to the counter and gets Queenie a coffee and bun. With eversuch nonchalance and glee she places them in the vacant setting at the table and pulls out the seat.

Yvonne, fond of putting French phrases into her written correspondence, is reluctant to actually speak it. Fortunately, Queenie is not the talkative type. They take her to London with them. They decide to deposit her at the travellers' squat in Hackney. Or rather, Yvonne decides that Sophie will.

It seemed to Queenie that she had entered a labyrinth of terraces, street after street of brick houses exactly the same stuck onto one another with some kind of glue, only occasionally broken by a group of shops and pubs with swinging wooden pictures. The corners they turned were meaningless and so many they must surely describe an ever-tightening circle. In the middle of it all, Sophie stopped her Mini at the dead end of a road, facing a broken-down terrace of three two-storey houses. Sophie conveyed the difficult information that this place is used by travelling women who will accept you because of how you look, and probably someone in there will speak French. She didn't move from her driver's seat, nor are energetic gestures Sophie's forte.

Queenie stands on the kerb of an East London street, *sans* false notions, *sans* learning of the academic sort, simply thrilled by the intensity of buildings around her. Strangely confident in a foreign land and glad to be alone, finally, with her own adventurousness. She feels no threat. Eight Mr Whippy vans are parked to her left and behind her four West Indian women talk and walk. Sounds of a fiddle playing an Irish jig from inside. Noise of children and a pushcart somewhere. A black and white kitten leaps down from a crumbling wall to curl itself around her legs with tail erect. It leads her in. Through the open door, down the narrow passage, out past some fallen timber and plaster, and smashed plumbing, to a yard where wild ivy blankets the crumbling garden wall and piled rubbish lies like a tea-towel thrown over the washing up. The kitten climbs over it, into the next yard, where, Queenie hears, there are voices.

She follows, her balance on the treacherous vine a little unsteady, her sudden appearance at the top of the fence a considerable shock to the naked feminists below, prone to the sun on striped and tartan rectangles of blankets.

——————in these septic conditions my knees are infected i do not think i am going to die here i have dreamed my death and i believe it will be by drowning i am convinced i will drown therefore i am not afraid and i have not even got to europe i attacked him about the subject of alcohol today i said you whipped her close to my cell so i could hear it all he is amazed i know what i am talking about he has a new respect for me because i am visionary i laugh and say i have discovered how to handle pain i become a sexual masochist he is horrified and anyway i am screaming i am not afraid for i will drown drown drown in oceans of sweat he felt my forehead went out__________

HACKNEY

Dear Trees,

Thanks for the letter, I'm sad and lonely. Xaviera is leaving soon. She really is a tourist. I'm not, I'm at home sort of, as at home as I was in Collingwood, or Springvale for that matter. Any city is everyone's home who's in it, and no one's. Don't say that to a Londoner, Etama.

Oh Lesley and her labyrinthine mind, I love that woman. Goddess-luck to her and her search for the crone!

Grundhilde wants me to turn a clay drum for her, both of us being of the earth and now finding it very difficult to communicate with words, must try our vibrations. She says my matter is too dense! It's not as bad as it sounds. I'm not very hurt, I'll make her her drum, it's a challenge. Zorro knows about a workshop I can use, around the corner somewhere.

There is a French Canadian living in the broom cupboard. Queenie. A Cancer. She doesn't seem to have any other friends, no memories, no destination. She does a lot of the shit-work around the place which I really appreciate. The kitchen in this squat can become so disgusting you almost throw up. So many people in and out. And no hot water. She doesn't speak English and I don't speak French. Zorro jabbers away at her and she listens with eyes like a really intelligent dog, drinking it all in. Zorro thinks Australians are racist. Half the time I can't understand her English, she speaks in long sentences with no Anglo-Saxon grammar and long words all of them.

I think Grundhilde and Zorro are cooking up something to do about Arachne. At least Grundhilde is trying to secure Zorro's services in some way.

I met a friend of Frances Furriskey's the other day. Sophie McKennan. I heard her sing at this Jazz Club, what: a voice! She's fat and has this long golden hair wrinkling over her large shoulders. Wears tent-dresses! But what an amazing voice. She must have vocal cords like cables and lungs like caverns.

It's really distressing, Xaviera going so soon. I have to let her go. It's like letting go the day at sunset, something inexorable and natural. Sad.

Loud words today. This English woman moved in and wants to bring in carpenters to fix her room! Men! She polishes her windows and her mirror, wears sweaters from Harrods, has a hi-fi with huge speakers. I reckon she is decadent. We won't have men here and told her so. Most of the vain people I've met are basically plain. Very sad.

The Sweeney Todd in navy blue Rover squad cars surrounded a women's squat the other side of London Fields yesterday. Looking for a member of the Baader-Meinhof gang. Freaky.

Zorro's cooking oily, potato-laden Spanish omelettes, and I'm starving. I'll keep you informed of all my doings, my good friend, and you keep well. Heard anything of Oona, lately? Did Jay Jay get my card?

See you blossom,

love,

Et.

——————revolutions and surprise bombings are making the world a fairly dangerous place i must be mad to travel by myself how do you know i travel alone he laughed and laughed each day is unique i thought i was accused of something to do with those shady folks in the van in which case i would not be travelling alone then he changed and interrogated me savagely so that i became worried about the note to et and trix and hoped they would be all right it was probably confiscated i began to cry___________________

18

QUENTIN MCMILLAN is one person who really enjoys the absurdity of it all—the madness of simply living. He has the witty, bystander mentality of the high camp sub-culture. Sweet homosexuality is like a resilient climber, with redolent, spiky flowers entwined around the old oak tree of patriarchy; and Quentin loves it so. Always threatening to become the more dominant culture, the refined plant, at certain times in history, seems the more fruitful in the arts, but a parasite ready to bring down warriors, princes and politicians if the secret code of dissemblance is broken. In short, Quentin knows everything about the darker side of fame, either first-hand or second. He is one of the lucky ones, troubled neither by morality or immorality, indifferent to age and judgment and genuinely fond of his mother.

Kate, for her part, tolerates his idiosyncracies and finds his spite amusing and the dirt on big names fascinating. She worries for his health and needs his loyalty. They are often together. They live in the same big first-storey flat on the Esplanade overlooking the Bay.

Winifred Stevens is having a small goodbye party before she leaves on a sabbatical tour in England for a few months.

—It's a jigsaw of psychology and conditioning, the hedge and track of relationship and loneliness.

Quentin is driving and they are making their way through the solid red-brick suburbs towards Hawthorn.

—But I dearly love interfering, darling.

—You haven't seen Iona Flynn for ten years, why on earth bother, Treasure?

—Quentin, if you are a student of character as I am, you soon learn to tempt the idealistic. And, if you like, make the pragmatic realist work for them—favours.

—Of course. I know Winnie of the chocolate brown stretch slacks and white ankle socks, court shoes and odd marquisite brooch…

—The little hobby horse with the blue rhinestone saddle? Given her by a long lost lover I believe. Her *affaire grande* with an older man when she was a student or young academic. I don't think she's slept with anyone since.

—But what about this other, Associate Professor Doreen Redman? Winnie had her nose put out of joint by her promotion, did she not? The poor possum.

—There's something obsequious about the young, apparently brilliant Doreen Redman. Winifred became quite sharp about her when she realised she would never be more than a Senior Lecturer, but I was amused by one of her stories.

—Oh?

—She has a vice, according to Winifred, that she would prefer her academic colleagues to know nothing of. She can deny herself television, sex, cigarettes, alcohol and valium, but she is addicted to the Mills & Boon Romance Classic. Faced with a choice between Pound's *Cantos* and the thin lavender paperback, she will snatch up the latter before the mechanisms of guilt take hold and force her to 'work'.

—Winnie's a dragon-lady and snob.

Quentin is laughing his easy laughter and the deep crease down the side of his cheek is attractive, his adam's apple prominent.

—Winifred herself has probably never even read anything considered popular. Inside, her soul is probably slowly rusting. But for the grace of Dante, there goes a shell of a woman.

—I take it she is an idealist once tempted. Like Iona?

—Take a left here, son. They've made a one-way street up there. It's such a small spark in Winifred. Whatever she finds in *The Divine Comedy* keeps her human. But in Iona, as a student, it was a blazing bonfire. She wrote poems about the Burning Dance, Tragedy, Truth, Beauty, all that. Naive, savage, anachronistic passion in words so corny they were too—um—feminine.

—I thought they were good.

—You were five years younger than her.

—I liked Iona. She was like a ball game. You could throw anything at her and it'd come back. She looks at you.

—Here, that place over there. I have another motive. This university treated her badly. Her essays were truly eloquent, heartfelt. They hated that. She'd get so distraught at the low marks they gave her. It was so unfair. And ignorant. I want to satisfy my own anger. I couldn't do anything. But you know, you were there, the girl was clever.

—Not so clever as sincere…you don't think Iona could turn out like Winifed? To stop that rot is why you're raking over old earth, Sweetness and Light? Who'll be here, anyway? Is it going to be awfully tedious?

Kate sighs, a rare and significant expression for her.

—The old parlour pinks of Melbourne, no doubt, whose chief bugbear is the Left Wing of the Victorian Labor Party. Drinking red wine and talking about their holidays or holiday houses or gossiping with a bitterness they've grown to love. Like the tannin in their claret. No matter what their age.

—Any queens?

—Doubt it, darling.

—Dare say I'll peek into a couple of closets, if we stay.

—Allow me the interest, my dear, in my autumn years, since sex no longer holds the glamour for me that it does for you, to manipulate others' lives. I want to make a surprise for someone.

—Funny she was your only gay affair.

—Dykes, for the most part, Quentin, are hopelessly dreary. We'd better get in there, nibble the cheese, identify the year…

The men, Quentin notices, are awfully butch, for intellectual types: young marrieds in wools and tweeds identifying with their subject—Keats?—or footy types who teach Aust. Lit. Drama. Old gossipy codgers who haven't looked in the text for years, Shakespeare, Ben Jonson, one or two classes a week, lots of lunches, expressing amazing naivete as to what goes on in the other two universities. All conversation eavesdropped sounds so local. The women loud-mouthed, opinionated, graceless. Poor Winifred, with her pepper-ginger hair showing some salt, seated in one of her mauve armchairs with a raucous green sweater, the marquisite brooch and—my god—a heavy stone pendant, has a neck-brace on. Whiplash. Just before departure, too. Doreen is, as his mother implied, one of those crawling, deceptively powerful women, busy talking shop to those senior and fending off questions from those junior to herself. Quentin amuses himself teasing a private school lad, son of a widowed Senior Lecturer.

Kate sinks to the floor, with the flexibility of someone half her age, beside Winifred's chair, and they chat.

—Well I thought I might look into some of the out-of-the-way women writers in the London library, as a sideline to Dante. Wander around Bloomsbury, read Woolf, retrace her steps.

Kate has her wandering gaze on Associate Professor Doreen Redman, waiting for the moment to pounce and convince. Meanwhile she is all ears for Winifred's obsessions.

—Any interesting…

—Willa Cather.

—Mmm?

—I find this immensely interesting. Gossip. Willa Cather, whose writing I find worthy, that of a compassionate, wise woman, wrote a story called The Birthmark. She refused to withdraw it from publication in McClure's magazine. Even though she was told—the story being based on the disfigurement and dilemma of a friend—that friend might be ruined. The story ends with a suicide, you see. The writer said, briskly, I believe, 'My art is worth more than my friend'.

—Really?

—Women writers are more worrying than men, in a way.

—Indeed.

Feeding her sleek Abyssinian cat on her balcony, Kate notices the spider in the jasmine has been industrious during the night. The dew in the crisp morning gives light in spherical rainbows to the roundels of the web. The cunning yarn is played out with beauty, there to hang, the sticky trap, a pleasure to behold. The lady wolf spider emerges from behind a pot-plant carrying a white ball, the same size as her body, on her back.

The burden, the sacrifice, the yearning to make martyrs, or to become The Maker's food. The game and the game. Kate smiles, the party was worth it.

When I awoke at five I was as fresh as a filly in a paddock of buttercups.

Dear diary, you are Something.

I feel like a child with candy under the pillow.

My unsightly face has meant for most people that I am intellectually handicapped.

Do they think the deaf, mute and blind are handicapped mentally as well?

Milton. Homer. Tieresius. Oh what the blind can see!

If this were a gothic novel, D.D., Winnie and I would meet up in the end after lots of climaxes and tragic events, the worst of which will have destroyed her eyes, and we would live together in deep friendship and contentment. She, perhaps, could dictate to me her epic journey into hell, and she would imagine me as beautiful as Beatrice.

Years ago I may have had a similar daydream about a non-existent brother. But Marion's sons have taught me. Boys will be boys, no matter how clever and handsome.

Before we were nine. Winnie and Ursey. Nipper and Skipper to my dad.

Still day, the bay is glass, a mirror grey to the sky. Only the slightest specks of colour. A scallop boat. A line of bathing boxes.

We are all alone really. Varnished wood keeps us from the worms in our graves.

The coffin is a vessel.

Ships and 'ships. It's interesting that marriage is not a 'ship. Companionship. Relationship. Friendship.

I am on board a 'ship with my mother. And Flush is my mascot.

The sea is like present participles, flowing, moving, the restless bones of the boxless dead. The fish floating, gazing, grazing.

It's all very well imagining a dream ending for Winnie and me, but it would not be so different from the present.

I light the fire in the evenings and we watch the TV news. British comedy. Then Mimbo snoozes. I take myself to the kitchen and the radio, the washing-up, the polishing, knitting, darning.

The kitchen is my castle.

I visit the TV room with hot Bonox, pills and biscuits on a tray, and gently remind Mimbo of the time.

The Pope is in Brazil.

Jazz on the radio. I put my head in my arms and dozed. Hobokon on the Hudson River, the towers of Manhattan. The hour was late and the rain coming down. I was invisible in this dream, in a long American car, a Dodge I believe. I.F. was at the wheel. This is a new individual, different from the Fiona I'd conjured up. This girl, in the wet violence of New Jersey, was vulnerable and frightened. I arrived to help her. Hence, she couldn't see me.

Instead of taking the Freeway, she turned down a smaller road which followed the banks of the Hudson. It weaved in and out and up and down, passing midnight factories and closed shopping centres until in front of us was a huge sheet of water. On the other side was a line of cars held up by a policeman.

She put her foot down and we descended into it, soaking the copper on the way out. I left her at Hackensack.

————————they gave me herbs for my festering knees they work i just press the leaves hard against the graze and gradually they dry it out i wonder if they are treating me better or whether the length of my confinement has lowered my expectations i have the coffee and water in the mornings and a small meal in the evenings when it is meat it is very oily and hot and there is unleavened bread to eat it with often there is just yoghurt dip they put my food in my room silently and bring dirt to throw down the deep hole which is my toilet————————————————

HACKNEY

Dear Iona,

Isn't taxi-driving awful? I'm writing because you met Xaviera before I did and Zorro wears your R.M.Williams boots. And Xaviera has just gone back to Mexico. I'm devastated. Perhaps I should go there. The world's a small balloon, isn't it?

You know Zorro keeps a box of your writing safe?

When I try to ask her what went on between you, she just snorts and says a line of poetry in Spanish, something about an island in the ocean…that North is South and South is North???

Went to Brixton with her yesterday. You feel the colour of your skin when you're with Zorro. It all turned out pretty freaky for me. Zorro strides through this doorway without knocking. When I go to follow her my way is blocked by two huge cockney West Indians. I said 'excuse me' and reached out my hand. The one I touched recoiled with disgust as if my hand were a slug, and hissed 'slut'. He let me past holding his nose. Eventually after feeling I was in some horror movie, I found the room where Zorro was. It was crowded with middle-aged black women, people she had worked with in the factory, when you were here (another reason I'm writing, one of them said hello). Zorro brought out of her bag bottles of vodka and tequila. I didn't even know she had them, nor when she bought them. Zorro was swashbuckling like Tyrone Power, unscrewing the tops while somebody got glasses. One who talked in real lah-di-dah English went at Zorro with a pair of tweezers trying to remove her facial hair. They started wrestling. The others were laughing. Hot-blooded people find it easier to get physically close. I wasn't even in a position to laugh. I felt if I'd laughed they all would have stopped, you know what I mean?

I was lonely, rooted to the spot, getting dizzy from all the smoke, sipping my drink. Racist are we? I was shy and angry.

I have just slept with a woman called Sophie who is a friend of Frances. She came here to study music, dropped out and sings with straight jazz bands. It was good, she is a sensual, overweight Taurean, got an appetite. Well, Frances never answers my letters and I was wondering if you knew anyone in Ireland. Actually Frances mentioned to her your cousin, Gwendolyn or Olwyn? She wants to get out of England for a while. She got involved with this woman who sounds like a nasty mixture of Miss Marple and

Sister George. It seems that poor, loveable Sophie is just around to be laughed at. Sophie shares a flat with a guy and is politically unaware, but she doesn't deserve that. What's your cousin's address?

A whole bunch of European women have arrived and Beatrix, I can see them coming down the street. I haven't seen Beatrix since Crete. Goodbye, regards to Rose,

Etama.

____________sometimes you are grateful to be left in peace it is like hibernation eventually your blood stirs like a bunny you want to poke your nose out of the hole and go round chasing daisies and all that and if the hunter is at the mouth of the burrow you still want to run off out into the sunshine now i have to find a bag of tricks in my head and treat it like a lucky dip i am going to lie on my carpet today and think________________________________

19

FRANCES AND SOPHIE were lovers at school. Between the nightmare which began their affair and the scandal which ended it, perhaps Frances lived some of the happiest days of her life.

To relieve loneliness in a large family, and with precocious intelligence, Frances taught herself remember-games to go to sleep by. In the third form she earned a scholarship to an expensive Catholic boarding school in a large country town. Nightly after lights out, she would recall every detail of the day: French verbs, geography, biology, chemistry, a look exchanged in the corridor, a smell coming from another girl in the ranks they had to form along the walls, the taste of a vegetable, a new way of balancing for a backhand, everything that happened, then carefully she would sift and evaluate. All while she gently caressed her clitoris. Her mind so stuffed with compartments like filing cabinets, the small orgasm of masturbation would explode it all into a kaleidoscope of fractured knowledge and she would sleep. Sheer exhaustion tossed her on her right side and she slept like a log with hard-earned and short-lived peace.

Then the uncontrolled subconscious, having broken the chains of the trained mind, sped off into primitive regions of violent action and ferocious honesty, making catastrophes and hideous monsters come at her. Frances was at the mercies of her pitiless fears. This night a searing pain in her uterus woke her. The bed was damp. She got up and leaned against the window.

The moon was a scimitar and the stars and planets the bits and pieces of the pure white body it had disembowelled in a passionate rage, laid out on the navy forensic blanket of the sky. Shivering there at the window she tried to know more, but her body felt like splinters of ice. She couldn't move. It seemed to her that one must always be a victim. Unless one could be both sexes at once.

She contemplated suicide as she thought of the dampness in her bed.

Unlike Frances, Sophie was a light sleeper, but a generally untroubled one. She was woken by Frances' stifled grunts of sleep-bound terror. She watched her fluorescent watch for five minutes, anticipating the moment she would go to offer comfort. Frances, the scholarship student, brainy, serious and withdrawn, topping the class in music theory, the only one to really like Bartok and Shostakovich, was not popular. She, Sophie, was big and played the saxophone, preferably by ear, listened exclusively to New Orleans jazz and did, where possible, the easiest subjects. Even if she was to be disappointed, for Frances might throw her off, abuse her, the waiting time was delicious. She would put her ample arms about that long intelligent head and press it into her breasts. When she heard the scrape on the windowpane and the sniffle, she could contain her friendliness no longer.

Nothing else could have saved Frances that night. The girls made love until dawn.

By Mass, at seven thirty, they were in love. As they filed up to Communion, all Frances' suspicions about Sophie's wealth and popularity melted before the glorious beauty she had discovered in this lazy, spoilt brat who was sneakily touching her hand. What she loathed before now made her giggle.

Sophie had taken many girls into her bed in her long boarding-school career, with gentle affection and innocent animal warmth, their ignorance of sexual finesse saving them from the horrors of sin. No such innocence was possible with Frances. She had discovered her nervy pleasure centres long ago, and was born with a respect for the body and the amazing intelligence of matter.

Six months of bliss. Sophie's wonderful voice rang out in the chapel with lusty holiness. Her comfortably large head of hair carried the blue veil of the Children of Mary as her right. She cheerfully deceived as they pursued their secret passion and remained popular with both nuns and pupils. She exuded an impression of overall goodness. Her great lungs gave praise to the godhead in the finest way devised by Christianity, through the hymn, and her love of singing compounded with her being in love. Whatever faith was, she had it, obviously. Theological analysis didn't bother her.

Frances began to understand truths she would never disprove. Real, palpable beauty was only experienced through matter. The pinnacle was a merging of mind and body and the sum was a whole beyond the parts. She hated the authority of boarding school even more, because they were wrong. Unjust. They said the finest thing in life was a sin, a vice. She did not fritter away her new knowledge in useless daydreaming and sentimental fantasies; she thought about love as she loved. The quality of Sophie's voice she sought to find in her body through sexual experiment in an environment of horrid hostility and hypocrisy. In defiance she thought of the devil as equal to god. He was the definer, the separator, the real father of humanity. The fall was a fall away from androgyny, a fall into two or multiple parts, as a single bucket of water falls into many drops and remains water. There was both male and female sexuality within herself. The real difference was between making love with someone and masturbating.

The scandal began six months after the nightmare. The moon was round but incomplete. A fresh-faced postulant was nervously checking the dormitories after lights out. The young woman brought from her sheltered home a noctophobia of near pathological proportions, so the spooky rounds, a part of her training, were a very real penance for her sins. She gathered in her insecurity and determined to shoo the girls off into their own beds if they were breaking house rules.

Her habit having no rosary beads, she crept along soundlessly. She heard movement. She flicked open the nearest curtain to see a neatly made, unoccupied bed, altogether an eerie experience in the moonlight. She shuddered, then flicked open the next curtain, and gasped. The passion of it was disgusting. There could be no mistaking what Frances and Sophia were doing. Sheets and blankets had been thrown off by thrashing legs. Frances' thighs were clinging around Sophie's long, damp hair. Frances' page-boy haircut was bobbing up and down on top of Sophie's belly not two feet from the postulant's eyes. The two girls evidently did not hear the rasping of the rings on the curtain-rod or the nervous cough of the young woman in her grey serge outfit. She, for a moment, was paralysed by such close iniquity. She watched horrified before she let out a scream and went running off to fetch a more senior nun.

Frances did not scuttle back to her own bed after the disturbance. Coldly conscious of the situation, she made the bed and placed herself in it beside Sophie, who had retrieved her nightgown and had its virginal flannel all over her Venutian flesh. Sophie could have lied, in fact the ecclesiastical authorities would have liked her to point the finger so that they could have a single scapegoat. Frances would have been expelled. But she was dismayed, caught on the horns of two self-sacrifices and unable to choose. Frances had decided. She was defiant and articulate.

The senior nun was not shaken to the core. It was the postulant who had seen it and her inadequacy in the language necessary, combined with the older nun's limited imagination in the field, gave an inadequate description of the crime.

The Reverend Mother called a special assembly the following day to shout hellfire and damnation and let off some steam.

—From now on, she bellowed, no touching. No seeking warmth in the beds of others. This sacred chore is saved for married couples who do it for God. Lesbian practices will not be tolerated in this school. They shall not cast their satanic shadows in these halls again, nor shall they degrade the grounds. Never, especially if you are wearing your school uniform, are you to so much as hold hands.

Et cetera, for an hour.

While the scandal shook the whole school, no expulsions were carried out. Frances' parents begged the Mother Superior to mend Fanny's dreadful ways with her severest penalties. From thence until the end of her school days, Frances was blamed and punished for all the misdemeanours done by others. In revenge she never denied, she never even deigned to answer. Ironically, her results in Matric were brilliant, the best in the school in her subjects. Sophie's well-off parents took it all in their easy-going stride. They happened to calm the Principal with a timely gift of sporting equipment.

Nevertheless, the scandal and the entire experience seared an indelible scar into Frances' soul. She would not forget a single detail of her treatment, ever.

——————when i was free i was not deaf but i used a hearing trumpet and deafened myself by hearing too much and became confused now it is simple i can listen to my own head and not be distracted by riches as far as the eye can see so what are the endless possibilities of my destiny i think i dreamed about janice and about my donkey and she drew up two equilateral triangles now what do they represent______________________

HACKNEY

Dear Trees,

Beatrix has arrived. So now we're organised and bulk buy rice, millet, peanut butter and honey from a wholefood barn in a little lane off Shaftsbury Avenue. Two bunches of women turned up within 24 hours of each other. One lot is on its way to Wimminsland in Wales. It's like a refugee way-station here.

Bounds and rebounds.

Let me explain. It seemed so peaceful before the battalions came. The mixture of nationalities was happily galvanised by Xaviera. Less organisation, everybody cooked for themselves. Yolanda, the Pom who polishes her windows, was always frying up gammon and leaving Heinz baked beans tins all over the place. Meat-eaters get threatened by vegetarians en masse! She really freaked when Beatrix straightened her out. Queenie doesn't have to do so much shit-work any more. What a woman she is! So tiny! Real energy. Positive.

I was silly to love Beatrix too possessively. She is 'plural'—it's good to be in her orbit again. I did not realise how alienated I was becoming.

These travelling women's politics are fantastic—you share everything, even clothes. It's fairness that matters, not personal possessions. If you have a problem about privacy or something precious, you all talk it out together. All decisions are made this way. It's time-consuming, but time is something we have, having sacrificed other things to have it.

When Grundhilde met Beatrix and heard her drumming, she put her head on the floor in front of her. It wasn't embarrassing, it was deadly serious. A couple of days later and Beatrix is sharing Zorro's studio. Grundhilde is sleeping with Greta who was with Beatrix…everybody else seems to get it on together so quickly and so easily.

I went wandering around by myself, reading in the London Library at Bloomsbury. Actually, I met an old Uni lecturer of mine, Winifred Stevens. We had a cup of tea together. She was milking my brains about recent women writers. She is sort of sly. But having tea in London with an academic older woman made me feel somehow mature. Too many years in the ghetto has made a child of me.

An American called Hettie has turned up. What an idiot! She paints her face up like a clown and goes down to Broadway Market, the local Hackney High Street, and begs! Meanwhile, she talks about the stock market and getting enough money to buy an island in the South Pacific! Amazon Utopia. Zorro hates Yanks and thinks she's a CIA spy. She won't contribute to the food kitty, only when she begs it off the poor Poms. There is no-one rich in this area. The way she talks about things and asks questions does sound like she's learnt it from a file.

In with the battalions sneak single spies!

She moved into Queenie's broom cupboard and Queenie and I are together.

Grundhilde, Zorro and Beatrix are hatching some plan. They have this way of talking which makes everything they say sound like conspiracy.

I don't know how I am, Trees. Perhaps getting a bit unhealthy, not enough fresh vegetables or fruit. I'm looking sallow and thin.

Dying for another letter,

Yours,

Et.

__________i have been doodling with straight lines i placed the equilateral triangles on top of each other once balancing on their noses and then on a side on the side it makes a one a diamond on their points it makes a chalice the diamond and the chalice are made of the same ingredients this is very interesting philosophically the diamond is coin and the chalice is cups cups question mark kindness spirituality and materiality__________________

20

ALL IN THE affront of attempting to be more or less than one seems, Iona is ankle-deep in the grime of pinching pennies, somewhere near St Albans. Longing for a camel, she rides a taxi, smelling the oily dust of the city's night people who transform in her cab to tired home-comers. They bend beneath porch lights to poke keys in their holes with chronic resignation.

Two bright planets playing triangles with the moon these clear nights, a Doris Lessing quote in her mind about the nature of the group-mind we are seldom prepared to acknowledge, Iona is lost in the identical streets of the suburban wilderness. It is ghostly. Victim of the grid, darkness then corner lights, she is a rat in a maze. Can there be so many square miles of this? The map in the directory is just as bad. There is no route out of the rut she is in.

She was less scared, less lost in New York City. Metropolis, Manhattan.

But it is not the names of the places, not even their mystique, it is one's state of mind.

—Am I gripped by a Western Suburbs state of mind, resignation to a rodent life in Doctor Strangelove's mighty laboratory? This could be really freaky. She turns yet another corner.

The shackles of Frances' possession are still on her, Frances' tricks still unsettling. Her dreams have Frances trapping her in houses, in cities. She clings to the rhetoric she spouted to Helen.

The last of her long line of overseas lovers, Helen had seen the thunder-clouds in her sky-coloured aura. Helen adores her. She is John the Baptist of the new era. When she has discovered the meaning, found the direction, many will follow. It will be a dance and Iona will be the centre. Helen listened to Iona's talk of Australia and the women and theatre and the freedom, and changed. She saw a star in the west, whereas I? I was probably homesick. I was impoverished and she took me in. She massaged my feet and had mysterious orgasms doing it.

Iona's cast of mind is tolerant, not fixed. If someone believes something with the conviction of consequent behaviour, she takes notice. All in the attempt to understand. Even though it was ridiculously egocentric, I went along with it. I thought Helen's love could drown the influence of Frances, but more likely I have driven Helen mad by letting her love me so much without returning it. Only trying to be honourable.

—I'm nowhere near knowing. I am not only a lost taxi-driver, I am metaphysically a lost taxi-driver, letting luck alone guide me. Taking no responsibility. Certainly not for Helen's spinsters' Elysium.

Helen had tricked psychiatry long ago, simply by learning more about the subject than most practitioners in the Tri-State area. But her time with the therapists had schooled her in examination of her inner life. The forces she uncovered were not, as they would say, manias and phobias, they were powers. Entities and deities. Psychic phenomena were of an ordered battle raging in the sphere immediately outside the human. The intelligences behind it were vitally interested in the doings of all inferior levels: human, animal, vegetable, mineral, gaseous. The practice of tantric yoga increased her paranormal awareness, she said, through controlling the vital essence of Kundalini in the spine.

When she saw Iona's aura of glowing Chinese silk, a transparent blue she could see through to the background of mirror and top shelf bottles, she was assailed by a new emotion, an angerless acceptance, a restless longing. The sense of wilderness she searched for and didn't find in Israel. She picked her up in a lesbian bar in Greenwich Village. She picked me up or I picked her up. I needed a place to stay, she needed release from that neurosis which she related to being an American Jewess, daughter of the holocaust. Having to have babies. Being so frightened of men. Relating sex to death. Educated right out of her brain. Resorting to three or four personalities. I soon cut the crap. She never knew she was funny until I laughed.

Now she is coming to The Great South Land of Humour.

Iona finally turns onto a major road.

—This is not good. I will not be able to cope, she's crackers.

Names, names, names, a circus of women's names. Zorro, too, Zorro loved me, and Yvonne…maybe. All since Frances, and now, Rose and I, we've slept together. Maybe will again. I, the beloved, feel like the prey. All this time working under the moon, I think I am turning loony.

————————the incredible simplicity of two equilateral triangles has blown me out for days but then i thought of the crescents again crescents question mark i was distracted thinking about my eccentric family you never knew what would be happening when you came home from school and i have been dreaming about the fresh bread and jam at susie's place and susie's mum and then of course rose because rose reminded me of susie's mum____________

Diary mine! Dear me! Jocelyn is such a bad driver. She should be allowed to drive a little biplane in the uncluttered sky where she could whoop and dive as much as she likes.

She flies over the railway line in Bungower Road as if it is a ski jump. And she laughs! The poor, poor pedigree dogs.

I still have a headache. Even though I've taken the sea air.

Winter suits me. I'm not afraid of the cold. I could carry out my tasks in Greenland or Lapland.

When the clouds speed across the moon like witches on broomsticks, I am most happy. The ghosts of galleons and highwaymen and landlord's daughters and shots of treachery and the threats of redcoats make me excited. I wish there were more…

stories.

Whipped through a Gladys Mitchell from the library, called *Late, Late in the Evening,* and one line I recall. Dame Beatrice, her detective, reflects, 'It is said that every person has it in his power to write at least one book and that we all hold the life of at least one other person in our hands'.

All the songs on daytime radio are about love and all the talkback never ever mentions it. The songs are daydreams and the talkback chats the daily grind of small miseries.

If I let Old Ursula's face go on telling its own lies, while my mind floats free behind it, then I have nothing to hold onto.

No consistent reality.

I read Kafka again to calm myself down. It is the immediacy of his judgment. It's not on some future day. End day. Therefore the defence and courage is always here and now. The accusation, the indictment, has been on my face for forty years, and I have not had the courage to protest my innocence.

The rot has set in. I've bruised something.

I've grown suspicious. And barmy.

My own words accuse me.

I think you, diary dear, are a crutch. Like a schizophrenic's alter-reality.

Tonight I went at sunset and sat for a long time on High Rock. Most of the sky was clear. The silence like a held breath. The moon mounting behind my right shoulder and the sun wrapping itself up for the night in pastel, mohair blankets.

Flush sniffing about, discovering what canines know through their noses.

Sea iridescent, blue-silver-gold, and lapping gently.

Cormorants flying close to the surface and seagulls calling and organising themselves in the sky.

I should have been relaxed. But no, troubled.

I felt someone watching me.

The TV whingeing behind closed door, looking helplessly at you, D.D., I think I should destroy you and write the one book I have in me and be done with living. Continue existing.

I am an active lady who has been forced into contemplation.

Miss Trap is not a Trappist. No no no.

Not Martha, nor the martyr Ursula, not in my soul.

——————i have figured it i have i have indeed the crescents are scimitars that is swords i have the chalice that is cups and i have the diamond that is pentacles and all the time over my head was the fourth side of my bag of tricks the boa constrictor is a wand see leo you have the four sides of the tarot and they are paths and they are channels and i just have to interpret their meaning_______

HACKNEY

Listen Mary,

You have no right to lecture me from 12,000 miles away! I'm really hurt. I know we're sisters and responsible for each other. I've lived the politics of feminism longer than you have. I must point out that the first I knew Arachne was travelling was when I heard she was incarcerated! How did she know where we were? You reckon I must give up everything for Arachne. You're crazy I don't care if I will earn a better karmic bank account, that's stupid. Europe must look pretty small from Aus, but I'm not so near the Middle East that I can just walk out and demand her release. There are wars and earthquakes and all sorts of things. You do something. Etama.

21

THE CRUST of the earth is as delicate as eggshell. Helen feels its fragility as she crawls around on the rocks and sand. Three Ph.Ds count for nothing when the mind is a hair's breath from madness. The wordsome knowledge that she writes to Iona—'the sexagesimal system was known to the Sumer-Akkadians in Mesopotamia as early as the third or fourth millenium B.C.E. as evidenced by multiplication and division tables found at the temple libraries of Nippur, Sippar and Ashurbanipal…'—cannot be understood without her presence. Sitting among sacred texts is no longer, as she once thought, journeying enough. There on the friable earth of the Nevada desert, Helen, in one of the vast compartments of her brain, realises that such sterile learning is the final patriarchal trick. It is up to herself to bring about the synthesis of knowledge and presence. The extent of her knowledge feeds off loneliness and insanity, in shape like a mushroom cloud. The extent of it needs the community to live, to mean anything.

She is suffering an agony of separation which the screeds of paper covered with tiny writing she has sent to Iona in the past few months only worsens. Her precursor is putting up psychological defences against the knowledge. Her return letters are getting more and more polite and materialistic.

Helen is surrounded by a black iciness she knows is the demonic. Her anger in the past was capable of flipping her personality, making her into an entirely different person. She feels the threat of its rebirth as she reads Iona's latest letter. Distant, concerned, saying that she believes the highest of the art forms is healing. The second, music. Her own, literature, is somewhere in the middle of the scale.

Trying to release the pressure of her rising torment, Helen responded—'in order to dance, we must have experienced a kind of paralysis'. And dance, because it is presence and knowledge in one and the same, is higher, the ultimate. A ridiculous argument about the class structure of the Muses crossing the Pacific ocean when she herself should be flying to her side, to be her teacher, to facilitate the transformation from within. She wrote another letter immediately after posting the last—'You must have a great task as my whole well-being is mixed up in you. Great tasks require commitment. You cannot do it alone. I realise you are the 50th, in the middle of the circle of the Sun. In holding onto what we think is reality, we lose something unless we simultaneously relinquish something, so that we might glimpse the essence. To fear even one aspect is to fear everything. You just want the positive aspects of intimacy without the trauma of risk. Consider for a moment that there is no reality external to you.'

Iona, obviously tired and spending time with a dilettante in spiritual learning, had written back that Mary thought that Pamela was the centre of the circle. Whoever Mary and Pamela are, it is Helen who is the teacher, as she herself knows. If she does not somehow get there, Iona is in danger of falling among false prophets. Helen's mental well-being would be shattered forever.

Helen's hair of henna-brown is cut neatly at the beginning of each season to maintain an order in the self in all aspects, as each being is a microcosm of the cosmos. Her eyes with twenty-twenty vision jut out from their sockets, permanently startled. Her shot-putter's physique, not that of a bookworm, has brought her close to catastrophe when the violence of her aggressive personality takes over. There is too much to control.

Whether from crawling around on the sharp rocks or, as Helen immediately believes, from stigmata, blood spouts from the palms of her hands. She feels her side, there is blood there, too.

In the paroxyms of stress and karmic isolation, seeking Iona in the aqua reaches of the sky, Helen has been rolling and scraping and punching the brittle earth. Her clothes are torn and blood stains her pocket-book. Knowledge accumulated over twenty years of exhaustive study bursts the banks of her psyche and she preaches to the landscape as if addressing multitudes.

—But Babylon of brick in beautiful dimensions... Tower of Babel...Hanging Gardens...the great Temple of Marduk! Bohr's principle of the correspondence between Quantum and Classical physics brings to mind construction of the unprecedented 3,000-foot bridge across the Euphrates to unite the two parts of the city. They called her Whore! Every block of buildings, because of the Sacred Marduk Building Code that none dared defy, would be incorporated into the same system spaced in integral multiples of Babel brick, the brick being the quantum unit. Babel brick...Babel brick...Babble babble ... This illustration of the paradox may give us new insight into the meaning of liberty!

Helen suddenly stares at the blood stains on her bag with amazement. Her cousin, Aaron, is about a hundred yards away and his car is parked beyond him. Helen runs.

—Are you okay, Helen?

—No, look. She shows her palms, her side, the blood and her clothes as dusty as a desert hermit's.

Driving back to California and stopping on the way to slot coins in a coca cola vending machine and buy gas, Aaron is persuaded to lend her money to go to Australia.

—If it'll make you sane...

—I'm not mad, Aaron, never call me mad.

HACKNEY

Dear Trees,

Things are hotting up. Yesterday in Petticoat Lane we were nearly arrested. The National Front was out. So the police were protecting him! We look like terrorists so we are terrorists. Let 'em bash up darkies and dykies, it's okay, they're all a threat to the state. We simply weren't allowed to go shopping. Are we paranoid or is it really happening?

About Arachne. We're not going through the authorities. Queenie provided the money. You know what Beatrix is like, persuasive; anyway Queenie was the only one with the cash. We went down to Australia House, inspected the vehicles for sale, and bought a campervan for four hundred pounds. We brought it home and parked it outside and came in to make plans. Zorro argued that it's summer in Europe, crowded and crawling with all sorts and the way not to be noticed is to be extra noticeable. We paint the campervan, make a name for ourselves, take instruments along and play music. A troupe de l'arte. Busking wherever. Guess I'll have to pass around the hat, not having any musical talent.

I am Queenie's first. Those Canadian lakes run very deep. She is like a William Blake poem. Serene and savage. I'm not worried about her money-wise. She's a Cancer and a worker. Been working in the toffee-apple factory around the corner. On the other hand, Zorro should be careful about what she says to her. I mean Zorro's the demogogue who wouldn't hurt a fly. Queenie could do anything. Zorro doesn't lack courage, it's not that. It's just something in her that isn't physical strength, childhood weakness, perhaps she has T.B. It sounds like she has weak lungs. She suggests, she hints. She theorises. Queenie listens, and it's all news to her.

We've decided on a name for the bus. "The rites of passage", and its colour shall be purple. Tomorrow Beatrix and Zorro are going to one of Zorro's emigre friends to do the spray painting. How exciting! On the move again.

I'll send this and write to you immediately before we go,

Love from, and Beatrix sends hers,

Et.

—————————i am going to use my bag of tricks to get out of here i will look at the hardest first scimitars power violence there is this violent fundamentalism of the muslim faith all round me and you have to be pretty bloody violent to beat that but i see from political cartoons that they are only small countries underneath the heavy clouds of russia and america a little western woman like me in here could have the entire might of the western world behind her the president of the united states could bring in his nuclear helicopters that is if my note got out_______________

A you is not passive.

Again a redolence of someone else.

Flush, with his pointy nose, he knows. He wagged his tail.

I started sniffing about myself, up on Nonne's Walk.

Then I saw. She was squatting to urinate. Her brown buttocks had no bikini line. Her clothes were unironed and yet silky, patterns of maroons and creamy greens.

I beat a hasty retreat.

I stumbled past a ring of rocks and a tiny fire.

Well I know this Council and they won't put up with camping on the foreshore.

Instead of to the sea, I've been walking out to Jocelyn's. She is pleased. She can put her feet up, and laugh even louder. Flush is not so pleased.

Where has my self-righteousness gone? My sense of Kafka and justice.

I went back today. The fireplace has gone.

My disappointment quite surprised me. I feel foolish, flustered.

I have to do something dramatic. I will burn my diaries.

Death sentence, diary dear.

She caught me on the beach. Still in floppy forest-in-the-Fall colours. I tried to run away, but she is as fast as Diana of the Golden Apples. My hand went up to my face but she grabbed my wrist. Her grasp is as strong as a man's.

I looked down. She held my jaw and turned it to the side. She examined my profile.

I thought I wanted to escape. But none of the destinations I could think of were freedom at all. I gave in after a struggle. The struggle was to admit my face and myself were one being.

I had no idea a person could be so familiar and demonstrative with a stranger. Especially as strange a stranger as I.

She put her arm around my shoulder. This was on Royal Beach. She led me around the rocks towards Fishies' Beach to the cave that is there near the overflow drain.

I said I have to go. She begged me to return there tomorrow.

——————with wands i would use some kind of magic call on that womanpower we used to sing about win with the bending of the reed rather than the intransigence of steel if i were to use the diamonds i would simply say name your price my granny is rich and so is my father for that matter just ask cups is more difficult i think it is my innocence justice and the argument and defence of the law intelligence and fairness i have decided that this is the most arduous and hopeless course_________________

The gift from Iona, a Mexican blanket, Oona loves. She pokes her head through the hole in the middle, *como los bandidos,* or huddles beneath it and her grey one to keep warm from the stiff breezes off Bass Strait.

The island is distinguishable for its grasses, though she was sad to learn from the local women that the snakes native to the Furneaux Group had been destroyed by the white men in their paranoid, biblical fear of the serpent. Otherwise it looks like good snake country. Wild boar, goats, rats and rabbits are a problem from shipwrecks in the early years. The Tasmanian Aborigines, not a full blood among them, but with as strong a culture as any, are to Oona's liking and they talk. She feels peace, as if she is on holiday. It's good to be creative; she has her leather-bound exercise book with the carefully printed lyrics to her songs, and a felt pen.

If you're a goddess daughter
what mother was mine
when you let me drink water
while you sip on wine.

She strolls underneath the low quacking Cape Barren geese and sees the sea from small rises in the land and thinks of all sorts of subjects for her opera. Ned Kelly, maybe.

On television is the series *The Last Outlaw* which Oona watches with the jolly mutton-birders. These people, truly blotted from the history books with heaps of grudges, are now slowly becoming politicised. Smart kooris from the mainland visit them and talk. It happens Oona is there and the lessons give her new life, a purpose and identity. She feels brainy.

After several weeks, she leaves in a small aeroplane which was hired by one of the mainlanders with whom she says she will work during her peregrinations networking for the new organisation, Link-Up, designed to reunite Aboriginal families separated by the Protection and welfare Boards.

She is on her feet again at Taree at the side of Highway One.

22

——————whatever the outcome thinking about means of escape has made me cheerful the english-speaker has not visited me for ages i feel optimistic i have become very close to great phoebus to whom i pray of a morning and this morning i swear i heard a reply i touch my head on the ground in respect in case i am making it up but he said mother earth is doing her best__________________

HACKNEY

Dear Trees and Jay Jay,

Thanks for the card Jay Jay. Yeah it's fine with Beatrix, you do what you think is best. She'll write.

I'm writing to you together because well I've been writing to Trees pretty constantly and have only received one letter back and Jay Jay has written…well…I don't know how you all are feeling over there. I don't know how my epistles are being received, whether they're being read round the campfire at night like the *Bulletin,* or whether you, Trees, just pick them out of the mail-box-fridge, read them straightaway on horseback and leave them to get damp under the kitchen tarp somewhere… I just don't know.

They left without us. That is Grundhilde, Zorro, Greta, Beatrix, Gertrud and Gunta left in "The rites of passage". Some pretty hairy happenings first though.

They argued that since neither Queenie nor I were musicians, we couldn't go, even though it's technically Queenie's van and I'm her lover. They want to make real street music, protesting that they have to live. Music became the only credential. Shit shit shit.

But weird. In the morning after we bought it we discovered the van had been painted over with yukko symbols, inverted pentagrams, upsidedown ankhs, even a backwards swastika. The camper was yellow right? These evil things were in black. It gave us the shivers. Grundhilde said Hettie could be something worse than a CIA spy.

Anyway, the Spaniards did a pretty good duco job on it and it has "The rites of passage" written in four languages on its four sides, and "We're a troupe of women singers, ask us to play for you", in Italian.

Hettie has disappeared.

Queenie is amazing, though. She wasn't hurt. She trusts Zorro so much, and I think some arrangement other than the one I know about—to meet them in Greece—has been agreed between them. Queenie has rocklike determination. Queenie and I have decided to go apple-picking in Wales to get together some money.

Address all enquiries about Arachne to Beatrix, she'll be the one looking in at every Poste Restante in the major European capitals from now on.

Love, Et.

——————the english speaker my interrogator came with one of those cold yoghurt drinks i have grown to love he certainly made me laugh crystal pendulum he exclaims spit opal cufflinks spit diamante butterfly spit clown-head brooch spit i gathered that he had discovered that all the costume jewellery that i had at some time or other was a goose chase for him it was the first time i have seen his smile his teeth are startlingly white he said you want to know how long you have been here and i shrugged he drew six short lines and one long one through them none of these he asked and i shook my head——————————

Well diary.

She crossed her legs and sat with a straight back. Her clothes falling off her. She had no panties on. The cave behind, her strong broad forehead, her wide lips, the line of her cheekbones, so beautiful, so beautiful.

I propped against a rock, facing her, tilting my head to one side, like a bird, birdlike indeed.

She told me of her dream, 'And in this dream this woman who I think was you had a perfect nose. When I saw this, or judged the nose beautiful, the ugliness washed away.'

I hardly listened. This woman is as gorgeous as a movie star.

Does my ugliness wash away?

No, she answers simply. Without coyness, with neither accusation nor apology, as natural as wearing no underwear. All of a piece she is.

I am full of questions. I am talking to a goddess and my throat seizes up.

Face to face with reality inner and outer. There were, diary dear, several moments of silence, perhaps even twenty minutes. We stared at each other. Then I realised I had to put up or shut up, or otherwise there could be no pretense of sanity, even to myself.

Hectic changes inside, hectic, frantic.

Any rate.

The Main Street came to mind, all those people who know me, who are polite and ask me how my mother is, addressing something over my shoulder, all those people should see I have a life of my own. They would fall over seeing me walking up the street with a beauty queen.

Do you want some coffee or tea? I asked, thinking of sitting in that new Shoppe in Barkly Street, ordering tortes.

So I did walk up the street with her and the usuals were aghast. No-one dared ask how my mother was.

Then we settled to talk.

'Incredible, you know. Dawn remembered seeing you, years ago. She knew it was on one of these beaches.'

'I remember her. The surfer girl.'

'You know, I reckon it's important. It's karma.'

'What is?'

'The coincidences. Everything. I've made it a mission to find you and I have. And you need me. It's great.'

She then asked me if it was a birthmark. She did not assume that it was.

'No womb would have such heat as melts the skin of an infant,' she said.

If I could blush I would have. There were Mrs Cole, Mr Wilson, the girls from the chemist, Miss Upright Bank Teller waiting for a takeaway, being discreet, but all ears. All ears, D.D.

What kind of conduit are you?

Now I had the opportunity to tell the whole Peninsula the story.

'It is a burn,' I said as loudly as I dared. Then giggled.

'Right, yeah,' she responded, with the care people take in things when it's their own life. 'There's a vital difference between a birthmark and a burn. You see, we assume, in searching for the meaning of our karma, that it's all controlled by an essentially good force. If it was a birthmark those higher forces chose that condition for you. You know? But there are strong negative forces too, whirling around in the stratosphere. For whatever reason trying to have their effect. See if you were highly evolved in the last life, you were probably shining very brightly on the other side, and they hate that. They attack.'

Even I had forgotten the locals by this stage. She was so convincing, so concerned. Evidently an occultist. I don't know whether I believed her but I was very pleased; also, with a part of my mind, about where the gossip about me would go from here. It's a burn. She's a witch.

'So how?'

'I can't tell you here.'

'Why not? Well, anyway, when they attack it's usually just before puberty, nearly always girls. That's why you get young girls in *The Exorcist* and so on. You know? Where there are paranormal happenings, young girls. To attack they have to find a vortex. Maybe someone's anger, or greed, or sexual activity, or jealousy. Perhaps a flawed aspect between Mars and Pluto, I don't know how they find a crack, but they need one. Then wham. Whoosh. They impede you.'

When I was walking home, I recognised each shop by its smell. The boot-maker, Nick. The barbecued chicken. The healthy oily working odour of the garage. Even the furniture and carpets reeked. And the stationery and the newspaper. The cake-shop so much so that I bought Mimbo and me a fresh lemon tart.

My nose.

Leafed through Dickens tonight. Don't know why. Felt like it. There's a terrific solace for one's oddness in fiction, especially if it's miasmic and miserable.

23

YOGA CLASS was an adventure into her own pain, a journey through stiff joints and lazy tendons. Dawn, eleven years younger and as supple as a sapling, stood beside her. At the end of the yoga session was a deep relaxation period of a quarter hour.

During this time Iona thought of Nola and her mother. She became inexpressibly sad. Many are the times she had been told by her mother and many the times she remembered by herself: 'I couldn't leave her in that place, Iona, no human being could. They had straw on the floor and cages!' Her mother had gone once to an institution for severely handicapped children, made her judgment and refused to go back there. 'Nola has the same genes as you. Michael's and mine. Neither her body nor her tongue obey the messages from her brain. We don't know what she thinks. But they don't even treat pigs like that. Nor criminals.' Her mother was talking of thirty-six years ago, but Iona remembers the lectures from her third or fourth year. Nola had grown bigger and bigger in her chair and giggled and gurgled to a rhyme and reason of her own.

The relaxation period ended and Iona stretched. Dawn's lithe body was upside down in a headstand. The abyss of taxi driving, waiting is like nothing. A void. She'd been on the Southern Cross rank when she read of Iambe, the buxom serving girl, entertaining the gods and goddesses or whoever with jests all of a vulgar nature. What are the chemicals in my own brain doing? She is inspired to think Nola has a nature like Iambe. Has the deep relaxation told me something I always knew and didn't recognise? Of course Nola is that kind of a character, different from Mum. Mum who doesn't even like toilet paper and nappy ads on TV. Nola loves them. Dawn folds herself down from the headstand like a road map.

Demeter grieves. Persephone's gone. Hecate hears the yowls from the one captivated, kidnapped into hell for the season. If a woman's depression is archetypal, then so is her humour.

Mrs M starts the dance class with some chat about Indonesia.

—The ritual of the Kore as played out on the island of Ceram involves the dancer being the maiden, Rabie, standing near a pit in the centre of a spiral of arm-linked men and women who dance her into the ground. Then they stamp the earth over her like a seed. It is the burial before the birth. She rises as the full moon.

—I've been buried, Iona whispers to Dawn, in the shadows of Melbourne suburbia at night.

—You don't have to dance like that. I'll put some Indonesian music on. I just want you to move with it. Imagine the spiral or imagine the maiden or imagine the earth or imagine the rising of the full moon. Remember the centre for the moon in your body is the small of your back. Dance from the small of your back. Centre your energy in that place.

It's scary at first having to dance without steps, without resorting to stamping out the percussion. Iona takes a few breaths and feels clumsy. Too literal. She does begin to feel freer. She begins not to care about anybody who might be watching her.

Mrs M changes the music, divides the class into smaller groups so that each indivdual has plenty of room. It is a Bartok choral piece. Dawn and Iona exchange glances, it's impossible to dance to that. They watch the first group of three women and a man. Then it is there for them.

Impossible, I can't think of anything to do, I'm tired, I want to be somewhere else. She is one of four on a huge space of shiny wooden floor. Gradually she listens, she stills the verbiage in her mind and listens. Voices. She remembers her insight into Nola of a few minutes before. Iambe. Salome. I'll dance for Herod. Ha, this is a woman's view, being inside the seven veils, dancing out from veils with sauciness and insolence. Her arms are whipping the web-like sticky veils from around her. She doesn't see her Herod though she knows he is there. Iona, in her mauve leotards and pale blue tights, has not an ounce of extra fat on her these days. She is not fit, she is panting and sweating. And everywhere is Bartok.

She was a sportswoman, co-ordination is not a problem. The singers intrude into her fantasy, she is drawn up and up but she must stay balanced until the end of the note. Every muscle is aching. She must touch that place the singers are. It is not as though her outer body could stretch any more but inside each joint she finds a millimetre more. The note ends and she totally collapses. Mrs M, who glides among her dancing students, kisses her cheek and whispers 'thank you'. What did I do? The music is finished.

Dawn and she lean against the barre shaking their heads in eyebrow communication. Neither has seen the other dance, and they both watch the last group of four.

The final piece of music is Handel's *Water Music*. It seems easy and flowing, rippling, but Mrs M wants more, she only wants them to walk, to walk from the throat chakra. To know nothing else but the forward energy pulling from vishuddhi centre. After she has given the instruction, Mrs M comes to Dawn and draws her aside, so that she is in the second group and Iona in the first.

I can do it. I can concentrate on the throat chakra and I can go forward without my feet. I can be the music. Up and back Iona goes, flowing, she is sea. She is her drowned sister, the soul of her suffering mother, the resilience of her vegetative sister. She is giving expression to the inexpressible. Her mind, body and the music are one. She does not remember a thing. When it is over she breathes air, whereas before she existed within the third dimension of water.

Both Dawn and Mrs M have tears in their eyes and the applause from the other dancers is spontaneous.

—Dance is something else isn't it?

—You did something tonight which was wonderful, answers Dawn.

—I don't know how. Only that my mind was absent, not elsewhere, inside my throat and silent.

—I know what it's like, but I didn't do it tonight. In fact it's probably the only worthwhile thing.

—Imagine Nijinsky. Wish I'd seen him. Or Isadora Duncan.

—Felt something similar surfing sometimes. But you did it, sport, you danced the sea. I ought to know.

—Dawn, seeing you and Mrs M with tears in your eyes was… Like I can feel the beginning of a potential I did not know existed.

Iona is blushing.

—That's dance.

—*Le danse.*

—Your new tights look good. Didn't know you had such sexy legs. You always wear jeans.

—I don't want to drive tonight. Do you want a lift home? No? Okay it's back to the shadows for me. See you. Reckon I'll do yoga for a while.

—Ciao, Bella.

You can't dance in the seat of a Falcon but a secret source of energy is exhilarated and exhausted and it is inside me. Yet you can't dance in front of any mirror, not really. You can never know what you've created. It's done and it's gone. It's the essence of the present. An understanding of time in which you are and you give but you don't know what you give, you only know the quality of giving within yourself. And that, and that,—what is it?—must be those extra millimetres inside the marrow of the joints. It is impossible to be selfish. To be anything. To be, intransitive verb.

There is more to think about. It'll take a lifetime.

____________something very frightening happened this morning very early the whole earth shook and trembled it lasted about a minute but afterwards there was still the sound of walls of buildings falling in i thought it might have been a bomb there was a lot of dust when the sun came up i discovered the most extraordinary thing the ceiling snake which must have come in an earlier quake now describes a circle with two tails and within the circle many thousand little cracks beside the door is an enormous fissure about six inches wide i do not think this place is safe anymore__________________

D.D. now stands for Doomed Diary. Doomed as the dairy you are, diary dear.

We've seen each other several times, but now she has gone.

Now I have unburdened my whole story, including Winnie and my dad and the economic conditions. Some history. Some geography. She assures me there is nothing in her theories which makes Marion in and of herself evil, she was just an agent, rather her anger was.

And Lesley, for her part, has told me of her friends. Of Dawn.

And she knows Iona Flynn!

She has given my loneliness back, the same as she took it away. She's gone.

Kali, detroyer and creator.

I have had hugs and kisses.

She smells of jasmines.

I told her because of her I can now burn my diaries. She doesn't think that's a good idea.

One evening I imagined Mimbo was dead. I came racing home. But found her asleep in the kitchen with the radiator two inches from her varicose bandages, and her mouth open. I welcomed the lively abuse I received for that one.

Well good morning and goodbye, D.D.

Who would have thought this dead sunset could kill?

I have seen so many real sunsets, and none has ever been as you. Beauty is movement. Is change.

I have ceased committing myself to paper. I am a doer.

I have Dawn's address. I have Lesley's address. I can write letters.

The lie of you was your passive sponge-like quality. The you I will address in letters will be active. Alive. Reactive.

Adieu, diary dear.

> There's the music and
> the dance and the
> dancer and the character
> she dances, the steps
> of memory and
> the freedom of forgetting, the
> being of body, mind and soul
> in a moment, a
> whole before fragmentation,

the extent of living which
could resolve in death
as sublime choice or
with equal sanctity
continue living

having danced.

24

SOMETIMES THE stringy spirits of the Australian landscape led Oona to places she had not stopped before. Here she is on the central coast of New South Wales, where the rocks are dramatic sculptures of arches and caves and the ocean suggests the total expanse of the seven seas. An inlet shelters her from the wind off the thundering surf. Trees as tall as mountain ash give way to scrub on sand dunes. Stands of paperbarks near billabongs hum with mosquitoes. Two parallel tracks worn deep by four-wheel drives and beach buggies appear well-used. The spirits in this place, Pacific Palms, seem restless, somehow crowded, bickering.

Oona is uncomfortable on the grey sand of the estuary beach. The paperbark is like damp rolled newspaper. She is hungry and the breeze across the water blows her hair into her eyes. She huddles into her brown duffle coat and reads. In some country town second-hand book shop, or was it that garage sale?, she bought, for 40 cents, *Women, Church and State,* written by Matilda Joslyn Gage, published in 1893, in Massachusetts, USA. The name Matilda attracted her and, as the book wasn't fiction, she bought it.

Now she reads and she cannot leave it.

Who will speak for the burnt ones, she once heard Janice cry. The unholy fire in Janice's eyes had always disturbed her, and now in this miserable morning she is learning white dykes' heritage, waltzing Matilda. Oh shit, there are times of learning never of teaching. Those intellectual lesbians who came and stole her mountain could have taught until they were puce in the face and she may not have learnt. She would have seen instead their suspicion of her, their fear of her bushy eyebrows over eyes showing some pain they had yet to discover, or of her downright laughter, her ridicule of them, her taking what she needed without asking. But now she was learning fact upon incredible fact, two million women burnt over two centuries. Not outlaws like herself, not blacks, not weirdos, but midwives, aunts, kids, friends, lovers, nuns, Protestants, Catholics. No confession accepted unless it was given after torture, recommended torture at least three days, gang rape, the strappado, and the confessions the most ghastly projections of satanic pornography she had ever read.

She pauses, listens to the sea crashing against rocks, sucking at the sand, and hears the time distant chatter of the local tribe at their midden eating shellfish. She is surrounded by agony. It assaults her natural serenity. Her mind grasps the scene of the strappado. The little girl raised high with her wrists tied behind her back and her weight supplemented by an extra fifty pounds and let drop the full length of the rope. 380 years ago she bore up heroically and confessed nothing. Ten weeks later, hoisted again after being told her mother accused her, she gave in and confessed to fucking the devil, killing children, eating their hearts, smearing old people with ointment to cause their deaths and raising five tempests, going to Sabbats and renouncing God and so forth.

It is fact. Fiction is, for Oona, an oral tradition, a make-believe in the listening state. She heard some dreamtime stories, but she would never read them. More than fact, Oona is knowing somewhere deep in her bones. She can't care for the hunger pains in her own stomach, the chill in the air and the long-gone bickering of the local dead ones.

She reads on. Pope Innocent VIII, in 1484, gave those Dominicans the ecclesiastical right to rage all over Europe erecting poles in bonfires, gathering all the girls and women who had some bond with each other, torturing confessions out of them and burning them in the village squares to the delight, by the look of the woodcuts, of the masses.

She has read enough. She remembers thinking of the humble outback windmill as an omen, a cause. The rotors circular, some teeth missing, it expressed a kind of sadness. She must have foreseen the sadness she feels now. That deserted windmill, the sign of the white man, is on the other side of the penny, the hurt and pain of half her ancestry.

The tone of the midden chatter changes. Here on this coast the massacres happened early. They stopped burning witches and came to massacre indigenous people all over the globe. Blood lust. Her own hunger echoing in the cavern of her gut makes her feel innocent and pure. She collects her eight separate things, the pearls, the little scales of justice, the books, the saddlebag. Always eight, this way she never leaves anything behind.

As she walks west, she carefully examines each woman in the Moonmare Collective, asking why she particularly would want to make it hard for herself.

They wanted to find their spirits. Their own spiritual tradition had been drowned in oceans of blood. Bleeding Jesus. Women's blood and coloured blood. They were desperate to make up for the subterfuge of silence, 'historical erasure' as Vanessa once called it. Now, having read Matilda Gage, Oona remembers the teaching they tried, but she thinks of it in relation to the personalities who had expressed it and with what level of vehemence and care. Janice crying out in that night, 'who will speak for the burnt ones?', had followed Vanessa's learned treatise on atrocities suffered by women in the past and Etama's emotional appeal for those suffering today, as if it were equal, even as if it were herself who would be burnt tomorrow. Yet it was Janice's histrionic words which became indelible, which, in some way, caused her to buy the factual book on the subject.

Her belly empty and her calf muscles past pain, Oona strides out along the deserted road in the midmorning towards Highway One. The road that rings the island continent is a private symbol not only of her known world, her personal journey, but also somehow of her inner circularity. She sees that squiggly line up there on a hoarding by the road, and she feels good. The abstract line of geography is for her physical. She chooses a bit, and visualises a known landscape, otherwise intends to go there someday.

Once Oona read in her tattered *Book of Wonders* of the strange phenomenon of spontaneous self-combustion. It is historically recorded that a couple of people have just exploded and left nothing but a pile of scented ash. While being absolutely fastidious with her facts, Oona nonetheless reserves the right to interpret them exactly as she pleases. The writers of the *Wonders* had implied that it was frightening, a terrible thing to happen to Professor so-and-so, sweet Miss whosemewhat. Oona thought it must be obvious, because of the pleasant smell, that it was good. An excellent way to go. There are boundaries of experience beyond which facts refuse to go. Facts flutter like moths to the candle flame, ignorant of and blind to the nature of creation and destruction, yet helplessly attracted to the light. The wherefore of existence. Pain alone turns them back. Pain is the end of the story of each witch, in the cases religiously recorded by the prosecutors with legalistic precision.

But is pain the end of the story?

Two women in a Volkswagan pick her up a couple of miles north of Bulahdelah. She squeezes in the back seat between the dog and a lump of doona and pillows. The women keep arguing with each other.

—It's not personal it's political.

—That's only partially correct, not everything that is personal is political, there's privacy.

—You're wriggling out of it, aren't you?

—Am I? Am I? I don't have to tell you the truth.

—What's the good of arguing if you're not telling the truth.

—Are you naive or what? You can talk, you play power games all the time.

Oona pats the dog and sighs loudly. They seem proud of their devotion to argument and don't mind displaying it to a stranger. They get off on it, decides Oona. When they start it up again, she interrupts.

—Could you two dykes buy me something to eat, maybe?

Their reluctance to stop, let alone spend money on their hitchhiker brings them to an accord which Oona assesses may well last the rest of the trip. Politically, if not personally, they feel obliged, pull into a roadhouse and hand her money from a purse on the floor, a twenty dollar note.

After she has eaten Oona goes to the toilet and sees them kissing under the trees. She fingers the change and pockets it. She hitches another ride, this time with a middle-aged man who, after two wordless hours, lets her off in one of the well-heeled, umbrageous suburbs north of Sydney.

She wanders down through the bush to a quiet arm of the harbour.

Inside the mangrove swamps the trees are above and below, standing on themselves. The bottom halves, the shadows, are made uncertain by the water. It is a dance of brown and green, shade and evening light. The brightness on the water is like darkness, you cannot see beyond it, but the dark reflections of the trees allow you to see beneath the surface.

She has opened her book again, even though the light is failing.

There is no silence in the unspeakable, the unsayable, which is pregnant with heart-rending pentatones, with sea-depth thunders which fall out the low end of our decibel scale. Oona intuits a music beyond her own knowledge, a music like silence in moments taken to mourn.

"In the strange mania—," she starts the paragraph again, turning the page to the brightness reflecting from the water. "In the strange mania which raged in the Neapolitan districts from the end of the fifteenth century to the end of the seventeenth and which was attributed to the bite of the tarantula, the women thronged in multitudes towards the sea, and often, as the blue waters opened to their view, they chanted a wild hymn of welcome, and rushed with passion into the waves. Tarantism, a hysterical malady, characterised by an extreme impulse to dance…"

An epidemic of madness! Lasting centuries! At the time of the rampages of the witch judges. The bite of the spider. The dance into the sea. Mass suicide. The songs and the throngs. Again Oona must pass the facts and go the flames of her own whys and wherefores. The choice, their only choice, their own choice. To burn or drown, to be judged, confess and be punished or to drown with your sisters in frenzy of dance, of ritual; to be seen to be evil or to be seen to be sick by the writers of facts. Jeezuss, choices were bad in those days.

Allu mari mi portati
se voleti che mi sanati
allu mari, alla via

cosi m'ama la donna mia
allu mari allu mari
mentro campo, t'aggio amari.

The Italian is a gift Oona felt she had been waiting all her life for. Her very own, her personalized mantra. She commits it to memory as she climbs up the dark bush path to the street lights.

Because of the bad light when she read it, because of her ignorance of the sense, Oona's personal mantra became: *allu man, mi portati, che voleti se sanati, allu via, cosi mia, allu mari*. In the future this idiosyncratic Italian will drive Grundhilde mad. But Oona, with her uneducated smattering of everything, will have placed Tibetan Buddhist connotations upon it by then.

Actually, to have had one of her deepest spiritual presents bestowed in a wealthy suburb of Sydney in the half light and not in the beauty of the wide open spaces was a strange irony, meaning, for Oona, that you never can tell.

Conviction is terrifying whatever way you look at it. Iona, unused to having a leisurely coffee outside her shed so late in the morning, reading the paper and a bit of astrology, notices the huge cobweb of the St Andrew's Cross spider. The cross in the centre sparkles with pearly rainbows from the earlier rain. She grins, just taking time.

She is to give a talk.

The Iraq-Iran war on the front page, ostensibly over the control of the strategic waterway, Shatt al-Arab, makes her think passingly of the rumours about Arachne being in jail in the Middle East. It is too hard to imagine. The best she can do is to let her fluvial mind rave.

Arachne playing her woodwind as history arrives clumsily at its brink, the present, frightening us all with its dark and pointless judgment, its monstrous violence as if Allah the divine decreed murder for his mortal sons, for the only way to save their souls is to kill and die for the faith: what company he has in his heaven! I dedicate my talk to Arachne, the fool, with her flower and flute on the precipice, for her to pass through those heaven-bound fighters unscathed, without even diarrhoea…well, at least she is free from personal bondage.

The astrology is as fresh as the news, for only yesterday had Mary worked out her progressed sun and lent her the book, *An Astrological Mandala,* Dane Rudhyar, for her to read and meditate upon: "A large audience confronts the performer who disappointed its expectations." This reading is wickedly appropriate.

Am I a taxi-driver or a writer? Am I just a woman who gives herself the time to express herself, and so doing must express more than myself? The revolution? The redress of all the forgotten facts of the lives of female genii, works burnt, bones buried in unmarked graves etc? How don't you disappoint an audience? She has already asked Mary, Rose, Dawn and Lesley to perform her writing. She will do only the talk, but first she must write it.

It would be best to seem to be spokesperson for a greater number, to inject meaning into meaninglessness, to generate a bit of hope. This is my supreme ethical choice, that my illusion is better than despair. Which anyway I don't have. Could have if I relied on research and not my natural optimism. I don't know myself or my ambition well enough to talk about my life, those facts are boring and which of the many little things that have changed the routes of my small journey are the important ones? Perhaps I could take the image of my taxi driving and pick up passengers, my cab, my self. No, I'll just wear my Yellow Cabs jacket. Use honesty, use idealism as weapons, seem to be what you wish you were. The light of the word in the darkness pointing the way to emancipation, the star. Breathe regeneration into the old whinge, the hysterics, the madness of hags on street corners, make the world as you imagine it to be and sock it to 'em. Give it, fill the cups. I don't get many opportunities, might as well flood, flood like the silver belly-dome of Ayers Rock when it rains. It is all, Yellow Cabs jacket included, a matter of appearance. They're not going to know me if I don't know me, so we'll all know what I choose to project, and I can control that by how I am and what I say. If I lose my ego in the subject matter I can't get hurt. *Argiope aetherea,* the zoological name, is in her writing pad from an earlier time of having to identify the spider of the magnificent cross.

This morning your cross is a beacon, Argiope aetherea.

So, starting with "Today I noticed a spider web…", Iona sits in her shed for an hour and ten minutes and handwrites her twenty-minute speech.

25

ARACHNE SQUEEZES her body through the length-wise crack in her cell wall.

Must move along, snakeroot and bayberry, pomegranate and heart song, must go, mosey on out of here. Muse on, one might say. Dance away.

The sun is directly overhead. Everything is motionless, as if the world never shook, nor spider moved, nor aeroplane landed. The whipping post casts no shadow.

She stands perfectly still, waiting, staring at the ground, at stones so white. No wind.

No movement. No orders. No shouting. No shoving. She senses her hands. Nothing in her hands. Her hands are free. Vacant, empty hands. She turns her palms to the sun. No things. No passport. No flute. No toothbrush.

Allah be praised. The Ineffable. Freedom right here and now is the choice to be free. My own ultimatum to myself. Ten weeks of social deprivation, of, to put it a better way, asceticism. How impressive! Women can't see holiness as isolation. There's always the womb, the other, even if you're barren, there's kith and kin, care. I must escape to care. Every woman has a mother's knowledge. Mobilisation of that spiritual virtue would save the world. It stands to reason. My hands are empty and my heart is a pomegranate.

Window-holes in the sun-drenched buildings are pure blackness, pupils without irises. Nobody evident.

Through a gap in the abstract of walls and shade, Arachne sees a gate and the corner of a sentry box.

The sentry wakes to find eyes looking at him without command, without judgement, without fear, without need, without urgency. Grey eyes like vast oceans and his eyes like agate stones. The prisoner is invisible. He picks up his telephone, dials, listens, does not speak, drums a forefinger on his cheek. Both wait, brother and mother. He replaces the handset.

Arachne solemnly closes her eyes, touches her forehead, her lips, her heart and bends. Blindness to see.

When she opens her eyes, she does not look at him, but walks towards the gate which is ajar. She hears the sentry's voice. Mid-step she stops and turns. He is gesticulating and his gestures point one way, 'Jeddah'. She repeats her forehead, lips, heart touching, nods and follows his directions with slow dignity.

She walks into the bazaar as it sleeps. In some shade she sits down.

A few years ago, frail white-skinned boys and girls wearing kaftans and Saudi Arabian sandals, smoking the hookahs and wandering through their markets, were a common sight. The shopkeepers are not amazed by the sight of Arachne. Quake damage, low prices, a cousin killed in a village, another with money from oil creating problems, family arguments and those of neighbouring countries concern them as they prepare for the evening's trade.

Arachne neither moves nor speaks. She sniffs freedom-scent, mixed in with that of spice and ground coffee and life alive and bustling, orange sunlight and long black shadows. She has only trust and empty hands. Sweet humour swims in her eyes. She is given food and coffee. Empty hands carry no weapons. She is given a mat to sit on. She accepts the wisdom of Allah and murmurs his praise. Her eyes are not vacant. There is nothing to say.

The merchant of pitchers and pottery sends off the boy with a message. Soon Arachne is disturbed by a little man in a stay-pressed American suit

—Jason Loren, ma'am. From the United States Embassy, would you like to come with me? he says, thrusting out his soft, clerical hand with the brash generosity of a man in a position to help.

Arachne bows to the merchant of pitchers and bowls, repeats her dignified, respect-for-Islam movements and leaps into the jeep. The words of her story from beginning to end stream into the ears of Jason Loren.

I,
ninth letter of the alphabet,
is of but not the whole.
She
cannot see the full soul.
One
with no mythology, no tribe,
an almost forgotten dreaming,
hers
is the experience
of a culturally confused individual,
yet
she is interlocked in a web.
The web,
tied by co-incidences,
is often invisible,
woven beyond our ken.
I is the ninth letter.
Nine,
a number of full expectancy,
is the stage in the count
before
the first return to wholeness.
Nine and the initial,
first person singular,
focal points no more
no less important than any.
The alphabet
is a tentative fiat
for a literary conspiracy,
implying a wholeness, an equality
among individuals.
Each of the characters stand
in the place of nine,
I, in their own circles.
A circle composed of overlapping,
unfinished circles,
through which spins a spiral
and another spiral,
time.
In the circle of our alphabet,

each is urgently aware of a 'more'
in the scheme of things.
This 'more' is complete in the dance
foreshadowing the narrative at the number 50.
But that is arbitrary.
50 is a wholeness and a half wholeness,
and so on.
And the 'more' is beyond the end,
the possibility of many endings.

26

THE GREEKS compared nine to the ocean. They said it was like water surrounding the other numbers. Nine is the circumference of things. Nine is six, the symbol of sex, turned on its head. Nine is five, the senses, the root races, plus four, the seasons, the elements. Nine is Teth, the serpent, the power of serpent wisdom. Love, incarnation, service, eventually freedom from personal bondage.

Mary is driving Iona and Rose along Dandenong Road.

—Pamela said you owe Frances Furriskey two hundred dollars and that Frances is telling everybody you won't pay it.

—I am more interested in my numerology, Rose, than lies Frances chooses to tell. She is not getting under my skin that way. It's not true. It's the other way around. But it was a gift. She doesn't owe me anything.

—Might as well tell you now. Pamela and I are going to Scotland.

—Just Scotland?

—Just Scotland. My Mother's family is there. In Kenneth Clark's *Civilisation* he said the island of Iona gave him more sense of peace and inner freedom than anywhere else. I'd like to go there.

—Since when have you and Pamela…

—A couple of weeks.

Kate McMillan listens to her moon-faced acquaintance on 3UZ while she sews. Nine months Quentin grew inside her. It was a magical vague time when talents inadvertently were released. Perfect pitch came for the confinement and went after the birth. He was a bookish, sensitive lad, too skinny, lanky, chestless, clever, fatherless, affectionate. Some time before his twenty-first birthday he told Kate he was a homosexual. She could like it or lump it, he certainly did. Her initial repugnance eventually softened, yet now the constant worry about the probability of diseases, even violence, tempered her vicarious pleasure in his apparently enjoyable promiscuity. Her flesh and blood threatened…

Good roles were few, and most parts, now, involve the problems of age and aging. She does them very well, with a poignant glow, as if the afterlife were being measured and balanced in her Muse, Melpomene. She acts neurotic, middle-aged women whose lives are falling apart more with her mind than with jaded theatrical tricks. Underneath the script contemplating axing the husband to death. The quarrels with daughters, the conflicts of exploding illusions come out as if she suffered the essence of Wrecked Nerves. Her temperance, however, allowed her neither the shattering of nerves nor dreadful disillusionment. The single line of sincerity between Kate and her characters is her devotion to her Muse. The gift. For this enchantment she had worked hard all her life, exercising voice and body, keeping her memory supple and retentive, her concentration ready, her brain sharp, her home and emotional life in shape.

This afternoon she will attend the literary lecture she arranged through the kind offices of Associate Professor Doreen Redman.

Time on the line. An hour on the train. Ursula entertains herself in the carriage of the red rattler with a book of Banjo Patterson's poems. Because of the rhythm. The way her dad, with his voice like Leonard Teale's, would read these rhymes brought tears to her eyes. As wild horses held their way, upwards ever upwards… In Bob Trap's household the bush poets were music, entertainment, sentiment, nights around the fire. Winnie and Urse each on an arm of the old leather armchair, galloping, flapping their elbows and leaping fallen logs, bending round mountain ash and kurrajong, skidding down vertical slopes… or riding like a new chum from Pommieland, with stiff upper lips and their backs arched.

Mordialloc, every day people on the platform with their cares and woes, pushing prams and shopping jeeps with difficulty onto the train. An old woman obviously going to a medical specialist in the city is careful of the way she holds herself. Ursula stares, and is stared at, but she doesn't mind.

At Caulfield she alights, to catch a tram then a bus.

Dawn has the dignity of a dignitary at all times. Lesley wonders how much inner effort goes into her grace and calm, because, when she speaks of the state of the world, it is impossible to understand how one so young could care and worry and know so much. How can anyone retain such a deep level of despair?

—Do you think she will come?

Dawn had arranged to go to Iona's talk with Lesley as a special date, including lunch at Pelligrini's. Minestroni and parmesan cheese, fresh Italian bread and fruit juice.

—I don't know, actually. I told you I rang. But I didn't speak to her. It was really embarrassing. She had told me her surname was van Trappe.

—What is it?

—Trap. Anyway her mother answered. 'Miss Ursula van Trappe! Don't be ridiculous. We're not Dutch! Who is it? Do I know you?' I have no idea of her circumstances. Anyway I put on my mother's—grazier's wife, you know —voice and everso politely asked to speak to Ursula. 'She's out with the dogs, and who wants to know?' Aggressive old bitch. So I said it was Monash University speaking, that I was the English Department secretary and could she please take down a message for a Miss Ursula Trap. And I spelt out the details slowly and clearly. What do you reckon?

—I reckon she'll come.

—We'll see.

—I remember she looked at me as if I were the risen lord. In constrast to my alcoholic mother who hated my guts. I was a nugget of gold in the mud.

They squash up the red serviettes and toss them on the table.

Lesley refuses Dawn's money and speaks in Mrs Trap's voice.

—'Don't be ridiculous. We're not Dutch!' I'll pay.

With Rose on her right and Dawn, Mary and Lesley behind her, Iona walks along the corridor. Associate Professor Doreen Redman instinctively steps to one side. Kate McMillan stands her ground. Thirteen years. A fleeting impression of Iona cloned into five. Kate instantaneously knows them all. The intensity of familiarity shocks a little. But Iona never had rich brown skin and curly dark hair, nor was she very fair, nor very tall, nor very beautiful. Not remarkably graceful.

They walk quickly. They are upon her. Iona in front of her, hair greying, face, though more mature, somehow younger, impish.

—Hello.

Kate and Iona lock looks in mutual curiosity. Then embrace.

The seven shuffle a moment before exploding into chatter and small talk and introductions. It is unbearable. Rudeness is in the Flynn family blood alongside the blarney. Iona turns on her heel and runs away. She skids on the polished floor in front of the lifts. Pain sears through her knee and she must limp. The others laugh at her and wave.

Nine minutes. To loathe. To observe the mostly Asian or mature-aged students handling the wind channel between the library and the union building. Graffiti on a wall—Lesbians love dogs—amuses, puzzles. I suppose it's meant to be an insult.

Redman has hushed the hall. There are quite a few to hear the writer. Her breath is wrinkled. The soreness in her knee feels like David's, knocked deliberately with the sculptor's hammer. It's good. She is introduced and looks at the crowd through her glasses, then takes them off. She does not see Frances Furriskey enter by one of the back doors.

The Muse, Polyhymnia, takes her in her grasp and she talks with ridiculous honesty, with little reference to her notes, relishing the power of having the floor; of being the one in front of many. One and another, exactly as if she were at a mirror staring at her own eyes seeking the meaning then the words.

—It's a dishonourable profession, yet it's the only one I have. Except for taxidriving. But writing is like taxidriving, anyone can get in your cab, anything can happen. So it is with fiction. Anyone can get in. You can be taken anywhere, and anything might happen. You're on your own, you're responsible. You're in charge of a vehicle of sorts.

Possessed by the Muse of Eloquence, she is hardly aware of what she is saying…

—It is written on every DNA cell in my body. The DNA doesn't care if I fail at it, fight against it, make lots of money from it. I don't know anything about the DNA, except its structure is a double helix. If I'm happening to say a writer is born and not made, I'm wrong.

She laughs with a delight that is infectious. The mystery of two contradictory thoughts that somehow must end in a single truth is the real challenge of talking publicly and thinking on your feet.

There is a lot to say. The solving of an immediate intellectual problem makes the speaker passionate, grasping at the real. Present. On show, attentive to herself thus demanding of attention, even if the concentration of the audience is merely upon the performance impromptu.

The Associate Professor is leaning forward in her chair which is on the dais behind Iona. Mary gazes serenely outwards. Dawn gives her a stage wink. Rose glares at her with a worried kind of fury.

—The writer's cry, then, is a cry in the wilderness. The wilderness of individuality. Struggles with improper ecstasy, like the temptations of St Anthony. It always remains the question, not the statement. The question is please. The plea is to the many. That a few may love it, you know, share the life of it…believe you for a while.

The stillness when she pauses snips the thread.

—Now I'd like you to hear Rose sing a poem I wrote in Madrid. Then Mary will read a couple of small pieces. Lesley and Dawn will perform a radio piece about two women and the sea.

Somewhere in the audience, the clapping is enthusiastic. Iona is grateful for it. She is ready to defend, explain, carry on. The magic of Rose's voice, however, she did not expect. It glistens unaccompanied in the air like strokes of Japanese ink on silk. Notes fully achieved rest on the silence with the simple correctness of the golden mean.

Mary reads her old short stories as if from the inside, crumbling on certain words. Dawn and Lesley are relaxed and humorous with their material. To some in the lecture theatre it is a display of cloying incestuous love. Especially repulsive are the few tears that escape Iona as she listens to her own work.

Doreen Redman asks for questions.

A bearded young man in the second row is ready.

—Barry?

—Can you tell me why you didn't read your own work? Why you needed your friends on stage with you? Could this be political, as in Feminist?

—Phew. Iona plays with her spectacles. I can't sing. It is just as sincere for me to be one of a number as it is to be the unit, writer.

—I suggest, Barry responds, that it's politically intimidating.

—I assure you it was far more pleasant for the audience. And why shouldn't my friends be here?

—Most writers have to show their weaknesses…

Mary takes over with authoritative self-confidence.

—Have you heard of the Chinese understanding of Yin, the female, one of whose attributes is community, as opposed to the Yang, male, individualisation, hierarchy? We do have a sense of community. I'm not a writer, but I read what Iona wrote as if I'd written it. At the risk of sounding pious I feel a religious wholeness with some women's work. Feminism is fundamentally spiritual. If it isn't, then I don't care for it.

The young man jumps to his feet, enjoying a fight.

—We all feel this at times. Although my writing is nothing like Tolstoy's, but when I read, say *The Resurrection,* I feel I could have written it.

Spontaneous laughter. Barry jackknifes back into his seat.

—Zoe? Zoe is a Politics tutor with velvet-heavy curtains of hair and bony round shoulders.

—I'd like to take up Barry's point. What specifically is the difference between your 'community' and the empathy that one might experience reading Tolstoy?

—There isn't any, Rose mumbles.

—I don't know if this has anything to do with it, Lesley speaks. But I had this hypersentience-trip once. Past-life travelling. It was this incredible dance, around a hole dug in the ground, fifty women and a harvest moon. It was something to do with menstruation. You don't feel that kind of thing reading.

—I do, Ursula is beside Zoe and Xian, a Chinese Politics academic. She whispers. Zoe bends to her left.

Barry is calling out again.

—What do you feel when you read Tolstoy?

—My favourite author is Georgette Heyer, Mary replies with her customary poise.

Barry groans. Iona grins. Doreen Redman leans across Rose to say, Really? Mary nods. Kate McMillan in the front row notices an odd light in Doreen's grimace of a smile.

Iona takes up the forum.

—How I see it is this. Tolstoy on his lonely mountain looks across the centuries to Lao Tzu on his lonely mountain who looks across the range of centuries and countries to Michelangelo on his, and you on yours, albeit maybe a molehill. The last few thousand years have created hierarchical pyramids all over the place. Very Yang. As Tolstoy said of Napoleon, history throws up the single individual male to express its tide. A gynocentric way would be different. I don't think it will be individual women who lead future centuries, it will be cooperation, not coercion. If it is going to remain in the hands of individual men, disaster is a foregone conclusion.

—What about the warrior woman in China? Xian queries sweetly.

—What was her name? Where is the tide of change beneath her? Perhaps there were many warrior women in China, Iona quips.

Kate McMillan speaks from her seat, legs crossed.

—Lesley, in your dream I presume all fifty women were equal, if not in talent at witchcraft, at least in their role in the dance. It is a long time ago, and there are no written records. Perhaps you have a lesbian femininst romantic attachment to times you actually know nothing about. No doubt life was hard and probably brutal. I personally like being an individual.

Mary returns to the discussion.

—All individuals were equal. They were but a cell in the organ of community. Like an ant colony. The whole is the central purpose for living and dying. Big funerals and monurnental tombs all over the earth only came into being after the patriarchies were established, and sun religions dominated.

Dawn clears her throat. She is so fair the light on her eyelashes is white. She address the back wall.

—The particular dance was something else. It created a vortex on the occult plane which bound the souls of the fifty women together for their entire karmic journey.

Her certainty silences everybody. Even Lesley is surprised that Dawn knew the dance. There is general restlessness.

—What about such individual traits as strength, intelligence, justice etc? Are these bastard talents born of the patriachy, too? Zoe shouts over the confusion of anger, awe and opinion.

Iona knows she just need lift her arm to still the assembly, but the action is of a type she abhors.

She speaks quietly.

—Who ever accuses the lefty Aussie male writer of being responsible for the massacre of the Aborigines in this country, heh? He is an individual only responsible for himself, isn't he? Is he? Innocence may have deeper implications than guilt.

She has her lenses on her nose and she sees Frances sneering at her.

—What are you going to pay, Star, for the lives and thoughts you rip off in your writing? Anyone can get into the cab, can they? Anyone can get into fiction? Bullshit. You with your notebook sneak around brain-picking and quoting and copying and eavesdropping to become famous. What about those whose faces, words, actions you've stolen to make your lies look real?

She is walking to the door.

—The writer appropriates others' lives.

She leaves.

Doreen Redman, Associate Professor of the English Department, resumes her part.

—On behalf of everyone here, I'd like to thank Iona Flynn and her friends for coming and their thought-provoking discussion. Thank you.

—The poser, Iona makes a posture, must have the opposer. Who's right? In some cases the best that can be done is the book.

Rose, to whom she is speaking, smiles and draws aside as the meeting breaks up. What had been one thing with a single focus becomes a chaotic many-centred movement. The formal rows rustle into disorder. Rose is disturbed. Noise everywhere. She notices Iona is not left alone. Whatever they were up there, it created enough centrifugal force to keep attracting particles of the audience. Rose has a natural curiosity about after-the-event momentum.

She sees an incredibly ugly woman, grotesquely made up, push her way past a little Chinese woman and the anorexic, curtained Zoe, making a slow dash to the lectern through the lingering groups. She arrives as the crowd thickens around Iona. Rose is held in suspense, for she knows Iona is capable of cruel indifference when her ego is swelled. The creature is the loveable style of freak like someone Diane Arbus photographed. Rose fears the lakes behind her eyes might spill if she intuits too much pathos.

Ursula digs through the throng with sharp, fast elbows, to be stopped by Doreen Redman as if she were a security risk. She dismisses the academic's arm with a thrust. Now Rose sees the surprisingly youthful back of the body and hat. Iona's eyes, as she listens, flicker over her shoulder to Kate McMillan. She moves impatiently. Iona smiles pleasantly enough but there's panic in her lovely eyes. Irrelevantly Rose asks herself, did I love her? If it weren't for those eyes I'd have had no trouble denying myself. The hatted figure is somehow like Arachne from behind. Rose recalls Etama's letter and phone call and her decision not to phone Mrs Farr. Too embarrassing. She moves closer.

—That piece Lesley and Dawn did, dear, it's mine. You wrote it for me, because it describes my longings and captures my sea…

—What? I beg your pardon?

Lesley, Dawn and Rose in eye contact feel protective of Ursula.

—The radio piece, dear.

—Oh that. I wrote it on the anniversary of my sister's death. She drowned off Cape Schanck when she was thirteen. Imaginative nostalgia, a bit shallow, really. Excuse me, I've got to catch Kate.

Mary is discussing Georgette Heyer with Doreen Redman. Rose is introduced to Ursula by Lesley. The few folk left speak of drinks and bites to eat, lectures and future dates. Shoulder-slapping, bicep-tapping, hooroo ta-ta time.

Ursula is affected by some kind of sorcery, the magic of the many and the image of the reincarnated author. Rose asks her questions. Ursula imagines politeness to be mumbling about her bus. To express aloud her secret mission would be ridiculous, yet it is brimming out of her, and she, in the absence of Iona, is the centre of the small group near the lectern.

Doreen Redman looks at the watch under her shirt cuff.

—Well I have about twenty minutes up my sleeve. Grimaces at her own wet joke and briskly invites them to share her personal jar of Nestles Instant Espresso in the staff room.

—Did you burn your diaries? Lesley asks as they usher Ursula along the corridor of neatly-labelled doors.

—Some, most of the others drowned.

—Drowned?

—They were waiting in the wheelbarrow, under the leaky spouting. It rained you see, which was why I had to stop burning. Any rate, they swelled up, all went pale and bluish. Most of the words and indeed all the sense washed right out of them.

Iona and Kate are already in the staff room.

—Why don't you dye your hair? You look so old.

—I am old, Kate, older than you'll ever be.

—So it's all rubbish, this matriarchal stuff?

—I don't know. Maybe it is and maybe it isn't.

—I want to know what makes you tick.

—So that's how it works, this acting trade, is it? People are clocks, open their backs, see how they tick. That's how you play characters is it?

—Sometimes I only feel real when I'm someone else. Strange. Or when I'm arranging carrots on sticks for donkeys.

—Ah. Well, did my mule of an ego pass the test?

Ursula is hovering. Apart from the scarring of her face, Iona has met many like her. Diary-writers who love to hear her speak because somehow whatever she says gives them courage. She suspects, however, that this one probably wants to meet the famous actress. Sophisticated, successful people like Kate don't have to listen. Iona wants to shock them both, to be a ratbag, unpredictable.

—Ursula, wasn't it? This is Kate. I was about to tell her that once I slept with her son, like brother and sister, two spoons, when she, this voyeuristic old pervert, was imagining we were… But no, Kate, it was you and I making love in the mornings with Handel's *Messiah* on the stereo full blast. Remember?

It is clever. Kate is a match for it. She smiles and lets herself see again the shadows of the pot-plants on the window sill, screen-printing the wall, themselves encircling in the sacred music, turning spirals around each other with magic fingers sliding smooth paths in and out. Wordlessly she kisses Iona and departs with a wave and a promise to ring for the Associate Professor.

A flock of seagulls appears flying over the Arts Block on their home journey from the tip. The silver/pink wing scatter rhyming and syncopating will now become scattered white birds on the green lawn vying with sparrows for meat pie remains and the crusts of wholemeal sandwiches.

—I must get back to my mother. She's not well. Of late, she…

Iona is more beautiful than Lesley at this moment, beaming full attention on Ursula, looking through to the pain of living behind a birthmark like that.

—You came because you like my writing, well, I love you for that. The most gripping thing, I mean when you've had five packets of cigarettes and ten black coffees and it's three a.m., is the gift of it. The thing that you don't talk about is that you're giving, that is why you're careful with your craft, why you agonise over a single word, why you double-check the philosophy behind it.

You've got to give. That's the energy and courage behind it, the drive to be a saint.

—Oh I hate being a saint. I just like to be entertained.

Iona feels she has come on too strong. She leans back against the pigeonholes and thinks what the heck, it doesn't matter.

—Winifred Stevens! Ursula reads the name of her childhood friend beside Iona's right ear and feels faint.

—Yeah, she's an academic here. On leave at the moment.

—That does it. It does. My life is changed.

27

WALES

Trees, Trees, I'm sorry. I was just in a shitty mood with everybody. And thanks for your letter. It was very newsy and I want to be home in the endless blue ranges to listen to the whipbird and the howl of the dingo. What's this about Amos?

I haven't written to anyone for about three weeks, though Beatrix has written here. They're making their way, busking on the streets and in the piazzas. I suppose she's writing to you, too, did she tell you of their mysterious stalker, the man following them?

I couldn't have written even if I had known you were reading my letters in the way you say. As if they were a story in instalments.

Well, here's a narrative, the tale of my last three weeks. I think it has changed my personality.

After the others left in their pretty purple bus, Queenie and I went to the station and caught a train for Wales, travelling at night. I thought we were leaving the American, never seeing her again. Queenie had an address of an orchard employing casual labour.

We arrived and our accommodation was/is no more than a shed, a single room. He warned us before we went in there that we'd be sharing with another lady. When we did go in, there were notes pinned everywhere, in Hebrew. One in French: PEEL ME A RABBIT. And another in English: I'M EXPECTING YOU GIRLS. This, the beginning of a psycho-drama.

The orchardist took to Queenie straight away. Well, you could understand that, she has a kind of careless, sexy charm. She made a deal with him, to get more money, shooting hare. Poaching, I suppose. So she got this gun. A shotgun is in the place, hanging up like a phallic symbol.

The other 'lady' was Hettie!! The first night she was all sugary sweet and cooking for us. Queenie was cheeky. She wanted to make love with me with that woman in the room.

About the third day, the first couple we were so tired—(weakened by city-living)—the rabbit incident occurred. Queenie came with three rabbits hanging off the scarf which she uses as a belt. She carefully put two aside for the farmer. The third she skinned about a centimetre from Hettie's nose. She had sprays of blood on her face. I was paralysed, horrified. Was it the skin or the rabbit you desired? she asked in French. All bravado, Hettie replies, the rabbit. Queenie gives it to her and demands 50p. Then she went about skinning the other two and salting the pelts.

Later in the week was what I call the Semitic Incident. Hettie had left work earlier than us. I didn't know why. When we were coming up the path to the cottage, there she was standing with the gun held up to her shoulder in firing position. I'm about six inches taller than Queenie and her steps did not falter. She kept walking. We both kept walking. I didn't want to, I wanted to hide, but I didn't show it. We called her bluff, like they do in the movies.

She let the gun fall and broke down crying. She was sobbing that she intended to play russian roulette, or to kill herself outright. She accused me, 'You don't like me, you're anti-Semitic. You hate Jews. You hate Israel. You hate me. You're always torturing me'. I didn't even know she was Jewish and debated whether to say so. Queenie humphed and ignored her and began preparing supper. I let Hettie talk to me for a long time. But it was all crazy, scrambled. It was giving me a headache. She was playing, and I had no choice but to be a sucker.

Queenie said one thing, a question. 'Are you a CIA spy?'

No answer. But she stopped bullshitting.

The work is hard, back-breaking, and that's numbing. Your mind is taken up with pain and determination. I would go to the cottage at lunch-break to get a ploughman's sandwich and read for twenty minutes. I'd asked them both to give me this free time or otherwise I'd go mad. One lunchtime from outside I heard these regular thuds on the back wall. Queenie had her skinning knife and was throwing it into a makeshift dart board. Hettie was standing there. There was some ugly challenge in the sinister silence. Queenie was carrying out Zorro's orders and frightening Hettie, whom she was convinced was as dangerous as Zorro said she was. This had been cooked up in London. And I was no-one.

I was bugger-all in their scheme of things.

I screamed, Either you go or I go, Hettie.

All the Tai Kwando training came back to me.

'She's not the only one who can whip you.'

I showed them. Anyway Hettie left that day.

Since, well it's been okay. Having the cottage to ourselves. The funny thing is that Queenie really loves me. That's total, but it doesn't include telling me anything.

Hettie yelled as she was going down the path with all her gear, highly-coloured American stuff, 'Tell Iona Flynn you met a friend of Helen's.'

Got to go to work. At least I'm getting back into pretty good shape. We won't be here very much longer.

Love to all, Et.

Cerridwen, in her solitude, sucked eggs. Frances remembers the plovers' eggs, and hens' eggs, pierced and carefully sucked dry. With a fine-pointed brush, then, she would paint, usually snakes. Ovoid snakes and ladders in miniature. The characteristics and colours of tropical snakes were copied from glossy magazines like *National Geographic*. What Frances sarcastically called ladders were in fact intricate triangles and the snakes spirals.

The tables turned on Iona in Dublin. Cerridwen took to Frances, whom she saw as a woman with an integrity so strong she refused not to show her unmitigated unhappiness. The Flynn wit and sparkle was lost on another Flynn. The cousin had obviously had a stomach full of that duplicit Anglo-Irish charm, so Frances let rip with venom and sting. And scored herself an invitation to the cottage in County Wicklow. Cocaine, gold tops and grass made it a dream holiday. Cerridwen, herself a snake between skins, was as delicate as her eggshells and as graceful in movement as her black cats. Each day was a discipline of reverent slowness; a hermit, she could be cantankerous and abrupt.

Frances challenged the little colleen's world of extrasensory awareness with rude realitites of the world: the polluted rivers, the proximity of nuclear war, the stupidity of government leaders, the prevalence of mental illness, the torture of women in South America; whatever she read in the newspapers she criticised with intense subjectivity. She let herself experience anything painful and frightening to the point of masochism. The surrounding peace allowed her desperation full expression. Cerridwen listened, gave her herb teas with fresh honey, took her walking along the beaches, hiking into the Wicklow Hills. She borrowed another bike and they cycled to stone chapels and castles blanketed in aged ivy. She sympathized. The meanness was a response to the theft of magic, in Cerridwen's opinion. Iona had stolen her style, her actual tastes, her thoughts, her love and placed them on the table to sell in a short story. She understood that Frances belonged with and involved, that relationships were a vital avenue to the meaning of life for her. She did not drain her. Being with her was like being at a film festival, Cerridwen felt, exhausting but worthy.

Frances was a political hero exiled, in the wrong body, from the wrong part of the world. They discussed Nietzsche, Hegel, Wittgenstein, Che Guevara, Allende and Sartre as Cerridwen sat at her craft, an oasis in the desert, and Frances agonised and proclaimed the necessity of criticism. Cerridwen liked her, Frances knew, and, whether real or illusory, she inspired Frances' trust.

Frances had usurped the cousin's place. It was a part of a general revenge on the Flynns, mother and daughters: the Veronica whose namesake she was and whose looks she had and whose death held the family in the clutch of sentiment which meant Iona could never love her as she deserved; the Nola whose crippled condition meant that everyone danced attendance; Iona herself, so gorgeous in body and soul, stolen from her by the state of things and her martyrish desire to be good; the mother who symbolised everything she hated in women of the previous generation, flushing their excessive brains down the loo of domesticity to become, in that small place, harridans of power, prejudice and manipulation. Plus there was jealousy. Somewhere in the genes Iona could do it, whatever she wanted. She had the choice and she did not choose to give all to Frances. If she had, the sheer force of their happiness would have beaten everything.

Being her nastiest self, and, despite that, achieving the respect of Cerridwen Flynn and putting Iona out in the process, was an addition to the arsenal for revenge.

If there cannot be love let there be worthwhile hate. Iona, star with overflowing cups, was worth an all-out campaign. The choice is simple, madness or action. The point was to implicate her. Let her cast the stone.

It was Iona not Frances who gave Sophie Cerridwen's address at Etama's request.

Cerridwen felt she could disappear from the Sophies of this world. Simply not be for them. A heat haze, no more.

Notwithstanding, one comes on the four o'clock bus from Dublin, interrupting the sucking of eggs and the painting of spirals and triangles. Sophie, whose popularity and friendliness make Iona look shy, irritates Cerridwen immediately the way she sits down. It is a wide-beamed yacht mooring, sighing at anchorage in a sloppy sea. Having gained the armchair she stays enthroned in an excess of flesh. Seven weeks' work destroyed and Sophie doesn't even feel the broken eggshells under her arse. The relentless chatter rising and falling like tamed sea in a rich man's marina; Cerridwen can hardly bear it. Her sitting room is no such harbour.

Cerridwen points to one of her completed eggs on the mantlepiece.

—Very nice, says Sophie.

Even her Welsh witch of a great-grandmother is no help, the triangle is an arrowhead and she herself conjured it.

—I don't actually know your cousin, Iona, but I've met…

—If you don't know her then why are you talking so much about her?

Cerridwen's violet eyes stare at her, begging her to understand: I don't give a damn for your pretences, can you not see? You bargain too much on social niceties. Mustn't offend so let's pretend.

But Sophie's inattentive sight is taking in the handmade surroundings. No crisp edges, no primary colours, no hard lines. Even where the ceiling meets the walls the plaster is rounded seemingly by hand. The doorframes smoothed with the palm then whitewashed, crooked. The window-glass is thick and uneven, distorting the view of outdoors with wobbly refractions. All the furniture is old and brown, remnants of the thirties. The light is blurred, not bright enough for Sophie. She takes out the bottle of port stowed in her bag and removes the duty-free wrapping.

A sepia photograph of Cerridwen's mother's grandmother, sitting in a garden chair in pale crinoline and lace, erect in her high collar with New Forest dense behind her, is framed and hung on the wall between kitchen and lounge rooms. The hostess stares at it, trying to calm down. The apex to this triangle is absent; intuited by her, yet unknown to Cerridwen, Etama. Between the large Taurean, Sophia, and the petite Aquarian, Cerridwen, the chemistry is reacting badly. She had warmed to Frances, not because of her tastes, traits, friends. It was her inner conviction to be the adversary at any cost which, in Cerridwen's scheme of things, must have a special purpose.

Sophie feels that now she has slept with the radical, separatist Etama she can be with any woman and fuck if necessary. She graciously offers the port as a present.

No wonder, thinks Cerridwen, life deals Frances a poor hand, if she is attracted to or intimidated by this superficial charm. The great-grandmother's eyes look unerringly into the camera lens, straight at Cerridwen. The confessional gossip goes on behind her.

—Do you like mushrooms?

—Oh, yes, please. Sophie is eased by the thought of food.

She had been apprehensive of radical women, macrobiotics and hard drugs. She never wanted to lose her mind. She has no idea the offer is the hallucinogenic fungi.

Cerridwen shakes a generous amount of dried mushrooms into a tureen of vegetable curry, a lesser amount in the other tureen, and places the spiked one on the right in the oven. She dry fries some brown rice in a cast-iron skillet until it is almost burnt, then covers it with water in her pie-dish and puts that in the oven also. Sophie is fiddling with the cork of the port bottle.

—Do you mind if we don't open that tonight?

To Sophie the question sounds unreasonably sharp.

—Would you be very hungry, now, do you think?

—Starving.

—Yes, starving. You've been to India, then?

—No, not yet. I expect I'll get there some day. Sophie adjusts her back in the armchair in a gesture towards turning around.

—Did you ask Frances if she has been to India?

—No, she would be terrified for her own health and dreadfully depressed by the beggars, lepers and cripples.

—What did you think of my dear Frances?

—I think she could kill herself if she had the mind.

—Do you think she is unstable?

—Mentally unstable? Now I didn't say that, did I? Frances might consider that taking her own life is the only sane response to the world.

Cerridwen leaves Sophie in ignorance as to the contents of the curry, while she herself gets mildly stoned.

—My papa was a diplomat. 'Poor old Fred' Aunt Nisaba calls him. But he is retired from Her Majesty's service now. Once in Rio I met Iona's father, my uncle. Monica, my sister, and I thought the very world of him. He ran away from his own family, said he had a girlfriend, the colour of whose hair was that of cooked turnip. She giggles. You've never met Iona, you say?

—No. I feel strange. Suddenly I don't care for the snivelling bitch. Fuck her!

—You're not speaking of my cousin are you?

—No, Yvonne. Yvonne Smythe, librarian extaordinaire.

—Don't get to telling me of your love affairs. I can read them in the colour of your aura.

—What colour?

—Maroon, dark like coagulated blood. My mother is different from her own mother and her sister-in-law, Nisaba. She believes in Franciscans. High in the Andes is the Inca city of Machu Picchu, when I was twelve, I decided to be a hermit. I was nibbling on a leaf of cocaine and I was high, high, and thirdly, I was high. As we are now. I was disturbed by my father who was red-faced and panting. Worried. In all his years in South America he never learnt to trust the Indians. In fact, he calls all black people Indians. Are you seeing anything beautiful in the fire, Sophia?

—I see them playing panpipes. I see twelve thousand virgins walking up the golden steps to give their blood to the sun-god. They are garlanded in flowers and feathers, gold bracelets, necklaces and belts. The sword that pierces their chest is gold and red. The steps are steep. This is death. They rocket from their bodies and become cherabim. My mind is electric. It's wonderful. I feel like a genius. There is so much happening in Machu Picchu…

—You were seeing one of your past lives. I say that because you mentioned the death and the afterdeath.

—I want to sing.

—Aye, shall we sing? My mother and I sing the folk songs of the Gaelic peoples. Apart from Franciscans my mother has her piano. Shall we start with Danny Boy? The Mountains of Morne?

A weary traveller passing anywhere near Cerridwen's cottage this night between eleven and one would hear such sweet harmonies on many familiar tunes he would swear in the morning he saw the little people wending their way to a wedding feast no less, in a wee carriage with tiny horses apulling and all. It's the whisky, Paddy, and don't give us none of your tomfoolery. And they were singing a treat, aye, 'twas to the feast of a wedding they were aweaving, to be sure.

Cerridwen finds the richness of Sophie's voice unexpected and frightening. Sophie in giving voice could blow the thatch right off the roof.

—Hum Mani Padme Om, chants Cerridwen. Sophie takes it up.

Sophie leaves to discover Ireland several days later.

The Jewel in the Lotus, a spiritual centre for Cerridwen, becomes bodily and erotic, a possibility she hadn't dreamed of, even though by accident once she bought a Tibetan Buddhist text by that name and it turned out to be a sex manual of sorts.

In the weeks following Sophie's departure, Cerridwen perceived a change in her meditations. At first it was a warm sensation which grew into apprehensions of such beauty she was brought out of slow deep respiration to breathlessness. If she began her journey into stillness by imagining a rural village with a church on the hill, a priest would suddenly expose himself in midst of male voices performing a Gregorian chant. The sexuality of Christ on the crucifix would become evident. The spirit vibrated her body. A flaming orgasm would surge up her spine, breaking through the crown chakra while no part of her would move except small muscles in her face. She began to read books on Tantric Yoga and the kundalini. Her visions became ugly. A large-headed dwarf would wield his long member as if it were a hose spewing a putrid slime over everything.

Now she watched the clock, the rhythms of her routines became rigid. She started a bank account.

She could not blame Sophie, who was all innocence. She could not blame Frances. Nor the invisible third, Etama. The other side of the jewel in the lotus was rooted in her own being, her own hermitage. She was twenty years old last January.

28

GRUNDHILDE'S EYES see through to the lethal. The upper sides of the irises reside under the darkness of the upper lids leaving a band of white eyeball above the lower. They want summation. Her entire body, with its prominent dowager's hump, slopes around the eyes. When she drops her chin, in a tussle of wills, she magnifies the impression of her bulk. Zorro's eyes are as black as coal, the whites but four glistening triangles.

—What is this, with my papers? demands Zorro of the border guard.

The others in the van notice that in one of the cars behind them is a man they saw at Dover and one other time crossing the garden of Europe, France. All eyes flicker with the question of treachery.

The guard flicks her passport with his thumb.

—Female? The sarcasm of temporal power.

Zorro's vocal cords are too precious to use in the circumstance. She nods.

He laughs at the mountains. Immaculate, meat-eating teeth laugh, the eyes don't. Then he shrugs as if she had been wasting his time.

The musical crew of The Rites of Passage' are unsettled by this as it is as by a number of curious incidents.

Beatrix, in love with health, interprets Greta's slightly yellow, disagreeable look as liver trouble, and treats her with dandelion salads from plants growing along the way. The three other Germans in the back discuss women's lands about the world and practise their instruments and voices; itinerants for the rest of their lives. Beatrix has no guilt for illegal deeds. Music, health and women's-love are her politics and the natural outgrowth of who she is. Her only guilt is for the trail of broken hearts suffered by women who shared her wonderful single-minded commitment to her life but were left behind. Her intelligence is at the disposal of her current lover, Zorro.

The bone of contention, the identity of the man.

—We saw him talking to an official when we were in the queue. It was the same man.

—We were not stopped. There's nothing to worry about.

—But he looks so much like a movie spy.

—Then why us?

—Yes; why us? Zorro?

—Why us, Greta? You are hiding something from me.

—You are paranoid.

—That's three times we've seen him and we've been travelling in a crazy route, with unusual timing and stops. Why did the guard call Zorro into his office? Then let her go?

—Zorro was interesting to him.

—No, I am not interesting to him because of myself, but because I am travelling with some German women. The man following us is from the British Secret Police…

—I can't tell his nationality.

—They do not want to stop us at a border. They want to do what they are doing. Spying.

—We are in the great free West and we have done no crime. We have nothing to hide. When I see him again, I will approach him and have this matter out, no?

—No.

—Greta has a twin sister. They are not identical. But they are very mystical, these right-wing creeps. They think there is some biological drive for twins to see each other and work on side.

—And what does the twin do?

—Who knows what Gertrud does? She has disappeared off the face of the planet.

—She is in Poland.

—You do not know for certain.

—Whenever I cross a border, they probably think I am going to see Gertrud.

—But she is never going to see Gertrud. They have quarrelled badly.

—*Mi madre, mi madre.* All war is civil war, all violence is domestic.

—Does it mean that every one of you has quarrelled with Gertrud?

—No.

—Why is it me, anyway? In Dover it was the van. He did not see us before he saw this vehicle.

—Maybe he is a friend of Hettie. Maybe Hettie told him some lies.

—Hettie did not see The Rites Of Passage' after we painted her. We made sure of that.

—Beatrix, you have a false passport, why is that?

—A man's full-time salary chasing me!

—Australian Social Security fraud?

—I just needed a supporting mother's benefit rather than unemployment benefit so I could travel and still get a cheque. They just want to know what I've done with my non-existent child.

Zorro shakes her head and wonders about the sister-twin. She has a sister who is a communist with whom she has quarrelled, too. Gertrud has probably sacrificed much to keep this little sister safe. It is possible.

—Little sister, she asks softly, are you being followed?

Grundhilde responds with, And Zorro are you being followed?

—It would be very serious if I were being followed. Many people would be in danger, not only this little coach of troubadours. Especially if I don't know for what, or by whom. Therefore I approach him, next time, suddenly by myself on a street corner. Cowardice is not my way. If something happens to me it is a warning shot. Ringing through the darkness. Giving some light.

—Zorro, let's stop and get something for your cough.

Their quest to save Arachne, the antipodian fool named after the spider, seems sour for the moment.

—I saw it in a dream, to find the innocence, to follow the innocent. In the dream it was holy communion with the holy grail…

—Well I don't see why one man should divide us like this. The question, who he is, should bring us together.

—It might be stupid to visit my friend, Zanzibar, in Milan.

The Mediterranean Sea is dull grey glass to the right of the bus. Tables holding up umbrellas in the open air are nearly deserted in the early morning. The tunnel into Monaco starts a joke about gynocentric symbolism.

—The youths in Milan shot up a radio station. I must see Zanzibar.

—You dramatise yourself, Zorro.

—I will see her in secrecy.

—This hard road is a wooden stage for your scene. All the time.

Going to Barcelona had seemed a part of Zorro's make-believe to several of the women. They busked and waited for Zorro to whirl in and out of their company like a fickle zephyr. She did not explain even to Beatrix that she had been in bed at her mother's house. Beatrix, to whom loyalty to her lover came naturally, was troubled. But on the road, climbing through the Pyrenees, Zorro had been romantic and nostalgic. She had shown them places she had loved as a child bivouacking with the girl guides. She had been sexually passionate.

The shock of seeing the man again at the border had brought up some residual resentment at her being so uncommunicative in Spain. The second time they saw him, the time before the border, he was two legs protruding from underneath their van. Seven women abreast stood still and watched him come out and stand up. Not seeing them, he inspected the paintwork and took down the Dutch number from the plate. Then Beatrix yelled, Hey!, and he put his notebook in his back pocket and hurried away. Beatrix checked the petrol and oil, tested the spark and ignition and looked in the engine for a device that shouldn't be there. The Germans considered her actions foolhardy.

At the border he showed some identification to the official and jerked his head in the direction of their bus. Short, sandy hair, stocky type, his very ordinary clothes, nothing about him gave any indication that he could be German, English, American,

Dutch, Australian, even Italian or Spanish of a type. They hadn't heard his voice.

Busking brought mean pickings in Nice and Marseille. They have their sights on Italy. The conversations of the women about the fights of European politics confuse Beatrix somewhat. She thinks all women exist anarchistically and their one politic is to nurture everything, children, each other, the earth. If she uses the word 'power' she means games of manipulation within the group, otherwise power is irrelevant. The thuggery of governments and multinationals is another, more horrifying, thing.

The Italians and the holiday-makers along the Gulf of Genova love the music of these women. The weather is kind. They are allowed to stop anywhere, and bring out of the lurid purple wagon all manner of instruments for strumming, blowing and beating. They are given food and coins. Zorro, standing with her shepherd's whistle glinting from the shade of her sombrero's wide brim, Grundhilde, sitting with a zither on her lap or hugging a guitar, singing songs of the agony of the earth and the suffering of women and of love, Beatrix, in gold satin pants and tapestry vest, changing from one percussion instrument to another from all over the globe, Greta, in her faded red tracksuit pants and sloppy sweatshirt, looking beautiful with her violin tucked under her chin, her eyes under their long lashes catching the others' for the moments in the music when the tide is strong, the clarinets, recorders, saxophones, bamboo pipes and trumpet of the others adding depth and divertisement, they are galvanised into a unit of folk entertainment. Their spirits lift as they travel in small hops along the Italian coast, having argued Zorro out of the idea of going to Milan.

In Rome, it is impossible to find a place to park the van and sleep, so they busk all night. Tired the following day, falling about the crowded interior of the van, Greta strikes her hand on something sticking out of the floor.

A little flat handle had worked loose and is standing up.

—What is it?

Beatrix treats the wound from her medicine box. Zorro goes on to her knees to examine the trapdoor.

—Look, there is a compartment.

—So, we travel on top of a secret hole.

Grundhilde's guttural laugh.

—You want a mystery beneath us, in the bowels of the vehicle?

—Yes, for the time being.

—Well, we'd have to remove the seat to open it.

—A box in the bottom of 'The Rites Of Passage'!

—We don't have the tools...

—It's good.

Overlooking the Bay of Naples, eating cheese and drinking wine, Grundhilde hums the melody to her new song; *To An Italian Sea,* Beatrix reads about volcanoes, a couple are arguing about going to the Isle of Capri and Greta and Zorro discuss the airless cavern in the underbelly of the bus. A lethargy and acceptance swamps all disagreements. Grundhilde's song seems to dismiss the paranoia that caused discord through France and Spain. The Bay of Naples ripples in brilliant blue and silver. Evening approaches. The man watches from the seat of his BMW. Plans are idly discussed.

—The map.

—Here.

—Right, Salerno, Taranto, Brindisi.

—The Ionian Sea?

—The Adriatic.

—Catch a ferry to Corfu.

—There's the man!

—Zorro, come back.

29

ARBOUR AFTER arbour of street lighting, hectares of shiny cars for sale, hacienda-type offices islanded in the middle of crowded motor-ranches, bitumen paddocks of swell duco jobs, sassy chassis; oversized retail outlets; swimming pools like baby baths for giant infants; food-to-go, hamburger joints; dead cat in the gutter; insane bird-chatter in the palm fronds; humans on the conveyer belt grabbing wheels, faces lit from dashboard dials; sportsgrounds flooded with white light, joggers on electric avenue; Oona walks into Sydney, lines of dirt around the calf muscles where the boots end, jeans as thick as suede, eyes arrowed by crow's-feet, brown hair stiffly rooted in skull-skin, swag, kitbag and duffle coat.

It is a long way. Oona arrives at Kings Cross where she sleeps like the swaggie she is, uniformed to receive whatever safety hoboes have, on the street, all night. At dawn she wakes. She has a coffee in a cafe with white-faced women, wrecked by the penetration of needles and pricks, smoking filter tips held by puce-enamel nails and ordering T-bone for breakfast, eating the meat, leaving the salad.

She goes down William Street. Sleep they may by day, but the park-dwellers are up and about in the early morning, carrying their cartons of milk or plastic two litres of orange juice somewhere like stray dogs busy with a sense of direction unknown by anyone else. Morning powwow on the bench near the railway line, now is the hour of agreement, the cockroach humour of city corners, later the arguments. Oona walks down to the Roma.

Silver bottle tops on the pavement make a twisted sculpture of waste, garbage waiting to be collected in trucks. The smell in the Haymarket is vaguely Chinese. The barn of the Capitol reminds her of Covent Garden, though she has never been there, and of old black-and-white movies of Manhattan.

Her dallying in pretense is stopped by the arrival of Cheerful Charlie, the German drunk. Hooking his thumbs into decrepit lapels, he declaims to non-existent crowds, pointing a wavering finger at the skies. He is Laurence Olivier playing Giordano Bruno delivering an eloquent defence to the Inquistion.

—I haff held and hold ssouls to be immortal. Schpeaking ass a Cath-o-lick, zhey do not pass-ss from body to body, but go to Par-a-dicse, Purg-a-tory or to Hell. But I haff reasoned deeply and schpeaking ass a phil-ossopher since zhe ssoul iss not found wizzout a body and yet iss not of zhe body, it may be in vone body or anuzzer, and pass-ss from body to body. Zhiss if it not be proved true, zhis sseems zhe most likely according to zhe opin-i-on of Py-thag-or-us… I haff held and hold ssouls…from the sspir-it zhen which iss called zhe life of zhe universe … I haff held and hold ssouls… I undersstand to be immortal, zhere being no uzzer death zhan div-iss-ion and con-greg-ation…in Eccl-esi-asticks vere it iss said zhere iss nozhing new under zhe sun. Zhat which iss iss that which wass.

The creases about Oona's mouth deepen, her eyes seek in their watching. A flicker of shrewd sanity from Cheerful Charlie, he performs some more. It is nonsense. Then he begs.

—Piss off, mate, I haven't got any money.

He is angry.

—You vere burnt as a vitch. Bitches and vitches.

He mutters as he wanders on, still quoting Bruno, but stopping at every litter-bin conscientiously inspecting each white paper bag for sandwich remains.

Oona's shadow is long on the footpath as she walks around the Capitol, reading the theatrical posters in their grimy glass cases.

'FREEDOM FOR VIOLET & BRUCE', a huge banner in the forecourt of the Roden Cutler Building. The pebblepave is a lounge room, mattresses, armchairs, kerosene heater, TV set, an electrical cord slithering inside to the cleaners' room. Women will be women. Even here, in the protest against flagrant injustice, adopting the radical course of living on the street outside the Department of Corrective Services, there are brooms and sundry evidence of housewifery. Oona recognises the tactic. She has seen it before, five years ago, in Chifley Square, to free Sandra Willson, the strategy of anonymous numbers.

A couple of policemen stand idly keeping guard near their wagon. A woman sits on a folding chair reading *The Thornbirds,* another accosts pedestrians with petition and pen. A stack of pamphlets on a small desk, where someone is knitting and laughing with someone else. Two serious lesbians on a mattress frown together trying to make a drama, transcripts of the trial caught under a brick near their feet.

Oona feels comfortable with numbers of women, and stays.

The police, constantly trying to find the inner cell, are bemused by the innocent yet cynical response, 'We have no leader'. The absence of an organising governing unit, there being no boss-hen to grab, bothers Special Branch the most during the hundred days. 'We need no leader.' Communicating in a network of modern-day Etruscan, the ratbag fringe oozes out of the depths in never-diminishing numbers, gathers on the streets, rattling the scales of justice, slashing its sword of rage, speaking with impeccable logic and behaving in riddles. Hell hath no fury as arrested are Sarah, Kerry, Cathy, Kristine, Rose, Monica, Toni, Jillian, Rita, Christine, Meredith, Mary, Georgina, Jane, Wendy, Jenny, Cathy, Julie, Dianne, Megan, Margot. In any ingenious way they can think of, the women make the media tell the story of Violet and Bruce…the family poor, the kids bashed by the father, twenty years of fear, the violent, constant demands for sex in drunken midnights, the mother more and more desperate and damaged, the place Pacific Palms, the police with thousands of calls about domestic abuses are useless, put off at the door by the man who seems reasonable to them, the doctors treating bruises and broken ribs not heard in the trial, the mother and son shoot him and are convicted with heavy sentences. Incompetent legal preparation invalidates an appeal.

The women march their very long petition up to Parliament House and run into a full-blown police security set-up; scuffles break out. Terrorists wish to upset the opening of State Parliament, while overhead a helicopter flies the message: 20,000 PEOPLE SAY LET THEM GO FREE.

One day Oona wanders into the Art Gallery of New South Wales to see Sidney Nolan's Ned Kelly and stands in front of Hans Heysen and Fred McCubbin, tiny characters and animals in the big, soft bush. She wants to be back there. The thing is, she says to herself, there can never be justice in punishment. This is a problem. The trundling juggernaut of power lumbers after someone and it doesn't matter about innocence, and it doesn't matter about guilt. One way or another the guilty get away with it.

She leads the city women, who drove her up from where they parked their car at the most remote orchard's fence, past the soldierly pines and up a steep incline, single file. On a special boulder which commands an expansive view of treetops and impressive rock faces, Oona stands feet apart and sings the cry of the crow, signalling her presence to Janice. They are at a point behind the Brigadoon gate, higher up. 'Arwk Arwk' echoes back. Oona points the way down for the eager city-slickers, and continues upwards.

Jay Jay's black fringe shines like raven feathers, she waits at Oona's camp, staring at a collection of ten gallon drums carefully stacked under a tarpaulin. A red-bellied black snake is comatose on a log, warming up in the sun.

The ordered calm of letting go is like water flowing through her fingers. Iona is relaxing for the first time in months. The countryside murmurs away beneath, beside and around old Torpid, rolling, humming, pleasant, changing, the sky a comfortable balance between cloud and clarity, the tones of the landscape merging and refraining with the soothing regularity of a Mozart air.

A snap decision. Syzygy. Of why and why-not. The correlation of opposing accidentals and incidentals. All Melbourne was dominated by a brumous mantle. Her mother's misery. Nola, the anchor, threatened to pull the entire ship to the floor of the sea. Mary would be returning from Sydney in a week after checking out the latest Indian guru and Lesley was leaving for the bush in half an hour. She rang her partner, Dennis, who assured her he could find someone to take over nights while she was away. Some taxidriving superstition held that she must keep Gay One Seven.

It was a nice car and Dennis, as a partner, was okay, always leaving it smelling as sweet as a florist shop to smother the tales the odour might tell of the nature of his smoking habit. He specialises in carrying packets from factories and big companies to each other and the airports. He has a pretty cool routine worked out. Her mother, despite the dampness of her mood, was magnanimous on the telephone.

She threw her tracksuit, three T-shirts, a pair of jeans, a couple of flannelette shirts and her Canadian lumber jacket into her pack and was back in time to bus bushwards with Lesley.

Between Iona and Lesley no sparks fly and most of the time they don't need to speak. Nothing to prove to each other, no contention, no question of sex, yet both feel a love, like the motion of Torpid, an integration of the surrounding scenery with the mathematics of music. They agree as reflections do, in the challenge of mirrors, and, in refractions in the prism of the group soul each seeks to find expression in her own way, almost as a life work.

Water and air.

Even though they look uninhabited and uninhabitable, the mountains scarved in winter mists, great rocky scarps jutting out in stunning terracottas, unimpeachable majesty and powerful serenity, that is where Lesley points.

—There, she says.

Steep and densely covered with eucalypt, the mountains defeat Iona. The bush seems dusted with a powder from the feathers of wild teal. A green-blue softened by cool pink which is grey. Impossible, no language for it. They address her with mystery.

—In there is the valley.

Iona can't respond, she grunts.

—Don't worry you won't have to walk. Lesley grins.

The road now twisting around and climbing a heavily wooded pass darkens. It is late afternoon. A little fear and depression.

—What do you reckon about Mary's theory that you don't like the time of day you were born, Lesley?

—It's true.

When they get out of the car at Bilpin, the wind is brisk, spiked. Lesley has parked off the road, under the pines in someone's yard.

Five horses with sheepskins girdled to their backs crop in a one-acre paddock behind the restless moaning trees. Beyond are orchards bare of leaves, blossoms and apples. They walk up to the tea rooms beside a garage on Bells Line of Road. Lesley, Iona notices, has a sneaky smile playing about the corners of her mouth. I simply don't want to be told. Or I'll be told by the ululating conifers. What can be shown shouldn't be said, didn't Wittgenstein say? There is a tide in the affairs of woman that she should just plane along, meanwhile kid just breathe in the negative ions.

Inside, an open fire blazes warmly, lighting the faces of Janice, Therese and Vanessa with orange-gold.

—Have you been waiting for us? Iona's question is spontaneous and eager with the beam of genuine surprise.

—Of course.

—You don't know how many years we've waited for you to come.

—Yeah, well. Great. I'm here. On the tide or the wind. Feels good. Iona blushes.

—A brandy? Vanessa is offering, There's a long ride.

—Am I going to ride in?

—Sure, didn't you see the horses?

—Thanks Vanessa, a brandy, yes.

The hugs the women exchange are long and concentrated. Lots of out-breaths in lieu of words.

No-one is in a hurry. Iona recalls how she used to work race-horses at Croydon in the frosty dawns of her teenage years, how she went to a hunt at Cranbourne once. Trees tells the story of their mob of mares and geldings.

—We were going to sales. Everything was too expensive, until one Thursday Jay Jay and I happened to see a yard full of horses all going under the hammer at once. The auctioneer was obviously expecting the knackeries to bid. We counted, thirteen. We looked at each other. Both of us sort of decided at once. We got thirteen horses for six hundred dollars, plus transportation.

—Then we let them out to run like brumbies.

—Until they started making friends with us. Choosing who they wanted.

—Except Nancy got sick.

—Misty throws the women off. Quite serious falls, too.

—Who's Misty?

—He's a roan and white gelding who belonged to an old man who loved him and spoiled him. Died on his back so we were told.

—There's Bowen, who is mine.

—Yes, Lesley wanted a beautiful white horse with a flowing mane and tail, and ends up with brown, gentle Bowen, who is perfect for her.

—Church is Jay Jay's. She used to be a racehorse, thoroughbred, bones and skin. Gave birth last Spring to Isis.

—The sire must have been wild or jumped a fence, because we never had her mated.

—Vanessa's is a bay stock horse from Wallerwang. He must be twenty-two. He doesn't know how to walk.

—And Trees?

—Nancy, she's okay now. And Visshnu-Kali who has the Queensland Itch. I think Tipsy is pregnant too.

—The others?

—Well, some of them prefer to stay free, and the rest are turned out for the duration.

—But useful. Old Patch on the hill. He is a huge black and white draught horse. He's like a flag. He keeps the mob in sight.

—He, for some reason, is never behind the trees.

—But Church is the boss.

—Mares actually lead a mob of horses from the inside.

The strongest stallion is out the front, the weakest at the back and the others on the flanks. Pregnant mares, brood mares and foals are protected in the middle of the herd.

—Let's go.

—Who have you brought for me to ride?

—Misty.

—But you said no-one could ride him.

—He saved himself for you, Iona.

—And we brought the bridle.

—We all ride in halters.

—Home-woven halters.

—The women are superstitious about him. He doesn't understand them. Etama had a really bad fall, and Quince.

—But both times he was the only horse available. He got excited and took off.

—A case of misguided trust leading to superstition.

It is just on dusk and each single leaf is gilded on its Western edge. The light is flattering to complexions and the wind has dropped. With respect for Misty's spoilt lad's personality, the others relieve Iona of the duty of carrying her own gear which together with everything else is stuffed into makeshift saddle packs made from hessian chaff-bags.

The bush has many gods and many voices. They go across country to Mountain Lagoon following the fire road to the Upper Colo. It is sandy and soft on the horses' unshod hooves. Iona is a responsive rather than bossy rider. Misty is exactly the sort of mount she likes, educated and energetic. She can imagine him dumping people who feel like a sack of pumpkins on his back. She has only to apply pressure with her right calf and he is wheeling to the right. She needs only to press down with her bum and squeeze and he is into the slow rocking canter much favoured by stockmen.

—This boy has a soft mouth. I feel safe on him.

—That's what Jay Jay said. She said you have a way with animals.

As soon as they branch off the fire road, the atmosphere changes. It is very dark. Iona must rely on Misty. The others are ahead of her, progressing at a walk, single file. The bush has altered. Sudden pockets of warm air engulf her like a lizard spirit which slips away and darts back. She is confused. The trees feel more like those of the rainforest.

—Bush gods are very shy and very powerful.

The women in front are chanting.

—My mare's feet beat a low rhythm, the soft thunder of Thoth.

—I hear a music between the earth and the scythe of moon.

—The fine vibrations of the air, the air.

She cannot see anything, only shade and darker shade, like gaping mouths of caverns. She is surprised when the horse makes a turn, disoriented yet trusting. She listens.

—We have avuncular spirits who like to chatter and clammer.

—Into your ears at night, well-mannered and kind-hearted.

—Close to Aborigines, they ride on the bodies of mosquitoes stealing bites of blood.

—They recognise each other's territory, tree-plants, flower-plants, mammals, insects, reptiles and rocks.

—All in the right parcel.

—And birds fly messages from one invisible parcel to the next.

—The rainbow-bird, wirrit-wirrit, gave us the secret of fire.

—From the fire sticks poking out the end of his tail.

—The rainbow-snake, from her head to her waist a woman, from the waist down a serpent.

—She is sitting down, all coiled up, waiting, hitting the song-stick and singing.

—Wings of birds whirred.

—So few humans heard.

—An egg of the Giant Green Ant cracked and the discord thwacked the harmony.

—All bush gods got rankled. Disturbance rustles in the Bush.

—Willy-wag women gossiping, gossiping in the she-oaks.

—Danger, disaster. Has this nonsense reached the dreamtime, too?

—Ooohoowooohoo.

—The dingo howls with strange starvation.

—The Tasmanian devil has lost its body and prowls.

—Prowling about for a new one to wear. Is this devil a devil?

—How far does he travel?

They stop in a clearing near a gate. The new moon is brighter. An iridescent light catches the yellow leaves of a poinsettia. Wild waratah traces the fence-line. Out of the weeping bank to her right grow bleeding hearts. The pain in her upper thighs from sitting astride without stirrups bothers Iona slightly.

—I smell a rat, says Janice.

They have picked up the old "Brigadoon" sign and are reading some graffiti spray-painted over the name of the Scottish village which appeared and disappeared in a mist but lived long enough for Gene Kelly to dance and fall in love. Just such a quality of romance had been in Iona's daydreaming as she rode.

—'If your tits are too big you will fall over unless you wear a rucksack.' Lesley reads, then laughs. Her laughter is unaccompanied.

—It couldn't be Amos, he's not that clever.

—He probably heard it somewhere.

Some metres down from the gate, Vanessa finds a tree has been lopped, crushing the fence.

—He's cooking up something.

Near the felled tree the wire is cut. There is severe soil erosion immediately after the gate. Misty leaps and canters down into the paddock. Alone there, Iona hears a harmonica played in D. Someone behind her cooees. After the space of about three beats, the cooee is answered with drums. The air is too warm for this time of year and the altitude. Misty is champing at the bit, glad to be home and eager for some hard feed. The drumming echoes around her. Trees is beside her.

—This way.

The horses splash across a creek and there on the other side is the kitchen tarpaulin lit by an enormous fire. The sheepskins are taken off the horses and thrown on the ground for seating. Therese buckets out bran and oats onto the emptied saddle-bags and equine faces are lit beyond those of the women. An iron pot of soup gurgles on the glowing coals. Iona is exhausted and immediately after eating sleeps on the sheepskin.

Lesley and other women stay talking.

First Jay Jay then Trees take Iona out on rides through the bush, showing her the waterfall, the ridge which once was Oona's home, the vast views, the hideaways. She sees the birds, the roos, and everywhere she rides she is accompanied by butterflies.

The second night she is there it is dark already and no one has prepared supper, even though everyone, and that is almost twenty women and children, is hungry. Iona feels strangely humble as if she must ask permission to cook. She looks at the scattering of wooden plates and chopsticks, the wicker basket of vegetables. She finds in a tub some buckwheat noodles. Is there enough food for an army? She wanders over to the herb garden where scented thyme forms a ground cover and sniffs around to identify oregano, basil and parsley. Trees is bandaging a sore leg of one of the mares. The new moon is fatter. I feel I have to ask, yet why shouldn't I be chef? Whose guest am I?

—Trees, she yells, is it okay if I make a meal?

—That would be nice.

—Can I borrow your knife?

She finds a candle. With its own wet wax she sticks it to the chopping board secured in the mud, builds the kitchen fire into a blaze between two solid logs, selects vegetables and arranges them around the board, puts the handful of fresh herbs in a mug and washes a large camp oven in the creek. Kneeling on the ground, she chops. Thank the goddess for yoga, without its meditation my back would be killing me, thanks for Dawn and her zen reading, for here is a zen occupation, thanks for Helen and her kundalini giving strength to my spine and Mrs M for the knowledge of prana and here goes. Soon it is as easy as pouring water. Hunting around the makeshift shelves for tastes, she throws in peanut butter, tamari, miso, even a touch of honey and curry powder, all with a flourish and a kiss of good luck. Pumpkin, swede, potato, onion sizzled in oil, then fresh water and cauliflower from the vegie patch, then garlic, grated ginger, raw herbs garnishing the end. All the time swishing the mixture and spreading the taste. The buckwheat noodles she does separately. But there is not enough of those for everyone to have her own helping, so into the pot and the overall stew. With a prayer and a blessing. Care for the texture.

After they have eaten, after everyone has eaten, Iona finds Janice staring at her. Seventeen people are quiet.

—Amazing meal!

—Thanks Iona.

I tasted it myself. But what is it? The food was like ambrosia, like excellent claret, it reached the dizzy heights of art. Shit this is interesting.

—Let's have music. Quince is behind the big conga.

Jay Jay hands Iona a couple of singing sticks.

—What do I do with these?

—There is music in everyone.

—Just clap them together.

Iona plays. She counts out the fifth beat with an off beat adding her own unique bit to the music and it is as fresh an experience as ever she had had. Entering the company of it. The placement. The rightness. The balance between concentration and freedom is that between being and existing. Becoming.

The kitchen camp is about half a mile from the house in which no-one sleeps. The women prefer to live outside. The house is where things are kept which need to be dry and safe. The hut where the first five found Oona is much higher, on the plateau at the top of the mountain. Dotted between the kitchen tarp and the stone hut are the camps of the different women, some couples with children, some alone, all slightly off the track, with tracks of their own. During the day, one might see strings of smoke weaving up through the musky colour of the trees, but no other evidence of settlement.

On the night before Iona is due to go to Sydney to meet Mary and return in her car to Melbourne, thirteen women are making music at the kitchen fire, singing feminist ballads with breaks for Vanessa-solos on the harmonica. Iona is not able to repeat the rhythm of her second night and she has begun to hear dissonance in the harmony, to find people she simply does not like, whose ideas and manners of expression draw her contempt.

Amos and the boys are indeed cooking up something. A huge pan of Tom Piper Steak 'n' Veg is bubbling on a fire near a tree. Toohey's Draught, Carnation Milk, Heinz Baked Beans cans are blackened in the ashes. Mac is smearing slabs of white bread with lavish hunting-knifefuls of margarine. Ring-pull crack and hiss as beer meets the air, there's excitement in the camp. They're priming themselves. Mac brought along a few sticks of geli. Others have their kangaroo-shoot rifles. The four-wheel drive, with the four spotlights, is permanently streaked with old roo blood. Snap, shuffle, click, rifle-loading. They're claiming their power. The plan is to move the log, get through the fence, cut the engine and roll in. When real close turn on the spots and start firing. Scare shit out of those university sheilas.

Bangs in the air, shattering nightsong, disturb the horses. The men assumed the women would be in the house and come running out. They hear and see nothing but their own noise and each other. The spot shines on the vacant house.

—Let's take it, fellas. Amos screams.

The explosion blasts the house into flying rubble. Another blast takes the water tank. The old timbers of the homestead go up in pyromaniacal glee, dried food, guitars, fiddles, passports, cash, mandolins, bankbooks, extra blankets, coats, toys, books and sarongs dissolve into flames and smoke.

The women standing silently in the scrub are moved by the destructive beauty. They begin a wordless hum, a sort of hymn to Kali. Tearing emotion and suppressed hysteria, one of the children cries remembering her painting, a present for Lesley, in there being destroyed.

The men, suddenly taking fright, can hear but not see them. Several, scared of the criminal charge of arson, throw coats over their heads and run. The house-fire makes the landrover's spotlights look weak. Amos gets behind the wheel. Its journey is slippery up the grassy hillside and past the severed fence. The dykes are sly and brainy. So just to scare them and to prove his lack of fear to himself, Amos stops the vehicle, gets out his gun and shoots into the air.

After the shots, the women hear the men crashing through the undergrowth, squashing wild flowers. They emerge, and, as if of one mind, hold hands in front of the flames and keen for the loss. The huge fire is exciting and terrifying and amazingly quick. Each person spends her hysteria in anarchistic ritual and dance, becomes a dervish circling a kind of exorcism, unashamed of inappropriate bursts of hilarity.

In the Kurrajong Hills, still trying to find a word for the colour of the eucalypt forests which cover the Blue Mountains National Park, Iona looks back to where she has been and it looks as if it couldn't possibly exist. She doubts and knows in one smile. She catches the train at Windsor.

HEATHROW

Dear Jay Jay,

Ta for the card. Well that's witchery heh? Oona steals my things, turns up again with them. They're fine and they wouldn't have been if she hadn't nicked them. Oh shit Jay Jay I don't know who to trust after recent events. Just keep rowing Captain Bligh.

I'm at the airport, the parting of the ways, homecomings and departures. In the actual waiting 'where' becomes irrelevant. I've just watched an Aussie movie on the video, starring Kate McMillan, but I guess I wept more for the photography than for her sad character. Our cinematographers are at the Heidelberg school period of their development, but it's nice.

Where? Athens. Then, I reckon, home. I miss the land, the gum trees and the grass trees, the rocks, the craggy outcrops. Bushwalking. Also I want the dole. In that way it must be a lucky country; for me anyway.

You would have read my letter to Trees. Well, we finished picking and Queenie gave the shotgun back and got a kiss on the mouth! Yuk! We got the night train and arrived at Paddington to see front page news about Saudi Arabia. 301 people killed in an air crash at a place called Riyadh. When I get to Athens, I'm definitely going to the Australian Consul, if nothing else has happened. I went back to Hackney to pick up my mail (your postcard) and found the squats we had lived in smashed up again. Tin all over the windows and planks and boards across the doors, and mail in the mail box! Memoirs of a survivor!

We wandered about London Fields and had breakfast in a dugout tea shop: baked beans on white bread. Hot strong tea in thick heavy cups. Spent the day getting visas and stuff. Queenie's got one for Australia. You'd think she'd find it hard, the way she looks. Maybe it's because she's Canadian. Anyway she got a work permit. So you'll meet her. You'll like her.

See you soon. Do something about Amos and friends.

Love to Trees,

love always,

Et.

30

YVONNE TURNS thirty-seven in the midst of a games-playing party at Islington. Among the guests is a visitor from Bradford, a vehement North Country socialist, Yootha. Yootha always wears a black leather flying jacket, even inside, and carries to her chest her thesis, *Sexual Abuse of Children in the Nineteenth Century*. So uniformed, yet so mysterious, she intrigues Yvonne.

In the morning, a Sunday, she follows her. Yootha strides with a kind of aggression, stooped forward over her loose-leaf folder of photostats, maps, photographs, diagrams, ruled pages and underlined articles, hole-punched and secured to centre, just.

It is a great question mark.

The tube to Aldgate, then walking through the street-market crowds to Whitechapel, semi-circling the London Hospital. Gumshoe Yvonne, in love with detection and secrecy and clues, proceeds like a private eye a hundred yards behind. The map Yootha consults is the location of disembowelments in the foggy, sinister past. To be the one to unveil the true identity of Jack the Ripper for good and all is Yootha's mad ambition. Yvonne deduces this from the terraces looked at. She remembers a story of Iona's about a lover of hers spending his entire life hunting the extinct Tasmanian Devil. She meets Yootha on the banks of the Thames, suggests, teases and queries, but Yootha smiles with half her mouth and lets her eyes travel over Yvonne from head to foot.

Meanwhile, Sophie waits to board the Flying Express at Fishguard. She is dying to see Yvonne. No longer is Yvonne's yoga stupid, nor are her twenty-minute twice a day meditations the fun she made of them. No, Yvonne is right. Now Sophie could listen to her talk of the stars and eccentric religions with excited interest. She could try to understand the implications of having her moon in Cancer, or was it Scorpio?

The wings enamelled on the sleek sides of the express unfold and lift her into the freedom of the skies. She is coursing along the tracks of her destiny to her destination, electricity poles rush past, whither goes her individual railroad? She writes, in elated impatience to Etama in Athens, a missive full of strange imagery, glorious phrases and far-fetched generalisations. The clatter-whack-ack of the wheels only eggs her on.

She will be as passionate as Yvonne desires, she will sing a serenade under her balcony in the snow if necessary in the voice of one so pure.

Yvonne's letters had stopped shortly after her arrival in Ireland, true, but those that had come were so delicately redolent of romance, so luscious in language, so generous in spirit, Sophie is certain all her new intentions will pave the way to Heaven. Generally letters were not Sophie's style, but after her couple of days with Cerridwen and while she made her obligatory tours of the west coast and Tipperary, she wrote daily, detailing every little thing that happened to her. In Dublin, she was lyrical about the children of the tinkers on the bridges over the Liffey and in St Steven's Green, all observations embellished with how she felt.

At Kings Cross Station very early in the day, Sophie is full of nervous energy and aching in her joints. She hails a taxi. She falls against the door of Yvonne's flat, lending her weight to her fist, banging. She is leaning, she is looming, in the door frame. After some time, Yvonne answers, frowning wickedly.

—Could I have a shower and breakfast? Sophie smiles.

—No. Yvonne begins to shut the door.

—Hey, Yvonne, why?

—How dare you wake me up at this hour, knocking like Special Branch? And how dare you write me all those self-indulgent letters, all about your aches and pains and this woman you met?

—Please, Yvonne, I'll explain.

—Also, how dare you assume that I'm alone?

—Aren't you?

—No. Yvonne slams her door with a decisive finality even Sophie cannot mistake.

Sophie wanders away, stands in the shade of the barn of Sad-dlers Wells and waits for a bus. She is chilled to the bone, a stunned marlin.

The hairy muso with whom she shares a flat has shoulders rounded from the constant weight of a guitar. He irritates her. She sits at the filthy kitchen table and completes her letter to Etama.

Needing to see Etama, or some Australian like her, several days later she makes her way to the squat. It is all tinned up. The loss seems complete. She recalls the days of the travelling dykes, the little French Canadian she deposited here. It seems a century age. The lively comings and goings, her night with Etama…

31

THE DECAY of the Angel by Yukio Mishima. Iona marks the place in her paperback with a fine rice paper envelope with Irish stamps, a good bookmark.

At Tullamarine International Airport, on any of the three taxi ranks which are roads in themselves, it is possible to wait an hour. The highly moral Mishima suggested contemplating death for ten minutes each day, and ten years ago he did it. Aggressively nostalgic for the chivalry of Nippon's past.

Depressing, along with Cerridwen's strange letter. It was both polite and rude, besetting Iona with questions of blood, and, in mentioning her unknown father with a familiarity Iona had no suspicion of, it hurt her. She felt like one robbed rather than one receiving. The melancholy and envy lurking in her murky depths was stirred. She was jealous, jealous of darker lives.

She gathered that her cousin had also written to her aunt.

Frances, dancing in the ice culture of smack, the devil's dust, rocking down the sweet highway to hell, leapt in the cab earlier on behaving like a junkie, demanding a ride. She liked to be truly squalid sometimes. It distressed Iona.

Heroin smelt of suicide.

—Remember Cerridwen? Iona asked, tapping the bookmark in her paperback between them. She wrote.

Frances laughed.

A laugh can be horrible as you remember it. It is as if Frances touched my pretty cousin somehow and she had to change. I don't know what Cerridwen's asking or what she's telling or why she's written. And I don't expect her ever to write again. Should it be me who doesn't write? Actually, let's grapple with this.

Iona finds the rice paper envelope with the Irish stamps empty.

32

ETAMA AND QUEENIE fly into Athens in the morning. The light on the pollution sickens Etama. They take the airport bus to Omonia Square. A chill wind blows, seemingly, from the Parthenon. They head down into the Plakka, searching for a cheap pension.

Queenie feels invigorated from flying. Her first flight. The Mediterranean! The islands! She loves Athens from the air.

Etama is tired, having had to wait overnight at Heathrow. Queenie's unadulterated joy at being a bird chills her, as if her own sophistication were a cool cloak around her. Duty, not adventure, brings her here. As goddesses go, Athena had never been a favourite, chiefly because of her phoney birth from a man.

Queenie is enchanted by the classical building. Examining its proportions she longs for it to be taller, yet she is satisfied that it is wide. She wants to learn everything about it, even though in her whole life she has had cause to use the word 'architecture' less than a dozen times. Something inside herself, in her own clean white bones, is at one with the elegance, the simplicity, the endurance.

They sit down at an outdoor table. Etama orders Perrier Water and Queenie coffee. Queenie ignores Etama's world-weariness. She asks for answers, knowing that Etama's learning will pull her mood around, if not totally, then for a little while. Their packs and coats are strewn near the legs of the table.

—It is the theorem of Pythagorus.

Etama picks up a paper serviette and takes out her purple felt pen, and draws a triangle and the numbers 5, 12, 13 in the stylish lines of an artist.

—It was really his wife, Theana, who discovered the Golden Mean. Pythagorus himself was probably just responsible for the decad as a basis for mathematics.

Queenie is not interested in academic feminism, nor even in names, but she stares at the geometry in front of her.

—More, she begs, offering another serviette.

Etama draws a snail with a spiral pattern and writes the numbers 1, 2, 3, 5, 8, 13 and then straight lines with arrow ends, the 1 measuring the centre, 2, the first circle, 3, the second, 5 the third, etc. Silently working in response to Queenie's intellectual naivete and blissful curiosity, she traces the lines of a transparent pyramid with the appropriate numbers. Finally, on the last napkin, she does the pediment and front columns of the Parthenon with the relevant numerals. The handiwork of her left, drawing hand is more explicit than words and Queenie carefully folds the tissue pages and puts them in her coat pocket.

For Etama it was a doodle in the feeble sunshine, for Queenie it is the first study in initiation to the mysteries undertaken by a young priestess, or something similar for modern times.

Etama feels both lumbered with and dependent on Queenie when right now she needs someone from her own culture, like Frances, Jay Jay, even Iona, with whom she could talk and talk through the complexity of emotion and input, the worry she is feeling.

Queenie is approached by a man, a Greek gigolo. Urbane, handsome, intense in a self-serious way, he addresses her in fluent French. Queenie chats as if she were a chatterer. They are laughing. Queenie is being complimented on her looks. He says he chose French because of her dark red hair and freckles. There is an irresistable serenity in her face. Queenie is flattered and gracious.

Etama knows Queenie wants to go and look through the Parthenon, but she is too tired, or bored. This odious type is a regular hazard in any travel through Southern Europe.

—Do you know, she interrupts in abrupt English, any cheap pension? Running the risk of his knowing where they are staying, she wants a bed to lie down on.

—Of course. By the way, my name is Dimitrios. Let me take you. It would be my pleasure.

The pension is a building they had passed on their way to the tourist section of the Plakka. It is a rabbit warren of narrow corridors in tesselated tiles. The room itself is ugly with three single beds parallel to each other like dormitory bunks, separated by side tables covered with plastic lace. The tiny window at the far end of the room is ajar, permanently, sucking in the bad Athenian air. Too many heavy wardrobes line the wall opposite the beds. There is no table, no desk or mirror. Etama has a bed to lie on.

Queenie is out, wandering delightedly through the ruins of the Acropolis, with other tourists and with Dimitrios. The insects hum in the dry grasses and the light in her Titian hair is luxurious. She laughs at his stories. A more willing, trusting listener he could never have hoped for. They climb up to the Parthenon and Queenie examines each nook and corner with an uncluttered wonder.

When the tourist season ends, Dimitrios tells her, then he goes to sea. They share shipping anecdotes.

Towards evening they climb over the wall into the Theatre of Dionysius. It is stunningly, historically, endlesssly empty. Queenie is spellbound. He finds her innocence of her sexuality so desirable he is gallant. Tender. They sit together on the tiers of stone and he relates the stories of the great tragedies and comedies. He knows snatches from speeches in the ancient language and translates them into French. It is all new to Queenie. Darkness comes upon them without their noticing until sudden garish lights spring up on the Parthenon above them.

In the unreal, theatrical glow, Dimitrios becomes a hero in the classical mode. He touches her more often, and plaits his own soft words of romance into the tales of Agamemnon, Cassandra, Helen and Troy. She looks through the poetics of passion and his elaborate antics and suggests they make love. She says she has never been with a man. He is charmed.

They walk hand in hand to a sheltered corner and lie down on the hard stone. Queenie enjoys Dimitrios as he comes to his orgasm but does not reach her own. She asks permission and brings herself to climax with his flaccid penis. Oh Medea, Antigone, why must I experience delicious castration with a French-Canadian virgin, this classic impotence with a fair-skinned savage? What has happened to Greece? he moans in Greek.

There is to be a rehearsal, he remembers.

The actors come, and the director with his megaphone. The lovers escape through the shadows out the main entrance.

Etama watches the froth of the water and soap course round the ancient porcelain sink backwards. Clockwise, the wrong way. The spirals in the Northern Hemisphere do not suit Etama. She feels a nauseating homesickness, as dark as the depths in the awkward plughole, a black constriction inside falling around incorrectly. The way the water flows away at home is correct.

—More correct than familiar. At home, down under, the invisible spirals to the infinite would therefore go to the right.

This discovery of the clockwise vortex into the sewer is ominous. Things are probably worse than her suspicions.

She walks back to the room along the dimly-lit hallway. Nothing welcomes her into the homeliness of this hired room. She throws herself face down in the grip of emotional gravity, sucked, circling in and in on herself. The phlegm from crying has made her sick. The strangeness of the city, with its heavy corrosive air, the kitschiness of modern Greeks and the now unpleasant darkness outside creates an agoraphobia in Etama. She is being pulled down into self-harming jealousy. Jealous of everything like the unity of colour in all-encompassing dark. Putrifying in suspicion, where the hell is Queenie?

Whenever the gravitational pull of unsatisfactory emotion gets hold of her, all the past gets washed around her brain the wrong way. The desperate cry for a fair deal in the absence of another has only downwards to go. Jealous of Iona Flynn. She wishes that around the corner was Frances' flat and outside in the gutter the brick that she threw to interrupt their love-making and that she could do it again. Express her rage and frustration like on that other night when she rang the fire brigade and hid in the bushes to watch their humiliation and embarrassment. The sweetness in Frances's shout through the melee, in her knowing, 'Etama you're just a fucking idiot!' being the revenge, hearing her name in that voice. But it is Queenie she waits for.

—Queenie was so…so biddable.

Sounds in the corridor. Footsteps. Queenie, whose shoes are soft, it couldn't be, yet Etama hopes. She looks at her watch. Only an hour since her last wash. She shudders on the white cotton bedspread and the room is hateful.

—I think the situation for women today is worse than it's ever been, Etama writes to Mary several days later, but not for us, not for university-educated white feminists. Then why, why, do I feel so damn depressed? I've been bored to paralysis, and agoraphobic, and homesick to the point of nausea. I'm as bony as a starving dog. The magnetic poles are askew as far as I'm concerned. The radial rose of the cross is reversed.

Always the post.

—Begging the best out of a bad lot, I bought a bowl with the most stunning glaze. There are little female dancers circling around it. When I get home I'm getting back into pottery in a big way. This bowl is precious to me, an inspiration.

—Not many drachmas. You know what Cancers are like, careful with their money. Well I'm with one at the moment. It's not that her economy is bothering me so very much, it is that she is in a completely different headspace from me and it's irritating. She's out all the time and comes in looking maddeningly radiant. While for me, each day, it becomes more and more improbable that Beatrix and the others will turn up in their campervan. For her, well, she just smiles with bland certainty. Meanwhile I wait. I'm impatient and I long to come home.

—I do have some good news for you. A note from Arachne, at Poste Restante, can you believe it? She is uncanny. Herein, quoted in full:

'Been having a ball with diplomatic Americans for the past few days. (No date mind you.) New passport being arranged, in new name, Angel, and new identity. (How does she get away with it?) They're going to fly me to London. See you there, though it's not likely you're still in Greece, is it? Keep it together Et, love A.'

—If Beatrix were here, we could have laughed for her eccentricity, guessed her plight, felt compassion for the little fool and just blessed her luck. I needed someone to share it with me, to make it for me, you know. Anyway, I'm glad she's safe.

—I'll fly to Melbourne when I come. Expect a telegram.

Missing you all, Etama.

She posts the letter, and finds to her surprise a long missive from Sophie. She walks all over Athens trying to find an Australian newspaper, only to discover in one that they are drilling into the sacred Aboriginal site at Noonkanbah, spiralling into the body of the living earth. She has an urgent desire to be chained to the wheels of the bulldozer, screaming abuse at the bastards. Nostalgia for all-out battle.

Sophie's letter is incomprehensible, fragmented, scattered. Etama gathers that the silly bitch is into dope now. However, simply thinking of Sophie brings pictures of Frances and herself, brown as berries, as women in a Gauguin painting, having a holiday on the Barrier Reef.

The tiredness that has been with her since touchdown at Athens weighs like a lump of stone on each foot. She is anorexic.

Earlier she had had a fight with Queenie. Her tension and frustration had burst in a fit of temper which Queenie could not understand. She struck her across the cheek in front of the crowd outside American Express.

—Cry. Cry all you like, she shouted. Tears are easy for you. It's me who should be crying. This city is full of fuckers and pollution.

Queenie had stood perfectly still while Etama stormed off. Etama looked back to see a group of onlookers cheering up Queenie and taking her off with them.

Suddenly, outside the palace, near the guards in their crushed blue and white uniforms, she is sure. It is Greta! They're here. Faded red tracksuit pants, same hair, same walk, back view. She runs, yelling. Faces the woman. She is nothing like Greta. The stranger disappears, a mirage in the city.

When she comes into the room of the pension, Queenie is there. Etama feels too fragile to eat, yet hungry. Queenie goes out and brings back salad, cheese, olives and bread, then stays for about twenty minutes. Etama says nothing. She just holds her bowl of circling dancers.

Queenie returns at midnight. Etama pretends to be asleep. Queenie emits a small humming sound as she undresses. With only a towel about her she goes to the window to look out at the crisp Grecian night. Etama's eyes burrow into her milky back. Queenie turns, catches the open eyes. She quietly climbs into Etama's bed. She presses her big round breasts into Etama's lean, unresponsive back. She sighs, brings her right hand down over Etama's hard flat stomach and into her pubic hair. Etama neither turns to face her nor hinders her ministrations. The physical, mechanical climax releases Etama into a heavy sleep.

Queenie, now lying so close to Etama, needs long, slow loving. She needs the woman. Etama brings her knees up into a cramped foetal position for sleep. The bones of her spine jab into the sleepless Queenie's arm. Her period is five days overdue. There is no room for Queenie in the bed. She balances on the edge, gazing into the gloom.

Her feeling for Etama dies. Realising this, she carefully moves her weight out of the bed, hoping not to wake her first love. She backs into the bedside table, nearly tipping it over. There is a crockery crash on the tiled floor. Queenie catches her breath, but Etama only grunts in her slumber.

In her own bed, Queenie is sure she is pregnant. It is intuition. She enjoys imagining the growth of new life deep in the mysteries of her own system.

When Etama wakes in the morning she is gone.

—It looks like lightning struck.

The fragments are undisturbed, shattered outwards in an oval of eighteen separate parts. Each bit still beautiful, but flawed by severance, by a raw terracotta edge. The whole destroyed. The one artefact from her five months in Europe a broken piece of pottery. Everything seems pointless. That the finger of fate should choose this tiny thing to strike makes her weep. She hadn't been everywhere, hadn't done very much, but it was over. She collected the individual bits one by one. Used the carefully saved, drawn-on serviettes from Queenie's coat pocket to wrap them. Her exhibition would be different now. Not complete bowls at all, not complete circles nor complete dancers.

33

THE WOMEN who rent out rooms on Corfu look like overgrown crows. Their black clothes shine even blacker against the pristine whiteness of the block-shaped buildings. Their incomprehensible squawking, alert eyes and shrewd simplicity of financial objective is something Queenie understands well. She could give savagery for savagery but there is no need. The universal language of arithmetic is enough. Grundhilde respects Queenie and leaves her to it. *Her joie de vivre* seems to have doubled since London. Queenie's confidence, bright with life, is in contrast to Zorro's growing morbidity.

Queenie sees that Zorro is not well and bargains even harder for a warm, comfortable room. Or two rooms for five. The others wait. Beatrix has tried to heal Zorro but it is a sickness beyond her physical cures. It is impossible to treat a martyr. Her medicine relies on the patient wishing to be saved, but stubborn idealism is fatalistic. Beatrix gazes out towards the blue Ionian Sea.

Queenie settles with the landlady.

They go down to a wharfside cafe for supper.

—I received the postcard and I did tell Etama, but she wanted to go home. She gave me this note from Arachne which I cannot read.

—The spider is in London! About-turn for me, for me alone.

—Alice is always all right, and now she is Angel. I remember her once carrying rocks in her pockets all the way up our Mountain of Moon Mares, thinking they were precious gems. She wasn't even high.

—The more I must know her.

—Now we are here.

—Queenie we should tell you the tale of the follower.

—Oh yes, our paranoia!

—Beatrix has your money, we sold him the bus. The Rites of Passage.

—He is a Dutch journalist.

—A trouble-shooter.

—He recognised the numberplates.

—It was a van suspected of gun-running. We don't know to this day whether the secret compartment in the floor was an empty niche.

—Or full of rifles.

—He had been on the trail of these crooks for years. The leader of the pack was a woman.

—A Tasmanian!

—My friends in Italy are interested in nothing but their own success and going to California to make women's movies. Dreamers…

—Zorro, you are a dreamer yourself.

—But my dreams have been dealt a heavy blow, things change. I will have to go to Lebanon, or Israel.

—Can you have a side in that struggle? Are you Jewish?

—People suffer. My mother is Sephardim. I don't care where but I must work eighteen hours a day, perhaps on a kibbutz, or perhaps for Palestinian refugees, and think. I must think while my back aches and my stomach rumbles. A refugee in a refugee camp. A pilgrim in the promised land, who knows?

—The Israeli Army diet might help you, but you are suffering already.

—I don't care for my own health.

—We do.

—I read in *Bild Am Sonntag* of a bomb at the Munich *bierfest* killing twelve and injuring two hundred and eleven and right-wing terrorists are pleased to claim the responsibility. And last month, this woman who is proud of the eighty-four corpses at Bologna Railway Station, she says 'We are against the Reds…and we will strike again'.

—Greta Greta Greta, don't get so depressed.

—Your quest for this Australian fool is stupid.

—It is my karma.

—How do you know?

—I know, I think. At this rate it will take me everywhere until I find…

—It seems here in Corfu we must part ways.

—Beatrix, what are you going to do?

—Would you like to come to India with me, Queenie? And from there to Australia?

—I will tell you of my romance, with Dimitrios, in Athens. Always we made love outside in the ruins of temples, and now I have a baby growing.

—We can be up on the mountain by summer.

—India. Bon.

—I am going back to Germany.

—Me, London, and Beatrix, give me every detail about this Alice Farr.

—And I, to Israel.

—Keep in touch.

The five women, like gypsies who travel the world without much money, have no place of their own by choice, always exiles, having started as aliens in their own families. They walk up the hill in the dusk, passing dark-eyed youngsters playing soccer in the narrow streets. They are kin through knowing and trusting one another and parting is small pain for all follow destinies of their own which, like separate threads, braid together for a while then separate.

34

WHAT WAS the life of this Hungarian Jewish female psychiatrist before 1950? A few years in Vienna as a brilliant young student, flying through Medicine then up to the arched black eyebrows into her speciality, fascinating documents and theories—the science of the human mind. Suddenly, Nazism. Everything destroyed. A destitute journey to the United States of America, treated as sub-human, having to lie, cheat, betray, hide and starve. Months on Ellis Island as a refugee, being no more than a woman with the worries of food and clean clothes. The war years at a Kentucky clinic. Eventually, through hard work, becoming in the fifties what she was, a talented therapist. In the sixties being thought greater than she was. By the seventies, her practice was almost exclusively famous, artistic women. Those disgusted with Otto Rank and the neo-Freudians finally reposed with Harriet Mendelsohn. White-haired with no grey in those eyebrows, finally, in nineteen eighty, Harriet had lowered her sights and become the most superb, peace-giving listener in New York, metropolis of the Western world, with no pretension to analysis.

Preservation of her sense of wonder, Harriet felt, was worth many times the value of a world-renowned name. Besides, she had as much work as she could manage in her seventy-fourth year.

Nisaba Diana Kirby was a patient, and Nisaba was a friend. Friendship, if theory were ever to be peeled back, is, fundamentally, Harriet Mendelsohn's psychiatric style. Love, marriage, war, famine, civilisations may rise and fall, but friendship was, is and will be, like the water of mountain springs, a curious marvel of life. Successful women came to her, and friendship was as complex as all the people one knew, as complex as the acrostic of time and place.

Harriet's tortoiseshell cat, Anya, has a space on her desk, another on the heavy pile carpet where a square of sun falls, another in the earth of the pot of the rubber tree and sometimes she would occupy the third comfortable armchair, all within eye contact of the venerable psychiatrist. Harriet's habit is to gaze at her cat as she listens. Who knows whether astute feline insights are conveyed by subtle body movements giving the therapist wisdom as old as ancient Egypt?

Anya always stays out of Nisaba's sight when she is there. All three silently conspire to forget the presence of the puss, because, Harriet suspects, Nisaba has an eerie effect upon animals, and they on her. The leaves of the Chinese maple outside the window detach themselves now and then to rock-a-bye down to the ground.

Harriet is possessed of a fine collection of ashtrays. Her sole preparation for each patient consists of choosing an ashtray for her otherwise bare desk, and its placement. Sometimes there are flowers in a vase.

Now, a crystal ashtray, sprays of dried honesty and pampas grass in a tall glass jug and Harriet in a woven peasant skirt and raw cotton top tied about her slim hips with a strip of Navaho webbing from New Mexico.

Nisaba nervously pokes her cigarette into a tar-catcher.

—Anything particular, babushka?

—Dreams, crises, the lot, my dear Harriet, the full complement. Dramas and dreams, and I'm being assaulted by others' spirits. Or their spirits are being assaulted and I must needs know about it. Blah.

—Let us start with a dream. Harriet smokes long, thin, brown cigarillos in shallow puffs, like a pipe.

—Dishes, Harriet, dishes, recurring and recurring. I am washing up after a particularly murky feast, judging by the remains on the plates. Yet I am not me, I am someone who washes dishes every day, efficiently. Juanita does all that, not I. Anyway, I do in the dream. I am getting to the end of the pile and the nightmare starts. I pick up some dishes I know I've done, and they're still dirty. I redo them. Go back to the original ones, and continue, to find after a while the others are not only not clean but worse. The dream starts quite relaxed but soon I am frantic. I wash and I wash. There is no multiplication of the plates, the same ones simply don't clean. I don't question that it's my duty to finish the job. It is unsolvable. I go mad. It's godawful, Harriet.

—Dramas? The cigarillo burns undisturbed in the ashtray and the straight hair of smoke becomes curly several feet above the desk in the still room.

—I really must leave Armand. Who am I? Why am I here? There is the dreadful pressure to keep working, painting the very marrow out of my bone. Each is a discovery, a mystery, I cannot repeat myself to eternity. Three grown men. I keep three grown men. Armand, I'm sure, believes he eats apples from the Garden of Eden. Manuel and Dominic, my darling twins, are nearly thirty. Is that my sickness, Harriet, I can't let go of my sons? I adore them. They could use my back as a carpet and I would be grateful.

—Whose spirits are attacking yours? Harriet kills the slow incineration of Virginia tobacco, the wispy lines disappear from the air.

—The young women. Horsewomen of the Apocalypse. My two nieces and Juanita's daughter, Xaviera. All equally inspire me with a sense of combustion. Cerridwen, little drug-taking hermit in Ireland, with slow and gentle ways, she writes. She asks me for something. She says there is no-one else who can be her mentor. I'm nobody's mentor, Harriet, I can't even keep myself on track. Anything I say I know will extinguish her constant candle flame, yet it seems to be flickering in a dark night in the valley of squinting windows.

—Are you still afraid of fire?

—I am neurotic about fire in New York City, Harriet. I fill all my ashtrays with water. I nearly have a heart attack when one of those red trucks goes screaming past with maniacs in uniform hanging off the corners. Imagine if fire took hold in this city, Harriet!

—Does this have anything to do with your sense of attack, of combustion? The girls?

—In my opinion we've had pestilence, famine and flood. We're waiting on fire, Harriet, and it is upon us. Flames on all levels of awareness. The insidious invisible burn of radiation has already happened, and will continue.

Anya hops from the pot-plant to the armchair behind Nisaba's.

—Michael's youngest, Iona, is as bright as a button, yet something of a two-year-old. Laughs at everything like a toddler gurgling. And yet she has an amazing melancholy, a sadness, Harriet. Stares through you when something is a deliberate joke. I think she wanted to change me.

Harriet is not her guru, not her teacher, but her listening through the reams of trivia the fortnight Nisaba is in New York to see her, helps Nisaba uncover the swami in herself. The last hurdle of existentialism, she figures, is the monstrosity of living towards no final resolution, which is the only alternative to immolation in the greatest fire. The veils of surrealism and absurdity she embraced in youth to accommodate her secret earnestness now split into two, nihilism and holiness. Choosing holiness forbids so much. Confused by high-mindedness, sometimes she is driven to pour whole bottles of expensive red wine down the sink. Packets of cigarettes she would throw away, only, on her next walk in Gomorrah, N.Y., freshened by a breeze of careless nihilism or humour, to buy another and smoke ten end to end. She has read the complete works of Carl Gustav Jung and Helen Blavatsky and Douglas Baker, whom she had met in person some years before. The surreal, the shifting patterns of veil upon veil of illusion which informed her painting of mysteries, now teases her with visions on the street. Her art alone could heal the crack in her sanity, yet it is with utmost difficulty that she finds the proper paints, or linseed oil. She worries about money to the exclusion of all else for a couple of days, then spends with abandon.

Harriet Mendelsohn, with her long, yellowing fingertips silently tapping each other and studied gentleness in her eyes, watches the cat and confesses that she, too, loves Armand.

It is the sock in the jaw that Nisaba needed. The jealousy that woman must have felt over the years while she patiently let Nisaba's madness flow over her now finally shocks Nisaba into sanity.

Nisaba walks to Weisers' Book Store to browse and study the advertisements for meditation classes. Secretly she would go along, secret from Armand and secret from Harriet. Just watching the breath at the end of your nose must be about as close as you can get to basics.

She gazes at the glass figurines in a store window in Fifth Avenue, crystal pigs and dragons, fish and horses, wolves, the nagual…the breakability, the line, the light behind them. The light behind, through and within, the achievement she has tried all her life to do with paint, simple in another medium. She buys postcards of the figurines and dashes off a line to Cerridwen.

—The light behind. Love Aunt N.

—The light within, she writes to Iona.

—The light through, Armand, I achieved that, didn't I? H.M. loves you. I'm fine. Nisi-Nike.

It doesn't matter whether they understand her. The cryptic is the riddle and making logical sense of anything is a great exercise in hypocrisy as it is all a riddle anyway. She continues gazing at the animals of glass. The nagual that disappears through walls as it is seen, large for a wild dog, a foreign dog in Mexico, whose biggest native canine is the chihuahua, is a part of the lore. She is one of the few white or Anglo-saxon women to see it, yet the Indians live with it daily, live with the sight of it and the riddle of it. They cope with it to excellent advantage, in Nisaba's opinion. Yet the godawful whites in their statutes in the honoured age of Humanism declared having an animal spirit accompanying one was proof of witchcraft. What was it called? A 'familiar'? If the worthy citizens of a town could give evidence that the woman had a pet answering only to herself then she was evil. The conclusion is wrong, oh god, so wrong, while the fact is true. They could prove many a woman a witch with that one. Especially black cats like those of Cerridwen. Iona's uncanny, naive ability to inspire trust in creatures, and, of course, Xaviera, who has them at her command. She tried to curtail animal imagery in her painting because they began to have anthropomorphic faces and this was logically wrong and strangely spooky. If painting were glass-blowing she could break her creations. The shattering would be mere violence and noise. The fight within the self would go on. The 'familiar' would be torn from limb to limb, warts would be gouged out from the roots and all magic, healing plants burnt in a bombfire like books.

A fire truck screams down Fifth Avenue, covered in Keystone cops and scattering pedestrians and Nisaba feels no urgent fear in her breath. There are more fearsome fires than that which could consume New York City. The mad thing is the worst of practices will go on in Manhattan and no fire will take it. Nothing could be so logical. Best get back to Mexico.

Waiting outside the Boxhill station, sipping a scorching cappuccino from the pizza shop, Iona watches the man in his red tea-towel apron swish flat cigarette butts out the door with a broom.

—Have they no notion of Lesbia's pain, "a skirmish in the whole tremendous conflict between body and soul"?

Lesbia Harford's slim volume of poetry under the dash, the ease of rhyme impresses her, and forces her to admit the label 'poet' is not hers…

'I have a sister whom God gave to me
He formed her out of trouble and the mists of the sea.
Like Aphrodite she came to me full-grown,
Oh, I am blest forever with a sister of my own.'

A resurgence of grief at the finality of death, the loss of it, and then the conjecture of belief alone to comfort. Belief and interpretation. She was playing Gin Rummy with her brother, Terry, when she first felt the grief of her sister's drowning. Veronica gone. They could not even find her body in the treacherous sea of Bass Strait. An absence like a clean rectangle on the wall where a picture had hung for a century, a palpable absence, loss. She felt nauseous and her enjoyment of the game evaporated. Terry and her mother there beside the fire, and deformed Nola in her wheelchair, Iona, at the age of seven felt alone with her personal loss. Yet had Vronnie lived she would have been trouble…

The fresh darkness outside the cab is disturbed by a presence, a man in a well-cut woollen suit opening the passenger's door. The intrusion of the male, the seducer, a man with whom it is possible to make love, is strangely archetypal—possessor of the teeny seed to penetrate her tiny egg. He wants to go all the way to Williamstown.

They discuss theories of the origin of the universe. The Solid State hypothesis, wherein galaxies recede from one another and eventually topple over the edge. The Big Bang idea supported by the evidence of radio telescopes which detect a constant chatter of cosmic static. The expanding universe, exploding forever, in which, inexorably, all the lights of the sky will go out.

—The Oscillating Universe differs from the Big Bang theory as to how much matter there actually is. In any case, this Milky Way of ours is condemned some 50 to 100 million years hence to die of either ice or fire.

He is so smug I could snip his balls off.

—You're dispassionate, aren't you?

—We should permit nature to reveal the truth to us. The next few decades will determine the fate of the universe.

—Through your experiments?

He nods.

Iona feels immobilised between two tight sheets in her brain. What is it that makes him so sure that observation will reveal the nature and fate of the universe? That human beings possess such superb intellectual capabilities of which computers are such a grand expression? So anthropocentric! Yet another part of her is singing, hold me, you prick, just hold me.

—How can you be so convinced that our cosmology is so very different from the Greeks? You deify man, like they did.

—No gods. Just an enormous engine, physical laws…

—What about the nature and fate of hearts and bodies—souls—in the next measly little decade?

—Cosmology is an experimental science, no longer up to the theologians.

But you don't reckon on the daughters of Demeter, who have slid down the snakes to Diabolus, in the earth, climbed the dizzy ladders to Christos, in the air, all full of vertigo and virginal, who have danced together to death in the primitive sea. And the steel phallus, named Apollo, has struck the moon. Rockets and bombs of nuclear fission all cocks, stealing, striking, destroying and trying to penetrate and, now, to co-opt all meaning.

Iona sighs to herself, and you here, in my warm cab, ejaculating words into my intelligence, with your penis hidden behind neatly pressed trousers.

The chemistry of lust, which could turn to love, which could induce Iona to take on a husband and produce a family of her own, is electric in the taxi. His hands are long and narrow and the nails are better manicured than her own.

She, however, refuses his invitation to come in for a coffee.

35

LAWFULLY THEY raped the forests, lawfully they dammed the creeks, flattened the homes of satin bird and possum, beetle and tree snake. With bulldozers they dragged long logs through the native flora and brought erosion. Breast-round hills they bared to the beating sun. Parched and loose earth, pitted and furrowed, emptied by the root-tearing sheep. One law obeyed, another lore desecrated. The earth spirit groans and kooris feel it in the stomach. Along the east coast and in the highlands in from there, the indigenous people seem long forgotten, seeking solace in booze and bashing; this land is bought and sold, exchanged from name to name legally. If his name is on the paper he can do anything he likes, and he likes profit best of all. The hardwoods have all but gone, lantana and gympie gympie rush in, bringing with them the lawyer vine with its fishhook fronds. The cow cockies peck at their patches of scrub like chooks doing their best. It is a trick to think in detail, and a comfort doing something. The white idiot is confused unless he is getting more than he has had. Play the game of detail, sign a cheque, sign a loan, the edge is off the hunger. Just keep three steps away from real desperation. Don't hanker for a village life.

Excuse me, the women said to the foliage, as they shouldered their way into the land which on paper was theirs. Several pythons made their homes near foodbins and kept away the rats. It seemed serene. A floating, rootless neighbourhood of tarps and fire rings, dull for some, relaxing for others, disturbing for a few. A web of relationships settled on the acres where the dreams of a Scottish couple, grandparents of Amos, were hard and fruitless. The pastures return to scrub.

It is not possible to be off the map. There is always the town, the electronic media, the news, and the other way of knowing things, their own grapevine of gossip. Along with the abundant creativity, music, craft and children, hatreds run strong. Politics depress and excite. Those with the tongue-gift wielding power, getting followers, others resenting it, the fight often turns inwards.

—Such a fight breaks out after Amos bombed the dwelling, after the Smith Family had given synthetic blankets and bedding, at a meeting to discuss it all. There are many there. The strategy of the collective is argument. It is daytime. Twisted corrugated iron and blackened beams litter the ugly devastation of the fruit and flowering trees planted by the Gaels. Stinging nettles regrow in an instant. The burning of the house has symbolic importance. The flames, some women claim, came out of themselves.

—We live worse than the boongs, the policeman said.

—We would be dead if we couldn't laugh.

—At what? At ourselves?

—Why not?

—That is too hard.

—Oona is beating out barrels to make herself into Ned Kelly. What a farce!

—I have his letter which was printed in *The Argos,* the newspaper in Victoria, in 1880.

—You have his letter and his suit.

—Why not?

—He was a man.

—He was all right.

—I feel the need for retribution building in my bones.

—Let's get 'em.

—Sheila is an archer.

—Every cell in my brain is burning with the electricity of revenge. I want it. Judgment is mine.

—I say we use legal channels. Get him an arson conviction!

—Us, use the cops! The system! That is disgusting.

—Fuck the world.

—In this instance we can avenge through it.

—Fuck the world.

—Are you going to lie down and take it like a girl?

—That is ageist.

—Let's be imaginative.

—Sheila takes her bow and arrows…

—We find them down at the lagoon, round a fire, drinking beer…

—The moment their dog barks we start an ululation. It doesn't matter how long we keep it up…

—We circle them, ululating eerily.

—We spook them.

—What century are you living in?

—You will just get us more trouble.

—That's all right.

—Tall paperbarks surround the billabong. Everything is in silhouette.

—Sheila hides, we all hide, Sheila lifts her bow, and takes out their lamp with one accurate arrow.

—It's frightening.

—It's ridiculous.

—We really confuse them.

—The frogs are croaking in the swamp.

—Mosquitoes are buzzing around ears.

—They know who it is. We move fast.

—Why are we doing this?

—To steal their rifles of course.

—Why?

—To rob a bank in Lithgow.

—Are you crazy?

—Yes, but very clever.

—We take their landrover as well.

—Yes, but only to dump it in a creek.

—So we rob a bank in Lithgow, then have a fine eight years in clink.

—We're not caught.

—We do it well.

—Early, soon after opening, a smoke bomb explodes. The smoke clears and there I am, Ned Kelly, ghostlike, using an Irish accent I say everything…

—Give her the speech, Oona.

—'If I get justice I will cry a go. Fitzpatrick knew the weight of one of these fists only too well as it run up against him once in Benalla and cost me two pound odd as he is very prone to fainting.'

—We are as cool as the proverbial cucumber.

—Oh yeah, it's a fantasy.

—How do you get into the bank dressed like that?

—Avenging angels find a way.

—We only use Ned Kelly's hat.

—I dress up as a nurse and I wheel her in in a wheelchair. Under a blanket over her knees is everything she needs. She pops the helmet on during the smoke bomb. Stands dressed in a long coat. And holds the rifle at her hip.

—'I said I did not blame the troopers for doing honest duty but I could not suffer them blowing me to pieces in my own land…'

—Great!

—While Jay Jay's saying all this, they, the clerks and clients, are surprised and intrigued. It's real theatre. We get behind the tills and into the strong room and collect only cash money.

—'They knew Fitzpatrick wronged us and why not make it public and him but no they would rather riddle poor creoles.'

—How long is this speech going to take?

—A few minutes.

—Listen to this bit: 'I think the public will soon find the police are only in the road of good men and obtaining money under false pretenses.'

—We will get away with it. Everybody loves Ned Kelly.

—Because he is safely dead.

—It is so crazy it's got to work.

—I think you are really stupid to even think about it. I was about to say…

—You would tell on us. But you can't because it's politically unsound and you would be branded a traitor.

—If you are really going to go through with this, I am packing death right here.

—It's… Fuck the world!

—Who's got the courage?

—Who's got the cool?

—Fuck the world, we can do it.

—The vault is unlocked, the tellers have their mouths hanging open and we're as fit as deer. We leap over the counter and out the door and into the ladies' loo across the park. While Jay Jay finishes Ned, totally ignoring us, just concerned with delivering the words, the smoke bomb and holding the rifle.

—In another puff of smoke, she is gone.

—The rifles…

—The rifles we put back in the four-wheel drive in the creek, right? Everyone who's handled them has worn gloves, right?

—I don't want to hear any more of this.

—If it goes farther than this meeting, someone might find an arrow in her thigh.

—I am registering my objection, my absolute rejection of the idea. I think it's greedy and stupid.

—That's your right, but my threat holds good. No gossip on this one.

A mist crawls up through the valley. The scene of the meeting by the burnt-out house dissolves into silent whiteness. Each must pick her own way through it to her own camp. The slow progress is time for contemplation on their place in the scheme of things and how far each individual is prepared to stick out her neck. No-one is heard talking. The excess of words and colour is followed by thought in the monochrome fog. Those who do the deed might not be those who imagined the scenario.

Arachne arrived in London and went to Fleet Street to visit the ANZ bank. There, for her, were letters and money. One, from Etama, written months before, gave her useful addresses in England. A few by her mother ramblingly told of the wasting sickness of Grandma in morbid detail. No one seemed to know she had been in jail.

—It's really incredible, she told the bank clerk. She sat on his desk and ruminated on how unbelievable the whole world was.

And here I am, talking to you as if I have just had a dream and I'm telling you about it. Now before I go, just explain to me how I get to these places.

The clerk made a couple of phone calls to Australia, which Arachne willingly paid for, and satisfied himself that she was Alice Farr and had a perfect right to the substantial account and to the new name, Angel Farr. He doodled out some bus and Underground routes with a kind of boastful pleasure.

Henceforth, Arachne was lost only once in London.

From the list of Etama's addresses, she found a place to live. One day, Wendy from the bush came. They sat on her bed and described to each other the lemon scent of a eucalypt near the hut, the sound of wind in 'big bad banksia trees', the beaches, Sydney, the women that they knew, wanderlust and Wendy quite forgot to ask whether the rumour of her incarceration was true.

Sophie, not quite as big as Mama Cass, belts out the blues on her tenor sax in a London dive surrounded by the smoky faces of jazz enthusiasts, casually hooks the saxophone on its stand, flicks her long soft hair over one eye, curls her mouth around the mike and lets her voice fill the basement with soul. Wendy and Arachne watch. She joins them at the end of the bracket. Something about this friendly Australian reminds her of the French-Canadian whom she left standing at the end of a dead-end street in Hackney. Because her attitudes have really changed, because she is now sadly in need of security herself, because the blues are summed up in these sea-grey eyes, she begs to go home with her.

Soon she is fully resident in the Albion Road squat, grasping morning coffee mugs with both hands and beginning a new love. This one is a little deeper, a little wider, less selfish and more reckless. They are snug in their room as London outside grows bleak and dark. Neither being limited by lack of money or troublesome parents, they look at the atlas as if the world were theirs.

Like Laurel and Hardy in second-hand fur coats, with bundles of luggage about their feet in the shape of musical instruments, they are at Gatwick, with tickets to Lima. Wispy snow floats down outside the plate glass windows.

Great journeys start with simple exits.

The gumtrees in her garden full of the squabbling of crows and magpies, the magpies losing, Ursula cannot say her lawn is a bowling green. The garage has junk in it, and beneath the eaves cobwebs restlessly swing. Inside, the two-bedroom bungalow is neat. Slipping out the back door, with her latchkey in her handbag, her good felt hat pulled down Greta Garbo style, Ursula has no notion of the outcome. Flush, controlled by his chain, tied to his tea chest kennel, is confused. He threatens to knock over his water in pique. Busy lace-ups on the way to the bus-stop, thirty denier stockings and raincoat against the unpredictable weather, the mind inside is feverish with intent.

A bus-train-tram-bus trip she has made before.

Winifred, looking at one fictional birthmark on the faded page of *McClures* could not expect to find another staring at the name-plate on her door.

The questions of identity and individuality halt Ursula in her steps. Ironically the self who gives can spread about her misery, the smothered ego grasping for sustenance transforms into the self who takes. A self cloaked and unknown exhibiting a need to take, for no other reason than her own gratification, is something she has not been for forty years.

She taps with her knuckles.

—Come in.

Ursula carefully grabs the handle, gently pushes in and peeps into the office. Winifred looks up.

—Well, come in if you want to see me, and don't if you don't. Winifred runs her freckly hands through her ginger and grey curls, then leans on her elbow and prepares to listen.

Ursula stares at her.

—My good woman, please make up your mind.

—Excuse me, I'm sorry. I hoped to be recognised.

She quietly pulls the door closed and scurries off along the corridor. She has seen and done enough. Winifred is someone else, the same person and someone else. To bother to know the someone else would eventually lead to the same person who is already fully known and best kept in the time capsule of memory. Ursula is dolefully satisfied with her journey. She does not want to destroy Winnie's own capsule with the ghastly impression of her face. She could not be that selfish.

Flush is howling. The crows are crying along the rooftree. There are no magpies warbling within earshot.

—Mimbo!

36

'YOU ARE THE Hermetic force—the Messenger—the karmic trickster—and you will have to be as swift as your horse...you will move like the grey wolf perhaps in oblique patterns separating out, alerting those who recognise you that the long trek must begin... I would prefer to consider us as conspiratorii—those who breathe together—The dominion is only over self but a unity exists beyond the individual... You stood alone and gave meaning to it, and it necessitated an acute awareness of solitude so profound that few people even begin to apprehend. The true priestesses never give or take but rather they provide unchangingly—in harmony with the fire above and the water below.'

Helen's letter goes on to explain the Fibonnacci sequence that attempts to describe the proportion of the spiralling Phi and Pi found in all aspects of nature, in plant and flower shapes, in butterfly patterns, the factors and sums of the musical octaves and the guiding principle of the pyramid.

The letter is in response to one Iona wrote after her trip to the bush describing her experiences of the Mountain of Moon Mares, where butterflies followed her, the gelding, Misty, responded to her gentlest pressure and the place seemed to disappear once she was back on Bells Line of Road.

'The messenger is ultimately nothing less than the very process of change, and the story-teller gives the pattern of movement backwards, so it is possible to recapture what has been lost.'

Near the signature is the date and time of her arrival at Melbourne, Pan Am. Iona sits in the passenger seat of GAY 17, re-reading snatches, sharing one of Dennis' joints. He was easily convinced to take her to Tullamarine at their shift changeover. Then he will speed about his taxi-day with a fare from the airport at the head of the list. Dennis is an unemployable mathematician, and they argue merrily as the queue of cabs in front shortens.

What is visually and aesthetically obvious to Iona is logically imprecise to Dennis. While the formula is the same, its implications, for each, are irreconcilable.

Iona feels more comfortable with Dennis and their intellectual stalemate than the exalted expectations of Helen soon to be met outside Customs.

Five international jumbo jets arrive within two hours: from Athens, from Singapore, from Tokyo, from London and from Los Angeles. The build-up of welcoming crowds is enormous.

Mary had received Etama's telegram and Ellen had planned a theatre of reception. Each dressed as a clown. Chris juggles and Dawn contorts in yoga postures. Louise has sweets. Erica is a housewife clown with rolls of toilet paper and a mop. The women carry on in front of the multi-cultured Australians, to the delight of some Greeks and their children, the Asians, poms and ockers.

Etama attracts the suspicion of the Customs officials and they search all her baggage and question her movements. Her impatience makes her angry and uncooperative. She can hear her friends and when the doors open she catches glimpses of them over the sea of black-haireds.

Helen slips through Customs with ease. The dancing, clowning, musical women do not recognise her, though she knows them. She stands transfixed by the Hertz desk. Frowning. She has seen them all before, in her dreams and nightmares. The reality is different in one salient factor, Iona is absent. In one of her dreams Iona circles this group on a monocycle.

Etama flies through the swinging doors, hurling her bags in all directions. The theatre dissolves into the hugging and kissing of lesbians at travel terminals.

Helen is paralysed, cemented to the spot. The display heightens the agony of the past eight months.

The airport is a familiar place to Iona. She has wandered many times about the shiny spaces indulging vicariously in the atmosphere of constant transience, with cardboard cups of coffee, feeling like a worker, the cleaner or the cafe attendant. Too much familiarity makes her generalise the crowds and become vague and daydreamy. It is an effort to recall Helen's features. She has forgotten it's Etama's arrival time also.

Iona sees Mary ferrying the Etama-welcomers towards the doors. And panics. She passes in front of Helen, calling.

—Hey, wait. Where are you going?

—Hi, Iona. Breakfast is arranged back at Mary's.

—Right, okay. You don't know Helen, but she must be here somewhere.

—Bring her. It'll be an all-day party, probably.

—Okay, see you.

To get away from the messianic mission Helen puts on her, to dismiss from her heart fake romance, to stop feeling phoney, Iona goes into the toilets, to sit down and to give way to inexplicable tears.

Helen follows her.

Helen does not smell good, the sweat of a long plane journey on the dreadful perfume she thinks she needs to wear. The perspiration of tension is the scent of fear.

—Welcome to my home town, Iona sounds pathetic.

—You weren't there. The others danced and horsed about. They don't know me.

—Give it a go, Helen.

—Listen…, Helen begins to shudder. The saliva in her mouth whips itself into a foam. Her eyes roll back into her skull. Iona reacts as if her friend is having a fit. She straightens her shoulders and slaps her hard across the cheek. Helen screams and blathers. She cowers into the basins, throwing petrified looks at Iona, trying to beat off an invisible demon.

—What's wrong?

—You're a monster. I see about you a hideous flying creature.

Iona tries to lift her. The big, muscular body shakes her off with the strength of a weakling.

—You hate me.

I'm… I don't. I care about you. Calm down.

—You don't know, do you?

—Okay, I'm ignorant.

—Women who don't know their own power are worse than dangerous.

—Sure, Helen, you know all these things. But you've got to get it together. Right now, let's be practical.

Helen nods like a toddler who knows that nodding is preferable to adults than screaming.

—I'm more afraid of your power than anybody I know is of mine.

—You don't know you've got it. You can reduce me to a screaming heap.

—I don't want power, Helen. I don't want power over anyone.

—You have got it. Didn't you see what happened then? Great black wings were beating at me. Your wings.

—No, you're freaking out because of your own sight. I'm helpless.

Iona is aware of other ladies, using the water taps and mirrors and emerging from the cubicles. She is embarrassed. Helen is a giant baby needing a bath.

—Come on, let's get you into the shower.

—I don't want a shower.

—I do love you, Helen, but I'm only on the verge of knowing what love is. Your teaching, I'm afraid, only teaches me to love myself.

Helen pulls on a brightly-coloured parka. There has been a cleansing thunderstorm. Now the Melbourne weather is crisp and sunny. Helen shivers. The taxi ride is tense.

At Rose's, an antagonism sets up between the Queenslander and the American. Iona has to ask politely if Helen can have a shower. Helen wants to go.

—Let me go to a motel. She screeches.

—No, you're our guest.

Iona must handle Helen as if she were shattered glass, with sharp splinters. She cannot bear it. Rose makes it no easier.

—First, before you go to your motel, please come to Mary's, meet my friends, just relax.

On the way over to Mary's new house, a rented, single-fronted terrace in Carlton, Helen tells Iona of her stigmata in the Nevada desert, and shows her the spots of blood on her handbag. Fire sirens whinny in the air and the bells on the shiny red engine ring out, signalling disaster, but Iona does not notice. She must get Helen off her hands.

A dark narrow corridor leads past the bedrooms to a small living room, beyond which is the kitchen. Outside is the bathroom and toilet. The lounge is crowded with the clowns from the airport and half-eaten quiche, dips and corn chips.

Iona introduces Helen with pride, and welcomes the glass of champagne put in her hand by Louise. She drinks, chats, worries, and thinks she must escape.

—I have been driving all night. I must go home and get some sleep.

Mary and Etama agree to look after Helen.

The freedom walking along the disused railway to North Fitzroy is temporary but delicious. Iona tastes it on her tongue in the incomprehensible need to laugh. Contributing to the laugh is the post-storm sky dotted with woolly cumulus cantering in front of the wind. They are an atmospheric trigger, an abreaction of the emotions to an earlier time when she adored her sports teacher and won her regard by scoring winning goals for the team. Her body is her friend, its light coordination. Balancing on the rail, she imagines she is a funambulist. Problems, something to think about in 'pine fresh' Gay 17. The comforting knowledge of having to do a job is a respite from personal duties.

Kate spent a day and a half making Winifred a pair of silky pyjamas, though for the life of her she couldn't think why. A homecoming present? For the love of sewing? It was a school play in Hobart once, an obscure thing, in which she played Klotho. It required her to chant a couple of lines with two other girls. Since, she has played Cassandra who prophesied the destruction of Troy and why. Medea and Lady Macbeth with blood on her hands. But none seemed to have the nice meanness, the homely resentment of Klotho, the threader, the unsung piece-worker of Greek tragedy. Bitter, oh so bitter at not winning the lead role, then. Then, in the soft, desperate ambitions of youth anything, no everything, dented her vulnerability. A long time ago, way way down, at the bottom of many ladders. Anyway, shot-silk PJs, beautifully ironed, await Winifred in dark brown tissue paper on the settee.

Ginger-and-salt-haired Winnie, red in the face, pants at the top of the stairs, dressed like a prison officer in civvies. Poor Winnie, all brains and no sense, no common and garden sense.

—You didn't have to hurry, Win.

—Don't mind. Do it all the time. Run the stairs. Fifty next month. Nice of you to call, Kate.

—Well let's settle down with a drink. Scotch?

—No ice, chilled water.

—Fifty, yes, well I'm a little further down the track than that.

—Look at us, and you'd think I was the senior. Half a century, more than half a life, and only in love once. Oh, I'm a damn fool. Been reading these new women writers in London, and you know, I should have bunked in with a woman when I had the chance.

—You had the chance?

—Perhaps it isn't too late. Though not quite sure how to go about it.

—In love once… Kate muses. Something inside feels battered and bruised, used.

—Michael. Michael fitted so nicely into my grand notions of romantic, ideal love. Beatrice, you know. Ah, Dante, Spenser, the infinite sadness of the lost love, something to keep an academic happily at her desk until retirement. Perfect.

—Michael who? Kate really doesn't want to listen. There is a reason why sewing ladies keep in the background. The garment is now a rather embarrassing present.

—Flynn. Michael Flynn. For years I held onto him. In a fist. Suppose I squeezed him dry. At the time it was my *grande affaire,* an older man, a charmer, an adventurer. A liar.

—You've never mentioned his name before. Kate feels unaccountably angry.

—Same birthdate, we had. Though he was twenty-five years older. Born 1905. He left his wife and children for me.

—How many were there?

—About four or five. The youngest he adored. One, if I recall, was retarded.

—The youngest?

—You mean how old? Oh, I'd say she was born about the time we met and that was my first year here in Melbourne, now she would be thirty-three. The wife bashed him. Winifred laughs. She was stronger, physically, I believe. It lasted many years. We would travel about together. Sometimes I'd get letters, sometimes he was there on my doorstep. After a while it suited me that way. I had my career. Never wife material, never desired to give birth myself. I haven't heard from him for years, but I still expect a letter or a visit from a very old man.

Winifred is comfy on the settee, complacent with her dreams of old. Her elbow leans into the brown tissue treating the parcel as a cushion. Her legs in synthetic stretch slacks are apart.

Kate is furious, almost to the point of tears; tears shed in the past listening to Iona and tears like those she cried for herself when she missed out on the part and had to settle for Klotho, one of a chorus. Winifred has a dead love in a safe, like a miser's diamonds.

—Your life is more perverse than Quentin's, Winifred. Even though he suffers the threat of venereal disease all the time, his life is healthier.

—What on earth do you mean?

—It's disgusting calling a myth love, yet your kind does it all the time.

Kate escapes into her kitchen, leaving Winnie mildly bemused. Arranging the water-biscuits and olives, she weighs her anger against its possible causes. Bending into the fridge for another cheese, a blue vein, she realises the only possible origin is her emotion. It is still alive. Her tenderness towards Iona was triggered by her fatherlessness; but it was also her lack of self-sorrow, the matter of fact way she had of recounting the most difficult upbringing, having to be wise from the age of seven. Precocious little brat.

—Is love so cheap it can bought like pearls? Kate is rhetorical as she emerges with two plates of antipasto. I loved her without regard for gender. Now you've made me mushy and sentimental, a side I never showed her. I was a substitute father!

—Pardon? Ta, very tasty. Winifred's features squirm around a cold artichoke heart.

—Didn't you ever consider the wife, the kids? But most especially, didn't you ever encourage him to go and see the one he adored, the youngest?

—Actually, no. I forebade all mention of his family in my presence. He had that terrible Irish facility for being maudlin beyond reason.

—You don't even ask me how I know Michael Flynn is dead.

—Oh, I assumed you meant it metaphorically. Of course he is dead. The myth is dead. My necrophilia is dead. One could say. In the past.

—Life is danced in the dark for the most part. We don't know what we do. I loved that daughter, and only now I realise it was a real, genuine love, nothing mythical about it. I care like hell. Your disregard for her years of hardship and her mother's courage brought it home to me. Half the time I considered it a game. Like her schoolgirl crush on the sports teacher. But for me it was real, because now I could claw your jugular vein out. He was safe, heh? No demands, no interruption to your career. It's not the infidelity I mind. I would be hypocritical if it were that. No, it's more likely the career. It's all in the head and it teaches you nothing of life, in fact, it lies about it.

—I couldn't have the whole family. They are certainly not my responsibility, never were. I chose to be independent. Now, of course, I'm quite wealthy and can do whatever I like, I suppose. Oh dear, what's this I've squashed?

—That? I owe your colleague, Redman, a favour. Perhaps you could take it with you, put it on her desk, mention that it's from Kate McMillan.

A Sunday. Nola, Iona, Mrs Flynn gaze at the Red Bluff across Shire Hall Beach. There are bathing boxes separating the sand from the tea-tree and banksia bush at the base of the cliff. Several show the ravages of time, sea winds and vandals. There was a time when each winter they would get a fresh coat of tough bright paint. In the other direction is the jetty and the yacht club, spiky with the tall masts of keel boats high on wooden stands, corralled for the winter by a high cyclone fence. Standards flutter from the flagpole. Behind them, church bells. Along the shore line a woman walks her dog. Hobby-fishermen put-put out into the Bay.

—Thea tsee thee, Nola cries, banging the arm of her chair.

—Yes, it's the sea. Or rather, Port Phillip Bay. See straight across, that mountain is Mount Macedon, and down over there, the You Yangs, and there, see, there are the Dandenongs, where we've come from.

—Og og. Nola frowns.

—Yes, look at the fluffy dog.

—Pluffee pluppee. Keke…

Their own dog, Kevin, an old smooth-haired part-Kelpie, is off, head down, tail up.

—They won't fight, don't worry.

Mrs Flynn strolls back to the car.

Nola begs to be pushed closer to the edge. Flush and Kevin inspect each other on the sand below. Her mother sets the large wicker basket on the council table and sits down on a matching bench, anchored in a slab of concrete. She watches her daughters, silhouetted against the pale grey sky. Iona looks tall, and slim. But strong. She had lifted Nola into her chair almost easily, whereas she herself now has to brace arms and legs and use a practised swinging action. And yesterday, Iona climbed into the roof of the house, helping the pest-control chap seek the errant possum, like a gymnast. The contrast of Iona's physical and mental prowess with Nola's vegetative state brings to mind Veronica. The selfish sea.

—Iona, she calls, holding up cork screw.

—So soon? Her daughter laughs over her shoulder.

She pulls Nola's brake hard, and leaves her on a flat part of the path. Behaviour, thinks Iona, is one of the few things in life that can be controlled by a code. One doesn't need to compromise oneself with a code, although there are times when sincerity must break through the surface, being of a different essence. Hence one's code should be clearly worked out beforehand to accord with an underlying sense of who you are and what you're about. Chablis and orange juice.

Ursula walks up the hill. Iona recognises her and gestures.

—Hello.

—Iona Flynn!

—Come, meet my mother. This is my sister, Nola.

Ursula's stare at Nola lacks conventional sympathy. She nods.

—Some wine, Mrs Flynn offers her a plastic mug.

—All right.

Ursula is abrupt and shy as Mrs Flynn asks polite questions about the district, such as, where is the best place for a picnic?

—Here is as good as any. It won't rain, the cloud is too high. About four o'clock perhaps.

Iona pulls the cork. The dogs compete with each other as to which is the quicker at sniffing behind and which avoids being sniffed; Nola rocks with enjoyment.

Impertinent and awkward, Ursula interrupts Mrs Flynn's gracious conversation with a direct question to Iona.

—That Doctor Winifred Stevens, tell me about her.

Iona is shocked by a complete change in the atmosphere, her mother. She wasn't that rude, what is it?

—I don't know her, so I'm afraid I can't help.

Frank's station wagon pulls up on the skidding stones. A fresh generation of Flynns scamper up and around the table. There is familial humour and the pleasure of genetic loyalty. Frank is, as always, genial, his wife large, sighing.

Ursula is disgruntled. She leaves her wine and walks off, whistling Flush.

—Bye. Iona is mystified.

While the two Mrs Flynns lay out a cloth and plates and cold chicken, leg ham, tomatoes, lettuce, thermos of soup, Frank wheels Nola, and with Iona and the kids they go off for a walk.

—Does the name Winifred Stevens mean anything to you, Frank? Mum nearly collapsed when her name was mentioned a while ago. Larry! Cut it out, you little devil!

—Is Terry coming down?

—Frank, I asked you a question. Yes, he's saying Mass at eleven, after that. Might be here about one.

—How are things with you? Been getting good fares?

—Not bad. Things for me are too complicated at the moment. Let me take that, she wants you to hold her hand.

Frank's refusal to answer her answers Iona's question. The family is one where emotions are kept under fierce control, otherwise violent passion would have consequences none desires.

Later in the afternoon, lightning forks over the high-rises of Melbourne, beautifully, splitting the iron grey build-up of cloud. Then a water wall blots out all view of the hills. Nola screams with delight, almost stands up as she reaches towards the massive string of sparks as it gets closer. Iona runs. The kids are hurrying up the cliff from their sandcastles, and their mother is yelling 'buckets!' Thunder claps. Iona catches Nola's chair and pulls it backwards against the drag of unresponsive wheels. She fights to unlock the brake, pulled on earlier by Frank. The older Mrs Flynn is white, paralysed, staring. As Iona brings her sister through the rain, she catches the eyes of her mother, and realises the meaning of a lifetime of worry. Terry lifts Nola, leaves the red vinyl seat to get soaked and Iona and her mother both move to fold it up.

—You get in the car, Mum. I'll clear everything.

37

THE RAINFOREST is a garden, and the garden is a jungle. As Lesley glides, embracing the circles of the lost, looking for Buddha, Vanessa grieves and resurrects the dream of her youth to be a farmer. Spots of blood on the white page. Mosquitoes by the lagoon buzz through the halo of meditation to be slapped like gunshot. Argument after argument, like lightning striking, in equinoctial storms. Declare the drought broken in the west, barefoot in the mud and slush, anarchists in search of rightful duty, wet leeches grow fat on the ankle veins. Therese stands, one leg straight, one resting, biting the nail of her little finger, worrying. The trees around Janice wall a finite space she struggles to maintain as a utopia. The battle of underlying disagreements brews as in a cauldron.

Vanessa is impatient to be away from the consequences of an illegal action they all know is done, though none speaks of it. The small town press did not take it up. Banks are robbed often in the State. Still, it is a blot on the conscience of the community. It releases an irresponsibility, an anything-goes. Dope plants multiply. Vanessa is furious. Janice struggles with words to explain to the younger women ideals which seem to them dated. She shows her age. The dreams of her generation are scorned. History runs past her feet like the hard, driving water off the slopes.

Vanessa, whose name is on the deeds of ownership of Moonmare Mountain, goes into town, applies for another loan and goes out along Old Putty Road seeking land of her own. Janice hears about it, and it's the last straw.

Therese bites her nails away.

Janice, a warrior without a war for so many years, feels the pent-up violence peaking to an eruption. Her sanity, as thin as the earth shell over a faultline, crumbles. Words have totally failed her, words will not be spoken. Junkies have taken over the stone hut on the mountain top. There they shoot heroin.

The night it all comes to a head, Vanessa is playing Mah Jong in the hut, and several bottles of white rum are being consumed. Those at the table clicking tiles, building and destroying the wall, seem to the others so bourgeois, so stuck-up and straight. There are two camps in the tiny hut. A storm beats outside.

Through the lightning and the rain and the thunder, Jay Jay rides her mare called Church. The metal sculpture of the headless Ned Kelly hanging on a post near Oona's camp rattles like the ghost of the Green Knight in Gawain. Oona and Trees try to shout sense into her, but she feels betrayed. The night itself exhilarates her mood. She canters off along the slippery track, until sweating and puffed, horse and rider reach the shack.

Though the atmosphere of discord is sliceable, Vanessa jokes while she plays her game, creating hands called Heavenly Paradise and Lily of the Valley, Imperial Jade or Buried Treasure. Four conspirators, it seems they whisper 'Red lantern, the limit and the twittering of sparrows' in a code to mean There is a property at Scone we could get with the collateral of this place. No-one else can go there. We will be happy'. The others feel jeopardised and resentful. Sarcastic jabs and teasings are ignored. They continue clicking tiles and talking Chinese in English with a tranquility which is repressed anger.

Jay Jay kicks open the door. The wind and rain rush in. She has smashed the catch. She vowed to say no words, she says none. It is down to naked antagonism, to frustration with everything. She picks up the side of the table and throws it over, sending two of the players backwards, screaming. Vanessa is immediately pugilistic. Her friends are hurt. The brawl is vicious. Some shout 'stop it', others add fuel to the fire with their own resentment. Vanessa is strong. Janice is agile. They tear each other to pieces and the hut is wrecked.

The community on the land splits in two. Nothing is resolved. Those who want to stay can only pray that Vanessa and her mates will keep up the payments on their new place when or if they get it. Otherwise, the mountain and valley of the moon will disappear like something caught in a time warp.

Janice returns to her nurturing role, wiser and more cynical. She and Trees move to a place on Crown land beyond Oona's camp for peace and quiet, and all the horses are with them. A mob of brumbies picturesque against the distant plains.

The whispered needs of her mother encroach more than the requests of her friends into Iona's lot. Come back to the tradition, revolution destroys too much that is good. Kill then be killed and who has the right to know? Free the plants in pots who have coiled and tangled roots like forgotten wool from unravelled jumpers saved in a bag, let the quiet earth soothe with its moving worms. Helen crumbled in front of her, and she could do nothing, except run away. Etama, the lover, would love her.

No car but a taxi.

In Iona's taxi, at her own expense, is Helen, shivering, terrified of meeting Mrs Flynn and Nola.

—It'll be okay, Helen. It's comfortable at Healesville. If you want privacy, there's the rumpus room out the back. Spring is superb there, new leaves on the English trees, the orchards bursting into bloom.

—The physically disabled undo me, Iona.

—They don't. You undo yourself. They can't do anything to you. I really must keep driving tonight, you know that don't you?

Her mother is weary. The fire is down to the last log. The night is crisp and the brightness of the stars seem to sharpen the chill. Gratefully, Iona chops in the light of a bare globe and comes in with her arms loaded. Helen is tightly seated, still with her parka on. Iona builds up the fire into a hot blaze, hoping to warm the emotional climate as well.

—Mum, Helen looked after me in America, now it is our turn.

—Fine. You can have the boys' room, Helen. There are clean sheets and towel. Relax. A brandy, Iona, before you go?

Helen refuses alcohol but removes her jacket. Both Mrs Flynn and she stare unabashedly at each other. Something has been said.

Iona sees the naked honesty in their looks—their *look,* it is identical. She fears, above all, that her mother will attack Helen as she did Frances. If Mum can get past Helen's social discomfort, she will find her entertaining and helpful. It's just got to happen.

—I'll be back at the weekend.

Her mother is more resigned than ever, and she merely nods goodbye and accepts the kiss on her forehead from her armchair. Helen comes to the verandah.

—I told your mother that we were lovers, Iona.

—Oh, Iona bites her bottom lip hard. How did she take that?

—She said no woman could love you more than she does.

—While I was outside chopping wood?

—Your mother and I have something in common. I will teach her about your karmic path, Iona.

—Just be kind to Nola, Helen. Don't...don't hassle yourself.

I want to escape again; smothered, it's smothering me. What is this bloody love they're talking about? If one were a pet, one could be owned and indulged, but this requires something of me. Christ I've got to think. I don't want Helen to touch me. I want to be exemplary in my mother's eyes and now that is impossible, perhaps it always was. Must get away from this haven of shattered individuals huddling by a fire and Nola snuggled in bed like a monstrous baby and get out into the hard night, serve strangers and hustle a living.

—Got to go, mate. Get well here.

—Without you.

—Please Helen, go inside. Goodnight.

Most of the rest of this night is spent in the South Melbourne depot. The paperwork of a minor accident. Talking with the lads. Driving Don 74 to Dennis's, having a cup of tea with his girlfriend, smelling the milky poo of their baby. Agitated, thinking, hungry, rattled, nervous.

Mary is in love with her new guru and talks of nothing but pooja, bhoots and practices of the queerest nature to achieve nirvana. Her advice to Iona is to take a dozen lemons, cut them in half, seal them in a plastic bucket when she is awake, but when she sleeps leave the bucket open so the lemons can suck the bhoots out of her, and then after thirteen days and nights of this, throw the sealed bucket into the sea, where Grandfather will dispose of the bhoots, which are little spirits that live under fringes and such places.

Smothered, again, I'm choking.

38

YOU ARE LIKE the Olgas, my darling. They are magical. Your muscles, your curves, your breasts, your belly, the angles of your whole shape remind me of the Olgas. The Olgas are beautiful, back views of bums like the mango shapes of arse and top thigh, delicate visualising, in immense conglomerate rock. You can feel that place was sacred from the men of the tribe. The Olgas, Katajuta, meaning many heads, was described as monstrous by the first white men who saw them. Monstrous, get that. Aboriginal men weren't allowed within cooee of them. Perhaps there is a certain beauty that only women can see. It's bigger than their sacred place, Ayers Rock, half as high again. Uluru is stunning, impressive, but Katajuta is inscrutable and powerful. She hasn't been as abused as Uluru either. You know the dreaming air is clean, and the song of Old Gaia is strong. Too strong for some women who have gone there. My darling, you are like ancient sculpture to me, and your wisdom is astounding.

Etama beams adoration over Helen's body. Her touch is careful. She means what she says. Her brown eyes glow. Her face is chiselled in lean lines of smooth monochrome tan. Helen frowns.

—I don't know why you think she's the centre. She is too slippery.

—I know.

—For goodness sake Helen, Iona is not the only woman in Australia. We're all equal here. Don't you love me? Even a little. A little would do.

—You don't understand little, Etama. But you do know the extremes. Iona doesn't.

—I can love you with everything I've got.

—Okay, we will be lovers. My heart is as big as Katajuta, and it, too, has many heads.

Etama bounces on the bed, yelling yippee.

—Great. Oh shit, I forgot. Fancy me forgetting Frances. That proves I've never loved a woman more than you. You are my chariot.

—Frances?

—Yeah, we'd better get up, she'll be here soon. Etama is already slipping her jeans over her hips and reaching for her once bright orange windcheater. Mm, I met her yesterday in Smith Street and invited her for coffee.

Helen frumps naked down the passage to the toilet. It is a little terrace in Collingwood in the shade of the towering Housing Commission flats. The back yard, chiefly concrete, has a narrow strip of a herb garden, a rotary hoist and a freestanding dunny, Helen stretches her big, white body into a four-pointed salute to the sun under the clothes line.

Frances glares at Helen, aware, from her conversation with Etama the day before, of her relationship to Iona. Helen, also cluey, stares back shrewdly. Etama, happy to have the great love of her past and the great love of her present in the one room, bustles about preparing morning tea. She ignores their uneasiness and chats as she works.

—By the way, Frances told me that your blessed Iona owes her two hundred bucks, Helen. She lived off you, too, didn't she? Cunning rascal, that one. Milk, honey, oatmeal cookies, homemade?

Helen leaves the room.

—I remember Iona at talking a koala out of a tree. Etama pours, and smiles at Frances.

—Well, she has a way with animals. Why did Helen leave like that?

—I don't know. We are always having arguments about Iona Flynn. I put her down all the time, what else can I do? Anyway I reckon it's healthy.

—That was the front door.

—Don't worry. She's pretty moody at the moment. It'll blow over. Did I tell you about Hettie? I must have. She was this very weird American we met in London. In fact we thought she worked for the CIA. But Helen's told me all about her. What a person!

Helen and she shared a lover called Hannah who was into S 'n' M. This kid gave them both the run-around so they got friendly. Hettie is a transsexual. She was a male. She has done everything. Had homosexual relations when she was a boy, had heterosexual sex both as a man and a woman, and now she's a lesbian. No wonder she's so fucked up. Helen thinks she has her own sperm in deep freeze, so when the technology figures out how to give them wombs she can give birth to her own clone! Etama laughs like a racket of crickets.

—Was she into the sado-masochism, too?

—Probably. But she was mental.

—Americans have to have everything, don't they?

—Not Helen. She is amazing. You don't realise it when you first meet her. But she just gets deeper and deeper. She's mad. Beautifully and magnificently mad. I love it.

—Still, Hettie could have worked for the CIA as well as the rest. Helen doesn't like me.

—That'll be her, now. Helen! Where have you been? Helen marches into the room, drops ten twenty dollar notes in Frances' lap, and sits down.

—But Helen, that's all you've got. Etama blurts.

—I don't want your money.

—I will pay Iona's debts.

—Okay, thanks.

—Frances, you can't take it. She hasn't got any more money, honest. I know she's American, but she's stony.

—You said you would look after me.

Etama is rocked back into the lounge chair, silenced.

—Right, well, thanks, and I had better go, so you two can have a fight about it.

There is an air of establishment. Wood panelling in the hall, soft armchairs around the large fireplace, tables and sideboards of dark varnish, photographs in standard frames, the house creaks like new leather boots. The dining room has a setting for six, never-closed double doors give out to the sunroom where the furniture is white cane. The reedy roll of blind is rarely pulled down, shade being given by the trees outside. The kitchen is big and square with an old oblong butcher's table in the middle and a woodstove converted to oil. The bathroom is on the other side of the hallway with the three bedrooms. The boys' room, the girls' room, in the third, her mother's room, Iona does not remember there ever being a double bed. The middle one, the girls' room, is Nola's. The mother's is at the front with its own door giving out onto the side verandah. The steps around the house have all been changed to ramps. The masculine room looks over the backyard where an old-fashioned line either seesaws with the washing or is tied one way down with a rope. The toolshed was converted to a rumpus room for the grandchildren and there is the double bed. The masonite washhouse is a lean-to on the kitchen wall. There are bookcases in every room, including the rumpus shed, and many chairs and lounges scattered about the place.

Iona takes the boys' room. She packs up her mother's desk and moves it into the front room. Incidentally she discovers her mother is writing some kind of history. She does not sneak. Perhaps she will read it while Mrs Flynn is away. She has her list of instructions behind a magnet on the refrigerator. She has the keys to the old Ford Consul. Kevin, the dog, can't stop wagging his tail. The huge grey cat is indifferent. Nola's fish glide in their bubbling tank by her shady window. A couple of Scarlet Honeyeaters are nesting in their little cup in the turpentine tree by the western fence.

Her mother is excited. Mrs Crookall comes to have a cup of tea and her husband will take the travellers to their bus. Iona, in her way, is excited, too. The challenge of Nola on her own and the house full of books and the song of birds from outside, the ease of being gracious is nothing to the vicarious pleasure of seeing her mother like a boarding school-girl on the eve of the Christmas vacation. She has chosen, after much thought and worry, after finally wearying of the constant hustle of the night roads and the stale emotional drag of her friendships, to be here. Not forever, for three months.

—Don't lose too much money on the one-armed bandits, she teases her mother. By the way, did you want me to read that diary you are writing?

—Today I am saying yes, tomorrow I will probably regret that, but as you are trying to be a good writer you should know your own background.

—Are you writing it for me?

—Who else? Who else would care? Now, just relax, put on a bit of weight, get that frown off your face, and I know I can entrust Nola to you. I am going to forget you all for the summer.

—Watch out for dingos. Though you're both probably a bit tough for them. Regardless of what you say, I'll expect a postcard. Iona slaps the roof of Mr Crookall's car.

—Remember, her mother struggles with the window, Frank and family, be hospitable.

—Yes, Mum, have a good holiday.

The white Commodore pulls away. To Nola's delight, Iona pushes the wheelchair at a great rate around and around the yard, as Kevin barks. Iona calls race commentary as she runs, until all nearly come a cropper.

Another reality, I can do it, I can be it, I've just got to enjoy it.

39

THE REAL sorcery of words is done with digits in the sand, welcoming the broom of the wind and the mat of the sea. They may never be read. They exist, however, on a Pacific coast.

Arachne writes her story on the beach at Pisco, in Peru.

'Arachne pursued her shining path with trust, never carrying food upon her back, a spirit in search of experience, body like a homeless waif, too intelligent to be cunning, Arachne crossed Afghanistan, the high country. In Saudi Arabia she was arrested…'

At first, Sophie was amused by Arachne's unconventional ways. She would stand back, fluffing her long golden hair with an ironic air of assumed indifference until the situation became ludicrous, then, pragmatically, she would step in and find a place to sleep or eat, or the directions to transport. She was travelling with an idiot, a child, and took the responsibility. She had never in her life felt more like a big sister. It was fine until she found herself prey to irritability, bossiness, impatience when faced with Arachne's near catatonic wonderment. Arachne was not to be pushed around.

Touring to Sophie was seeing things consecutively, the grand, the indigenous, the unique, whereas Arachne would be quite happy sitting still in some unprepossessing village.

At Sacsayhuaman, where the carved stone blocks looked like thrones for giants, Arachne became transported and Sophie dispirited. The ritual was unlivable and she, distressed by mystery, finally gave way to exasperation. Her eyes were full of Peru. It was insane. She was hungry and her saxophone could not be tuned.

—Remember those big holes?

—Cajamarquilla.

—They were dropped like bombs, one after another. They had orders. Two hundred and nine brave heroes from another planet. It was a suicide mission, don't you see? All this is vanity, the higher lot showing off.

—You're bonkers.

—I've worked it all out. The reasons for the poverty here…

—I don't care what you've worked out. I'm sick of making all the decisions.

—We will go south. Pisco, Nazca, Mollendo, right to the Chilean border.

—I never saw you consult a map.

—I don't have to. I can't get lost.

Arachne played her recorder, and Sophie shook the shakers in rhythm and her voice was as reedy and thin as the pipes of Pan in this landscape. Sophie decided to go to New Orleans.

The tide is out and the words are read. A person searching for shellfish along the shore after the ebb, before the flow, sees the English, 'shining path' and 'arrested'. The food-gatherer scans the beachscape for some clue.

Footprints in the sand, the texture of intrigue, zigzag along the grey beach where there are some dead seagulls. Whatever Arachne's destiny, Sophie wants no part in it. Arachne walks towards the phosphorescent landmark, swamped with sadness, wanting to sit through the night in the cold and think.

—I need civilisation, Angel, please. I'm going to Louisiana, as soon as I can.

—Okay, you go there and sing the blues. I want to walk towards Chile.

Frustration at the pointlessness of experience for experience's sake tips Sophie's good nature and she weeps. Exhausted, beaten by something, Sophie catches a bus. Then, at Arequipa, she buys a ticket to fly in a small aircraft to the capital. Even the most superb view passing beneath and beside her cannot relieve Sophie of a small voice inside repeating 'the soul of man is naturally religious' and outside the oppressive beauty of the Andes. She wants to scream hysterically, or escape quietly.

Alone, Arachne is stopped by a stranger in a Che Guevara beret. Zimena sizes Arachne up and down with a ferocious, fanatical gaze. Arachne displays empty palms, shrugs.

—I'll come along. Arachne bends to lift up her grubby canvas bag.

Zimena is tall, dressed in man's clothes, with an air of authority and fire in her eyes that reminds Arachne of Janice.

Arachne returns to Lima in the car of freedom fighters, feeling safe and excited. She negotiates her wish for theirs. Zimena will take her Australian passport and they will find for her the journey she wishes, to cross the Pacific under sail. Her new friends laugh, they have a genuine fool on their hands. She is taken to a bank where she picks up a large thick envelope from her mother informing her of her grandmother's death and her own personal wealth. At the Australian Consulate, she repeats her lost passport procedure and gets a new one in the name of Alice Farr.

Zimena is transformed into Angel Farr, with a current, authentic, slightly altered passport. She flies to San Francisco, with the intention of going to Australia, all in the cause of gathering money for freedom for the people. Spreading the word of suffering with song and oratory, while Arachne is introduced to a playboy with a yacht. From death to birth to death, and dust unto dust. Mrs Miriam Trap is lowered into the earth at the cemetery at Mount Martha. Birds twitter in the tea-tree above the sombre mumblings of the pastor. Her tall grandsons in well-fitted suits stand together, hands clasped respectfully in front. Their mother's frock is a pattern of grey, white and black. She carries herself with dignity. Ursula, in her ordinary clothes and old felt hat, stands well back, gazing at tiny wild orchids. In the bush she notices the brown and white coat, the pink tongue, the flash of her little dog, Flush, who must have followed the hearse. Jocelyn looks pompous in her black mantilla and grey stockings. Her lovely sheaf of red roses is the one placed on the coffin as it descends. Allan spades a hunk of clay on top of Jocelyn's roses. Ursula hears the sound, the note of finality.

As the mourners pick up threads of seemly chatter, Ursula takes the chance to disappear. Like a truant, she glances back as she squeezes herself through the strung wire fence.

She walks along the Nepean Highway past the Master Builder neighbourhoods of brick veneer which seem to be overtaking the paddocks daily. She talks to herself in a severe manner. If I don't live my own life now, I never will. Sooner or later they will confine me to a mental home, no, I'm not being too harsh on them, it is possible. Indeed it is probable. All creatures die, and I am not going to die in a Home. I'm only fifty. It's not I who has died, but it's I who must rise. By golly, Flush, by hook or by crook. They'll need to put me into an institution for their own safety. I'd be a fool to stay, a fool to stay. We're not staying, Flush, by no means, not now.

Fortunately, the wake was at a church hall in Barkly Street. The number of people attending would not fit inside their bungalow. Regardless of how they felt towards her mother, they would not feel comfortable in the house of Ursula Trap. Mrs C and Mrs M were only too pleased to prepare sandwiches and pots of comforting tea. Ursula has time to pack and go. She does so with surprising ease and speed.

An hour and a half later an erratic spinster with a terrier on a leash and a cardboard suitcase strapped up with a leather belt stands out on the Hume Highway. Rolling hills stretch for miles, the wind gusts, lamb-like cumulus gambol in a sky blue with promise.

Suddenly they are inside the air-conditioned atmosphere of a Mercedes Benz. From limousine to limousine in a single day! Flush sits on her lap watching the white lines on the road disappear underneath him. Behind the blessed scar of uncompromising bad temper, she wonders what will become of them. She suspects her driver is a member of the marihuana mafiosa, but she does not mind, nor does she feel the need to chat. She snoozes. She dreams. She is running over the hot, dry earth chasing someone. It is the whitest of women whose red hair is of darkest gold. Every time she dozes this image of movement and excitement returns. The wonderful car is going so fast. They stop only once for a short toilet break. She, no ordinary hitchhiker, he, no ordinary motorist, they arrive in Sydney about ten at night. He drops her in George Street.

She buys half a dozen dim sims at a Chinese takeaway, bites them there in the street and throws the end of each to Flush. She hears a Country and Western singer, a husky male voice, recognises in the song names of Australian towns. She goes into the

Palace Hotel. The Aboriginal man in his red shirt, leather hat and dark glasses, with his electric guitar and percussion box, smiles at her. All around her the faces are dark, Fijian, Maori, Aboriginal, one Chinese alcoholic and a couple of painted white ladies having a whale of a time. Flush is trembling in the whirl of exciting scents on the footpath. Ursula orders a Pimms No 1 and the barman leaves her change on the wet towel. The singer adjusts his box to Reggae and soon Ursula on a stool at the bar is swaying, tapping in rhythm and sporting an idiotic grin.

Opposite her on the other side is a very drunk, very pretty Aboriginal woman. Their eyes meet every now and then. Soon it is necessary for Ursula to relieve herself. She slides off the stool to discover that her walking is difficult to control. With careful high-kneed steps, balancing on an invisible tight rope, she finds the Ladies and releases a gallon of urine with pleasure. When she emerges, the Aboriginal girl is there.

—Hi, I'm Lucy.

—How do you do, Lucy. This is my first trip to Sydney and I'm bushed. I've been bushed all my life, my dear.

—Okay, come on.

Ursula wakes up in a Sali Herman terrace on a Chippendale morning. Instant coffee never tasted so fine. They're playing Nashville Skyline on the stereo. Ursula did not know such good sound could come from a machine. Her own dear radio was over twenty years old. Her saviour, Lucy, is lying on her bed flipping through a magazine. Her bed beneath political posters has dark brown sheets and a doona cover of the Aboriginal flag, red, gold and black. Flush and several other dogs are curled up asleep on the floor. Ursula feels at peace, in a piece of art.

For three weeks she stays in the house, washing up, organising the inward and outward flow of paperbacks and manifestoes, asking questions and discussing land rights and other issues, learning fast and making them laugh. Always lots of people about, a little too much alcohol and some loud arguments, but when you understand, thinks Ursula, what they've gone through, you must bear with it. She takes her dog for walks in the city's parks and makes friends with the people who sleep in them. She recognises their need to scavenge and collect things and admires the distances they walk. In the middle of the day, there are story-telling sessions in which the moral is always mateship. Somewhere in the dregs I've found my level, Flush, and it is not at all murky. They like me.

One day a very big black man with a voluminous beard approaches her on the subject of money. She fears she has none. She is embarrassed. He has a sympathetic manner. He explains she must go to Social Security and get some. She is terrified of the humiliation at answering the Department's questions. I've never been employed. What will they make of that? He puts her inside his '68 Valiant station wagon, along with a few others coming for the ride, and drops her at the DSS, mentioning that it might take all day. And just tell the fucking truth.

As she waits, she smiles at the weary faces near her on the benches, puffing on cigarettes, bored or angry faces, cottons flopping over fat, cold legs, the drone of worry in the undercurrent. Myself and the unfortunate. My facial scar is here as much as it is a masquerade. I am real. I am poor. I am homeless. They shan't put me away.

Ursula speaks, in her interview, with withering precision. She lets her monster emerge just a little, under a strong hand, that mental rigour, the life of apparent nothing, those inner depths, the humiliation of it all, so much so that the young man inverts his original attitude and bends over backwards to insure her an income for the rest of her life. He sends her to a doctor, a personal friend of his, with a note, and Ursula returns with something signed. She has a pension. She blesses the young man for his good deed. The Valiant pulls into the kerb at peak hour.

In nets it is not all plain weaving and smooth plaiting. There are knots and ties. Beatrix and Queenie find this out as they work in India. They travel from job to job. Some people work wherever they go, and turn their hands to anything. Building captures Beatrix for a while. The women, she writes to Etama, are the builders' labourers in India, with their thin wrists, fine bracelets, they carry buckets of mortar and bricks. Queenie sits at some strange macrame with American nuns.

And so on.

The ticking of the clock is a rhythm to Beatrix, who can pick out the beat in the most complex timing. The bounce, the stress, the release, the intervals balance in Beatrix like a pendulum. Meanwhile, Queenie balloons with what time has in her womb. The small and the tall, the blossom and the metronome, the immediate and past-present-future, two time bombs, taking a season through India, threading through the likes and dislikes of the rest of the tribe, don't find each other hard and carefully plan their arrival at the bush to give Beatrix time to settle Queenie comfortably before the birth; the natural birth she looks forward to midwifing. From the Indians she learns and becomes, even more than before, a walking apothecary.

40

WHEN ZIMENA, the Chilean revolutionary who travelled under the name of Angel Farr with an Australian passport, came to Melbourne, she strode about the place in her Che beret.

She is the real thing. Her husky voice is heard at Women's concerts and events crying in song for her suffering people over the sound of her fingers on guitar strings. She is the angry passion personifying all social realist protest posters. Her message the world should hear and no message is more vital. If she were in her own country she would be 'disappeared', she states with ferocious conviction.

—Why don't you fight at home where it would be effective?

—Ha, she would cry to the crowd, take a photograph! She would point, here is someone who would have me murdered!

Frances falls in love.

At first she would crave her from a distance, relishing erotic daydreams and following her. Then her hunger becomes urgent and cannot be satisfied simply by the sight of her. In her obsession and frustration, she cannot sleep. She cannot masturbate. She would go to feminist social occasions which she hated on principle, knowing that Zimena would be there. She would have to swallow her distaste and become seductive. One night it happens. She asks and Zimena says yes.

At her place, Frances, usually so cool in matters of sex, wilts like a femme, serves like a femme. Something of the violence, the knowledge of atrocities happening to close relatives and friends, an understanding of the junta which came from fighting it so long, hits Zimena in the blood stream, like body-lust, like blood-lust. She grabs this fair Princess by the wrists.

—You want it, no?

Frances nods.

—You want me to tie you? No?

Frances finds some purple tights she has. She damps her lips, wondering what will come next. But there, ready for anything. Her hands are caught and thrust behind her back. Zimena kicks a chair upside down with more drama than violence. Frances is loosely tied into a backbend. The pain is nothing, the energy everything. Zimena laughs. They are playing.

—*Te gusta, no?*

Zimena sits down, rolls a cigarette, feigns indifference as she sips the scotch Frances had served earlier. With exaggeration she yawns.

—No, no.

She unties her, and places her over the other way. She stares at Frances' backside.

—Like fresh baked bread.

Zimena goes into the kitchen for the plastic bucket of honey. She pours the honey over the loaf of bread, bends down and licks.

—Yes, breathes Frances, yes, more.

—Get up.

—I can't. I'm tied. Let's…

—Enough.

They look at each other for a long time. Frances with her bum sticky and buzzing. All pretense has been stripped away in a moment of an extra-normality.

—I'm sorry.

—Don't be. I'm going to have a bath.

In the bath later, the two of them, knowing they are both capable of more than they show, Frances confesses her long-term crush on Zimena.

—Me, I'm going back. I don't belong in this middle class country.

—Until you do, I'm here.

The sexual exhilaration. They have much to discover, each has met her match. Their eyes are shot with sparkling questions.

41

MANY OLD MEN and Cerridwen are drinking in Kiernans. In a Dublin bar, it is nothing to bring out an old hardback and read out loud. This Poor Old Fred does, from his 1922 Egoist Press edition of *Ulysses*.

—'Onward to the dead sea they tramp to drink, unslaked and with horrible gulpings, the salt somnolent inexhaustible flood. And equine portent grows again, magnified in the deserted heavens, nay to heaven's own magnitude, till it looms, vast, over the house of Virgo. And lo, wonder of metempsychosis, it is she, the everlasting bride, ever virgin.'

Cerridwen listens, sipping a stout, her smiling Irish eyes crinkled in appreciation of her Da's rich recitation.—'It floats, it flows about her starborn flesh and loose it streams emerald, sapphire, mauve and heliotrope, sustained on currents of cold interstellar wind, winding, coiling, simply swirling writhing in the skies a mysterious writing till after myriad metamorphoses of symbol, it blazes, Alpha, a ruby and triangled sign upon the forehead of Taurus.'

Monica and her mother enter with bags of shopping.

The entire family subside around a table with a foaming jug of Guinness.

—When Da read about a ruby and triangled sign upon the forehead of Taurus, I got an idea. Let's go to Mexico. See Aunt Nisaba, and Armand.

—The days of the likes of old Fred Flynn in the Diplomatic Corps are over, I'm afraid. Still it gave us a taste of wanderlust, didn't it dear?

—Indeed. A champion thought, well worth a mighty consideration.

Monica insists they go, secretly glad to be rid of the parents for a while and the necessity of lying and self-justification. She begs out of the mighty consideration, which decision is actually being made speedily.

—Well, that's settled then.

—We can afford it, can't we, dear?

—I'd say so. Why not?

The face is familiar. It is some time before Sophie realises this is the face that interrupted her lovemaking with Etama in Hackney some months ago. She is not pleased to see it.

—I arrive at Lima, and I wait at the airport. Biding my time, waiting for Arachne. Australians should stick out like the Sydney Opera House.

—How did you know she was here? Sophie would prefer to be anonymous under the horsey papier mache dragons in the glossy Air Mexico poster. She is feeling sore.

—I return to London. I seek out this Yvonne, and she seems to know everything about everybody. I hear Sophie is gone to Peru with Arachne. So, where is she?

Sophie shrugs. She is too lacking in curiosity to bother with the braid of intrigue which plaits Yvonne and Grundhilde and Arachne and somehow leads to herself. The reckless Arachne, her erstwhile Angel. She reverts to her customary mental laziness, and yawns.

—I don't know.

—Pooh, Sophie, I am not interested in you. This Arachne will lead me to paradise, do you not think this is true?

—No. Unless you've got some precipice in mind, of course.

—So the jazz singer knows something of the labyrinth after all. Grundhilde digs into her faded denim shoulder bag. Is the labyrinth the place to hide? The mathematician says no. It is the place to lure your victim. We live in a world of lies.

—I suppose so.

—Sophie, in holding the key, you become a person in and of yourself. Here, I will read some Jorge Luis Borges to you.

—If you like. Sophie makes a show of looking at her wrist watch.

—'Yes. It wouldn't surprise me at all if the spider web (the Platonic spider web—let's keep this straight) may have suggested to the murderer (for there is a murderer) his crime. You remember that al-Bokhari, in the tomb, dreamed about a tangle of snakes, and upon waking found that a spider web had prompted his dream…'

—How come you knew Yvonne? And how come Yvonne knew Arachne? The reading of Borges has uncomfortably reminded Sophie of Cerridwen and her hallucinations. Vibrations, vibes, I never believed all that hippie junk before, but now, I feel some. Trembles which have nothing to do with music. Grundhilde, I've got to sing. I've got to become famous. I deserve it, it's written on my slate.

—Ugh, it may be fame, or it may be another destiny. We each of us could have chosen fame if we wanted to suffer the web of lies. But we are ridiculous. We want nothing, but to create another truth.

Sophie sighs again, and looks at her watch.

—You're like Yvonne, you like puzzles. She wants nothing out of life except more problems to solve. Mysteries to unravel. Why, why, why, the living question mark. But give me a fair go, I know what I want.

—I, Grundhilde sits down, In this life have one problem, not many puzzles. Maybe it is made up of many. The one and the many. Has the elusive Arachne found someone else?

—How on earth do I know? Last I saw of her she was walking south along the beach to Chile. She is so stupid. She is not afraid of anything. Off her rocker, that kid.

Grundhilde pulls her legs up under her. The two big women make an odd contrast sitting together. Sophie wears a bra, a tailored dress, crosses her legs and her ankles are slim. Grundhilde looks sloppy, heavier and more comfortable.

—Here in Peru! What a place is Peru! Perhaps this circle of the maze started in another great place, Crete. Etama splits up with Beatrix. Beatrix is seduced by something bigger than another woman. Etama comes to Belgium and cries on my shoulder. She is jealous. Emotions are an easy way out of the labyrinth, but they do not free you. You panic, you cry, you indulge your feelings.

There is a phone call, about a woman called after the spider. Who would change her name to Arachne? Borges' mathematician's answer is, of course, the murderer. So she does not kill, this little sweet thing from the Antipodes, she is the opposite of murderer. She is the divine fool. Sophie, I have been seeking the divine fool through five or six lifetimes.

—She is certainly an idiot. Now she is raving about spaceships and giants being dropped into Peru in cannisters. She's never even read von Daniken.

—Arachne, the fool, becomes very important to me. I stick with Etama. She leads me or we lead each other to the other fool, Zorro, saviour of the human race. Martyr-fool, again, no murder in her. Zorro could not kill a fly. On my wild goose chase I create a band of fools. You see, Sophie, again it is the many and the one. Like Yvonne with her many puzzles and me with my one. Here we have many beautiful fools rushing across Europe, singing and dancing to our death.

—My friend, Frances, would like you. She has an apocalyptic cast of mind too.

—Perhaps it is Australian. Etama made me read your Nobel prize-winner, White, the book, Voss. About the German explorer, Leichhardt, and his soul mate, Laura. Terra Incognita. Maybe the place is the fool. Grundhilde laughs.

—I had better get my seat allocation. Mexico City, then New Orleans. What are you going to do?

—Look at the big map of airline routes around the globe. That is my labyrinth. Connections and dead ends. I am a follower, I follow threads, and you seem sure of your destination. You are stubborn, Sophie. I will come with you to Mexico.

Walking heels first with toes outpointing, the two cross the shiny floor, Sophie's bra doing a fine job as she carries all her inches and ounces with pride and purpose, Grundhilde showing her weariness in each stride.

In Armand's opinion the women's revolution will be the greatest in the history of civilisation. He sits in the corner of it, witnessing, his sympathy flowing over the charmed landscape. Now, driving along the Avenida de Insurgentes in his Volkswagen, with Cerridwen beside him, he is assured of it once more.

—You remember Xaviera? She has become a sorcerer's apprentice. *Una bruja*.

His face as he turns has an amused, questioning smile, the identical of her Aunt Nisaba's. She wonders who copied whom, and how much it says of their love. She remembers Monica and Cleopatra, Xaviera and herself playing with Manuel and Dominic in the garden at Cuernevaca when young. She remembers the hummingbirds nesting in the fragile bamboo and the butterflies being bigger like gaudy, floating paper.

—Is she still at Cuernevaca?

—Well, she is a governess to some rich Iranians. On her days off she disappears into the volcanoes.

—Come on, Armand. Tell me the truth.

—I won't tell you. Let her show you. Your father, by the way, is a racist, right-wing, colonialist pig.

—Are you getting sick of him? Is this a trade?

—Suggest they travel some more, no?

When Armand telephones, Xaviera tells him to take Cerridwen to Plaza Garibaldi at midnight on Friday.

Much tequila being drunk, much marihuana-smoking, lovers and whores eating hungrily, the trumpets of the various, flashily uniformed groups of Musica Rancheras vying with each other to play love songs, the Plaza Garibaldi teems with exhuberant life. Cerridwen is approached by a young, bosomy woman with glistening long black hair adorned with a red gardenia. She wears a tiered Spanish dancer's frock of black satin with red lining.

—It is I, come.

Xaviera leads the slightly taller Cerridwen over to a food stall, where she draws attention to herself like a prostitute. She clicks her castanets and swings her hips and offers the back of her shoulders in the time-honoured Andalusian way. Later she must do her act in a nightclub. Cerridwen is confused by the subterfuge.

The bracket immediately before Xaviera's is a cowgirl in a shining white and gilded outfit, with golden colt pistols strapped to her fish-net stockings and white leather boots embroidered with well-horned bulls' heads. She sings of bandits on the Rio Grande. After Xaviera, there is an all-female country and western group, who sing in accented English with a Nashville twang.

Cerridwen awakes in the morning in a hut on the roof of an apartment block near the University. Xaviera brings her coffee. She is robed simply in pale blue silk. Cerridwen feels boney, white and breastless. She pulls the eiderdown up to her chin.

—What pretty eyes you have.

Whatever the reason for the night before, Cerridwen suspects the draining of her will was part of it. She is lethargic. She has no desire to fight the subtle alteration to consciousness, she feels. It is not drugs. It is a closer, more personal surrender involving trust in a human being, which, she realises, she has never experienced before. Neither like falling in love nor a high, it emanates from Xaviera's laughter. The soothing mesmerism leaves her relaxed, and alert.

The room is extremely untidy. She is lying on the only mattress, a double one on the floor. The door leads to the open air, rooftops. There are glasses and bottles on all available surfaces, and an electric kettle with long flex weaving a complicated path to its plug. A solitary sink. One bookshelf. Pictures cut from magazines all over the walls, many of fair, white women in erotic poses.

—*Como,* Xantippe.

A woman stands in the doorway. The silhouette she cuts against the diffused morning light is of a squat Indian, bird-headed, Egyptian in its squareness. Cerridwen feels a sinking in her bowels, her naked body feels like the soft porn on the walls.

—Who, she whispers, paper thin.

—This is my son's room. The matron speaks slowly.

—You can use Spanish. That's all right, isn't it Cerridwen?

—Yes, I speak Spanish.

—What he studies I do not know. Flesh, money, agriculture, the language of North America, what does he tell his mother?

—Cerridwen Flynn, the niece of Nisaba Diana Kirby.

—Yes. *Barrio,* no. Not this weekend. This weekend is for the city. You, my pupil, have others of your tribe in town, now. What is this international tribe? All girls, heh? The double-headed eagle. Yes. *Jungfrau, der Stieifrau,* you know?

—'Onward to the dead sea they tramp and drink…'

—Virgo and Taurus.

—Grundhilde? Xaviera queries.

—How do you expect me to know her name? The other?

—'A ruby and triangled sign upon the forehead of Taurus', Sophie? It couldn't be.

—Begin to trust your mystic self, little Celtic *chiqua*.

They make their way to the Zocale, amid the architecture of three cultures. Cerridwen, watching the pigeons and the postcard sellers, the grubby, colourful children begging so that they might give, decides that the Indians are different from the tinkers. Their look is not so degraded. Xantippe squats in the shade of the cathedral and becomes indistinguishable from other old ladies doing the same. To know the single one in a crowd seems just wonderful to Cerridwen. She receives a cheeky wink. Without a trace of stiffness Xantippe rises and gestures that they follow. She shows Cerridwen the foundation wall of the Aztec temple to Quetzelcoatl, the flying snake.

—The winged serpent.

—Yes, so what's new, heh?

In one of the *glorietas* on the Paseo de la Reforma, they see Sophie and Grundhilde. Sophie is carrying a many-zipped travelling bag trying to ignore her companion. She buys a slice of pineapple from a *criada* under an umbrella.

Xantippe makes a face of disapproval.

—Don't worry, she has the constitution of an ox, says Cerridwen.

—Go on. Xantippe pushes Xaviera at them and grabs Cerridwen by the forearm and thrusts her away.

Xaviera greets Grundhilde warmly.

—Come. I'll show you real food.

—Xaviera! Good god!

—Ha Grundhilde, you are not so clever. Xaviera speaks in German. You come to a city this size and not expect to find me! You wear yourself out looking for a needle in the haystack and all the time it is sticking in your knee.

Over the food which Sophie enjoys with bovine contentment, Xaviera hears the story of the purple bus, and of Zorro's weakening health. She shakes salt onto her upturned fist, licks it up, squirts lemon juice on to the top of the can and takes a long draught of beer.

—Better than the German stuff, no?

—You know where Zorro is?

—She is here. Xaviera taps the newspaper, where the name Sidon is clear.

—The refugee camp?

—Uh huh. Where are your travels going to take you next?

Grundhilde stares at Xaviera to lock in a combat of eyes. A word would be a dropping of her guard, a movement, perhaps a weakness. The table is tiny, the taverna crowded.

—Where should I go next, Xaviera?

—Onward to the dead sea they tramp to drink…until, lo, it looms over the house of Virgo…the dear, the radiant, coifed in a veil of, what do you call it, gossamer.

—The Middle East?

—You will see the flag of Lebanon entangled in barbed wire. A bramble around the cedar tree. The death of old men's dreams and the realisation of their prophecies in one sad turbulent hole. Do you want that?

Grundhilde shakes her head.

—Then go west, young woman. Xaviera laughs her mesmerising trick. She taps Sophie on her upper arm and waves her fingers. She is gone.

42

ETAMA HEARS about Queenie's pregnancy and her guts cramp. On a certain date in a certain place she had been cuckolded. No amount of flattery or lovemaking could ease the pain of retrospective jealousy. She cannot rid herself of the cockeyed plughole in her own being.

Helen says she must face Queenie, see the pregnancy, and, ideally, also the birth. She must stop looking so irretrievably glum and get off her backside.

—Who wants to stay in this concrete pit for the summer?

—You do! You want to be near Iona. Everybody cares about someone else as well as me. Never just me.

—That does it. We're going. Plan and pack.

Etama has a note from Grundhilde saying she is arriving at the address she gave her.

—Grundhilde relies on me to take her up the bush.

—Well, pull yourself together.

—I can't face Queenie, knowing she was with a man while I was suffering in Athens.

When Etama is depressed she finds it extremely hard to change. She wants to stay in her bedroom, brood and let the vast tide of her emotions swamp her until eventually she is thrown on the shore of something new. Helen is exasperated.

—When I said we would be lovers, I meant to act honourably, Etama. I am a woman of my word.

Helen leaves the house. The screen door slams. The kids from Collingwood High at their sports yell and the traffic is constant waves of noise. Etama goes back to bed with a book.

Helen knows only one person can fish Etama up from her depths and knock her sensible. So she seeks Frances.

Frances, as Etama predicted, began to respect Helen more and more as she got to know her. She was a *mensch,* a 'human being' in the Yiddish sense, and, when it all boils down, Frances believes you couldn't be much better than that. She says okay.

Several days later all four are in Frances' Toyota on the Hume Highway.

The atmosphere in the car is a lot better than Etama expected. This, she suspects, is due to Zimena, who is like a warm-blooded, healthy, humorous Zorro. She trusts her. Frances is in love in that way that spreads happiness. It is the only condition in which she really lets her brilliance show, smiling and cracking jokes. Helen's voice is high and thin, tuneful. Zimena teaches them Chilean freedom songs in Spanish, then passionately translates.

In Wangaratta, they rest and eat their wholefood sandwiches in the park. The day is pleasant. Ducks honk on the river. Etama wanders off to sort through her feelings. She loves kids. She loves women and honours the beauty of birth, but still the lingering pain persists; sexual jealousy of the father of Queenie's child. She feels her blood quicken as she imagines the confrontation. It is imperative to speak her mind, to express her feelings even if that involves anger and violence. But she does not want to fall into abuse of the things she holds most sacred.

She goes into the lavatory.

As she comes out of the cubicle, a young man stands there staring at her with the preoccupied intent of the flasher. Anger is her ready response. He is not to be distracted. He pulls down his running shorts. His penis is erect, moving. Etama can break his wrist if he so much as takes a step towards her. He doesn't. He is young, fit, handsome, and getting, in Etama's opinion, some depraved turn-on from simply watching her face.

She is fascinated. Her heterosexual innocence and her political disgust are distant from some immediate earthy need. He pulls up his shorts and goes. He rides across the grass on his bicycle. She stares after him. Normally one to whinge and rage about such affronts to her personal freedom, she consigns the arousal of her own sexuality to secrecy. It has dispelled her jealousy in becoming a guilty feeling, a private disturbance like erotic fantasies used in lovemaking or masturbation.

I'm glad, she says, as she touches Helen's forehead, that Iona rejected you. Otherwise I… I'm sorry I didn't mean to put it like that.

I know what you mean. Frances lays her head on Zimena's thigh.

A few of us at the time turned the sands of long-running fictions, or dug ourselves into the diaries of our mothers, grandmothers and those older women who were no relation. We lie on beds we can find, and read.

Iona sits at the big kitchen table, unwashed dishes in the sink. Nowhere to vent an unnamed anger except upon the confining welts of words in a foolscap exercise book, an old ledger from school accountancy…a failed subject. Nola is drawn up to the other end. The wheel brake is on, and she slaps at and grabs coloured cardboard shapes that Iona made for her yesterday. A big, loose jigsaw puzzle.

Myself having to be gentle with the sensibilities of unreal characters, persons made up or never completely known. With Nola, even, I have to guess what is in her heart, what hurts. I remember Yvonne in England with her dark-framed glasses and aluminium eyes, her angular frame and fastidious ways. The chronometers of Western history have let her type go by for centuries. The history have let her type go by for centuries. The independent woman on a bicyle riding riding down the lanes while the soldiers take the roads. There were moments when she rose to be chained to the railings in a cause, or wrote books, or travelled the Empire, or nursed in the Crimea, or lived quietly on the Continent in a cheap pension, the eccentric, competent, articulate Englishwoman. The romantic Englishwoman.

Amongst the mess that has gathered on the table is a card from Yvonne; not a postcard, a folded, glossy pornographic one depicting a breasty bikie girl in the ultra-realism of heightened photgraphy. Yootha, the focus of her love, has dropped the search for Jack the Ripper with all its hateful research, for the real politics, the real fight. The peace live-in at Greenham Common. Mercifully free of irony and impartiality, young Yootha wants to act and use every mental muscle and ascetic conviction to stop the madmen in their lust for death. Beside the imagined holocaust of nuclear war or accident, the pyres that burnt the witches, the Cathars and honest heretics are but bonfires. Yootha cannot understand distance or indifference. While there's argument there's hope.

Yvonne writes that it should be interesting. The burning zeal of her lover attracts her more than mysteries, but, she says 'I'm still perverse, sarcastic, a cheeky devil's advocate treading the knife-edge…'

Will Yvonne herself take on the men and the Americans? She may go there and become enraptured of the ritual of the demonstration. Her curiosity could take her anywhere.

Iona's great-aunt's loud-ticking mantle clock chimes twelve times. That means it is about twenty minutes past noon. It never fails to make Nola giggle and dribble. Is it lunch or the sound that tickles her? Nola also likes the untidiness that has grown around her like an unruly garden. She discovers objects she would not find in her mother's automatic neatness. There is an old bridle in bits, which several days ago Iona began to oil, underneath the books and papers. There is a circular tin of leather soap ready but unused. This Nola is reaching for. She likes to try to rub its smooth contour on her face. Iona surreptitiously pushes it closer.

When in my mind the refrain, she writes, making nonsense. Words on paper are an enormous excuse.

Another part of the rubbish on the table is Oona's half-written 'opera'. This work, because it is not slick, not the work of a writer, but something coming out of the spirit of more than Oona herself, is strangely important. Iona does her bit with care,…altering a word here, scansion there…knowing that others will also contribute. The music, the voices. Maybe for the moment of the performance, four choruses from four directions, in many harmonies, with ritualised actions, some magic will happen. The flowing liquid may settle into a pneumatological jelly, if not a more solid experience.

In my mind the refrain, 'when will our caravan be leaving for the west', jibbers and I see a ragged band of beggars trouping towards the sunset, as clever as gypsies, plucking mandolin strings and blowing into mouth organs, making fires and cooking grains, the sisters, the spinsters marching in freedom. Where, how, doesn't matter, that they march, that their existence is realised, known, respected, that's what I mean. And I see it as a caravan with camels. The discovery no cave of jewels, no inland sea, no big name in the history books, rather it is invisible to the eye. It is an inner sea.

The days melt into one another, but each day is intimate in detail. There's me, up early. Then, at nine, the gymnastics of getting Nola dressed, washed, into her chair and occupied. Well, it's all occupational therapy, for both of us. Yet, I am living in a treasure trove of sorts, like an opportunity shop where each little piece of crockery has a meaning. There is a tiny ashtray with 'Lucinda' painted on it with a spray of pink flowering japonica. This, I vaguely remember, was painted by my grandmother for my mother. It always sits beside another which was not painted by my grandmother but is very similar. That says 'Winifred' and has daisies. I suspect she was my father's lover. But how come it is in my mother's house? Her diary does not answer this question. The bridle I remember spending all my savings on when I was twelve, and I bought it at a sale at Myers' equestrian department. And Nola, Nola, Nola, this summer you and me, and you are thirty-nine. The summers of our childhood were spent in a holiday house at Somers on the Peninsula, until one horrible day the cloud of death hung and broke into that storm of shock and mourning. Veronica drowned. We all left this house, a happy family, Terry, Frank, Nola, Veronica, Mum and me, looking forward to the sun and surf, our friends coming down for the odd week or weekend, sand all over the floor, barbecues and games. All captured in frozen photographs, candid kiddyhood snaps. That's what we have of Veronica, framed snaps and one studio portrait. This house was spared her ghost.

The cat and the dog begin to move, especially the cat who expects, with the authority of the Queen of England, her plate to be filled promptly. Iona shuts her book and glances at her school handwriting and the pencil drawing of a pony under saddle on the cover.

Baked beans on toast, Nola's favourite. She probably doesn't realise the connection with her farts. But she likes farting as well. Kevin is old, and the radio vet recommends dogs over ten should have more than one meal a day.

In the afternoon a surprise visit from Frances.

43

ABE, A NEW York businessman, did not dream of a condominium at the Keys in Florida. He wanted to let his beard grow long and silky and retire in the promised land. He found a place on the border of Israel and Lebanon and bought a herd of goats. He wished to ponder, approaching death, the problem of Monotheism: why the Jews created God.

He spends hours with his goats studying sacred texts, thinking about the Beast, the Whore of Babylon and the coming of the Saviour. He wants to find in his heart a real forgiveness of the Germanic peoples. It is a hard spiritual task.

—The Prussians' Inquisition was more ferocious than the Spanish, he tells Zorro.

—Heh, they all burnt the witches. They burnt Bruno and the art of memory. They killed the wisdom of the Moors, they killed tolerance. In recent centuries we have lost more than we've gained. Zorro coughs as she looks across the bare rocky ground.

—It is not the Christians who hate Jews, it is the barbarians. Christianity became the excuse. Perfection is death. The Nazis wanted perfection.

—All myths are reflexive lies. Many things are perfect for a second. How long does a second last?

—To believe in perfection is to believe in a death that doesn't exist. Abe wittles his crook out of a long willow branch with a sharp knife and steady old hand.

—You have old men's dreams, Abe. You are a romantic.

—The Jews in making God, in making God perfect, impose an extreme guiltiness on everything else. Nobody likes to be told they are guilty. People take too easily to guiltiness, yes?

—The moral choice is with the individual. The self is the only one who knows whether that self is guilty or innocent. That is irrelevant to who is punished.

—The Divine alone has the power of retribution. Abe, waving his half-finished staff, looks like a Cecil B. de Mille Moses.

—I came to work on a kibbutz, to give myself to hard labour. But they have no care over there. They are shit. Exclusivist. There is no discussion. Zorro coughs, rattling the phlegm in her lungs, and spits. Abe sees specks of blood in the sputum.

—I think I'll go to Lebanon and work in a Palestinian refugee camp.

A convoy of tanks bearing the Star of David lumbers along a road in the distance.

—Zorro, you are to do something for me before you go, please? You are sick, already. You go into Lebanon and you will disappear with no trace. Write down all the names and addresses of your friends, your parents, your sisters and brothers, your comrades. They will be safe with me.

—Tomorrow. Today I will give you a quotation from a Russian aristocrat. 'I shall die and the worms will eat me, but I want our idea to triumph. I want the masses…of humanity to be really emancipated from all authorities and from all heroes present and to come.' *Adieu,* old man.

—Adios, hermana.

Abe watches the striking figure of the consumptive Zorro separate his goats as her body throws a elongated, shaky shadow over the tired ground. To be complacent, he decides, is to embrace Beelzebub. He looks away and when he looks back she is gone.

'I have never interfered with any persons unless they deserved it… But I am a widow's son and my orders must be obeyed…it will always pay a rich man to be liberal with the poor.'

Living is easier for some. Oona, when she sees a cobweb, first asks, where is your maker? She spends time to know whether it is a wolf spider, a huntsman, a red-back, always informing herself from a book of facts. The hanging headless Ned is home for several arachnid species, including a funnel-web.

Even though spiders' webs are of flimsiest silken threads, only seen when dancing light illuminates their intricate designs, they are tough. A Blue Warbler and his mate have made their little dome at the edge of her small garden. My friend, the wren. She has her exercise book and her inspiration. She is writing her opera, and from Lesley she has learnt the Tarot cards. The Moon. The Sun. Judgement. The World. Each an act, a chorus. For the moment she struggles with the poetry, carefully spitting on her lead pencil in the damp outside on a stump; she writes her ideas on lined paper.

Iona receives odd letters, cryptic in a strangely childish hand, asking her advice. In fact, Oona seeks assistance from everyone. Trees talks as she kneels with her hefty needle and expanse of canvas, making a teepee, responding sensibly and carefully, for before she tried to externalise, that is to live, her creativity, she wrote poetry. Oona is obsessed. The wrens and parakeets, her sculpture of the outlaw, the red-bellied black snake and the distant, singing dingo, contribute as much to her slow work as the community of women which rises and falls about her like a restless tide or a billowing-resiling cobweb of gossip in the wind.

Grundhilde's flight did not reach Sydney until five in the afternoon. She had been watching the desert continent unfold beneath her for hours. She has been mesmerized by the frozen sea of rock. It authenticated her science fiction visions. The magical games she played with herself and life and people were right. Correct. She wanted the flight never to finish. Even though she sensed timelessness, time was pressed upon her by the neurotic punctuation of the cabin staff at their work. Down below she had seen where her own death might be glorious and meaningless. Here was country gone beyond the cold valleys and high peaks of her homeland, impossible to rape or so it seemed from the sky. A place for her *frauerkinde,* where Nature must be adored and loved on scorched knees. She, a speck down there surrounded by dust and bones, need be only herself, and that self enough and all. And more. Such visions she had on her flight from Singapore.

She had seen the new world with her mortal eyes, and she dreamed with her mind awake the resurrection of the witches. Dots down there they walked in beggars' rags, practising herbal medicine and massage, eating the insects, lizards and roots, calling on the spirits of the earth and sky, with her among them in worn shoes or bare feet. It would be real. A bonding with the wilderness, true fruitful anarchy. She felt so powerful her seat belt could burst on touchdown.

Dumping her ungraciously into mundane reality, the aeroplane lands. Her vibrations are so fine, the comprehending of so much past and future and eternity, the thrust into the rude present makes her into a person having a nervous breakdown. She has to be helped into the arrival lounge, guided to her place in the queue for Customs. She cannot know any of this. It is some kind of hell. Mumbling in German, she finally screams, falls to the floor and hammers it with her fists, frightening her fellow human beings but not deterring them from their impatience to get beyond the barricades. A Qantas employee takes her to the Ladies Room.

She finds the nursing mothers' enclosure, and surrenders. The love of death now turns into a desperate sadness, she hears the cries of massacres, the grunts and groans of killers, smells the sweat of effort, of fear and of blood and the stench of rotting flesh. She glamorised death. Now her time-embracing mind must bring experience to imagination. She wrestles with her own powers. Supernature is all very well, but there's a job to be done, a life to be lived.

A job to be done?

She shudders out of her paranormal self. She is wet all over and the perspiration reeks. She goes into the toilets and strips and washes herself under the arms and over her pendulous breasts with cold water.

Back in line with her raggy old pack, guitar, and shoulder bag, dismissively nodding away enquiries as to her well-being, she returns to the job to be done. Whatever was it?

Arachne, the spider-named, the centre of the web she conceived, the wanderer whom she pursued all over the earth in the Borgesian game she constructed since meeting Etama, is surprisingly irrelevant. The task of pursuit has fallen from her, and the teaching of others to pursue also absent. Having her bags picked through at the Customs desk, usually so suspect, now she is light, guiltless, as if she really had arrived. As if the seeker had found. What?

The questions are mysterious and wonderful. Her face has an innocent glow, and she has forgotten and the Customs Officer misses the half ounce of Peruvian cocaine in the toe of her boot.

Thorough is Grundhilde, and before she brings out of her shoulder bag the address in Leichhardt that Etama gave her, she goes to a seat to meditate. She lifts her big legs into lotus and visualises…

The fate of Arachne.

She visualises the sea, the vast Pacific Ocean. The boat is a sleek yacht, twenty metres, with one tall mast and ample living quarters below decks. It beats into a blustering gale, the waves are so high, their troughs so deep, at one moment it seems the sailing craft is flying free of the sea and the next it is completely submerged. Right there on the foredeck, grasping the bow-rail with whitened knuckles is Arachne, resplendent against the steel grey sky and olive-grey sea in an egg-yolk yellow oilskin.

She is laughing-screaming as she would on a roller coaster. Her stomach lifts into her throat as the boat rises to the pinnacle of the wave, and descends. Her whole being is trembling except the fists on the chrome railing which express all her strength. There is thrill, not fear in her; the sea is a mother to her, *allu mari, mi portati, se voleti che mi sanati, allu mari, alla via cosi m'ama la donna mia, allu mari allu mari.*

The chant is Grundhilde's. She remembers it from lifetimes ago. But Arachne seems to be singing it to the waves, waves which are mountains. She is mad. She has been bitten by her self-chosen name. The yacht is holding out. Three black rubber slickers on three slipping and struggling figures around the tiller are managing to keep her bow up to the ferocious wind. The mainsail is roped to the boom and the jib is reefed tight along the centre of the hull.

Grundhilde has no idea how long it will last, and the visualising is exhausting her, for it is not her battle, neither her sea nor her suicide. The last remnants of Christianity disperse in her soul. This death of belief is her only way to depart before the finish. She still repugned suicide, thought a dark karma was associated with it, but now, as clear as the raging sea and the vessel with Arachne out on the bowsprit, teeth to the storm, she could see that the mortal sin of suicide was another conceit of the church fathers to stop the women choosing their own way of dying, of getting out of the way of witch judges, conquering armies and violent husbands. For all their faults the pagan Germans and the Shogunate Japanese were not wrong in ritualising choice of death, self-determination, allowing the act to be one of courage. Whether Arachne lives or dies in the terrible cyclone, it is good, Grundhilde decides. She was a fool to follow the fool, for no-one can share her path, and no-one else can love it.

In Borges' words, she understands. 'With relief, with terror, he understood that he too was a mere appearance, dreamt by another.'

—Leichhardt, she says to the taxi-driver and hands him the piece of paper written on in Etama's picturesque handwriting.

—Leichhardt was a German like me, come to cross the desert.

—Disappeared with no trace. More famous for the twenty-seven expeditions sent out to find him than for anything he ever did. And they never even found his bones, nor the bones of all the horses and cattle he took with him. A fool.

—Maybe he was not the fool, but those who sought to find his bones and the bones of his cows. Are you a student?

—No, a poet, that's all.

—Good, poet! You may have enough imagination to use a Swiss passport.

—I might.

—It will cost you my fare, okay?

—Mmm.

Grundhilde, with her dowager's hump giving her an ancient authority, leans back in the seat of the taxi. Following your dreams is a matter of trial and hard work, solitary, thankless and rewarding only in the eventual, inevitable understanding that, at least, you attempt to take your destiny into your own hands.

44

AN UNDERTOW of moral destiny drags at Iona's feet, a part of a tide within. A person is two thirds water, like the earth. It has been raining. The dog rolls in something rotten, a dead bandicoot. The sun is glinting on the dripping leaves, and Nola's chair is bogged.

—They're all gathering. My 'we' is gathering and I am not there. Let's sit here, Nola, and I'll tell you a story.

Nola rocks and the wheels dig a deeper groove. She looks worried, a slight frown plays on her not fully-controlled facial muscles.

—Nooni noni.

Iona sits on a rock. They have a view over paddocks and the hills.

—What is one woman's wine is another woman's water my friend, Oona, said, or sang. She smiles and holds Nola's ever-moving hand.

—Let's say I have a flagon of wine beside a water hole. It's a magical place, somewhere on the Docker River out-station. Water is hidden under a rock in the vast red landscape. I have on an army shirt with its sleeves ripped out; my arms are brown and my legs poke skinnily out from baggy shorts. I am drinking off the effects of my own guts. Intestinal fortitude. Around me? First there is the sky in all its blueness, a true, bright, infinite blue, no clouds. The ground is red, red except for some golden ochre. The plains stretch forever dotted with low, blue-green trees, though there are purple hills, worn-down mountains, on the horizon. Sheer laughter inside me, Nola. You know my Akubra hat? I dip it into the pool of clear water, lean over and let it wash over my face.

I have come to the Aboriginal settlement to buy a camel. All the cash proceeds from taxi-driving are sealed in my pack. In fact, it doesn't matter where I go from here. I trust my affinity with animals. This may be an anthropomorphic projection or it may be true. Soon I will find out. A wild young camel will soon be mine. I will stay and get to know her or him. Learning Pitjantjatjara is hard; evenso it is giving me insights. The main words of relationship, the moving verbs, the colour, grappling with a language so close to the land, the society and way of life is something for a white, urban Australian. I am a stranger, a wanderer.

In my generation, of my education, who isn't a wanderer, a borrower of others' space? A white among blacks. Everything is obvious. You can't hide, pretend to a politics, you are only yourself. I'm terrified, but it's my shyness, not physical fear.

You surely can't die from shyness.

It is late in the day, the weather is not so hot. I hear in the distance the roar of four-wheel drives, the thundering of camel feet, and see through the heat haze past dead tree trunks, dust rising. Maybe my camel will be penned tonight. Not any camel, a mate, a friend. My very own ship of the desert.

I see myself in flowing cottons astride the beast walking towards the many heads of the Olgas.

The mirage of herself becomes watery, the camel's legs disappear and reappear. Nola's wheels are about five or six inches deep in the soft black ground.

—There will be a mob of women at Pine Gap, and I'll arrive astride, out of the west, out of the heat haze. I ride there, and ride away. The movement reaching backwards, what was, what is. This is now. This is the new dreaming. We are the dreaming. We are the goddess. We give life to ourselves. If we dare.

The sunset brings a rainbow into the outer-urban landscape. The greens around are saturated, intense. She is surrounded by colour. She is surrounded by voices. She dreams and wakes. The penned camels are half her reality. The call to be with the soul mates for some significant rite is strong. It could take place in her dreaming brain, in reality at the Olgas, or it may remain shimmering between the two. To conceive it is to have it in some way, even if that way is a fiction.

The dog, Kevin, stinks. Yet he wants to praised for his aftershave. Iona lets down an arm of the chair and swings Nola onto the sopping grass. Kevin licks her face. Nola gurgles. Iona takes the chair up to the hard side of the road. She comes back and piggybacks the purposelessly strong Nola with her restless limbs.

—If you take your time you can do anything, she pants to give herself encouragement and to quell her sister's distress.

45

LUCY, LOOKING zappy in a blue denim waistcoat, blue and red pants and a black silk jockey cap, accompanies Ursula when she goes to meet Dawn in Leichhardt. The household will be full of women who, no matter what their age, will seem like adolescents. Odds and sods, musicians, print-makers, massagers, herbalists, clown-performers, poets, car mechanics, law students, refuge workers, others on the dole, with spiked coloured hair, or shaved heads, or hair just let grow any old how, women with serious eyes, strong mouths and sunburnt shoulders. Lucy gives Ursula an intimidating description and comes along in case Ursula doesn't fit.

The house, tucked away behind the relentless traffic of Parramatta Road, is cool with mess and plants and artwork. One wall in the kitchen is covered with mutilated Royal scenes cut from magazines, put in collages of postcard and poster sizes. Apart from the sound of a shower upstairs, Dawn is alone. A little flustered, she offers a range of drinks and a seat at the table. She looks straight at Ursula with coy friendliness. Ursula wonders how she deserves it. Lucy and Dawn sitting near the colourful noticeboard remind her of a UNESCO Christmas card showing the prettiest white and the prettiest black in front of an exotic background.

Grundhilde, all showered, joins them. Ursula immediately likes her. She is foreign and articulate and Ursula is curious about the world.

Through the back gate and in the back door with a carton of vegetables comes Oona in grimy jeans and cowboy boots. That weather-beaten face merely raises an eyebrow on seeing strangers and concentrates on arranging eggplants, pineapple, silver beet, apples, onions, potatoes, garlic and ginger root. She kicks the box over to take the empty beer bottles, as Dawn opens another.

There is a commotion at the front door. Etama, Frances, Helen and Zimena arrive.

It is about six in the evening. Dawn had bought a dozen bottles of beer. Frances takes the job of cutting the vegetables and putting them in a large bamboo steamer over a wok filled with water.

The conversations move, showing emotions, reactions, point and counter-point. There is short story upon short story in the layers of the party, vibration crossing vibration, swelling into waves and receding into many little endings. Freshness of intellectual engagement, a spectrum of accents and attitudes from cynicism to commitment are expressed, short of the need for disagreement. Eventually Grundhilde goes to get her guitar, and she sings her song, *To An Italian Sea*. Oona looks at no-one else; her mind races with a creativity inspired by Grundhilde.

After the food and song and towards the end of a long evening, Ursula makes another pot of tea. Here are the people of her dreams, or some of them, the dancer on the waves, bringing the realm of Art into the Real World, the muscular American, the powerful German, the hard-fleshed Australian. Lucy has gone home, finally sickening of the predominance of dykes, but Ursula has stayed to find her way, and seek her place among them.

Prompted by Ursula's story of the day she first saw Dawn, they discuss the sea. Helen asks Dawn about the waves, the living waves, which she understands mathematically.

—In the circular motion of water, molecules swing around like planets in orbit, rounding up and forwards and down and backwards. And when they come to the shallow beach, they have to squash up.

—They become elliptical. It's the orbital drag of diminishing space which causes the wave to break.

—The crest leans too far forward, curls, thins and crashes. Because it is circular in movement, half a wave down, the motion is only one twenty-third of what it is on the surface. Most surfers know this, instinctively I suppose, but we dive into the wave if there's trouble. It's quite safe.

—Even if they're huge?

—Being dumped hurts. You should swing your board back over the crest.

—It's the same with music. It is a wave pattern totally dependent, really, on numbers for its beauty, its harmony.

—One knows the beauty without necessarily knowing the numbers.

—How can we translate all this into the social domain?

—Birds and children sing in natural fifths and fourths.

—The spiral and the wave...

—You can sing, compose, play music without knowing why the sound is right, or why it is beautiful.

—Or you can dance on the sea if you know the mathematical rules, right?

—I don't know. Are you substituting maths for trust?

—Or talent?

—The rhythm of the sand-dunes is slow, but it follows the same dynamic. A dune is a whole, wondrous, creeping organism.

—So the desert is frozen music, frozen sea.

—Not exactly petrified.

—Technically it is music at an incredibly low pitch.

—And human beings, are we music, too?

—I don't know. Ursula, do you think so?

Very late, in the lounge room on cushions, they plan tomorrow. Ursula accepts an invitation to go to the Mountain of Moon Mares, with a smile. It has to be my home, as I have so often been a nightmare. Dawn has a ticket to fly out of Australia. Frances and Zimena intend to return to Melbourne. Helen and Etama are going to be with Queenie. It is Oona's munificence that makes land she never paid a cent for available. It is she who issues the invitations, enthusiastically. She needs a chorus of voices. She promises, after that, she will take Gruridhilde into the Centre.

The full moon rises high in the sky about three hours after Queenie's child enters the world. The women have been busy. Some rest while others prepare soup and rice and stewed vegetables. Everyone eats quietly with a warm contentment that approaches complacency. The baby is healthy. Queenie sleeps, not far from the campfire, Ursula by her side.

All her astral travelling led to the moment she saw Queenie, for Queenie was exactly as the fitful dream in the Mercedes Benz depicted. Ship ahoy, yelled the crone, and the kids all laughed. Devotion of her own free will transformed Ursula in an instant. Her bitterness was gone. There are no mirrors, except the faces of other women, on Moonmare Mountain and Urse, without regret, reverts to her prepubescent, sporty, happy self.

The generosity of logs to the flames is a way of celebrating and who can say what magic scenes are taking place in the red and golden depths of the fire's changing life for each individual woman. Everyone stares into it as if she were watching her own private hired show.

Then all videos finish at the moment when the mugs are dirty with tealeaves no-one wants to read. A restlessness ripples throughout the group. Beatrix stretches her long arm out for the bongos and begins a rhythm. Vanessa brings her harmonica to her lips and Grundhilde, Lesley and Janice pick up guitars. Etama looks for singing sticks in the mud.

Because of the latent happiness for the general fecundity of the earth and their closeness to it, the rhythms become exultant. Therese and those who hum and chant along can sit down no longer. They get up and dance. The drumming continues and guitars become finger drums or simply strummed so their players can dance. The flames play on their faces as they circle the fire. It is a mild night, the eve of the Solstice.

—Let's call her Eve, cries Etama. The chant becomes a chant of Eve. The Eve-chant becomes a chant of Lilith. The chant of Lilith becomes a chant of the spider, the caterpillar, and any other fond symbol they can think of.

—The wild goose, Hamsa, sings Helen.

A discordant sound clanks in the darkness. The exuberant chanting becomes a hum, a whisper. It cannot stop, its hold is too strong. But the women allow their ears the right of curiosity. It sounds like the twisted corrugated iron of the burnt house moving. It reminds them of the night Amos and his friends came and bombed the place. It reminds the more frivolous of a knight in rusty armour.

Lesley begins humming the dated pop song just as the figure comes into view around a clump of mimosa in the moonlight. Its progress is clumsy on the slippery clay slope, the sound grotesque. Others have taken up the jingle with gusto. In the trivial mystery of such things, the entire song is remembered and sung by the whole company. The jingle has dissolved into laughter by the time the armoured creature arrives in the circle of firelight.

Oona rests silently on the ground as jokes are addressed to her.

Dance is taken up again, this time seriously and flowing in the deepening night, the waves of sound rising and falling. Finally Oona, in her Ned Kelly suit, struggles to her feet and begins dancing too. She does a simple stomping shuffle, reminiscent of tribal dances of the Kimberleys. In its simplicity, Oona's dance in her beaten cans becomes entrancing. The others cease their movement. Etama pokes the singing sticks into her soup-canned hands.

She dances, she clanks, she clicks, she chants until clouds come close to the moon to make the sky dramatic. Queenie, under the tarpaulin on a mattress of sheep skins, yells bravo, as she feeds the newborn at her breast. Feeling like an Aborigine, Oona comes slowly and unobtrusively to her conclusion and when she does she raises her metal arms to the sky. The heavens open. It pours with rain.

Janice says, Trust you, Oona, you're the cunning one, you're dry.

Oona hears more than Janice says. She hears, You are always separate, Oona, it is power-mongering but it lacks knowledge of female power. There is no strength for a woman if she stubbornly stays alone, believing that her specialness is the major priority.

Oona touches Janice's sleeve with her soup-tin gauntlet as the rain pings off her and drenches the other.

Take my glove, her voice is muffled in the new silver helmet. Together they remove the gauntlet. The other women huddle near Queenie under the big tarpaulin, paying attention to the emotional duel near the dying fire in the rain.

Leadership changes hands. Oona signals and shouts the command and plea: Remember the tarantella!

Helen, Grundhilde and Etama remember instantly, and the words through the wall of water are inspired for them.

The tarantella, the tarantella, they dance a frenetic tarantella on the squelchy ground, until they are exhausted, until the last lines of rain are silken threads as the moon breaks through the clouds and stars reappear.

She thought sex, she thought clay, but Etama had never thought she could dance herself to oblivion. When she practised martial arts, Etama made her body into a strong, efficient unit. She had remained fairly fit since. Little alcohol, no smokes of tobacco, early nights and lean food, she thought she was as healthy and tireless as the next woman.

Helen had danced on and on, with round slowish movements, hardly breathing faster than normal. Not Etama. The bug of frenzy had bitten her. She danced like someone crazed, with nervous jerks and shudders throughout her muscles and sinews, her head and limbs thrashing in all directions. She was possessed.

She passed out.

She slept throughout the next day. When she woke and joined the women round the kitchen campfire after dark. The talk was of Pine Gap. There were plans to make a women's peace camp outside the American base there. A spy station run by the CIA made the perfect target. The chatter was excited, the potential stage of political action, full of idealistic talk. Etama had woken into a new world, a world which presented her with action, which could appreciate her talent for rhetoric and fund-raising. What's more it was an aim, including being in the desert with thousands of women, concentrating on saving the earth. It couldn't fail. Etama would put all her energy into it anyway. She would persuade every woman she knew to go, to make the journey; refusal would be seen by her, she said, as vicarious rape, co-operation with the oppressors, submission to the war machine.

Etama, the lover so often alone, had experienced something spiritual in her frenzied dancing, in her sleep and now in her waking into a group of Amazons preparing for battle.

It seems the end of a huge cycle in her life. Well, it is the end of her Saturn return. All the difficulties of the transit seem worthwhile. She and her karma had grown. There was the ten-year cycle as well, her love of Frances dominating the great year of conferences, then the buying of the land, the sweetness of Utopia and its souring, the trip to Europe, and now Helen and this: the great demonstration she could take a part in making. The first of many, hopefully.

Helen is everything Frances could be in bed when things were right. Her hunger, her drive could match Etama's own. They fit like driver in chariot, like butch and femme. Even infidelity won't shake it now, anything can be handled. Without Helen there, Amazon alongside Amazons, Etama may have felt less enthusiasm about taking on so much work. With her there, and with her new knowledge of the power of ritual, work is exactly what Etama wants.

She asks Queenie if she can hold the newborn. She cuddles the baby in her arms and becomes calm.

Etama is happy.

'Dear Frances,

Reviving memory and mystery, and remember when I wrote from Crete about forgiveness? Well that's irrelevant now, it's thank you. Thank you for ten years ago and speeding me on my circumference. For it's a full circle for me, never again will you find me a pain. You set up a whole chain of questions so that I've been busy linking up answers… I can't express it. It probably is a whole philosophy you won't agree with though maybe you, too, have changed.

Anyway, we're organising a fortnight in the desert for every woman in Australia who doesn't approve of American bases and the nuclear game. You'll hear about it.

I have in mind something to tell you. You were on with S at school, I had a fling with S in London, you were on with I who is cousin to C, friend to X (whom I loved as one loves the sun), erstwhile lover of Z, goddess to H etc. R is cousin to S. The world is a small place. Now I'm on with H who was on with I, and so on, something about the geometry of lesbian sexuality, the lesbian tribe, the puzzle of sexuality becomes clearer... It was so mixed with male rhythms. The lesbian body has its own rhythms. We participate in it, cogs in a great wheel. We've been discussing men and war. For men sex is a kind of death, they admit that. It is the completion of their biological role. They are, on a psychic level, ready for death. Look at the mess the planet's in and the necrophilia that has embraced all our lives. But for women sex is a beginning. It is new life. Engendering, giving birth, nurturing. Our psyche is so different from what we live in, the threat of death; so, lesbian sexuality. It does engender a new identity. A new archetype.

You see I always felt you beat me in our arguments about the nature of lesbianism. You thought I was some kind of hypocrite being a lesbian and fighting for abortion, child-care centres etc. You said I was only in it to have the fight, to be on the streets among crowds of women, to get arrested. Not so. I was aching for the new depth, the myth that got murdered, judged and silenced out of existence, but that's always been there, the archetype, Artemis, the lesbian goddess, and the Amazons who were the first feminist branch of the human family.

So if you continue to scorn separatists, I can only say I'm proud to be one, and I know, so excitingly know what; I am.

Maybe you'll come to Pine Gap.

Always here,

Et.'

46

THE KNITTING of souls is a freedom, no? Querida? It is wrong. Wrong. Iona handles Zorro's last postcard, from Barcelona, and the one before that from London. 'The C.N.T. members in London, in exile, they are dying … *Mejica lindo y querido? No se, si realmente, me quedo el desea de concer personalmente, esa tierra; pero hubo un tiempo*' She fingers the letter from Beatrix. Fists her hand, presses her teeth into her knuckles, she is unable to digest, to understand why…your lonesome struggle *para la gente,* you romantic, you idealist, you dead *mujere*. For Zorro had known the grand themes, she suffered a big love that swallowed the whole damned world. Zorro could shamelessly conceive Utopia and never betray her hopes. She made herself a sitting duck, I bet. Beatrix gives no particulars about how, just 'Zorro is dead' among words about other things, other people. Queenie? Grundhilde? Who are these women? Giving birth to themselves, giving birth in Australia, death and resurrection, oh shit, the tide, the surge, the memory of the grand themes, the fucking heroism of the woman, you dead *mujere!*

Oona in love, what is this? Go, go, go, said the bird… Going to the desert. Going to finish the opera. Oona in love with Grundhilde, who, in Beatrix's opinion, is a good composer. Beatrix would know, I suppose. What earthquake in Peru? Yes, yes, I know, Arachne is on the high seas; Frances, of all people, told me. Perhaps I wrote that to you, Trees. Where does gossip start and end? Here, here, here in the self, in the endless circle, self. Both Helen and Janice say I am afraid of my own hysteria, my Hystia, did you hear that, Nola? Me afraid of madness? Me, why I just mosey on in a gently insane way all the time, doesn't everyone?

—Mum will be back tomorrow, Nola. Back to the old dispensation for you, blood sister? Is that what you want? To weigh our mother right down into the earth, six feet under, having done fuck-all but carry you around all her adult life? Nola laughs. She is laughing at Iona's exaggerated performance, packing up the kitchen table and throwing things. How can you laugh? Do you know never once in my life have I called you an idiot? You would know that, wouldn't you? I have called myself an idiot, the ones that I love idiots, but calling you an idiot, well it's like calling Christ an idiot. You know how he comes in different disguises. Was it Saint Christopher, the one that had to carry a child across a raging stream, but the child got heavier and heavier until he was almost too heavy to bear, then he revealed that he was God's son and Christopher became a saint? Is that who you are Nola?

—Well, I'm not staying here for either of you. You've been happy, haven't you? With me? It wasn't hard, Nola, not for three months. But, Sis, this is not my life.

—Look, here's a letter from Mary. She is a saint now. She thinks she has been canonized already. She has met the goddess. Do you want to know the name of the latest incarnation of Jehovah, Nola? It is a woman this time. Her name is Nirmala Devi, Indian grandmother, the human manifestation of the crown chakra. The Second Coming. Well that would make her the Seventh Coming, but anyway. Mary, to whom I went for advice about matters spiritual, can't wait for serendipity. She's got to have it now. Now. Nirvana. There are a lot of divinities around these days Nola, you want to be careful. This lot don't care about the halt and lame, well not unless you're in their vicinity and catch a passing miracle. That is, if it is all in your mind, of course.

—We are all flies.

Iona dances around with the flyswat, backhanding and smashing the little insects as they square-circle about the light globe. Nola thumps the arms of her chair and gagas.

—All flies susceptible to be stuck in the honey, caught in the spider's web…oh, look up there, in the corner. I hate sweeping down cobwebs, and Mum hates cleaners who look no higher than their shoulders. Anyway, Mary is in India.

The table looks no clearer than when she began. I'm going to take this bridle. This, if anything, is mine. Two missives from Nisaba. I am flattered by that, you know. I have no response except I feel flattered. 'The light within.' Two, a diatribe, a disappearance into the mountains of Nepal, leaving Armand, Manuel and Dominic, finally. Harriet Mendelsohn has moved to Mexico. All the world is on the move. Me too, Nola, me too. You?

Iona takes the handles of Nola's chair and wheels her out onto the verandah.

—Now, this is serious. Let's talk. For once I'm going to listen. She takes both the jiggling hands. Remember the other week when Frances came and we went in her car. You can nod or shake your head. I'm going to ask you in a way you can say yes or no. Yes or no? Yes. Okay, You remember where we went? Yes. Where there were lots of people like you and lots of nurses and occupational therapists? Yes. Did that place scare you? No. Okay. Whatever you answer now I'm going to tell Mum, okay? Nola nods waveringly. Do you want to go and live there? Take your time, think. Oh, don't cry, Nola. What do you mean yes? Because I am going? Forget that for the minute and tell me whether you wouldn't mind going and living with lots of other people. The hard fact is, Sis, Mum won't be able to carry you very much longer. You are even too heavy for me. The answer is no, heh? Okay. I said I was serious, and I hope you were, too. Don't think, even though I love you and you are an idiot, I'm not going away. In a week, maybe. Meanwhile I've got to make this pigsty into a presentable home. I've got coloured crepe paper for you to rip up and we'll make it pretty like a party. Nola tries to clap her hands.

—Nola, I need my friends. Iona has taken Nola into the sitting room and is idly dusting. Zorro is bones in the bloody desert somewhere in the Middle East. I reckon that desert must be bonesand by now. Let's get out of the house for a while. I'll wheel you to the shops where I'm going to buy dozens of postcards. Later I'll sit down at the kitchen table and write on every one of them.

Iona scatters postcards on the wind, like butterflies of warning.

The Dance

The Dance

4553 B.C. fifty women gather for a rite beneath the full moon.

Is it the Spring Equinox? No, it is the Summer Solstice, because a bound sheaf of crisp wheat lies ready. It is a prop for the dance, a custom since the great changes brought about by farming.

Through a kind of mist I see and seem to know as I see. It clears.

Three pools of water and four cedars of Lebanon mark the sacred mound on a triangle of land between the Tigris and Euphrates Rivers.

The women are mourning the passing of an era. The growth of large towns has exhausted the land. The clearing of forests for grazing and crops has started soil erosion. A useless thorny bush grows unchecked where trees were felled and some inland lakes are becoming brackish. Dysentery, malaria and hookworm, unknown in the times of hunting and gathering, now attack the less fortunate.

These women seem wise, as if, in certain states of concentration, they possess past and future vision. They are moving in a deliberate way.

For the rites of passage in those times womb-huts were built for the flow of blood. But this month is unique. They have foregone their treasured relaxation to share the magic of their menstruation with others equal in discipline and memory.

Now I must concentrate on the shape they are making. The first woman mounts the gentle hill and squats beside a freshly-dug circular pit. The second woman squats with her back to the first some twenty feet due south of the pit. The third woman squats beside the first woman and faces in the opposite direction so that her left shoulder touches the left shoulder of the other. The fourth to arrive squats beside the second and faces towards the pit so that her right upper arm touches the right shoulder of the other. The fifth squats, touching right arms with the third, and begins the spiral outwards. The sixth, touching left upper arms with the fourth, begins the spiral inwards. Ah, it is two spirals they make.

When all fifty have come, the fiftieth and first face each other across the empty hole. The forty-ninth is twenty feet to the north of the pit, facing the pole star. The second is forty feet south of her. The geometry is exact, as if my hypersenient mind can hold the vision and see the abstract at once.

With the completion of these two spirals, twenty-five women face the pit and twenty-five point in a compass.

Now I am aware of the light. The beginning of the gathering occurs as the sunset colours the west and a huge orange moon breaks the eastern horizon. The general murmuring ceases as the forty-ninth and fiftieth come to their places. In the dusk there is such a silence that I feel it to the depths of my soul in my hypnotism and it lasts until all vestige of gloom is gone and the moon is pure white in a clear night.

As one they begin talking and fussing.

Again I am aware of the numbering. Twenty-four women in groups of six collect wood, food and implements, and go to make fires to the north, east, south and west. The other twenty-six are the members of the dance. They flex their muscles, shake out their hands, do breathing exercises, or pace in readiness. Some of those tending the fires rattle their simple percussion instruments and practise beats with the clapping of hands.

Before I am conscious of it, the dance has begun.

Except for a square of cloth in an earthy colour, the dancers are naked. Surely it is summer.

Because there are twenty-six and I have no other way of identifying the individual women, I will use the alphabet and, strangely, as I do, something in the sound of the letters agrees with the shape and character of the women, who, by the way, are of different ages, though none is a girl.

A emerges from the darkness with a single flame. She holds the torch at the height of her heart. The moment a spark, or a still-burning twig detaches itself, *B* leaps into frenetic action. She falls down, grinding the spark of hot ash into the ground with the bare skin of her stomach.

C and *D* are orbiting the first flame slowly. Then they begin dipping in and out of the light of it, each taking a posture, then dissolving it. *A* moves the flame and the four faces surround it; in unison they turn their heads from left to right. Their eyes stop on *E*. *E* opens her mouth and the sound 'Oooohhm' comes. Some others hum behind her. She sounds another, louder 'Ooohhm'.

A shakes the torch, a spark falls. *F* sneaks out from behind *B* and seizes the still-burning twig and touches G's skin with it. *G* reacts, backing away from the fire. She brings *H, I* and *J* to life. They dance as a threesome. As three, they handle out *K,* who is puppetlike. Where the trio leaves her, she stays permanently.

While she is still, the others in the dance move with anarchic energy, kicking up their legs and spinning around.

L dances forward with her square of greenish material billowing between her hands. *M* is hunched on the ground. *L entices her to grow. She rises, very slowly at first, then more and more rapidly until she is whirling madly. The rounded 'Ooohhm' changes to a wide-mouthed 'Aaaagh' and wailing. Their dance, though wild, brings them together. All the dancers form a ball of bodies. I can hardly tell one from another.*

Then like an egg it cracks open.

N emerges, frightened. The others goad her, force her out from them, alone. There she begins searching and seeking in the dark. She inspects each. Out of the hump she pulls *O,* who has both her hands about her head. She is pulled away from the others. Then *N* returns and entices *P* out of the writhing bunch of bodies. She places *P* back to back with *O*. Then, most violently, she grabs *Q* by the pubic hair and the hair on her head and pushes her into *P's* and *O's* backs.

R, S and *T* burst from the bunch, destroying it. They circle and circle the three who are standing backs together. The tone changes to 'Eeeehhi".

H, I and *J* circle *G* in the other direction. *A, B* and *C* face each other in a close dance around the flame. *D, E* and *F* circle them, facing outwards and going in a clockwise direction. The energy of the three groups circling attracts *U*. She flies towards the circling of *G* like a tangent, completes a circumference and takes off again at a tangent. *V* is slower to move, finding her body cumbersome. As *U* flees from one circle to another, *V* approaches gradually. She is assisted, enticed, prodded by *N*. When the two reach a circle, *U* reaches it too, and there are six in that ring.

At this point *W* begins a solo performance in the centre. She has grabbed the light from *A*. *W's* dancing dismembers the groups and upsets the order of the circles. The drums beat to a crescendo. The women dance. It is both integrated and chaotic. 'Uuuuugh.'

The tension climaxes and the drumming slows. Twenty-three women lie prostrate, in disorder. *X* begins to sing. The singing slowly warms them to movement. Their arms reach up, coloured rags flutter in their hands. *Y* dances in front of *X, encouraging her to follow. She does. Gradually others join her in following. The twenty-five make a long serpent weaving in and out of the fire's dancing light, chanting.*

Suddenly Z leaps out of the pit with a shout. She laughs. Her arms embrace the world. I feel tears on my cheeks.

The drumming stops. All the women walk in from where they are. *Z* is lifted up by many hands. She is relaxed to a dead weight. *Z* is carried to a tree and suspended by her right foot for a breathless moment. Then she falls.

The stalks are lit and sent flaring into the hole. The full moon is overhead. Each woman releases her menstrual flow into the pit of smouldering wheat.

I am exhausted, supine, with my eyes closed, dreaming or seeing these things. My spirit takes off from the group into the sky as if I died there. Around me, shooting stars are circling. On the distant orb of the earth I see the odd shape of the winged orobus.

Afterword

I wanted to write something that was feminist in aesthetic ... I chose twelve women readers, of different star signs, to read [the manuscript], and that took years ... The process of having those women readers involved for those three years is part of what [Remember the Tarantella] *is.*

Finola Moorhead

23

without a word. Beatrix, knowing Etama's shrewdness, sharing the same European addresses and aware that she would not spend much longer than travelling time on her own, deduced more accurately than Etama had told her, her whereabouts, however.

* * *

<u>The Moon Weakly Pictorial Review Centre-fold Tease</u>

Pics and pleas from the past! Test for literate ladies. Pictures and captions set out in eye-catching assymetry. Single initial and date of quotation provided. Consult your subconscious general knowledge or whatever you have at your mental finger-tips. Don't be afraid, ladies. Above all, don't feel alone. Remember some things never die and never change. But what?
It could be you.
Now: who?

Top Left illustration: a photograph. Light catches the profile front on; the face is long, the nose aquiline. The eye we see is musing on the source of light; morning sun through a window? Caught in a beautiful swirl are ribbons of smoke issuing from a long thin cigarette between two narrow fingers of the right hand, the elbow rests on the desk. The other arm hangs loosely beside the chair. It draws attention to the lower half of the portrait. We see she is knee-deep in a sea of crumpled paper.

"Shall I continue this soliloquy, or shall I imagine an audience, which will make me describe? This sentence is due to a book on fiction which I am now writing -- once more, O once more. It is a hand to mouth book. I scribble down whatever I can think of about Romance, Dickens etc. must hastily gorge on Jane Austen and dish up something tomorrow." V. August 12, 1928.

Left: a lithograph. We have an entire room. Elegant Regency; to the right a bay window, to the left a firepalce, in between an occupied armchair. The bodice of the lady's dress is striped. The hair is dark, parted in the centre and drawn tightly back. The head is tilted up, the eyes stare straight at the lithographer and they are the blackest thing in the picture, piercing. The hands are on the lap where an embroidery frame has fallen to one side revealing an open exercise book. Peeping out from the skirts of the chair's upholstery are a little inkpot and a pen.

"I begin already to weigh my words and sentences more than I did, and am looking about for a sentiment, an illustration or a metaphor in every corner of the room. Could my ideas flow as fast as the rain in the Store Closet it would be charming." J. January 24, 1809

The writing of Finola Moorhead's *Remember the Tarantella* was a vast work that spanned many years. This book has a revision history unlike any other book we know. It did not begin life as a plot, or a character, but as diagrams. As Moorhead writes in the book's preface: 'The first draft was a series of diagrams, and nouns … the second draft was flow-prose.' Through its early gestation Moorhead shaped the book according to patterns suggested by the Tarot, astrology, the double helix, and mathematics.

Remember the Tarantella was, as the author put it, written in the 'plural of women'; Moorhead showed the book at various stages to a large number of other women: 'Throughout the many drafts, I had readers, arguers, encouragers, critics, and researchers.' The changes she made are in part the result of the responses she got from these women.

In the extracts we've selected, we've tried to give a linear sense of how the writing of the novel progressed. There were about eight drafts altogether: we've chosen extracts from three different stages. The first consists of some of the diagrams that made up the first draft. Extract 1 is the first prose draft, and Extract 2 is a later prose draft. The extract from the final book, Extract 3, is transformed, but all the earlier processes are visible within it.

Woolfe's interview with Finola Moorhead took place in Sydney in July 1991.

INT: We've read that you began writing *Remember the Tarantella* with diagrams. Can you tell us how that process worked?

FM: I'd written a novel which was called *Lots of Potential*. Most first novels are pretty awful, so I thought, I'll make all the mistakes I can. And the book was totally chaotic. I sat down and wrote whatever I felt like when I felt like writing, regardless of plot or anything like that, figuring this was a first novel. I gave it to Christina Stead to read, and she said: 'You're really mathematical.' It was really chaotic but it was really mathematical.

That's why the first draft here is mathematical—diagrams. Consider the diagrams a draft, which I do, because it was the first work on it. I started *Tarantella* just purely from diagrams and nouns. No sentences because sentences bind you to themselves.

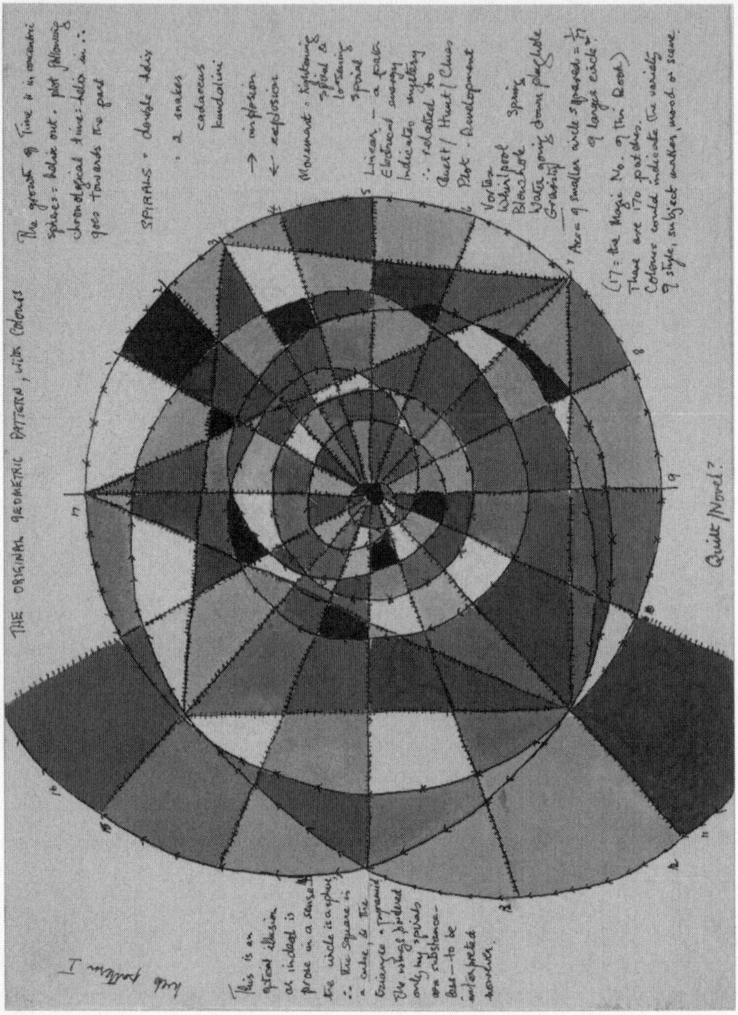

That was the first, that was done on big blotting paper when I was a writer-in-residence, and that was children's coloured playpaper stuck on a photocopy of it. I keep that winged circle going throughout.

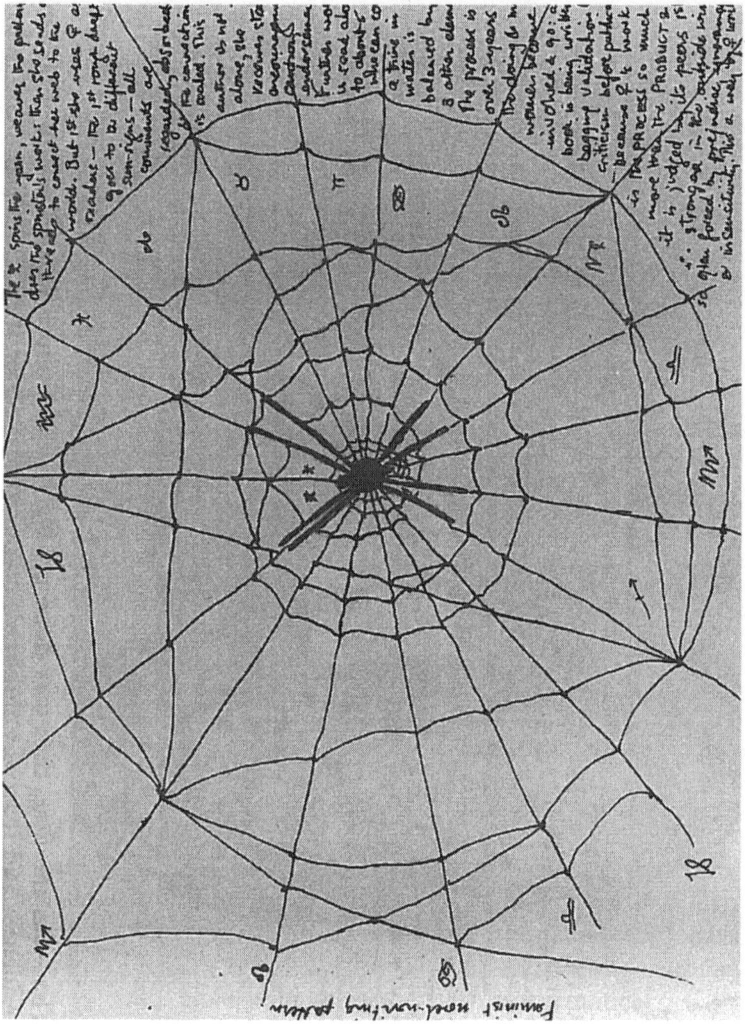

Then it's a spiderweb … (The words were written later, about 1984.) The female aesthetic was my main thing.

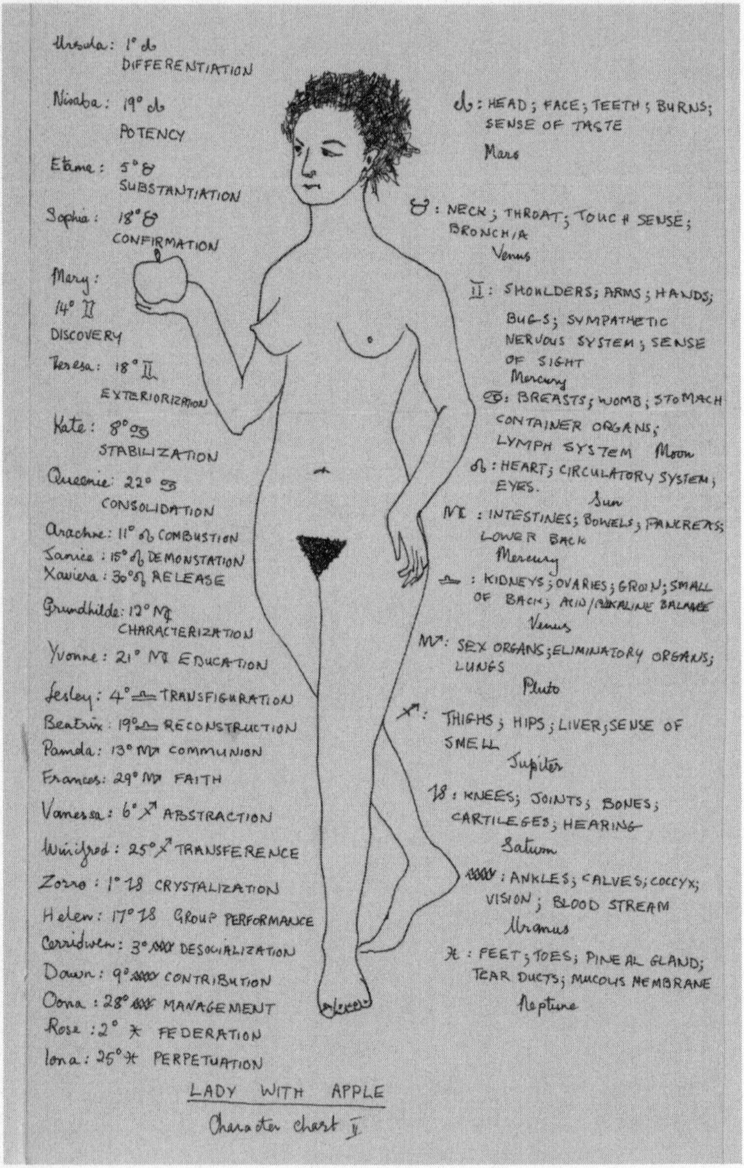

And that's the woman—sun signs and Sabian symbols for each character.

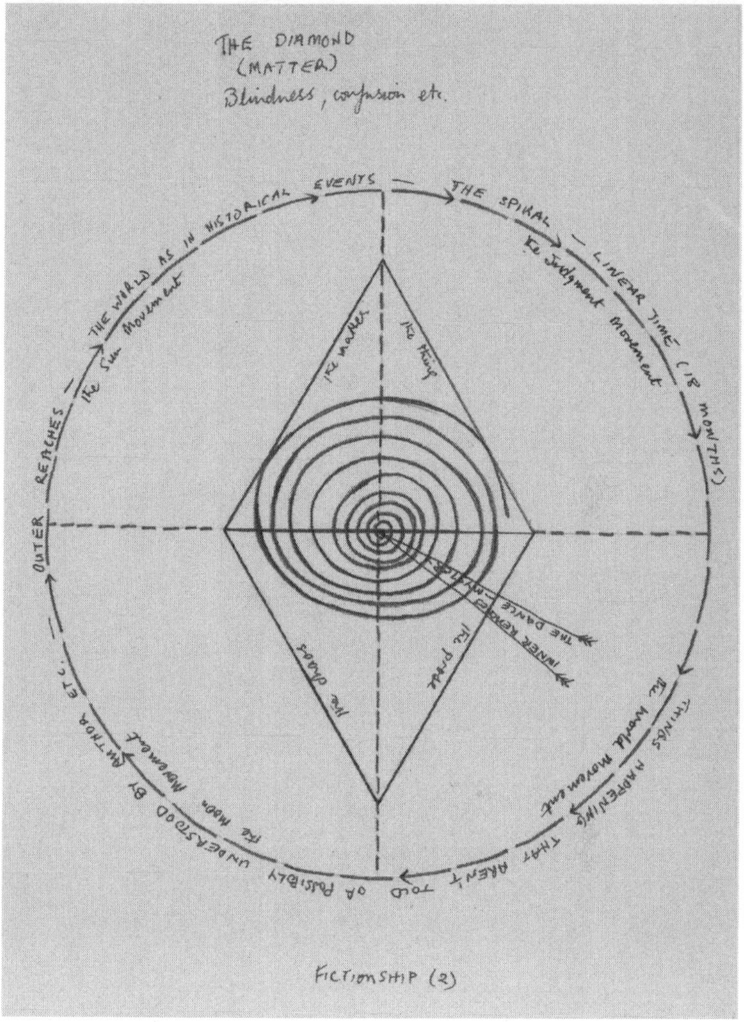

There's the diamond—an abstraction of the four movements. I wanted the book to have a symphonic construction.

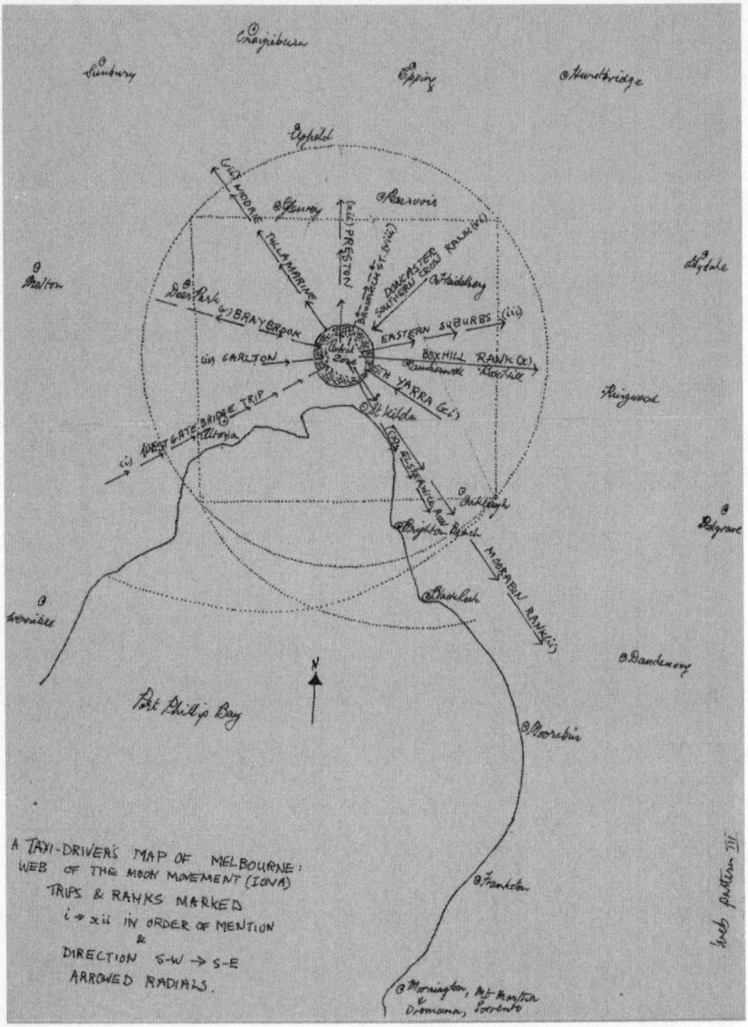

That's the spiral going through—the taxi-driving map—you get Iona going to Auburn and around about, spirals again. (Couldn't have that particular map in, say, Sydney. Melbourne, with its main radial arterial roads, works.)

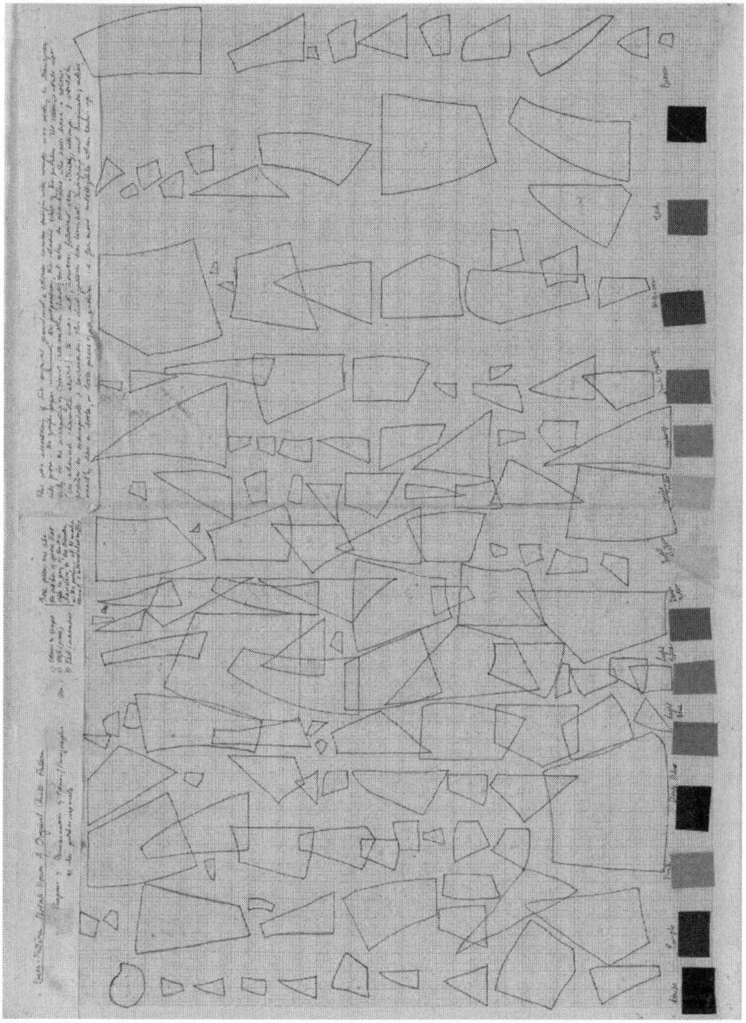

Here it is as a dress pattern—they're the separate pattern pieces of Diagram 1. You know how the Tarantella's got spots of one character, then another character: that was this one.

INT: Why a dress pattern?

FM: Because it's another female thing.

INT: What came after the diagrams?

FM: The movements. Prose and poetry. Four poems. There are about eight drafts. I was using so many arcane images. I was using the Tarot for characters up to seventeen, then I had the Moon, the Sun, the World and Judgment, and they became movements because you couldn't make those particular Tarot cards into characters. What I used Tarot cards for was to give the characters an essential moral of their own, the basis which they go back to. Like my moral might be freedom, or someone else's might be justice.

INT: So the Tarot cards stand for different…

FM: How I interpret them. How I use them. Because I couldn't be seventeen different characters, you know, they'd all sound like me. So I had to look at, say, Queenie, as the Tower. The Tarot informed me about how she would be in the world: solid, then sudden change. You remember Queenie, she's the one that shot her father, got rid of the old order. So seventeen of the Tarot cards worked for me like that, to give me something to go back to when I was not talking about me, but talking about the plural of women.

INT: So, when Queenie is represented by the Tower, which itself represents sudden change, that would make you think about the incidents that were important in her life?

FM: There's other things that inform Queenie too. Like being Cancer, she's the one that gets pregnant. The diagrams help me get to a deeper level than my life. My life bores me silly. When I'm talking fiction I'm talking something exciting, something that's elsewhere, in the soul.

Also, I wanted to write something that was feminist in aesthetic, not just coming to the climax and that's it. I wanted something like in the diagram, having many knobs. And something like music. I informed myself through the Tarot and also through the star charts and through colour and through number, all those arcane kinds of disciplines. Not that I'm an initiate of any of it, but I just used what came for me.

A friend of mine saw this and gave me coloured kindergarten paper when I was trying to sort out how to go beyond 58 pages, to write something big.

You start writing a novel, but my interpretation of it is, if you don't have an underlying theme, or spring, you can dry up. And the only reason to write is to be constantly excited by writing—by other than yourself as well.

INT: So the Tarot and the colours took you to another level?

FM: To the level of inspiration. It's the alphabet too, informing it. Queenie is quick, Ursula is ugly, the U sound throughout Ursula's pieces—so that informs me about the adjectives, verbs and so on. She might 'utter' rather than 'talk'.

INT: What did Christina Stead say to you about mathematics that gave you a kick-off point?

FM: She was writer-in-residence at Monash then, and she read *Lots of Potential*. She took me to lunch with a person called Crossley who was a mathematician at Monash. To sit down and have this conversation about absolute abstract purity! She and I knew each other to the tune of about five or six conversations like this, and how it helped was, it said to me: 'Go for it. Be it, be abstract.' That's why I go that way to start.

I can get music that way at the fundamental level of reverberation, and I can get a choral kind of thing going through the book—through the abstract thing. Such a lot of music is similar to maths. I don't have access to music really but I understand it on a mathematical level. Christina Stead wrote to me while I was at Monash—I was sitting up at a desk, now knowing what to do. Will I rewrite *Lots of Potential*? She said: No, forget that, write something else.

I'd been two weeks sitting up there as writer-inresidence myself, thinking about my own life, boring myself. Why should I relive it? What's to relive? Make something else! Create a concerto—which is what the Tarot is—a symphony or a choral work, something that you can read over and over again if you want to, a chorale of characters.

I proved my point about the female aesthetic, I can make a novel that does have very few men in it. I only had cut-out type men in it, without it being considered ugly. I wrote it too damn well for it to be dismissed. They do that a lot with a lot of feminist writing, they say: 'Oh, that's ratbag, that's heavy.' They dismiss a lot of feminist lesbian writing as marginal. I proved to myself the point that I could be central in terms of the literary values—I could take *my* lifestyle as the centre, not society's lifestyle, which is what most people get centred to. You get mainstream, you write mainstream aesthetics. That was my big challenge. It took me eight years.

INT: Eight years?

FM: The diagrams, and that work of research in the arcane, happened in 1980.

This next draft [Extract 1] is from 1981. I wrote most of that draft down at Mornington with my mother who had cancer, being a spinster daughter with her, and that was a very important time to just be with her, understand her frailty, and do something while I was doing it. I decided not to edit at all, I just went on. I just wrote it, and some of it's sustained right through to the end.

INT: Did you follow that principle all the time, that you'd write a whole draft, then another whole draft?

FM: Oh, they're all unique. The diagrams were followed by a 144-line poem, a quarter of which is the Moon, the Sun, Judgment and the World, and the poem informs me as much as the diagrams do. Then after the fast draft I wrote this 'slow draft'—I call it the slow draft, it's just type type type type—and the poem and the diagrams got thrown out in the very last draft.

INT: Was that a difficult decision, to abandon them?

FM: No. There were many refigurings. The artifice goes, becomes unnecessary—for example, *The Moon Weakly Review, Book the First*—the conscious, selfconscious pointing out the alphabetic position of the character. So does the naked inspiration of the writing. Ursula had to sit alongside other characters and take her place in the plot. So how, my question must have been, can I retain her internal romance cargo—that is, mine—when I'm first imagining Ursula see Dawn surf? And at the same time how to make her physical reality poignant? That's just technique and work and decisions.

But in the first place I set up such a broad blueprint with so many guidelines. Most of it was discarded—not really, it's beneath the surface—in favour of a decent read. Describing the bay, for instance. Hack work.

INT: What were the processes that took you from this extract to the rest of the book?

FM: That's the very first prose draft of the novel. There was no rewriting before that one. There may or there may not have been something written on the beach in the wind.

That first prose draft was written quickly in a fever of enthusiasm and consequently used basically as raw material. You see, I was frightened I would run out of inspiration. I wanted to create a block of marble at which I could chip away, make into a reasonable form and eventually polish. What one is looking for there is the guts, the gems, the jewels, which you can later set in a muted background, which, naturally, makes them shine the brighter.

Then I thought: I can't edit this without help. So I chose twelve women readers, of different star signs, to read it, and that took years. I started with just two readers, a Capricorn reader and a Libra reader; the Capricorn reader's a legal person and the Libra reader's into astrology, so they were informing me from different disciplines quite interestingly. They were reading that as I was writing it.

Then I thought, this is a good idea but as I've got so many broad-based women here, I'll need a broaderbased readership to tell me what is actually here. So the next draft was read by twelve women. After getting their comments on that, I had meetings for reading each new chapter as I wrote it.

INT: Did they ever meet all together, to talk to you, or did they come one by one?

FM: As many as I could get together I did, but some were up in the bush, some in Melbourne, some in Sydney, some were overseas.

I cast for traits as well as personality. I didn't ever care if the women liked me or not, I just wanted intelligent women readers. It didn't matter whether they were into literature or not, although a number of them were.

At that point the diagrams had seventeen segments, so there were only seventeen chapters. Big chapters. So they read that, I absorbed their comments, then they came and we read the new chapter aloud, like the old Russians or Dickens or whatever. In a weekend gathering we all read the new bits.

INT: Each reading a character, or taking turns to read a chunk?

FM: Taking turns. At a time there would be eight of them there. It wasn't exclusive—if their lovers were coming along that was fine too. At this stage no men were admitted, except Kris Hemmensley, I showed a bit of the first draft to him.

INT: How did you sift out the comments, the good from the bad, the useful from the useless?

FM: Well, I'm the boss, I'm the writer!

INT: Do you think you could ever be swayed … I'm just thinking how vulnerable I'd feel …

FM: I don't feel vulnerable because I love criticism. It's not me personally that would be hurt, it's that the writing is not adequate. They contributed heaps, they would get excited about the whole prospect of informing me of stuff I didn't know.

INT: About the characters, the scenes …?

FM: The world. Their brains … Their contribution was unselfish as mine was unselfish, in that I was sharing. You know you get that question: 'What's your book about?' Most of the time you think: I hate this question. But during *The Tarantella*, because I was experimenting, I would answer anybody who asked me: The book is about women, I'm doing da da da da. So by giving in that way, I received.

INT: It's an extraordinarily open way to work. I meant by 'vulnerable' that if someone makes a comment, I could write in a direction that in the end I wish I hadn't.

FM: Yes, well, I allowed myself to do that. You've got to constantly have your own critical faculty in gear, because you can throw out good stuff. You have to be able to say: 'No, that's a gem.' You can actually be blinded to what is a gem and keep things that are a bit of old rot. But eventually you know, because you just keep rewriting and rewriting and re-seeing, seeing from a different angle.

INT: Were you deep into the book by the time you got back all the responses?

FM: This draft of the women readers is 1982/3/4: those three years it took to make a big draft, which was a real fatty—so big, so amorphous, that I was pinned to the ground by it. I tried it with Jackie Yowell, managing editor of Penguin at the time, she said: 'It's brilliant, Finola, it's absolutely brilliant, but it's too hard for us to take on, it's too much editing.'

INT: How big a book was it at that stage?

FM: Well, then Paul Brennan took it on he said, 'You'll have to cut it by a third.' So it was a lot bigger than the book you've got.

INT: Why were you willing to cut the book?

FM: Because I knew it was too big.

INT: Did you feel the structure had become amorphous?

FM: The structure, yes, was bursting at the seams. Because while I'd had all these structural, blueprint plans—like seventeen chapters, movement of the Sun, Moon and World and all that sort of thing, and I'd been very academic or mathematical about it, there was a chaos within—the neutron within the atom if you like, the chaos within the simplicity.

For six months Paul and I would meet. And we did the final drafts on the computer. Why did I accept so generously his constant criticism? Because criticism is what I needed, flattery you don't need while you're writing a book, criticism you need—but I now had the male viewpoint. I gave my attention entirely to the male viewpoint of this female book that I was writing. I was very well aware that we now had the 'Yang' and I needed that, I needed to cut it, I needed the assertion, the self-assertion that a male presentation does. So what might have been a philosophical treatise, became a statement in the cutting, so five pages could become one paragraph.

It was a helluva job and it was distressing in certain ways. But Paul did not write a word of it. What Paul did was to show me what he understood, just as the women had shown me what they understood—but they also contributed. He didn't contribute, he just showed me … What he wanted to change, all sorts of things that never got changed, all of those were related to the myth, male myth.

The process of having the women readers so involved for those three years is part of what that book is, part of its multi-energy. And I don't think other writers should write like that. I didn't with *Still Murder*, it's not written in that style. Only *The Tarantella* is written with that sort of openness, because I had to make a great act of faith in women.

INT: Why didn't you want to use that technique in *Still Murder*?

FM: It's too hard. I had a couple of readers for *Still Murder*. I like to have a reader during the drafts because you don't see it like someone else does. I politely ask, 'Will you read it? Say what you like as long as I get some idea what's there.' *Still Murder* is just as long a book and it's just as big a book in terms of as many drafts, and the editing by Jackie Yowell for Penguin was just as intensive, just as much cutting, and my individual process was very similar—write write write write write, put everything down, then cut like crazy.

I really like the rewriting but I won't rewrite unless I'm just as inspired as I was to write the initial thing. I don't consider rewriting unexciting at all, I think it's fabulous, I love it. It's sort of like sculpture, you get closer, and closer and shinier, more detail and shinier, and then you finally finish and you're … it's furbished.

INT: As you write, do you have a feeling of discovery, uncovering something, or are you inventing?

FM: Yeah … Both. But within both is the mystery too, isn't it? You will get as much as your tiny mind can do, and then you trust … I personally think there's quite a strong moral thing in writing, that you're doing the right thing in terms of your own morals. You're trying so hard to express something well, and the words keep evading you, and then: Zoom! out of the blue a whole new thing you'd never have invented or discovered happens—not when you're actually writing but when you're reading through it. There it is! There!

So there's that mystery element that, personally, I think is related to your good intentions and your respect—respect for your characters, respect for the world, the earth, respect for the mystery of the human mind. You sit down at your desk with a certain level of humility, but arrogance at the same time because you're daring to do it. There are times when you think, look what I'm doing! But there are other times where you're humble in relation to it. It's 99 per cent hard yakka and one per cent … but that one per cent is so important.

INT: Do you despair at times?

FM: Not I!

INT: In all those years, you didn't have any doubts?

FM: Yeah, I went through that, a terrible down period in this at the end of 1984. The enormous fat draft was finished, and I had no ability and nothing to do—I just had this enormous manuscript, and an enormous lot of my life had gone into it.

INT: By then it was about three years?

FM: About four or four-and-a-half. There were other little short stories and things but I couldn't get into them because my mind was constantly trying to feed this one. I just ran down like a battery, and I didn't know whether it was a load of bullshit or whether it was a great book. I really didn't know. But I knew whatever it was, it was alive. I didn't like those years. The emotional journey to there was to the South Pole and back. A wiser woman ….

INT: So part of what you're saying is that after writing like that you come out a different person.

FM: You become more of what you may have been. A gum tree doesn't ever become a wattle.

INT: So it's a sort of transformation?

FM: I think any art is. It's a sort of mining of the self, and if you're going to write anything that's different from what anyone else is going to write, you don't copy, you have to go into your own uniqueness.

I become a relatively sick person when I'm writing, because I smoke a lot and drink black coffee, and wring, there's this wringing of the essential self. There's all that constant questioning, the 'Who am I?' of it. I am a writer because I write, therefore if I feel bad I'd better go to the computer and start work!

I don't have a work ethic in relation to writing. I work extremely hard out of respect for what I'm capable of, and what I've been capable of. I feel I've been initiated into something, in the sense of being given insights that I would otherwise not have, because of that work. It's not because you're published or because you're in the scene, something so artificial, I call that selling your soul.

But I feel that I've got the right now not to write. But I didn't feel that before *The Tarantella* was finished. The right not to write! Think about it! It is like I had been so trapped in the idea that I had to write—because I'd decided I was going to be an Australian writer, and an Australian writer with all the laurels that come, being recognised and so on. From 1972 to 1988 I constantly had this duty in relation to writing.

So the good reviews of *The Tarantella* and the acceptance of it finished my need to write. But then I got three grants in a row, which is the reason I could finish *Still Murder*. It's a good book too, just a different process, a different book. *The Tarantella* is written out of the pronoun 'we' and *Still Murder*'s written out of the pronoun 'they'. The 'I' book hasn't come yet. The 'I' book's the hardest of them all, but the 'I' book is what most first novels are. Me me me.

My mother was a very intelligent woman and a very good writer in her own right. She said: 'I'm sick of this first person in all these new writers, they're all "I".' That's why I've got an alphabet in *Tarantella*, it was she who gave me the idea. I thought: well, the 'I' has to go! If it's not an 'I' then which letter is it? So I'll use the alphabet.

INT: Your mother said that?

FM: My mother said she was sick of the 'I' in the new writing.

Extract 1 from a manuscript

This is an early prose draft of *Remember the Tarantella.*

A Constable Day & An Old Overcoat's Burden

No One could be a saint who dreams as Ursula does. For dreams are quite out of the reach of morals, ethics and charity; as Oscar has put it: 'Art is out of the reach of morals, for her eyes are fixed upon things beautiful and immortal and ever-changing.' As to morals and ethics and charity, what choice does Ursula have? The prison of her facial scar assured all three. Is sincerity a virtue? The Great Maligned, the signed-sealed worshipper of all nine Muses and priest of Plato crooks his finger to the horrendous virgin and brings his lips close to her ear: 'A little sincerity is a dangerous thing, and a great deal of it is absolutely fatal.' To give the Last Vowel her due, she has never indulged in sincerity, hence, has no pedestal for Blame in her heart. Her heart broke away from the Promethean chains of her visage long ago, fidelity to the daily facts of life took flight on the same date, truth became as fickle as beauty—as fickle as her married sister?—in that the Beholder's eye is the salient factor.

On an ugly winter's day ten used Roman calendars away, Ursula witnessed a scene that threatened to crack open the separate spheres of her life, and release passion into her daily round—a force antipathetical to its equilibrium—in such a case, a great deal of sincerity might have been fatal. For her married sister? For her mother? The wind was howling and the waves were rising high and cracking down on the shallow beach and the sky was a pack of ferocious grey bears, the temperature was bitter. No Scottish coast filmed for an introduction to Macbeth could have boded more evil. As the gods were angry, Ursula rubbed her purple hands into each other with glee and leaned her little body into the gale hoping to gain the headland to meet the worst of it. But her arduous steps were arrested. Divine Madness decreed, a moment from the depths of Art! In dark Victorian oils! Dramatic aloneness suddenly punctured!

Against the thunderous sky a figure on a surf board.

There were two: the watcher and the watched. The watcher watched, and was moved, so moved to stand stock still! Clad in black rubber, such a slight thing was flashing across the battling great waves through the spitting wind. The surfer seemed to dance. Dance in a Japanese stance. Speeding, then disappearing into the mess-mad whiteness and for goodness sake! The undertow, and the board leaping up like a shark on its tail. If ever such a light thing, it could still crash down on a skull. No. And lo, paddling out again to the treacherous deep where the waves were long giant ripples.

Never before, for Ursula, had /the/ Beauty of the living human being leapt out of Art and Dream into the Real World; she was so shocked she was afraid she might behave uncharacteristically. This was a moment of soul to soul, in /a/ region beyond the limited prejudices of the physical. She put the headland behind and made her way down onto the beach, where she stood feet apart, perpendicular to the graceful antics of the surfer, and waited, spellbound.

A solo ballet on the immensely restless seasurface; a folly performed entirely for her, for herself alone. She was reverent, she was transfigured. And when it was finished, she clapped her hands and jumped into the air several times to show her appreciation. The surfer squelched back the bonnet of the wetsuit, and a mass of hair, blond as sunshine, tumbled out. The board was heaved onto the hip and the young lanky girl approached her through the receding-encroaching-receding sea. Ursula did not recoil from this blondhaired, red-cheeked, blue-eyed, white-teethed apparition of Aryan health and courage, no, she rushed forward, lightly, as if she were as mystical a being as the Valkyrie coming from the ocean.

'My dear, my dear, aren't you cold?' Unfortunately sounding exactly like a maiden aunt, which part of her was, but not the part that was moved to speak. 'How old are you, you brave girl? O how I have loved watching you!' Dawn dropped her eyes shyly, kicked a lump of sand and breathed out, 'I'm thirteen. I'm a bit cold now, but I wasn't when I was out there. At least I didn't notice it, though I suppose I was. You see I'm going to win the Girls'

Surfing Championships in January. And to win I've got to train. I'm teaching myself on the Bay beaches. I can do anything if I put my mind to it.'

'I'm sure you will. I'm sure you will. My dear child, where are your clothes?'

'Just over there.'

The two walked up the beach together to where a green towel was hanging on the bushes, behind which was a neat pile of clothes and a childish bag.

'Well, excuse me,' said Dawn, 'And thanks for clapping. I'd better dress now.'

Ursula backed away, shaking her hand in an imitation wave. The girl smiled politely.

'I will see you again in the sporting pages in the summer,' called Ursula.

When Ursula reached the headland and stood with her body facing the weather, the teeth had gone out of the gods' anger and they—wind, sea, clouds and rain—were merely boisterous, matching this pure Beholder's playful mood. She opened her coat to let them get closer.

The coat was one of those made for a man in that honest combination of gabardine and wool to last /out/ long and hard wearing. No planned obsolescence about it, it was made in England during the war. 'My Rolls Royce' to Ursula, and what better model for the chrystalline spinster to wander around the winter cliffs in? She existed within /it/ with warm familiarity, comfortably taking it for granted. But now, this 1970 July day, the mauve fingers detached the large flat buttons from their holes; unused to such freedom the old coat billowed out behind her into a Romantic cloak, and thrashed and dashed as if she were galloping over the solitary moors two centuries back. Deep in an inner pocket something crackled. Curiosity beat the vision of grey turbulence, and old Ursula took herself off to shelter behind some boxthorn; she crouched down and unfolded the yellowed pages of newsprint. The 1949 Editorial of the Moon Weakly Review.

'The Moon is only about a quarter of a million miles away. It is believed that the Earth and Moon were originally one rotating fluid globe, round which the Sun swept a daily tide of molten matter. Eventually the pull became too great, and a huge mass departed, to swing around the Earth as a satellite. It has even been suggested that the great deeps of the Pacific Ocean are the gap left by the Moon's departure. The Moon has no atmosphere. Its gravitational pull is too small to prevent the swift moving molecules of gas from escaping off into Space.

...

No other object comes so vividly to life in even a small telescope as this dead world. For an hour or two, sunrise on the mountain tops may be followed, the peaks catching the light long before their surroundings, and showing as tiny glowing islands of light in the dark area. At full Moon, under vertical illumination, mysterious systems of bright lines, called 'rays', appear radiating from certain craters.

Some people suppose that a great shower of projectiles, perhaps meteorites struck and damaged the Moon, leaving scars which do look something like bomb craters, and which also resemble the few meteorite craters on the Earth.'

Extract 2 from a later manuscript

This is a later prose draft.
CHAPTER THREE
The Old Moon in the New Moon's Arms.

Unlike days at any other time of year, or unlike days anywhere else, the wind blows out in fierce, short-lived gusts, licking upon the waters water of the Bay to immediately spit spill it out. One is inside a huge breathing machine—a lung—on these days, an excited lung, panting. Flush, the terrier-dog, scampers on plasmic sand. Ursula, out for her morning walk, endorses ferocity of this sort. The beaches are hers alone, especially as it is Monday. She shrugs, our crow-faced saint, within the rhythm of her stalking along the tide-line where the sea must leave its worthless assortment of treasures caught in the black tangles of dead seaweed: the dome half of a tennis ball, bright colours of plastic all torn from toys and soft drink containers, white polystyrene, empty shells and encrustations, fish's bones, unbelievably beautiful sea-frosted glass of green and brown, cans and water-logged citrus fruit, and the smooth-skinned driftwood both of of both milled and natural shape. She stalks along the scalloping lace of the sea in the sand, the hemwork of the Bay. On these days cottonwool clouds gambol, for Ursula, on their way across a blue pasture. She doesn't slacken her pace to gaze: it is all familiar to her.

Some paper suddenly rises up, pirouettes and rushes full-blown towards her. She thinks at first it had fallen out of the bag of an errant pupil from the primary school behind the cliff, because it looks just like that. But As it stops close by, she picks it up to check to see what silly questions they ask them these days. Shiny foolscap sheets are stapled together in the centre of the lefthand long side. It is only a few pages thick. The purple copy is fairly faint, some typed, some handwritten; in the middle is printing of a different kind: off-set: with pictures, one of which Ursula promptly recognises. Such accidents please Ursula. A whole corner is sodden with sea-water. She decides to take it home and dry it out.

When you know Ursula better, you will wonder why the author did not say that she was thrilled on having The Moon Weakly Review dance up to her feet: why she was not excited, delighted and hurrying home to hang it over the radiator to have it dry enough to read with her afternoon cup of tea, while Mother snoozes in another room. In an earlier draft of this plot it would have been so … but as it is now, I must confess that Ursula felt an inexplicable nausea, a reluctance to continue her rapid 'constitutional'. When she reached the cliff, she sat on a rock and stared at the sea, angrily. You see her face with its horrid puce stain all down the right side, pinching in the skin of her eyelid and permanently spotted with whiteheaded, pimple-like protuberances was more than simply 'unfortunate', it had closed her off from the world as effectively as a Carmelite's grille, and she did resent it. So the left side of her face which could have relieved the ugliness through pure force of character wore, habitually, a most ungracious expression—that of deep-seated resentment. Activity must always be snipped in the bud, the instinct to be gregarious ruled off with a frown, the energy to gasbag on philosophy stifled at its inception. Her growth was somehow stunted, twisted, and the ordinary emotion of excitement, recognition, affinity—as that occasioned by the first words of The Weakly (…)—bent savagely into its opposite, antagonism, argument, loneliness.

After forty years, self-sorrow can descend intensely, but it is not indulged, defences against one's own vulnerability are stuck, as it were, on automatic, and set in motion soon after the stimulus is registered. As indeed, Ursula herself is soon in motion, excited, delighted and hurrying home to dry and preserve her new find.

Extract 3 from the published version

Remember the Tarantella, pages 15–19

"On days like these, we are inside the lung of a huge breathing machine. A panting, excited lung."

Ursula would seem to be a conventional old maid, nurse to her invalid mother, a spinster more unfortunate than most because of the right side of her face. The skin of her eyelid is pinched in and stretched through her eyebrow. The cheek is bulbous and pulls down the corner of her mouth. A slight dribble of saliva is always visible. The colour is maroon-purple, permanently spotted with whiteheads. It has closed her off from the world as effectively as a Carmelite's grille. The left side, which could have relieved the unsightliness by pure force of character, habitually wears an ungracious expression.

After forty years, self-sorrow can descend intensely but is not indulged. Defences against one's own vulnerabilities are stuck, as it were, on automatic.

She puts her diary back in her coat pocket and continues along the "plasmic" sand. Her dog, Flush, scampers ahead on the scalloped tideline, where caught in the black tangles of seaweed are treasures: the halfdome of a tennis ball, plastics of boys and soft drink containers, an abandoned set of dentures, waterlogged citrus fruits, white polystyrene, fish bones, shells and encrustations, green sea-frosted glass, smooth driftwood of natural shapes and hairy wood of the milled variety. It is the lace on the hemwork of Port Phillip Bay.

The wind blows out in short fierce gusts, licking up the sea into spitting waves. These equinoctial days suit Ursula's type of angry energy. That mark of Cain, the scar that forces her to be a saint, frustrates her. Growth has been stunted. Activity must always be snipped in the bud, the instinct to be gregarious ruled off with a frown, her desire to gasbag on about the meaning of life stifled. It has twisted in her, bent her character savagely into antagonism, loneliness. She pursues her rapid constitutional every morning at ten, covers miles of the foreshore in a couple of hours, with her diary in her pocket. The scavenging of her irrepressible terrier is a canine projection of her own searching.

"The wind cry, the wave cry, the vast waters of the petrel and porpoise" give Ursula her best communion. T.S. Eliot's words are Ursula's knowledge, for the sea is her great mirror. The sea is as she is inside, behind the shell of appearance, beyond the unopened door of her hymen. Virginity does not describe her state of mind. She dreams all.

For Ursula, waking from sleep is the running around of a small yacht from a turbulent sea. She is all a-shudder, having to take her bearings while being dumped by breakers.

In a bit of a pickle, panicked and brittle. She is racked with feelings, wave-motions, dismayed and bored by the heaviness of the body. Every night is the same. She's off adventuring on the high seas. Her dreams are crowded with personalities. Flying about the night sky with the fittest of astral bodies, she drops in wherever she is called, whatever the age, place, society, materialising and dematerialising. She is free in her dreams, but on waking, she is as helpless as a beached whale. Consciousness is an arrest of a velocity as could only be described algebraically. It is a slow clearing of smoke, a desolate landscape. Concussion.

During the day, what does Ursula have? She has her walks along the foreshore. And she reads.

With her cups of tea, she reads. When she has a moment, she reads. Apart from her mother, her sister and her sister's sons, Ursula has one friend in the world, Jocelyn, a demented dog-show lady with kennels. None of these give her the intimacy she gets from reading. Fine literature over the centuries has provided some great associates for the price of a book, a stop at the Regional Library. She keeps diaries, dozens of exercise books, each with a colour print stuck on the cover, a habit which started thirty-three years before with a couple of reproductions from *The Ladies Home Journal* of the artwork of Nisaba Diana Kirby. The picture, often cut out of a magazine, names the diary for Ursula, it recalls her mood, the date and the matters inside.

When Ursula goes to her church, to whom does she pray? Jane Austen, Joan of Arc, Cleopatra, Mary Shelley, Leibnitz. In her time, Ursula has talked to all the dead creators she has met. Ursula does not waste her time beating her breast. 'Mea culpa' would be a lie, her conscious life is a purgatory. She has nothing to say 'my fault' about. Neither Lucifer nor God would be interested in her petty sins, nor, if the truth be known, is Ursula. She has not conjured up heavens of purity and bright light and is scared of no hell she can imagine. Somehow salvation must be lived in the life she's got.

"Mimbo settled with tea and crumpet.

The other evening she said my diaries look like a collection of Dickens, an entire shelf of uniform height and spines of dark green canvas. I wonder if all mothers have such cunning ways with small flatteries.

On such a day as this I saw the wave-dancing girl. Oscar Wilde: 'Art is out of the reach of morals, for her eyes are fixed upon things beautiful and immortal and ever-changing.'

My façade puts me out of the reach of immorality. Another one, Oscar: 'A little sincerity is a dangerous thing. And a great deal is absolutely fatal.'

We were inside a Turner seascape on that day. In the winter of 1970, the wind was howling and the waves were cracking down on the shallow beach. I was wearing my gent's gaberdine overcoat, with the huge pockets, and my hat was pulled down at the ears. I was the watcher and she the watched. We were both in a moment of art, immortal and ever-changing. Clad in black rubber, she was such a slight thing battling with the surf. Her knees wide apart, her arms weighing this way and that, it was a performance just for me. To show me it could be done, ballet on the sea.

'My dear, aren't you cold?' I said. Her feet and hands were purple but she assured me that the wet suit worked. She was training for some surfing competition. She came from Bells Beach. 'It is not a girls' sport,' I said. But not for this androgynous creature, my shy Valkyrie, she could be better than the boys. 'Indeed, how old are you?' I said. Thirteen, neither man nor woman, boy nor girl, but an embodiment of all human potential, a spirit, a myth. How I managed to talk to her I don't know. The unique. She would not be taken aback by my looks. Or rather, that didn't matter a fig.

’80 – ’70 = 10. 10 + 13 = 23.

Now she must be twenty-three.

She instigated a faith I find returns every time the wind blows from the south-west. She brought to me a belief that my wishing life could by the one I live some day. I often trouble myself over how this can happen. Now instead of praying to dead writers, from which communication nothing can come, I have taken up hunting for a live one, listening to the radio and reading the newspapers, looking for the hole through which I might slip to meet the real … she must be great … no, I check myself, it is through her work I will know her. Her characters must be able to give me the intimacy that I know from so much reading. I have my rules and they are by no means easy.

The local library sadly lacks Australian work, except that of the most popular and vulgar kind.

Time laps in me like the seasons. My constant round, to the beach, to the shops, attending to Mimbo’s every need is monotonous, except for Flush. Every minute is new to him, that way he loves routine. Except for my secret expedition. Will it be an Elizabeth Barrett Browning? An Emily Bronte? I hardly think we’d hit it off. With one of her sisters perhaps. I fancy I’d get along with a George Eliot, actually.”